# Praise for *Breaking the Maafa Chain*

"The story of Sarah Forbes Bonetta, extraordinary even in extraordinary times, known to some in Sierra Leone, though virtually unknown elsewhere. Now Anni Domingo has brought her vividly to life in this richly imagined and compellingly told tale. *Breaking the Maafa Chain* is a gift to readers everywhere."

—Aminatta Forna, author of *The Window Seat*

"Part fact, part fiction, *Breaking the Maafa Chain* is an important book, beautifully told. Domingo's premise is a bold and uncompromising one—taking what is known, the story of Salimatu, the 'Black Princess', Sarah Forbes Bonetta, and weaving through it the story of her fictionalised sister, Fatmata, Faith. Domingo makes an eloquent point: that although the sisters suffered different fates, both were unfree: Fatmata enslaved in North America and Salimatu gifted to Queen Victoria, and utterly at her whim. It is a story that has resonance today, where Meghan Markle was expected to shape herself to a white institution, to belong."

—Guinevere Glasfurd author of *The Year Without Summer*

"Anni Domingo brings great sensitivity to her fictionalised account of the remarkable young life of Sarah Forbes Bonetta, the 'African Princess', who became a god-daughter to Queen Victoria. The internal struggles of Salimatu (Sarah) are movingly explored as she struggles to remain true to her identity as an African after being taken from her homeland and brought to England as a gift from 'the King of the Blacks to the Queen of the Whites.' A comparable story is told of Salimatu's sister Fatmata (Faith) who is transported to the United States before emancipation. Carefully constructed with a keen eye for historical accuracy, Domingo reveals a compassionate and affectionate Queen Victoria who is devoted to her

African god-daughter. This is also an epic story of two sisters who are separated towards the end of the transatlantic slave trade, but never forget each other."

—Stephen Bourne, author of *War to Windrush* and *Evelyn Dove*

"Anni Domingo's *Breaking the Maafa Chain* is so rich in detail and dialogue, it is simply seductive. She captures so well, a little girl, Salimatu, who recalls the security of her family life, who is transported to a bewildering future in England to become Sarah, where she has to stand strong and survive. Not only will this book be read for the sheer enjoyment of a beautifully written novel, but for the learning gained. It is a historical novel that cannot be ignored."

—Kadija Sesay, Literary Activist, author of *Irki*

# BREAKING THE MAAFA CHAIN

# BREAKING THE MAAFA CHAIN

*a novel*

# ANNI DOMINGO

PEGASUS BOOKS
NEW YORK LONDON

BREAKING THE MAAFA CHAIN

Pegasus Books, Ltd.
148 West 37th Street, 13th Floor
New York, NY 10018

First Pegasus Books cloth edition February 2022

ISBN: 978-1-64313-926-5

10 9 8 7 6 5 4 3 2 1

Printed in the United States of America
Distributed by Simon & Schuster
www.pegasusbooks.com

*For my beloved children Jem, Joel and Zelda*

# PART ONE

# PROLOGUE

A kì í dùbúlè ní ilè ká yí subú
*One cannot fall down when already on the ground*

## December 1846

Stripped of everything but our black skins, our ritual scars, our beings, we are tied together in rows and jammed into another *djudju* pit, packed in so close no one can move. We lie on our sides, rough wooden boards hard against our bare skins, rubbing our shoulders raw, chained to the living and to the dead.

Now I know what fear smells like. It is the smell of grown men, groaning, sweating, and stinking. Fear is women crying, wailing, and calling on the ancestors to save them and their children before they are lost to *Mamiwata*.

All around me chains rattle and whips crack as the sails flap, boards creak, and ropes stretch. The noise in the cramped space swirls inside my aching head, as it hits the wooden sides of the swaying ship, drumming wild thoughts and dark fears into my mind. I feel the howls of those beside me, those above me and those below me run right through my body. The call of the *Ochoema*, the bird of parting makes my heart pound holding me tight before fading into the darkness but leaving me in pain.

I sink down, and weep in a way I have never wept before in all my fourteen seasons. Ayeeeee. *Ogun*, god of gods, help me.

Through the tears, I see everything that had been. My heart aches for Salimatu, my sister, my mother's child, captured and sold, to Moors? To the white devils? There in the back of my eyes, way back, are the spiritless bodies of my mother Isatu and father Dauda, now gone to the land of our ancestors, without due honour. I see others too, Maluuma, mother of my mother, Lansana, my father's first son, gone too. I fear that Amadu, my father's last son, has also joined the ancestors. I have not seen him since he ran, but now can he be here in this pit, this wooden devil's hole, and not know that I am close by?

'Amadu, Amadu, son of Chief Dauda of Talaremba near Okeadon,' I cry out, again and again.

'Who calls for Amadu of Talaremba so loudly?'

'Fatmata, his sister.'

'They didn't get him,' he replies. 'He never stopped running. Santigie and the white man did not have time to chase after him.'

I recognize the voice. It is Leye, the man who speaks the white man's tongue.

The relief I feel flows through my words.

'*Olorun*, creator of the Egbadon people. I praise you; I bless you. I thank you.'

There are loud cries in many tongues from the different tribes of peoples.

'Now they will kill us and eat us,' says one.

'We're sacrifice to their gods and to *Mamiwata*,' says another, the shouts getting louder.

*Mamiwata*? I remember what my grandmother, Maluuma told me a long time ago. *Mamiwata*, goddess of water, drags those who disturbs her being down into the watery underworld to join the ancestors. Ayee, ayee.

'No,' says Leye, 'this big canoe, this ship, will take us far, far away to be sold to the white man's people. They've done this

12

before, many times. I was once captured, but I escaped and came back to the land of my ancestors, a free man. Now here I am again, tied up, a slave once more. I swear to all the gods, I will not go back to that life, I will escape again or die trying.'

The sound of wailing rises sucking up what little air there is left. Sorrow fills my nose. In the dark I feel for my amulet and stroke the heart-stone Maluuma, gave me before she journeyed two rainy seasons past. Maluuma, who had known all, heard all and seen all, even before she went to join *Olorun*, the divine creator of the Talaremba people.

'Maluuma, don't leave me,' I whisper. 'They're taking me away, taking me from everything. Help me find my way, for I am afeared.'

I hear my grandmother's voice, I am no longer alone, no longer afeared that I too would disappear, like Jabeza, Lansana, and Salimatu. Her words are in the wind that makes the shipboards groan and the flapping sails sing.

'*Listen, my child, fear is in the eyes, in the heart, in the mind. Fear stinks of sweat, rottenness, death. Face your aloe-bitter fears and they will disappear. I am with you, my child. I'll always be with you. I am part of you, so I will never be lost.*'

I know I must remember the words that come with the first cry of the baby and stays until the last sigh slips out of the spiritless body. I must remember the words hidden in my bones and in the blood that seeped into the ground under the mango trees. I must live so that I can hand the words to my yet-to-be daughters, to my daughters' daughters, to the daughters of my daughters' daughter, down, down, down. They will know that the ancestors were around before ships brought the white devil, before our own people sold us, before we knew the sorrow of the *maafa* chains that now binds us, before I became a motherless, fatherless child. No matter where the white man takes me, he cannot steal my roots.

Deep inside me I hear talking drums calling, shouting out my name, Fatmata, Fatu. My words, my thoughts, my life, are beaten into my bones, my smell, into my flesh, for all times. A deep feeling of loss washes over me, drenching me with sadness and sorrow. I try to push away the pain from the raw mark of slavery branded on my left shoulder. Instead, I touch the healing scars of the initiation tattoo I carved on myself, and on my sister Salimatu—the monkey tattoo that says no matter where they take us, we are Talarembans and warriors, even if we are girls.

*Oduadua*, god of all women, help me. I must remember, I will remember, I do remember.

SALIMATU

# CHAPTER I

*Then shall they call upon me, but I will not answer*
Proverbs 1:27

## August 1850

By the time the *HMS Bonetta* arrived in England, Salimatu was disappearing, and she was becoming Sarah. After more than four weeks at sea, Sarah had learned much, especially how to push back Salimatu, the slave girl she had once been. It was her Sarah self, not Salimatu, who could read simple words, and count out simple sums using the abacus. It was Sarah who loved the song of the beads as she slid them from side to side, adding and taking away. And Sarah too, who did not sing the *Odudua* song anymore, even as still, somehow, thoughts of her beloved Fatmata were always with her.

The dockside at Gravesend was very different from the one they had left behind at Abomey. Although Papa Forbes told her to stay below, Sarah came up on deck drawn by unfamiliar sounds and smells. She buttoned up her coat and pulled on her gloves. Even so she felt cold in the September dawn. She shivered and coughed harshly, holding her chest where it hurt her.

It was Salimatu's cough and Sarah wanted it gone. Papa Forbes had said it would go when they reached England. She was afraid she would cough until she spat out blood like Peg-leg Jed, the cook on *Bonetta*. He used to spit into a bucket in the kitchen or a piece of dirty rag all spotted with dark dried blood. She did not like blood. Sarah deeply breathed in the damp, smoky air and Salimatu coughed in response.

As the sun tried to push through the early morning fog, Sarah saw other shadowy ships, big and small, tied to the docks, hardly moving in the mist, as if drifted in from another world. Although the noisy dock was dirty, smelly and frightening, she stayed and watched the people laughing at the dockside; the *Bonetta's* sailors, running up and down the gang plank, pushing, and pulling the goods bound for enormous warehouses, moving them swiftly from ship to shore. After so long at sea they had no time to sing to her about Sally Brown. No time to say goodbye. They were eager to walk on ground that did not move, get to their homes and families. Those with no homes could not wait to get to the bars, Lieutenant Heard had said.

Now they had reached England, Sarah wished she knew where she was going. More ildly, she wondered, would Fatmata be there to meet her? 'No,' Salimatu, her other self, whispered. 'We'll have to go find her.'

Sarah shook her head, as if to shake free of Salimatu who she wished would disappear. She was tired of always having to fight with herself, always having to push her Salimatu-self down, into the depths of her being. She had to keep telling herself, I am no longer Salimatu with her old thoughts and fears—I am now Sarah with new fears. But keeping Salimatu at bay did not always work, for suddenly she would be there whispering or sometimes screaming in her ear.

Forlorn, she returned to the centre deck, sat down with the enormous sack and wooden crates, and waited for Captain Forbes to come to get her. Everyone had gone, except for Amos, the ship's bosun, who was staying on to guard the ship. He did not like women or girls on the ship. He said they brought bad luck. He glanced over at her sitting like a proper lady, her feet encased in soft grey leather shoes and, sneering, cleared his throat and spat. It landed with a splat close to her feet but did not touch her. All the same when Captain Forbes appeared, she ran close to his side, her eyes cast downwards in avoidance of the dreaded Amos and his filthy mouth.

As Sarah and the Captain descended the boat to the dockside Sarah, overwhelmed by the newness of everything, inched closer to Captain Forbes placing her head against his arm, her eyes barely open.

'Look up Sarah,' he said, clearly feeling sorry for her as she cut a figure of misery as they made their way.

His voice emboldened her and opening her eyes to the throng, she felt a sudden sense of calm, even a thrill of excitement, but when she saw the enormous horses, thick hair covering their eyes and puffs of grey air shooting from their noses, as they stood harnessed to the carriage, Sarah froze. Although it was almost five harvest seasons ago, she remembered how, after Santigie sold her to the Moors, she had been thrown on a large horse and taken her away from Fatmata, away from all she had known until then.

She whimpered, pointed at the snorting horses. 'No, no.'

'Don't be frightened. They won't hurt you,' said Captain Forbes, lifting her into the carriage.

She trembled and he wrapped a blanket around her legs. 'You're cold. You'll get used to our weather soon,' he said comfortingly.

Yes, she was cold, freezing, but that was not the only reason why she was trembling.

'Where are we going now, Papa Forbes? To see the Queen?' she said at last.

'No, no, dear child,' laughed the Captain, 'the Queen meets very few of her subjects. We're off to the train station and then home.'

Not to see the Queen? Hadn't he told her she was to be a special gift to the Queen? How can I be gift to the Queen if she won't even see me? Sarah thought. Her eyes stung from unshed tears. If she did not belong to the Queen after all then what was to become of her?

She clung to the long leather carriage strap that tethered her to her seat and peered out. There was so much to see. The carriage swayed and the sound of horses hooves clip-clopped noisily over the cobble stone. Buildings towered above them. Could they shake in the winds, like trees, then fall and crush them, she wondered. She had never seen so many people, all hurrying by, flashing past her eyes. The carriages criss-crossing so close they made her gasp again and again. She was sure they would crash into each other.

Arriving at the station, she clasped the Captain's hand, even more frightened by the size of the station hall, the strong and strange smells of people, the smoke, the noise. When the train arrived, snaking into the station screeching and bellowing, belching, smut and showers of steam into the air, she screamed and hid behind the Captain.

'*Djuju, djudu,*' Salimatu and Sarah cried as one.

'No. This is the train,' said Captain Forbes, evenly, noticing the curious glances of the people nearby, as Sarah's cries filled the air. Turning her around, he said, 'Stop it Sarah, stop it, right now.'

'No, *djuju* come get us,' cried Sarah in Yoruba, forgetting her newly acquired English.

'What is she saying Mama?' asked a smartly dressed little boy, tugging at his mother's red coat.

'Shh, Ernest,' she said, a long vertical finger firmly dissecting thin, pinched lips. 'She's a foreigner, she doesn't speak English.'

At this Captain Forbes scooped up a still wailing Sarah and walked hurriedly down the platform to the first-class compartment where he quickly boarded. He sat her down and shut the door.

'Stop crying, please,' he said, handing her his handkerchief.

'There are no devils here. And do try to speak English all the time.'

Sarah did not reply. Instead as the train moved off, she heard Salimatu whisper, 'ayee, we are inside the belly of the *djuju.*'

First the platform and people, but then the houses, trees, even clouds disappeared in a blur as the train sped away, shaking, and screeching its new song, *djuju, djuju, djuju, djuju.*

Sarah's whole body shook. 'Papa Forbes, Papa,' she whimpered, 'don't let the *djuju* take me to the ancestors.'

'No one is going to take you away from me, Sarah,' he said, putting his arm around her, 'you are quite safe.'

That word again. Safe. Her heart calmed.

✿✿✿✿

She had not understood any of his words the first time he'd said them.

'You're safe now,' the Captain had said, as he lifted her chin up and touched the marks on her face.

But was she?

Fatmata had told her that people like him, people who were skinless, were *djuju*, so she shrank from his touch, from his smell, but he had smiled and picked her up. As he carried her away from the 'watering of the ancestors' ceremony she trembled and, afraid the white devil was taking her to be his sacrifice, pissed all over him. Her white garment steamed and dried and smelled acrid in the sun, but he did not put her down. He took her to the missionaries.

'But what are you going to do with her?' asked Mrs Vidal.

'Take her to England with me.'

'Is that wise, old man?' Reverend Vidal asked. 'She's a slave.'

'I'm sure we can find a place for her in the Mission school,' interrupted Mrs Vidal. 'If she is bright, she could help teach others in time.'

'King Gezo has given her as a gift to Queen Victoria. He said to tell her that it was, "from the King of the Blacks to the Queen of the Whites."'

'The cheek of the man,' said the Reverend.

'It is not for me to decide her future. I will take her with me and hand her over to the Admiralty. But I will need to leave her with you until *The Bonetta* sails in a couple of weeks.'

'Do not worry, Captain,' said Reverend Vidal, 'we'll take care of her.'

'I'd better get sewing then. She'll need some proper English clothes if she is going back with you,' Mrs Vidal acquiesced.

'And what are we to call her?' asked the Reverend.

'Oh, I had not thought about that.'

'Well, those tribal markings on her face indicates that she is the daughter of a chief, so how about Sarah, meaning princess in Hebrew?'

'Hmm, Sarah was my Mother's name. Sarah, it is then. Sarah Forbes and I'll add Bonetta after the ship.'

# CHAPTER 2

*A kì í dá ọwọ́ lé ohun tí a ò lè gbé*
*One does not lay one's hands on a load one cannot lift*

## 1842

Birthing is women's business. When it is my mother, Isatu's time, Maluuma, my grandmother, leads her away from the men to the small birthing hut, on the edge of village. I am not yet a woman, but Maluuma brings me too.

'But leave that monkey outside,' she says as I follow her with, as always, Jabeza sitting on my shoulder, clinging to my hair. 'This is not a place for animals.'

'Yes Maluuma,' I say.

No one argues with her, not even my Jaja and he is the chief of the village. I tie Jabeza to the mango tree that shades the hut's opening and go in, to watch my mother give birth. We wait, the shadows getting longer, until they disappear, and still nothing. Madu's pain goes on through the hot, moonless night. I listen to the cicadas and watch her lying on the mat, panting and grunting, while trying to kick off the piece of cotton covering her body.

'Drink,' I beg Madu, putting the small calabash full of yarrow herb water to her lips. 'Maluuma says it will help wash the child out.'

Madu drinks but still she twists, turns and groans. I wave the palm leaf fan over her. It moves the air mixing the smoke from the oil lamp with the smoke from the herbal twigs and berries Maluuma is burning to help ease Madu's pain.

'You shouldn't be here Fatu,' Madu says between moans. 'You shouldn't see things like this. Go back to our hut. Go sleep.'

'No,' says Maluuma, 'by the time the sun has opened its eyes that one inside you will have come. Fatmata knows what to do. She has small hands and she might have to help me bring her into this world.'

'Her?' I say, doing a little dance.

'Yes' says Maluuma, nodding. 'I see the signs. It will be a girl child.'

And that is how I know I'm to have a sister at last. Although I find it hard to breathe, the smoke making my eyes itch, I would now rather let a lion rip off my arm than leave the hut. No, I need to be here for my sister's first cry.

When Madu starts to scream, I drop the fan, my heart beating fast. Her belly looks even bigger. Is she having twins again? Will they take them away too, like they did before, believing that twins bring bad luck to the village? I won't let them; I'll show them that I'm a warrior too. I can't lose any more brothers or sisters.

'Isatu, my daughter,' Maluuma says, 'you can push her out now.'

Madu pushes and screams but nothing happens. I sit by her side and whisper prayers to all the gods and still nothing.

'This is going to be a fight. Give her the cloth to bite on,' Maluuma says.

Madu chewing on the cloth, growls like a dog. But still my sister does not come. At last Maluuma says 'the opening is small. I will have to cut like last time.'

Shock grabs my belly and twists it. How can Maluuma cut when she is almost blind, her eyes covered by a filmy thin layer, the colour of watery goat's milk?

'*Ogun*, do not take my Madu,' I pray.

I've heard about cutting going wrong. What would I do without a mother? To be left with Ramatu? My father's first wife hates me, child of the third wife. No, no, no.

Maluuma pulls a knife out of her pouch, squats down at my Madu's feet and drinks from a gourd. She spits the drink into the air and over the knife before crying, 'Oh *Oloron* god of all creation, help my daughter, send this child safe to us. We praise you; we thank you.'

'Turn away,' Maluuma says to me, then she cuts and Madu screams.

I feel as if I am about to bring up everything I have ever eaten. When I turn around, I see much blood. I soak it up with straw and dirt while Maluuma presses on the cut until the bleeding stops. She gets some paste from a jar, rubs it on Madu's stomach and pushes down. My mother shakes, takes a deep breath, pants and pushes and bawls. She is covered in sweat. It seems that bringing my sister into our world will never come to an end. Madu gives one last screaming push and my sister slides out.

'Ayee! The cord's round her neck and an *ala* over her head,' says Maluuma removing the cord quickly before holding up the baby for Madu to see. 'Isatu, the gods are with you again. This one also has come with a message. She too will travel far. She has come with her protection, her gift. You've done well, my daughter. *Oduadua* we honour you; we thank you.'

I watch the baby stretch and wriggle and strain against the thin clear skin, the *ala*, 'white cloth' that covers her whole head. I cannot hear her cries, but I can see her face, flattened by the *ala* that moves up and down with every breath. I know all about this 'white cloth' because I too came into the world, ten harvest seasons before, with one over my face. Maluuma says those born with *ala* will travel far. Further than the marketplace, I hope.

Madu's whole body shines as if she has oiled the baby out. She tries to sit up, blinking as sweat runs into her eyes. I wipe her face and she smiles at me.

'You have a true sister now,' Madu says.

I nod, for until now I have pretended that Gashida, Ramatu's *cru* slave, was my sister. Madu stretches her arms for the baby but Maluuma is carefully peeling the *ala* off the baby's head without breaking it, without breaking the luck. It comes off with a whoosh as it rubs against the baby's hair. She opens her mouth and screams.

'Her eyes are wide open. No one is born wise but this one will see all. She will go far,' says Maluuma passing the crying baby to me. 'Give her to Isatu while I take care of this.'

I hold my sister, who is only a little bigger than my monkey. I search her face, her wide-open mouth, her flat, squashed nose. I blow into her face and watch her swallow my breath. She stops crying to stare up at me. I know then that we are one, and as long as I have breath, I will be part of her, and she will be part of me.

'What is she to be called?' I say, laying her in Madu's arms.

'Child, always you ask questions. One does not eat scalding stew in a hurry. Her name will come when the time is right. Until then we call her Aina, girl-child born with cord around her neck. Now, go get your Jaja,' says Malumma, pushing me out of the hut.

In the first light of day, I run through the village, to the chief's compound, Jabeza clinging to me as usual, chattering into my ear. 'Ayee, ayee, the child has come,' I shout. 'Madu has brought a new mouth to the village. Jaja, come quick.'

The villagers rush out of their huts praising the gods that has brought a mother safe through her birthing, brought their chief another child. All come except for Ma Ramatu, my Jaja's first wife and Jamilla, his second wife. Gashida, slave to Ramatu, my friend and pretend sister, crawls out of the hut. She rubs the back of her hand three times before she is pulled back. I smile for that is our special signal, our sign of friendship. Jaja walks slowly towards the birthing hut and I dance besides him trying to tell him about the coming of girl Aina.

'Enough,' he says at last. 'Let your madu tell me when she is ready.'

Men do not go into the place of birth; my Jaja, does not want to be made unclean so he stays outside and calls, 'bring me the gift from the gods, bring me my child.'

Maluuma comes out with Aina pressed against her flat chest sucked dry by age, with no milk to feed the child who opens and shuts her mouth, screaming in want. She hands Jaja the baby. 'Chief Dauda,' she says, loud and clear, so that all who are near may hear, 'you have a girl child. She came with a cord around her neck and an *ala*, over her head.'

'Ayee,' cry the women, 'such luck.'

Jaja looks long into Aina's wet face. I cannot tell what he is thinking. Had he hoped for another boy child to replace...? I stop. I cannot think of that at this time.

'And the mother, Isatu?' he asks.

'*Oduadua* helped her through the journey, praise be.'

Jaja nods and holding girl close he walks to the centre of the village, sits with the elders and waits for Pa Sorie, the *halemo*, the wise one, to throw the stones and find out Aina's true name. Only then will we know if the child has come to stay. I pray that the ancestors are going to send her name before too many sunrises.

'Come,' Maluuma says to me, 'we still have things to do for your mother.'

Several women come to the birthing-hut wanting to talk about the birth. When the blast from the calling horn sounds, we are all surprised.

The women call out, 'The name has come soon. The ancestors were waiting for her.'

'Praise be to *Oduadua*,' says Madu, trying to get up.

Maluuma pushes Madu back. 'You cannot leave here yet. Fatmata will go to her father and get Aina's true name for you.'

'Wait,' says Madu. 'Let Fatmata take the child-string to him.'

Maluuma nods, opens her goatskin bag and brings out two new plaited child-string braclets, one green and one red. She unplaits the green one and smooths it out, mumbles over it, and throws it into the fire. Then she passes me the red one, the child-string that says another girl-child has joined the clan.

'Go, give it to your father,' says Madu.

'He will give you the girl's name in exchange,' adds Maluuma. 'Go quick.'

I rush to the clearing and push to the front of the gathering to kneel in front of my Jaja. 'Chief Dauda, another child-string for you,' I say and wait.

Jaja takes the plaited bracelet from me and holds it up high. 'A red child-string, a girl-child has joined us,' he announces to the rest of the villagers. 'Praise be to *Olorun*. We thank you; we praise you.'

I watch him put it on his arm, to join the red one for me and the green one for my brother Amadu. I try not to think about the other green string that is no longer there, the one for Lansana, my first brother.

Although Lansana had six harvest seasons more than me, the daughter of our father's third wife, he never ignored me. Thin and tall, but not as tall as our Jaja, Lansana could pick me up and swing me around as if I was one of the sacks of yams he threw over his shoulders in one sweep at harvest time. Lansana's feet always pressed lightly on the ground, as if ready to run faster than the harmattan breeze. Whenever he was nearby my insides sang.

I do not want to think of Lansana now, for it is my disobedience that turned him into *osu*, a non-person. I only want to think of my sister.

Pa Sorie takes Aina and blows into her face. Holding her high, he walks her to the four sides of the village. Each time he stops and shouts, 'welcome Salimatu, girl child of Chief Dauda of Talaremba,' and a cry goes up. The drums beat out the news. The sound lifts the wings of the birds, up, up, as her name carried by the wind, rises through the trees, floating through the clouds to the stars.

'Salimatu,' I whisper, 'My sister, Salimatu has come.'

# CHAPTER 3

*Evildoers are trapped by their sinful talk, and so the innocent escape trouble*
Proverbs 12:13

## July 1850

As the train sped on, Sarah remembered the day her Salimatu-self left Abomey. She had stood at the water's edge, unable to move. The wet sand held her tight, refusing to let her go. Captain Forbes picked her up and she stiffened in his arms. His strong smell filled her nose, robbing her of the sweet smell of the pawpaw and palm trees that lined the edge of land. Salimatu shut her eyes, not wanting to see the marks she had made in the sand, not wanting to see them washed away as if she had never been there. She made no sound as Captain Forbes walked with her into the ocean, neither squealing with delight, in pain nor even crying out as fear, like a huge bird, swooped down and clutched at her inside. In the four harvest seasons since Salimatu had become a slave, separated from Fatmata, she had learned to hide her fear and be silent.

She was less frightened of Captain Forbes now. They had been together for a full moon cycle since he stopped King Gezo from making her one of his sacrificial offerings during the 'watering of the grave' ceremony. But the ocean did frighten her. Fatmata had told her, a long time ago, that *Mamiwata*, the goddess of water, lived in the big river and was ready to swallow those who disturbed her sleep. And here was the river in front of her, more water than she had ever seen, waiting for them.

'Don't be scared,' the Captain said, sitting her down on the plank seat in the middle of the canoe, before stepping in too. The canoe rocked and the rowers, big and strong, their bodies shining with oil, steadied it with their oars before pulling away. 'These Kroomen can get their canoes over huge waves even better than my sailors.'

Salimatu stared hard at the shore fading into the distance. The sun on the white sand hurt her eyes and they filled with tears that she refused to shed. This isn't my real place, she thought, so why should I cry. But once on the big ship that the Captain said would take them to England, the chance of ever returning to her village with or without Fatmata was gone. She took hold of the side of the canoe and tried to stand. She could not leave if Fatmata was still out there, somewhere.

The Captain grabbed her. 'Sarah, hold on or you'll fall in.'

She sat back down and thought, what if Fatmata had been taken across the big ocean too. That's what Ma Ayinde had told her, the day the Minos, King Gezo's women-warriors led by Akpadume, had come to take two women from the slaves' compound. Salimatu was afraid of the Minos. Whenever she saw them, she saw fire, for they had been part of the warriors who burned down her village and killed most of her family.

'Where are they taking them?' she had asked while the Minos dressed the women in long white garments of mourning that hung loose from their shoulders, and led them away from the compound.

'They've been chosen as sacrifices for the watering of the grave ceremony today,' Ma Ayinde told her.

'Why don't they use goats and chicken? That's what Madu used when making a sacrifice.'

Ma Ayinde's eyes flew open. 'To honour the King's ancestors?

No. When they put that white gown on you, know that your time has come. All the slaves in the King's compound will wear white one day and be sacrificed as part of the ceremony, one day, even you.'

'When King Gezo bought me from the Moors, he said he could see by the markings on my face that I was a chief's daughter, so I was safe here.'

Ma shook a head and sucked her teeth. 'Child, you've a lot to learn.'

'My sister will come find me.'

'You been sold and resold, captured during the war at Okeadon, to end up here three rainy seasons now, has she come? Your sister is gone. If she's not dead or sold to the Moors, she will be far away, across the big, big waters, by now. Don't know which is worse,' said Ma Ayinde, with a bitter laugh. She pointed to the marks etched into Salimatu's cheeks and added, 'you may have the marks of a chief's daughter but that won't save you. In this compound you are nothing but another slave and like all us slaves here, your time will come, then you will be sacrificed.'

Salimatu touched the face markings cutting deep into her cheeks. They may have saved her from being sacrificed, but here she was now, in front of the 'big water', the ocean with water as far as the eyes could see being taken away. Was that any better? The water seemed to attack the canoe, roaring loud, angry, and hungry, ready to swallow them alive. Then it backed away, slithering and sliding, hissing, only to come rushing back with greater power. It was like an animal with two heads that went both ways. Water splashed her face; she licked her lips and her eyes widened with surprise. It tasted of salt. All the rivers she'd known had never tasted of that. On the long journey to Abomey she had learnt that salt was important, not just for cooking but for buying and selling. Was there enough salt to make water everywhere taste of salt? Did the white man have so much salt they could put it in all this water? She gripped the edge of the canoe as another wave hit the canoe hard. Her gloved hand slipped into the ocean. She squealed, her hand shot out spraying her with water.

Salimatu pressed her wet hand to her chest and through the clothes she had been forced to wear by Mrs Vidal, she felt for her *gri-gri* pouch, tied with a string, around her neck. Inside it were bits of blue glass, a piece of her 'white cloth,' her *ala*. They will protect her. That's what Fatmata used to say. Salimatu wished she could remember more of the things her sister had told her as they walked through the forest so long ago. She had only four seasons then, now she had eight. Everything was fading away.

The shout made her look over her shoulder. There was the ship, *HMS Bonetta*, rising high above her head, up, up, up, its poles and ropes cutting the sky up into small sections. Did those poles reach right into the sky? The huge ship rocked and swayed, like a big dog trying to shake a monkey of its back. That brought memories of Jabeza, Fatmata's monkey. She wanted to hold on to that thought but it slid away. Other memories came, of Madu and Jaja, her parents. Could she climb up, squeeze through a hole in the sky and reach them? To ask them . . . what? Was Fatmata up there too? Before she could catch these memories and hold them, they drifted off like smoke.

Captain Forbes shouted to the sailors on the ship and they threw down a rope ladder. The canoe did a dance as he picked her up and began to climb the ladder. Shutting her eyes and trying not to breathe in his smell, she clung on, till rough, hard hands, reached down and grabbed her. The sailor put her down, her feet slid on the wet deck and she reached for a rope to steady herself.

The Captain rushed away, waving his arms about and shouting. Sailors ran all over the ship, fast and busy, like pink ants building a nest. She had to keep away from them. Ants can sting.

One man rolled a barrel close by and she jumped out of the way, falling into the side of the ship. It was wet, the water soaked through her clothes.

Above all the noise of the ship the call of the *Ochoema*, the bird of parting, could be heard. She wondered what would happen if she jumped into the sea. Would the men down there in the canoes catch her and take her back or would *Mamiwata* drag her down into the watery under-place to join all those who had gone before. She climbed on to a small box and holding tight, leaned over. The movement of the ship made her stomach toss and turn.

The wind blew her hat back and stroked her face. It felt like it used to when Fatmata blew on her face and say, '*Salimatu, I'm part of you and you are part of me. We have swallowed each other's air. We will never be lost to each other.*' She knew then that Fatmata had travelled on these waters. Why else had she come to her like this?

'Sarah, Sarah,' called Captain Forbes. 'Get down.'

She did not answer.

'Come, Sarah,' he said, coming up to her. 'You cannot stay here.'

She shook her head. 'Not Sarah,' she said, tapping her chest, 'Salimatu. Me. Salimatu.'

'No. I've told you. Sarah.' He pointed at her. 'Remember, you are now called Sarah Forbes Bonetta,' and tapping his chest he said, 'Captain Forbes, I'm Captain Forbes. You understand?'

She did not reply. The Captain grabbed her hand. 'I'll have to teach you more English words,' he muttered leading her below decks.

She understood some of his words now although it was not her talk. She had picked up the Fon language in the King's compound, now she was having to learn English.

Down in the cabin Captain Forbes wagged a finger at her.

'Stay here,' the Captain said. 'It is too dangerous up above. I'll sort out somewhere for you after we set sail. You will be safe in here.'

He gathered a few items and just before walking out and shutting the door he said, 'Sarah, stay here, understand?'

'My name not Sarah; Salimatu,' she muttered.

It was dark in the cabin except for the light coming through the small porthole in the side. She tried to see out of it, but it was too high.

'Ca-bin,' she whispered, then repeated the word again, 'cabin.' Liking the taste of the word in her mouth she said it again, faster and louder, again and again, turning around and around, spinning until she finally sank to the floor and her dress spread around her. It reminded her of the way Mrs Vidal had arranged the dress before painting Salimatu's picture. She had hated having to stand still for ages, dressed in her first English outfit, in shoes too tight, hat too big and gloves too hot. She had moaned and hid her face on seeing her image on the paper, flat, dead-looking, as if already with the ancestors.

Now Salimatu sat on the cabin floor winding the hat ribbon around her finger. When she pulled at it the hat fell off. She jumped up and threw it to the corner. Staring at the stiff black leather shoes, she frowned, not liking them for they hurt her feet. 'Shooes,' she said remembering what the missionary lady had called them. She tried to wiggle her toes, but her stockings would not let her. 'Shoes' she said again and kicked them off. She pulled off the stockings and spread her toes out wide. 'Stock-ings,' she said, waving it above her head, before flinging them too into the corner and whirling around. The frills on her dress twisted and turned, doing their own dance. She stopped and smoothed down the dress. The softness of the cloth, the satin bows, felt wonderful. She tried to undo the row of buttons down the front of the dress, but at first they were hard to shove through the tiny buttonholes. Pushing and pulling, tugging hard, one button went flying. It was easy, each button slid through its hole and in no time, she was stepping out of the dress.

Soon she stripped off everything Mrs Vidal had made her wear. 'Pet-ti-coat, pan-ta-lettes' she sang, throwing the garments around the room. Naked, but for the *gri-gri* pouch around her neck, she stood in the middle of the cabin and rubbed the monkey tattoo on her thigh. She was a warrior after all. Picking up the dress, beautiful, soft like the underside of a bird's wing, she held it to her cheek.

Although the shouts and running feet had faded away, the ship was still alive, creaking and swaying. In all her eight seasons she had never been alone like this. Salimatu held her *gri-gri* pouch in a tight grip, pulled the cover off the cot, wrapped it around herself and lay down on the floor. She faced the door, waiting, just as she had the past four rainy seasons, for Fatmata to come get her.

'Salimatu,' she said once more. 'Not Sarah, Salimatu.'

Fatmata will tell the Captain my name when she comes to get me, she thought. After all, hadn't she helped Maluuma, birth her; been there when the *halemo* called on the ancestors for her true name. My sister knows I am Salimatu.

She drifted off to sleep singing the song Fatmata sang to her during their long walk through the forest. It was the only song she could remember now. She had sung it every day while she was at King Gezo's palace.

*Odudua Odudua*
*Aba Yaa!*
*You know our plight!*
*Aba Yaa!*

# CHAPTER 4

*Blessed is the one who finds wisdom, and the one who gets understanding*
Proverbs 3:13

## July 1850

Salimatu opened her eyes, looked around and could not remember where she was. She tried to sit up but her stomach lurched with the rhythm of the boat, full and empty at the same time. She lay back and closed her eyes

'Sarah, Sarah, get up!' She opened her eyes again, saw a back, covered with long dark smooth hair like on a goat and trembled. Fatmata was right, white men were hairy devils.

'*Djuju, djuju,*' she cried, curled into a ball and covered her head.

The devil said, 'Sarah, Sarah.' It was the voice of Captain Forbes. '*Djuju?* Stop that noise. No devil here.'

He reached out, Salimatu shrank away and with the bedcover wrapped around her, fell. Captain gasped and stepped back when he saw that she was naked.

'In the name of God,' he said, grabbing his under-shirt and dropping it over her head before making her stand up.

She could not see her hands or feet. She was in white; he had turned her into an *osu*. She tried to move but got entangled and fell over, her voice filling the air as she screamed in terror.

Then in very bad Yoruba he commanded, 'there is no *djuju*. Stop the racket!'

She stopped screaming but refused to look at him. Instead she watched his hands roll up the sleeves of the undershirt. Then he picked her up and put her on his cot.

'Go back to sleep.'

Salimatu tried to stay awake, afraid that the ancestors would come for her if she slept. She must have drifted off, however, for suddenly it was morning and the Captain was sitting at his desk. He looked just as he had the day before. He still had the same short dark brown hair, brown eyes, long pointed nose with holes so small she wondered how he could breathe. His thin lips were almost hidden by his beard.

'Come and sit down,' he said pointing to a chair.

She did not move.

'Chair.' he said again and tapped the seat.

'Cha-ir?'

The Captain nodded. 'Yes chair,' he said, with a small smile. 'Sit down.'

She thought for a moment, got up, walked to the chair and sat down, trembling. If only Fatmata was there with her maybe she would understand this white devil.

'Good. Our lessons begin.'

She was still at the table eating a ship's biscuit and drinking a small glass of beer when there was a knock on the cabin door.

'Come in Lieutenant.'

Lieutenant Heard stepped in, stopped sharply and stared bemused at Salimatu.

'I've never seen a heathen sit at a table,' he said. Then peering closely, inspecting Salimatu as if she was a foreign specimen he remarked, 'You'll make an English lady of her yet,' laughing, 'but not her wearing your night shirt.'

The Captain sighed, 'that was all I could get her into last night. I practically fell over her when I came back to the cabin. She was lying on the floor fast asleep, naked under the blanket from my cot. I had to get her into one of my undershirts.'

'They're not used to wearing clothes, are they? You sure you've done the right thing, Captain, taking her away from her kind? Maybe you should have left her behind. The missionaries would have looked after her.'

'And what if King Gezo had sent one of his henchmen to get her? She would certainly have been the next human sacrifice. She's the Queen's property now, so I have to take her to England and hand her over.'

Salimatu did not understand what they were saying, but knew it was about her when she heard the name of the King. Was she to be sold again? Was the white devil going to take her back to be King Gezo's slave camp? She jumped up and tried to hide under the cot.

'Sarah stay. Not go back to King,' she cried.

'Sit down Sarah,' said the Captain, picking her up and putting her back on the chair. 'You'll never go back to that savage.'

The Captain sliced a piece of a yellow fruit, popped it into his mouth. He cut two more pieces, gave one to his Lieutenant and held the other out to her. 'Eat,' he said, 'I can't have you getting sick.'

She watched Lieutenant Heard suck at his and spit out the thick yellow peel. She took hers, put it in her mouth, closed her eyes and sucked. It was sour and screwing up her face, she spat it out quickly. Both men laughed.

The Captain went to the door and called, 'Abe, bring me some more water.'

The cabin-boy came with a bucket of water and poured it into the bowl on a stand.

'Wash,' Forbes said to Salimatu, 'then get dressed.'

Salimatu heard the word 'dress' and shook her head.

'Yes, Sarah,' he said, picking up the clothes and handing them to her. 'Get dressed.'

'You're going to be busy with that one,' said Heard. Captain Forbes glared at him and went out. Heard smiled and followed.

✿✿✿✿

In the days and weeks that had followed, Salimatu, sitting on the travelling cot that was positioned by the footboard of the captain's bed and where she slept, would watch Captain Forbes with twisting flicks of his wrist, shave and then trim, oil and wax his moustache. She liked catching him twirling the thin tips when he was thinking. She was getting used to his smell and sometimes would lean against him just to see if the waxed tip would prick her face.

Once Salimatu was able to find her way around the ship, she went everywhere, was into everything and got to know everyone, not just Captain Forbes and Lieutenant Heard. Every day, Salimatu learned fresh things. She was also learning that her name was now Sarah but she found that hard to remember. Her lessons with Captain Forbes began after breakfast. Abe, the cabin boy who brought them water to wash and food from the galley, would clear the table and they would start. At first it was, 'what new words can you remember Sarah?'

'Deck, ropes, sails, car-pen-tar, cook, bucket, sailor, money.'

'Money? Good.' He opened a small box and brought out a small, flat, thin piece of metal. It was round, and one side had a face pushed into it. She turned it over between her fingers feeling the markings on the flipped side. She put it in her mouth. It was cold, hard and resisted her attempt to bite through it.

'No, that's not for eating,' said the Captain, taking it from her. 'That is mon-ey, a pen-ny, for buying.' He put it on the table and pointed to the face. 'That is Queen Victoria, the Queen of England. We are all her subjects; we belong to her.'

Salimatu did not know what that meant but she asked, 'me too?'

'Yes, you too, Sarah. You are her gift and I will look after you like a father.'

'Father? You are my Jaja now?' said Salimatu frowning. She reached out and touched his face. It had no cuts, no tribal marks. He did not look or feel like her father, who she had called Jaja. No, this is different. 'I'm Sarah? You Papa?'

Captain Forbes threw back his head and laughed. 'No, Sarah I'm not your papa.'

'You are Papa. Papa Forbes,' she said with conviction.

'You are a funny thing. Fine, call me Papa. That's what my children call me.'

Sarah nodded solemnly. Yes, she could call him Papa. She did not want to call him Jaja.

I am two people in one, she thought. She'd answer to Sarah but inside she would still be Salimatu.

Whenever she could, Salimatu followed Abe around, helped him feed the chickens that gave them eggs, clean the fish caught to add to the never-ending salt pork or rotting beef, boiled rice with weevils and hard biscuit Peg-leg cooked for them all.

She picked up the words he threw at her and stored them for later. Maybe if she worked hard and pleased Papa Forbes, as she now called him, maybe he would help her find Fatmata when they got to England, then they could go back to Talaremba. At night lying on the travel cot, she repeated the new words until she drifted off.

Day after day the Captain would spread out large pieces of paper covered with lines and markings and stare them with heavy focus.

'What are you doing, Papa?' she asked one day.

'Reading the maps and charts and making calculations.'

'Why?'

'So that I can work out exactly where we are.'

'You do not know where we are?'

'When we are out on the open sea and can see nothing but water, it is the maps, charts, plus the sextant that helps to guide us so that we get to England.'

'What is a sextant, Papa?'

'This,' he said taking the instrument from Lieutenant Heard, who had come to the cabin armed with more charts, and instruments. 'We use it to work out the ship's position, the longitude and latitude. It tells us how far North or South we are. At night we use the stars.'

The Lieutenant laughed, 'Do you honestly believe she can understand all that, Sir?'

'Maybe not yet, but she will one day. She is bright, she learns quickly.'

It did not take Salimatu long to learn the names of stars and how to find them in the night sky. There was Polaris, also known as the guiding North Star, Ursa Major and Minor, Cassiopeia, Perseus and many more.

✵✵✵✵

Alone in the middle of the ocean, HMS *Bonetta* rocked and swayed, speeding towards England, away from all that made her Salimatu but maybe towards Fatmata. She soon got used to the ship's rhythm. Her stomach no longer wanted to empty itself every time she stood up, at least not until the day *Mamiwata* tried to drag them down, to join her and the spirits below. That day, the roar of the ocean, as swell after swell came crashing and banging into them the enormous sails flapping, left to right, in and out all frightened her. As the ship jumped and leapt, Salimatu crouched on all four in the cabin anxious that her whole inside would pour out and fill up the cabin. With each lurch of the boat her whole body rocked and she longed for her sister more than ever. Did she go through this? Had the sea goddess, *Mamiwata*, who punished those who disturbed her peace, got her? Salimatu groaned in unison with *The Bonetta* as the ship tried to resist the pull from *Mamiwata*.

Up on deck, the Captain, Lieutenant Heard, Amos the bosun, and rest of the the sailors, all fought hard with the angry goddess of the sea. It wasn't until Jack, a young, wiry boy attempting to tie down the sails that screeched and flapped like huge birds trapped in the howling wind, fell off the rigging into *Mamiwata's* screaming mouth that she receded, releasing them from the fight.

After the storm Salimatu learned to avoid Amos, the most experienced sailor, the bosun in charge of keeping the everything ship-shape on the ship. Whenever she saw him coming towards her with his rolling walk and bent back, his hammer in his hand she would turn and run the other way. She was not going to wait and see if he would knock her down with his hammer.

She and everyone on board knew that he blamed her for Jack being taken in the storm.

'God's truth, women should not be on ships unless they're chained up below, being transported. That devil of a storm came for her, the festering flea-bitten finagle. It sure be coming again so long as she be on this ship,' he said to the Captain as he fixed one of the broken planks.

'Hold your tongue, or you'll get a flogging,' said Captain Forbes, his voice loud and harsh. 'You do not tell me who I can have on my ship. Go below and fix the damaged futtocks.'

Amos held his tongue but Salimatu avoided him whenever she came upon him mending a sail or splicing rope. He would mumble a curse and spit at her. The other sailors, however, were friendly. The first time she saw them swabbing the decks, she sat on some ropes and let the cold water tickle her bare feet as she watched them work. When one started to sing, the others soon joined him, their voices strong and cheerful rose into the air. Salimatu listened and was brought back to her village and the men's celebrations, not nearby like this as girls and women were banished, but still the power of their many voices ringing out as one stirred her then as it did now with these devil men.

> *Sally Brown, she's a bright Mulatter*
> *Way hay roll and go*
> *She drinks rum and smokes terbacker*
> *Spend my money on Sally Brown*
> *Sally's teeth were white and pearly*
> *Way hay roll and go*
> *Her eyes were dark, her hair was curly*
> *Spend my money on Sally Brown*

Salimatu clapping her hands, jumped up and spun around, dancing. They were singing about Sali, they were singing about her. It made her feel happy and sad at the same time, only Madu and Fatmata called her Sali and they were gone. She listened to her song and when after several verses she too sang '*spend my money on Sally Brown*.' Abe picked her up and did a jig with her.

'She's a right corker,' said a sailor.

After that, whenever the sailors saw her, they sang a verse of 'Sally Brown'. One day a sailor brought out his fiddle. He played while the others sang and clapped. It was Salimatu, not her Sarah self, who took off her shoes and stockings and danced. As the music got faster, the men sang louder, and she danced wildly. She did not see Amos join the sailors as she danced and danced back into another world.

'Faster, faster,' Amos said, 'that's it, let the darkie dance, that's all they're good for work and dance, not sitting at table or learning to read, the skilamalink.'

Suddenly it was as if the music was lifting her up, up and she was going to fly all the way to the sun.

'Stop! What is the meaning of this?'

The music stopped and Salimatu was flying no more. She had been picked up by the Captain. She could see that he was angry, but she could not tell why. All she was doing was dancing. Was it wrong to dance in England? She wriggled to get down, but he held her fast. She was not free.

'Meaning of what sir?' asked Amos.

'How dare you make the child dance like that?'

'That's what the darkies do on the ships, isn't it?' said Amos, smiling.

Salimatu could feel Captain Forbes heart beating fast as he held her even closer.

'Is this a slave ship? You dare compare *The Bonetta* to those stinking hell holes? If I see any of you making the child dance like that again I shall flog you to an inch of your lives. She is not a slave.'

Sarah glanced at Captain Forbes but did not dare ask him anything at that moment. Salimatu too stayed silent as he strode away with her still in his arms.

Later that evening Salimatu said, 'Papa Forbes am I not your slave?'

'No Sarah. There are no slaves in England. It's been seventeen years since abolition.'

Not a slave? Then what was she, besides a gift. 'Not even *cru* slaves?' she asked.

'*Cru* slaves?' said Captain Forbes. 'There are different kind of slaves?'

Salimatu frowned. Until now she had thought that the Captain knew everything so how could he not know about the different kind of slaves? She moved closer, glad that she had something she could teach him.

'Fatmata told me that there are different kinds of slaves. *Akisha* slaves are slaves forever but if *cru* slaves work hard,' she said earnestly, 'they can buy back their freedom and return to their village.'

Captain Forbes pulled her to his side and said, 'I see, but in England you will not be any kind of slave. You are free to come and go.'

This was a new thought for her. She caught her breath and glanced at the Captain under her lashes. Did he really mean that she was free to do what she liked, go where she liked? She had not been able to do that since she was taken away from her father's village four harvest seasons ago.

'Can I go home to Talaremba then?'

'No. We're on our way to England.'

Salimatu frowned. England, England, England. Always he spoke about England. That word made her insides shake. Every time she thought of England her heart hurt. Sarah reached out and touched the Captain's arm.

'When we get to England, I am free to go look for Fatmata?'

'Who?'

'My sister.' Salimatu paused, then spoke rapidly, 'The women in the King's slave compound used to say that those captured are killed, sold to Moors or sold to the white devils and sent over the big water, like me.'

'Not like you Sarah. If your sister is alive and was sold to Europeans, we did not intercept their ship. We try to stop the slavers ships, but we are not always successful. In which case I'm afraid that she would have been taken to the West Indies or America.'

'Where's that?'

'A long way away,' he sighed. 'Now go to bed.'

That night as the sails screamed high and low, Sarah tossed and turned in rhythm with the ship, dreaming heavy dreams that soon became nightmares. She was Salimatu, not Sarah, running in a forest, calling for Fatmata. The forest was wet, and it became the sea. Salimatu could not swim. Sarah could not swim. Together they fought with *Mamiwata*. All the spirits from down below reached out. Sarah kicked and kicked, while Salimatu coughed and coughed. Then they had no more strength, they were sinking down, down, down.

A hand grabbed her. She tried to scream but there was no sound. She turned to see a boy. He pushed her up and shouted, 'go back, it is not yet your time.'

Was this her lost brother, Lansana the *osu?* The one Fatmata said had disappeared before Salimatu herself was birthed?

In the morning when she awoke, she smoothed her pillow and it was wet. And she coughed and coughed.

For the first time since she was captured more than four harvest seasons ago, she was free to do or go where she liked on board the ship, especially to the galley. As soon as she entered, Peg-leg Zed, the cook, drove her out swearing and cursing. But she always returned. She loved looking at his wooden leg, painted all over with bright blue flowers, yellow birds and best of all a monkey climbing a tree. It reminded her of—she struggled to remember—*Jabeza*, Fatmata's monkey. The name floated into her mind from way back in her past, and as soon as it came to her, she held fast to the fleeting memory.

Once she found Zed fast asleep, his leg off to the side of him, his snores pushing past the few teeth he still had. She wanted to pick the leg up, to have a good look at the paintings, and moving slowly, she crept up to the leg and stretched out her arms to pick it up, but it was heavy, so she entertained herself with tracing the beautiful flowers and birds and talking gently to the monkey as if it was her beloved Jabeza. She eventually grew tired, lay down and put her arms around the heavy leg, so the monkey appeared to be sat on her head, and she slept.

Peg-leg Zed woke up with a start, and seeing her wrapped around his leg, he shouted, 'Get out, get out. I told you, this is not the place of children.' She ran away as he coughed, spraying spit and blood, all over his chest. He terrified her, yet she hoped he would give her his wooden leg when they got to England.

As the time passed slowly Salimatu was left behind as she became Sarah, working hard to please Papa Forbes. She still loved to sing and dance with the sailors, even though Papa Forbes was set against it. It lifted her spirits to watch them and she would dance in her own way, out of sight, but in earshot of the singing and learned the words for her own enjoyment.

One day as they sat in the cabin enjoying the evening, practising her penmanship, she decided it was time she sang him 'her' sailor song. But she had hardly finished the first verse, when the Captain shouted, 'stop.'

'Didn't I sing it right?'

'Yes,' he said bemused, 'but that is not a song a lady or child should sing.'

'Lady?' This was another new word for Salimatu. 'What is lady?'

'You, Sarah. You are a lady. In England you must always act like a lady and speak in English. No Yoruba.'

Sarah nodded, Salimatu frowned. England. Again. That word made her insides shake. When she thought of England, she thought of Fatmata. She was sure that her sister was there somewhere. She had to find her. She would work harder, learn to write properly too. Now that the Captain was teaching her, even though it happened almost by accident.

'What are you doing,' she asked, sitting next to Papa Forbes, watching him dip the quill into the ink and making marks on the paper, night after night in the flickering candlelight.

'Writing in my journal.'

'What is a journal?'

'A book in which I write down all the things I do or see every day.'

'Why? Don't you know it?'

'Yes, I do, but others do not. Someday, others will read it and know my thoughts and my deeds.'

Salimatu thought about this. 'One day when I can read and write, I will write a journal too. Then I will always know who I am. Do you think that is a good, Papa?'

'That is good, Sarah,' he said smiling.

'Teach me, Papa.'

'I was not expecting to teach writing,' he said. 'There are no writing slates on the ship. You'll have to learn with quill and ink.'

One day the Captain gave her a little book. On the first page was written, *'This is the journal of Sarah Forbes Bonetta—August 1850'*

After that she wrote in her journal every day, just like Papa Forbes.

# CHAPTER 5

A kì í kò àgbàlagbà pé bó bá rún kó rún
*One does not teach an elder that what has been crushed will remain crushed*

## 1842

Always I think of my brother, the one whose name I must no longer say. Maybe, if Lansana had not given me the monkey he would still be here. I hugged Jabeza and remembered the day. Lansana and some of the other boys had gone hunting for monkey fur needed for their cloak of honour. I knew how important the hunt was for soon it would be time for the boys to go away from women and children, to go into the forest and join *Obogani*. There they train hard, in hunting, fighting, learning to become men. Later at the initiation ceremony, in front of proud grandmothers, mothers and sisters, they will be marked on their thighs with four long cuts, the monkey tattoo, symbol of our tribal animal spirit. Only then will the mother put a cloak of money fur around the shoulders of the new men.

So, when Lansana comes back, the one with the most fur, I throw myself at him so happy that he has enough fur to make his cloak. He also has something else.

'A gift for you, Fatmata, having seen nine seasons today,' he said, bringing a live monkey out of the bag slung over his shoulder. 'I have her mother's fur, but she is too little and has a broken leg, so I've brought her to you, our little healer.'

'Oh Lansana,' I say, fear sending a cold trail down my back, 'it's bad luck to kill a nursing mother.'

I hold the monkey close. 'Thank you, my brother,' I say, in a quiet voice, my heart bouncing, tickling my ribs, beating in unison with the monkey's heart. 'I will call her Jabeza, blessing of the gods.'

I do not tell him that I will have to go to the spirit-tree later and offer a peace-offering to *Oya* the god of re-birth, otherwise something bad is bound to happen to him.

News of the monkey spreads like smoke from a fire gone crazy at clearing time. The villagers, led by Ma Ramatu, his mother, rush to see it.

'How can you give a green monkey to that girl?' Ramatu screams at her son, breathing so hard her whole-body shakes and wobbles. 'What does a child know about the importance of such a prize?'

I say nothing because Madu has brought me up not to answer back to an elder, especially not to Ma Ramatu. I wanted to say to my father's senior wife, 'I know that the monkey is the royal family's animal spirit symbol and green the royal colour. Chief Dauda is my father and I have seen the monkey tattoo on his thigh and when he dies, he will be buried in his cloak of green monkey fur, as befits his royal status.' I do not though, instead I race away, broke off one new banana leaf from the tree before sliding past Ma Ramatu's and Sisi Jamilla's hut to my mother's. Inside, I go to Maluuma's corner and open some of her medicine gourds. I mix bone-knit and Fo-ti with honey and water just as Maluuma has taught me. I plaster Jabeza's leg with the mixture then wrap it with banana leaf. Jabeza bites me, hard, as I set her leg, but I do not stop. I am a healer.

☼☼☼☼

Two harvest seasons later, the *halemo*, Pa Sorie, and his helpers rush into the village at first light, before the sun has wiped the sleep from its eyes, banging drums, shouting, blowing horns. They have come to drag the boys who are over fourteen harvest seasons off to the forest for training into *Obogani* society and Lansana is one of them.

The "boys-huts", where those who have seen more than ten rainy seasons live, is past the compound, to the left of the village entrance, over twenty spear throws away, far enough for them to wrestle, practice their dancing, tell stories. The boys with fewer seasons went there to play and watch the older boys. Girls did not go to that part of the village.

'Why are there no "girls hut"?' I once asked Maluuma.

'The hedgehog does not live in the grassland, only in the forest,' is all she says.

I listen now as Jaja, my father, and the chief of the village says, 'go now as boys and come back as men.' He raises his staff, and the men line the boys up, tie them together with strong twine before sacks are thrown over their heads.

'Blue is the colour of wisdom,' Maluuma told me a while back. 'Blue ties sky and water, top and bottom, the ancestors and us. Blue drives away fear and keeps evil spirits away.'

So, I'm not surprised when I see each mother bring out a piece of blue glass and tie it to the village entrance post before falling to their knees and letting their tears give mother-earth a drink.

'O *Ogun*, Mother of All, you are everywhere, go with them,' they all cry louder and louder.

I watch Ramatu, as the c=-hief's senior wife, adds her glass piece, the biggest, last. The deep blue glass pieces dance in the morning breeze as the sun passes through, turning them into the light blue of the sky.

From where I'm standing, I can see almost the entire village, over twenty compounds set in a circle.

'There are villages much bigger than even Okeadon, with more than fifty compounds and many, many people,' Daria had said once when I ran around the circle of huts faster than she could peel a yam.

'Bigger than this village?' I had laughed. 'How can anyone know all that is going on then?'

No, Talaremba is big enough, I think. The twenty or so compounds are set behind low walls with the huts for wives and children grouped around the main hut, among coconut, mango, banana or pawpaw trees. I never want to leave it. I stroke Jabeza who is sitting on my shoulder searching my hair for anything to eat.

When I get back to our hut, I kneel by Maluuma's side and ask. 'Why were the mothers crying?'

'They know that their boys are gone from them forever,' she explains. 'They will never be the same again because *Obogani* devil eats the boys before spitting them out as men.'

'Eat them? How?' I lean in closer.

'It is not for the eyes of women. The water that you're not afraid of is where you'll drown. The mothers' fear that the devil might forget to spit out their sons. Your mother too will cry when Amadu goes in ten harvest seasons.'

'Will Madu cry when I go to *Zowegbe*?'

'No. Mothers don't cry for their daughters. Girls are on loan to the tribe until they are initiated into *Zowegbe* and are trained to be women fit to marry. After that they belong to their *oko*. Yours is already chosen for when your time comes.'

'My husband is chosen?' I say, jumping up so fast Jabeza screeches, pulls at my hair hard before jumping off my shoulder. 'Jaja has chosen a husband for me? Who?' This was the first I have heard this, and I start to shake. All the words inside of me rush to squeeze my heart.

My grandmother brings out a red kola-nut from her pouch and hands it to me. I know what to do. Maluuma has no teeth so although I do not like the kola-nut's bitter taste, I would chew it, breaking it into smaller pieces for her. Now I hold it tight and wait for her to speak.

'Your madu should have told you, but a bird that talks doesn't eat rice.' Maluuma sighs, then without looking at me she says, 'once your blood begins to flow, you'll join the *Zowegbe* society and become a woman. After that Jusu will take you for his third wife. He'll be next Chief of Gambilli. Your Jaja has done well for you.'

'But Jusu has almost as many seasons as Jaja. I don't want to marry him or anyone.'

Maluuma pulls me down to sit at her feet. 'You want to stay unmarried with no children of your own, no fire stone to call your own?'

'No Maluuma, but why can't I just stay here. Why can't I have a monkey tattoo and fur cloak like Lansana.' I cry.

'Stop talking such foolishness. That is for boys. You are a chief's daughter, and this is your destiny. There are many paths open to you. Make sure you choose the right one. Always remember that you can be taken away to another place, to live with other people but no one can take away the things that go deep down, rooting you to your inside place.'

'I hear you, Maluuma,' I say but at that moment I wish I was a boy, like Lansana, or a warrior chief like my Jaja.

'Maluuma, what would happen if I followed the boys into the forest?' I say and bite into the kola-nut

She pulls me close and stares, with her milky eyes, into my spirit. Though half-blind she is all-seeing.

'Child, why must you always question what is? A chicken egg should not strike its head against a rock. Listen to me,' she says in a voice that strokes my heart, 'my child, never, ever do that. It is against the gods for those who have not gone through the ritual to know or to see what goes on between men. It is against *Ogun* for women to go near such a place. They will make the place and the men, unclean. It is right that men and women have their secrets. If anyone breaks the laws of the ancestors, they and all they hold tight to their being will be crushed into more pieces than there are stars in the sky. They'll be taken to join the spirits, not the ones above but the ones below. Look upon their man-spirit and you'll pay the price. You will not live to see another day. The Kwa-le forest is taboo for the next three moons until *Obogani* is over. Do you hear me Fatu child?'

When she calls me Fatu, my baby name, I know that she is worried about me.

'I hear you Maluuma,' I say, giving her the chewed-up kola-nut and for the first time I swallow the bitter juice.

✣✣✣✣

A few days later, however, I do see parts of the boys' training. It is Jabeza who gets me into trouble. She goes everywhere with me. When I go with Maluuma to gather herbs, my monkey comes with us, wrapped around my neck staring at the world over my head. When I do the planting and digging, sweeping and pounding, carrying water from the water hole, she is with me, tied to my back with a wrap, like the village mothers do with their young.

If I am not with Maluuma I disappear into the forest with Jabeza. She leaps from tree to tree chattering, calling me to join her. I have just chased her up a tree when I hear the drums. I hide among the leaves and remain as still as a stalking lion, waiting for them to go past. The noise does not fade away, however, for they stop.

'Don't look,' I tell myself, but I do look. I shift and peer down. There they are, the boys naked, blindfolded, being led, by the

53

*halemo* into the clearing not far from my tree. I see Lansana and the other boys standing in line, like soldier ants. The drummers stop then start up again and the boys begin to sing and dance. They dance until their feet bleed and the earth is fed with their blood. From high up in the tree I lose track of time, mesmerized. I can see their blood-flecks fly out screaming for life. When at last the boys stagger out of the clearing, their bodies and their feet weep red tears of pain, tears that should not, must not, come out of a man's eyes.

Once they are gone, I scramble down, run home and wait to die. But Maluuma is wrong. Nothing happens to me or to Maluuma, or my mother, or my father, or my brother Amadu or to anyone I hold close to my being. Praise be to the gods.

After that I go to the forest every day. I follow the boys, but not close enough to get caught. I watch, I listen, and I learn with them. Then it is time for them to be taken one by one even deeper into the forest and left alone for their final test. I can no longer trail after them and I think all is well for no one knows what I have done.

But my action must have put a curse on my brother for Lansana is the only boy who does not return from *Obogani*.

'Lansana, forgive your father for turning his back on you,' Ramatu cries, when after one moon cycle Jaja makes him *osu*, an outcast for having failed his manhood test.

Raising her hands and voice to the skies, Ramatu cries, 'hear me, O *Olorun*, god of creation; forgive this man who calls himself a Jaja but refuses to bury his child.' Then grabbing Jaja's right arm she shouts, 'look at this, look, only three child-string bracelets.'

Everyone knows, but dares not say out loud, that more child-strings should be on that arm. A great man should have many children to show his prowess, his wealth. Jaja has but two green child-strings for Lansana and my little brother Amadu and a red one is for me. There is no child-string from Sisi Jamilla, Jaja's second wife. They say she is barren.

I know those strings. I learned about colours with those strings. Red is for girl-children because their knowledge is small, and they bleed on their moon cycle. Green is for boy-children, green is for strength. I want to be green not red.

✴✴✴✴

Jaja taught me about right and left with those strings. Right arm is for the living, left arm for the dead. Jaja's left arm has nine white plaited strings. Seven of those strings are for Ramatu's children, the six that came before Lansana and one after him, all children who came and quickly returned to the ancestors.

'Why are these two twisted together?' I asked Jaja once, as I tried to untangle them, like I did when I helped Madu with her weaving threads.

Jaja had slapped my hand away before saying, 'these two white strings, twisted together, are for your sisters who came together, sent to Isatu by *ngafa*, evil spirits.'

And that is how I got to know that I had had sisters, twins, who were taken deep into the forest and left there to return to the ancestors.

✴✴✴✴

Now, no one moves as Ramatu shakes Jaja's arm again and cries. 'Why didn't you give me more living children?'

The women suck in air and let out a long hiss through their teeth. Of the seven children Ma Ramatu birthed only Lansana has stayed, still she has said what she should not have let pass her lips. The men move closer forming a wall of disapproval. No one is surprised when my Jaja, Chief Dauda of Talaremba, raises his arm and strikes Ramatu. She falls to her knees, screaming. He hits her again and again. It is only when the *alagbas*, the old men who've seen much, shout 'enough' does Jaja stop. He wipes the sweat off his face with a shaking hand, and steps back.

'Hear me,' Jaja says then, 'listen, O people of Talaremba. As your Chief Dauda, I say the name Lansana will not be said in this village again. Not until I see his face, either here with the living, or on the other side with the ancestors, will that name pass my lips.'

Then Jaja snaps one green string and flings it to the ground. It lands in front of me. I understand then that the gods do not forgive. They always demand payment.

'O gods of gods, O mighty *Osain*,' I pray, 'forgive me. I, a girl, should not have tried to learn things fit only for men. Punish me, let me pay the price for my disobedience, not my brother, not my father. O great *Osain*, send Lansana back to us.'

I pick up the green broken child-string and hold it tight. I want to run after Jaja as he walks away, his head bowed. Maluuma grabs my arm and Madu, her hands resting on her swelling stomach says, 'leave him.'

# CHAPTER 6

## Igi kì í dá lóko kó pa ará ilé
*A tree does not snap in the forest and kill a person at home*

# 1842

That was seven moon cycles ago. Now a girl child has come with her red string. I watch over Salimatu as Maluuma pours a little more warmed cocoa-nut oil into her hand and with long slow strokes, pulls, squeezes, and rubs down my sister's body as she wriggles, kicks her fat legs and gurgles.

'She always laughs when you do the rubbing, Maluuma.'

'You used to laugh too.'

'Me?'

'Yes. I did this for you too, for twelve moon cycles. So, I must work on Salimatu for six more moon cycles so that her back is good and straight for all the loads she will carry,' said Maluuma pulling and pushing at Salimatu's legs. 'This should make her legs strong to walk and run fast.

'Like mine?'

'Yes,' laughs Maluuma, 'just like yours, but I hope that she does not use them to walk into trouble like you, my child.'

I laugh too. I like Maluuma teasing me. She is always saying, 'slow down'.

'Fatmata, come and help me,' Madu calls from inside the hut.

I shoo away Jabeza, who is sitting on my shoulders and clinging to my hair, because Madu has banned her from being taken into our hut. The monkey had knocked over pots of blue dye Madu had spent weeks getting from knotweed and tangled the weaving threads, ruining the cloth Madu had worked on for three days.

Madu hands me one end of the woven cloth. 'Help me fold this. It is big and heavy.' I hold on tight as we put the ends together then pull to make it flat. 'I must take them to the market,' she says, putting the folded cloth into the basket by her side.

'Ayee! What? You know you can't go to the market yet?' calls Maluuma from outside.

Sometimes my grandmother's hearing is very sharp. Madu says she was sure Maluuma could hear a worm sneeze.

'But worms don't sneeze.'

'That is so.'

Maluuma must have very special powers.

'You are in the middle of your moon cycle,' says Maluuma, coming into the hut. 'Your blood is still flowing,'

'It's almost over, Maluuma. I didn't think I would start my cycle again so soon after giving birth. She's still taking my milk.'

'It comes when it comes. You're ripe.'

'Well, I can't wait until after the rain season. We need to get some things from the market, but I must sell the cloths first. I'll go with Kendi and the others. They leave before the sun has risen.'

'Ayee, you can be as headstrong as your daughter. One does not eat scalding stew in a hurry. You can't leave the compound yet; you are still unclean and have this one to take care off. No, I will do it. I have many medicines and herbs I could sell there,' said Maluuma laying out bundles of dried herbs and plants.

'You've not been Bantumi for many moons now, Maluuma. It's a full day's walk. It'll be too much for you, my mother. We'll manage.'

'I will take Fatmata with me,' says Maluuma. 'The time has come.'

'Fatmata? What does she know about selling?'

'She has to learn. She's ready. She will be my eyes.'

I don't know how hard I am biting my finger, as I wait for Madu's answer, until I taste blood. I had begged Madu to take me with her so many times and always she had refused, now she has no choice for Maluuma has spoken.

When we are leaving, before the first cock has crowed, before the waking sun has pushed away the darkness of night, Madu brings water for ritual blessing. I kneel in front of her and wait.

'*Oduadua*, god of all women, lead them on their way,' she says. 'Go but come back.'

I sip water from the gourd she holds to my lips.

'*Oduadua* will bring me back,' I say, standing up.

Madu places the *shukubly* basket full of her woven cloths on my head. It is heavy but I smile at my mother and follow Maluuma. Six of us journey out. I walk behind them, with Maluuma. Although they all have larger, heavier loads than mine they walk at speed, even Khadijatu who never wants to do any work. They are soon lost in the dark.

Leaning on my shoulder Maluuma, walks slower and slower seeming to place each foot down with care as if afraid to disturb Mother Earth. The sun has woken up and gone over our heads before we get to Bantumi.

By the time we arrive the others are already selling their goods. I make Maluuma sit down in the space they have saved for us. I chew some kola-nut for Maluuma and give it to her. Only after she is enjoying her kola-nut do I spread a plain blue cloth and lay out some of Madu's cloths to sell and Maluuma's herbs and potions.

The market is crowded with more people, than I have ever seen, buzzing around like bees, speaking in many tongues, the sounds strange to my ears. Traders are shouting, calling, selling their goods brought from near and far away. There are foods that I know, and foods that are strange and new to me. Fish with dead eyes and wide-open mouths are mixed with eels and big snails. The taste of spices is in the air and I sniff their worlds into me. There are leather goods, straps and sandals, woven and dyed cloths. Iron goods push for space next to old women like Maluuma, selling medicinal roots and herbs, amulets and potions. Amongst all this are piles of animals' mess, dropping of pigs, goats and cows waiting to be sold. The many dogs run around barking, snapping, searching for scraps.

'Ayee, go, go away,' I scream and throw a stone from my sling at one of the dogs as it lifts its leg against Madu's basket that is still full of cloths to sell. I think I broke its legs for he yelps and drags itself away.

As the sun rises higher and higher its heat feels like fire on my skin and not even sweat can cool me down but still, I shout and call as loud as any other trader.

Then everything seems to stop and a tense silence descends, pierced only with the cry of 'Moors, Moors, the Arabs.'

As people move back and stare questions pepper the otherwise shaky calm. Arabs? The men who capture, buy, or steal people away? *Oduadua* help us. Some mothers stand in front of their children to hide them from the Moors. Two of them, in robes white as the clouds above, crack long leather whips as they ride through the market on large horses with wild eyes, flying spit, sweat and strong smell. The next horse thunders by with four naked men running behind. They are tied together and when one of them falls he drags the others down. The Arab sitting on the horse turns and hit them with his whip again and again, even as they try to get up. No one goes to help them; instead, some of the women throw rotten food at them and laugh. I bring out my sling that I always have with me.

Maluuma grabs my arm and hisses.

'What do you think you're doing? Put that away. You want to join them?'

'But why are some of the people laughing? Why won't they help them? What if it were their brother wouldn't they want someone to help them?'

'They laugh because they can, my child. Those slaves are not *cru* slaves like Gashida whose freedom can be bought. They are *akisha* slaves and will never be free. The Moors buy and sell people all the time. Do not let their eyes pass over you.'

So that is what it means to be an *akisha* slave. You can be tied up, beaten, laughed at, dragged through the market and no one will help you. If such a thing ever happens to me, I would fight. I would save myself. Even if no one knows it, I am an Talaremban warrior. Have I not followed and copied the boys as they went through their initiation rites?

# CHAPTER 7

*Do not forsake wisdom, and she will protect you; love her, and she will watch over you*
Proverb 4:6

## August 1850

Even though it was dark outside the room Captain Forbes took her into was bright, with the soft lights from candles, lamps and a blazing fire.

'Home,' he had said to her earlier. 'To Winkfield Place.'

Sarah blinked and gazed around the large room that was full of things she had never seen before. She could not take it all in. The walls were covered with paper—bright green, almost yellow, the colour of new leaves, with many-limbed trees on which vibrant coloured birds perched on branches that reminded her of Peg-leg Zed's wooden leg. She approached the nearest wall and sending out an arm, she stroked it feeling the thick, almost warm paper under her fingers and, overcome, she slid to the floor.

The floor covering was as soft as new grass. She frowned and looked down. Red grass, inside a house, and covered with small yellow flowers too! They reminded her of some of the flowers she had seen in the forest with Fatmata and her lips trembled. She bent down and sniffed but they had no smell. She pressed on them; they were not crushed. She tried to pick the flowers but could not.'Oh, Frederick look, she's trying to pick the flowers on the carpet. How sweet.'

'Sarah,' Papa Forbes called. She looked up to see his arms around the woman. 'Sarah, that's the carpet. Those flowers are not real. Come. This is my wife Mary.'

Sarah stood up; her gaze fixed on Mary Forbes. The woman was almost as tall as Papa Forbes, with dark hair pulled back, blue eye and a big smile.

'Good Evening, Mama Forbes,' Sarah muttered. She stopped speaking as the woman's smile faded.

'Mama Forbes?' Mary asked looking at the Captain.

'She calls me Papa Forbes,' he said.

'Oh! I see.'

Something was wrong, but Sarah did not know what. She moved closer to the Captain.

'Well, she had to call me something.'

Mary took hold of Sarah's chin, raised her head up and stared into her eyes. Her touch was gentle. 'Good evening, Sarah,' she said, with a little smile.

Sarah saw eyes the colour of the sea and her lips trembled. Mama Forbes pulled her close. Sarah pressed her face against the woman's soft, dark blue, silk dress. She did not want Papa Forbes to see her tears.

'Sit by me,' Mama Forbes said, taking Sarah's hand and leading her to the sofa opposite the huge fireplace. Sarah still felt cold and peered into the fire wishing she could sit closer to it and be warmed through. When she lifted her gaze, she saw a large painting above the mantelpiece. She knew what it was because the missionary lady had made her stand for ages while she painted Salimatu in her new 'English' clothes before she had left Abomey with the Captain.

Sarah had only looked at her painting once. So that was what she looked like, her face round, eyes a deep brown and wide apart, nose broad and flat. She had put her hands to her cheeks and felt the marks that told all who she was, the daughter of a chief. The girl in the painting had no marks on her face. Was the painting really her? Or had it started to take away parts of her? Would she soon disappear altogether? It had scared her, and she never looked at it again.

She recognised the man standing behind the chair as Papa Forbes; he had his hand on the Mama Forbes shoulder. The three children grouped around them smiling must be Papa's children. All the time as they crossed the big ocean, he only talked the most about England and his four children and she felt that she already knew them all. So, that must be Emily on her mother's lap, with Freddie sat crossed leg by Mama Forbes' feet and Mabel stood by the chair, looking up at Papa Forbes.

Sarah was afraid for Papa Forbes, for all of them, as she stared at the painting. Had they lost part of themselves so that they could be up there, looking down at themselves? And what about Anna? She wasn't there. Was she completely lost unlike the others in the picture? Then she remembered what Papa had told her on one of their nightly talks in the cabin, her eyelids drooping as he spoke, the ship swaying slightly in the calm of the coming night.

'Anna is almost two years old and I haven't seen her yet. She was born after I had sailed. Mabel is eleven and Emily seven years old.'

'I am between Mabel and Emily because I have eight seasons.'

'You know when you were born?'

'Fatmata told me. She was there. She helped Maluuma birth me just after the start of eight rice planting seasons past, just before the new moon.'

'That must be towards the end of April. I will look at my charts. My mother's birthday was 27th April. I will make that your birthdate.'

'How many seasons has Freddie got Papa?'

'In English Sarah.'

'How old is Freddie, Papa?

'Good girl. He's almost fourteen.'

Salimatu looked away now. She was not in any family painting; she did not have a family. One day she would find Fatmata and all would know that she belonged to a tribe of people she thought, stroking the hidden *gri-gri* hanging around her neck on a ribbon.

'So, what are we going to do with her?' said Mama Forbes.

Their voices faded away as she nodded off.

'I don't know, Mary. But I could not have left her behind. Apparently, she was captured for a second time during the Okeadon war and only lasted the three years or so as Gezo's captive because of her status. The marks on her face shows that she is high-born, the daughter of a chief. Gezo was saving her for a special occasion. I guess our presence was it.'

'Oh dear, the poor little thing.'

'You should have seen her, Mary. Dressed in white, she sat silent and still, carried in a woven basket high above the people's head towards certain death. I could not let that happen.'

'Oh, stop Frederick. How horrible.'

'I have sent a report to the Secretary of the Admiralty. They will decide what is best. She belongs to Her Majesty.'

'But look at her, Frederick, how is she ever going to fit into society?'

'Her English is quite good already. She is very intelligent and quick to learn. She never stops asking questions and although that can be tiring, she always remembers the answer.'

The sound of a bell ringing woke her up.

'Edith, take Sarah up to Nanny Grace. A bed has been made up for her in the girls' room,' Mama Forbes said to a young woman in a black dress with a white apron. 'Take care not to wake the girls up.'

'Goodnight Sarah,' said Papa Forbes.

'I stay with you. Sleep in cabin with you.'

'No Sarah, from now you sleep in the nursery,' said Mama Forbes.

Edith led her across the hall. Sarah stood the bottom of the stairs and shook. She had never seen such a thing. Were they going to climb all the way to the gods?

'Come, I'll help you upstairs,' said Edith.

Together they climbed the pile of wood that went up and up.

✻✻✻✻

When Sarah woke up that first morning at Winkfield Place, she wondered why the ship was not moving. Instead of seeing a calm sea through the port-hole, she saw a sky as blue as the sea through a small window and for a moment everything was upside down.

'There she is,' Sarah heard.

She turned her head and saw two pairs of pale blue eyes staring at her. She shut her eyes quickly and lay still.

'See, Emily, I told you she was not dead.'

Now Sarah remembered, she was not in the cabin with Papa Forbes. She was in bed at his home.

'She's very black, isn't she Mabel?' said the one called Emily.

'Silly, she's from Africa' said the first girl. 'Mama says it is very hot there and they're all black.'

'Do they get burnt? I wouldn't like that.'

'I never want to go to Africa.'

Africa? Was Papa going to send her back? She wanted to stay with him. She couldn't go before he helped her find Fatmata.

'Open your eyes. We know you're not dead,' said Mabel loudly.

'I don't think she knows what you're saying.'

'Yes, I do,' Sarah said and opened her eyes to see the girls in their long white nightdresses sitting on a bed across the room.

Salimatu, who was with her as always, whispered, 'be careful, they're in white.'

Sarah stared at the girls opened mouthed. Surely Papa Forbes would not sacrifice his own children. Would he? She pushed back the bedclothes and noticed that she too was wearing a long, loose, white dress. She plucked at it not wanting it to touch her body, trying to keep out Salimatu's voice screaming in her head. 'Ayee. They've got us. We are all dressed for watering their ancestors' grave.' There was no help for her. Tears she could no longer hold back fell.

'Why is she crying, Mabel?' asked Emily.

'What's your name?' asked Mabel

'What are you doing to your nightdress?' said Emily. 'You'll tear it, then Nanny Grace will be very cross. You won't like that.'

'Salimatu,' she whispered, still trying to rip off the white dress.

'Sali what?' Mabel said, laughing. 'What a strange name.'

'She can speak, she can speak,' said Emily jumping up and down on her bed.

'I'm Sarah, Sarah Forbes Bonetta' she said pushing Salimatu back. This was her place now.

Mabel frowned. 'You can't be a Forbes. Uncle George, Aunty Caroline and Aunty Laura have no children.'

'I am. Papa says so.'

'Who?' asks Mabel, stepping closer.

'Now, what is going on in here,' said a woman, marching across the room, the skirt of her grey dress swinging from side to side. She was short and round, with grey hair under a bright white cap, red cheeks and a mouth that seemed very small on her round shiny face. 'I told you girls to be quiet and not to wake up the poor thing,' said Nanny, putting down various items of clothing. 'Now go and get washed. Edith has brought up hot water for you. And then breakfast. Be quick, Freddie is home early from school and will be up in a minute.'

Mabel suddenly understanding shouted 'Papa,' and ran into the nursery next-door. Emily squealed with delight and dashed out after her shouting, 'Papa, Papa is here.'

Sarah jumped off the bed.

'Where are you going?' said Nanny grabbing hold of her.

'I want Papa Forbes,' said Sarah pulling away then she stopped abruptly. Through the doorway she saw him with his arms around Mabel and Emily, holding them close. He didn't see her.

'Oh, my dears, how you've grown?' she heard Papa Forbes say.

'I was just getting them ready to bring them down to you, Sir,' said Nanny Grace, walking into the nursery.

'Sorry Nanny,' said the Captain, cuddling his daughters. 'I know you would, but I couldn't wait to see the girls any longer.'

Mabel had her arms around his waist. Emily tugged at his coat. 'Papa will you stay and have breakfast with us, please?' she begged.

The Captain sat down on one of the straight-backed chairs by the large table and pulled her on to his lap. 'I'm afraid not. Mama is waiting for me to have breakfast with her. You can have breakfast with Freddie and then come down to the parlour for a little while after.'

Just then Mrs Forbes came into the room, a little girl clinging to her hand. 'I knew I would find you here,' she said with a laugh, 'so I have brought someone else to see you.'

'Anna,' said the Captain standing up so fast he almost dropped Emily onto the floor. 'My baby girl. Hello, little one, are you going to come to your Papa?' He reached out to pick her up, but two-year-old Anna, who could not remember her father, ran behind her mother's skirt. Then suddenly she started to scream, pointing at Sarah who was still left on the outside, standing at the bedroom door.

'Ssh, Anna,' said Mama Forbes picking her up, 'it's just Sarah.'

'Oh dear, I forgot,' said Papa Forbes holding out his hand to Sarah.'

'Papa Forbes,' she cried and ran to him.

'Are you her Papa too?' Mabel asked her father. No one heard her question.

# CHAPTER 8

*Open thy mouth, judge righteously, and plead the cause of the poor
and needy*
Proverbs 31:9

## September 1850

Sarah did not like the daily walk in the park, especially on cold wet rainy September days but she went without fuss.

In the short time she had been with the Forbes family Sarah knew one thing with certainty: that Mabel was not her friend. She would never be an older sister ready to look after her.

'Everyone is looking at us because of you,' Mary said walking away, refusing to hold Sarah's hand as Nanny had instructed.

Alone, Sarah walked past four boys in raggedy trousers and torn jackets, they stopped playing with their hoops and sticks and ran after her. They surrounded her, pointing and shouting 'tar baby, tar baby.' They were like animals circling, about to attack a prey. She shut her eyes and waited for the blows.

'Get away with you,' shouted Nanny, shooing the boys away.

'Nanny Grace why were those boys being horrible to Sarah?' asked Emily, moving closer to Nanny.

'They don't know any better,' said Nanny Grace, putting her arm around the shaking Sarah. 'They've never seen anyone like her before.'

'What is tar?' asked Emily.

'It is black and sticky and smells,' said Mabel, staring at Sarah.

'But Sarah is not black, she is brown,' said Emily.

'And I'm not a baby,' said Sarah shrugging away from Nanny and kicking at the puddles.

'No, you're not, so we will have no tempers,' said Nanny. 'Come, walk with me.'

'I thought they were going to attack her,' said Emily.

'Of course not. Whatever put that idea in your head? The good Lord says, "*For I am with thee, and no man shall set on thee to hurt thee: for I have much people in this city.*" So nothing will happen to any of you.'

'Maybe she should go where there are more people like her,' said Mabel, 'then she won't be different, and they won't stare.'

'Mabel Elizabeth Forbes, what an awful thing to say. How many times have I told you, as the good Lord says, "*clothe yourselves with compassion.*" This is Sarah's home now, so come along home, it's teatime.'

Sarah's face was wet but she kept her head down and no one, not even Salimatu could have said whether it was from tears as she whispered in Sarah's ear, 'remember, don't let them send us away before we find Fatmata.'

As soon as the front door opened Sarah heard the music. The sound tickled her insides. It made her feel like laughing and crying at the same time. She ran up the stairs and pushed open the parlour door, rushed across the room, crying 'Mama Forbes, oh, Mama Forbes.'

Mary stopped playing. 'What's wrong?'

Sarah stared at the big shiny, smooth box, with its black and white blocks sticking out in the centre.

'The box. The box makes music?'

Cautiously Sarah stretched her hand out and pushed down hard on the blocks, but instead of the music that had made her heart pound there was a high-pitched jarring noise, like glass bottles exploding in a fire. Sarah jumped back.

'Don't be frightened,' Mama Forbes said, seeing the look on Sarah's face. 'This is a pianoforte, and these are the black and white keys.'

Mabel, who had come into the parlour with Emily and Anna, laughed. 'Why is she frightened of the pianoforte, Mama? That's silly. It's not going to hurt her.'

'She does not know that. She has never seen one before,' said Mama, playing again. 'See, Sarah, it's just music. You must be gentle on the keys. Come, have a look.'

The music drew Sarah in and held her tight so that she had to sink to the floor. The notes washed over her like a shower of sound. Leaning her head against the pianoforte Sarah held on to its leg and rocked while the music dragged at memories. She heard the drums, the *shegbureh*, the *balangie*, the *cora*, sounds of long ago and tears rolled down her cheeks. From deep within her Salimatu's cry came out and then another and another until Sarah joined her, crying.

Mary Forbes stopped playing and sent the others away. She sank to the floor, her yellow dress spreading out, a circle of warmth and wrapped her arms around Sarah who lay there just as Salimatu used to lie in her sister's arms and cried herself to sleep.

'Mary,' cried Papa Forbes when he came in later, 'Is she hurt? She's not...?'

'No, my dear, we're fine,' said Mary. She got up and shook out her crumpled dress. 'I must look a sight. A good thing there were no visitors this afternoon.'

'What happened?'

'I was playing some Beethoven and it moved her to tears. Sometimes music can touch the soul. I will teach her to play the pianoforte. And who is Fatmata? She kept crying for her.'

✿✿✿

Later that afternoon Sarah dipped her quill into the ink and watched the ink bubble at the tip of the nib. She waited for it to drop, like a single black tear, back into the ink pot. Every time she picked up the quill, she was amazed that she could make marks on paper that were mysterious and secret from those who could not read. She loved the way the words looked on the paper, the feel of the paper, even the smell of the ink. Slowly she started to write.

*Wednesday, 4th September 1850*

*I had my first lessen on the pianoforte today. It talked to me. I can stil feel the keys under my fingers. Mama says I am musikal and it will be a plesur to teatch me. I am happy Mama thinks so but I wish she had not said that when Mabel was there becoz it made her cros. Freddie says that Mabel is always cros now because she is jelous of all the attenshun I get from Mama's many visitors.*

'What are you doing?' Mabel asked. Sarah jumped, and her hand shook.

'I'm writing in my journal,' she said, careful not to look at Mabel. She covered her writing hoping it was dry.

'What do you write in it?'

'Things I've learned. New words, sums, spellings. Things I do not understand.'

'Emily and I just make scrap books. That is far more interesting.'

'What is a scrap book?'

'We make a book then paste things we like in it. I can help you make one.'

Sarah frowned. She did not know what to say. It was the first time that Mabel had offered to do anything with her. Maybe Mabel was trying to be friends, so she said, 'O thank you, Mabel.'

'Emily is playing with Anna, so we can start your scrap book now, if you like. We cut out pictures from these old magazines of Mama's and put them in groups, animals, or birds or butterflies. Later we can also put in things we find while out on our walks, like flowers and plants; anything we like.' Sarah's heart began to pound as she thought about their walks.

Mabel brought a box from the cupboard. 'I'll show you mine,' she said taking out a large book and opening it. 'See, it has post-card pictures from our seaside outings and the programme from the circus too. Everyone keeps a scrap-book you know.'

'Do Mamas and Papas?'

'Yes. Mama's is pretty,' said Mabel as she cut a picture out of one of the magazines. 'She lets us look at it sometimes if we are careful. She keeps pictures of angels, birds, butterflies and many other things. She writes in it too, lines from poetry or songs. But what she like most is to write letters, lots of letters.'

'I don't think that Papa Forbes has a scrapbook. He just writes in his journal.'

Mabel snapped her scrapbook shut. 'How do you know that?' she asked.

'I saw him do it every night on the ship.'

Mabel bit her lip. She looked around. Nanny Grace was busy with Anna and Emily was playing with the alphabet blocks. Mabel stepped closer to Sarah.

'Why do you keep calling him Papa Forbes?'

'He told me to.'

'Well, he's not your Papa,' she said in a low voice so that only Sarah could hear. 'He's our Papa, not yours.' She pushed the magazines across the table. One hit the ink pot and tipped over the primer. Sarah snatched up her journal and stared at the ink spreading dark and wide, like the knot that started to grow in her belly.

'Nanny Grace, Sarah's spilt ink all over Miss Byles' book,' Mabel said with a smirk.

✣✣✣✣

Sarah loved all the lessons with their governess, Miss Byles who lived at the vicarage with her father, the vicar and came in every weekday to teach them. Everything about Miss Byles was long and thin. Her hair scraped back into a bun, feet in laced up boots, fingers long and thin like sticks dried and whitened in the sun, even her voice all was thin. Mis Byles' head, however, was full of things that Sarah wanted to learn. Things to make her into a proper English girl, free to go wherever she pleased, free to search for her sister. That is what she told Salimatu, reading the alphabet book with its rhymes and pictures and practising her writing, over and over, after Miss Byles had gone home.

She was ready when Miss Byles asked her, 'Sarah, have you copied out the rest of the alphabet rhyme?'

'Yes, Miss. I have.'

'This is very neat,' said Miss Byles when she saw Sarah's copy book. 'See Mabel, this is what your work should look like.' Mabel turned away and only Sarah noticed the tears at the corner of her eyes. 'Now, Sarah, you must learn the rhymes off by heart, then you can recite it to the Captain and Mrs Forbes.'

'I know them all.'

Sarah didn't tell Miss Byles that Papa Forbes had taught her the alphabet. She stood up and looking just above Miss Byles' head began to recite. She did not see Mary's frown, she just kept going.

*X stands for the cross,*
*On which Christ died in pain;*
*How great was his loss!*
*But still greater our gain.*
*Y stands for the young,...*

Sarah stopped. She could not remember. But she knew it, she did, she did. She had whispered it to herself again and again. When Mary laughed Sarah felt her heart start a dance of pain and shame.

'She does not know it. Miss Byles,' said Mabel, jumping up. 'I've learnt my poem off by heart. Do you want to hear it?' Before Miss Byles could say anything, Mabel started to recite.

*Little Lamb, who made thee?*
*Dost thou know who made thee?*
*Gave thee life, and bid thee feed,'*

Mis Byles held up her hand. 'Now Mabel,' she said, 'you must wait your turn. I was listening to Sarah.'

'I wish she'd go away,' mumbled Mabel glaring at Sarah.

'Mabel! That is unkind. How would you like it if that was said to you?'

Sarah opened the book and followed the words with her finger.

*Y stands for the young,*
*Such as you are, my dear,*
*Who should keep a still tongue,*
*And be willing to hear.*

She stopped. Tears burned her eyes so that she could not read. She wished Mabel would keep a still tongue sometimes.

# FATMATA

# CHAPTER 9

*Ayé ńiọ, à ńtọ̀ ọ́*
*The world goes forth, and we follow*

# 1842

The beat goes from drum to drum, from village to village, all the way to the market in Bantumi to wrap itself around me. I listen hard as the drum sounds skip and jump in the wind and my soul shakes. It tells me Pa Sorie, our *halemo*, our drummer, our keeper of stories has started on his last journey. I open my mouth to tell Maluuma but somehow, she seems to know.

'*Ogun*, we hear you,' she says. 'On our way here, I felt the ancient ones were near, I thought the signs were for me.'

One of the ladies seeing us packing up shouts over, 'Aye, Ma, you done?'

'Pa Sorie has gone to the ancestors. We have to go back, now.'

I pack quickly and lift Madu's basket onto my head, it is lighter, easier to carry. We walk through the night. The moon and Maluuma lead the way. Not once does she stop, not once does she seem to need my help. I walk beside her and with each step the distant drums pull us closer.

By the time the sun is high enough to eat into our minds we are back at the village. There drums mingle with the wailing of women. Salanko hits the drumhead like Pa Sorie taught him but everyone can tell that it is a different hand squeezing the strings around the *fange* drum, sending the message of a journey to the ancestors.

Seven times the earth swallows the sun and pushes out the moon hidden by the nightly rain, the gods weeping for our loss. Then it is time to make the last offerings. We gather at the far end of the village, waiting for the spirits, the *muunos*, to come. Their carved faces, fine, sharp, lips made red with berry juice the bodies made from strips of palm tree raffia, sway and rustle noisily as they move. The drumbeats change, getting faster and faster, the dancing gets wilder as the main spirit comes into the centre led by the elders. The women scream and start to run.

'Come,' says Maluuma walking slowly back to our compound, 'this is man business now. Fetch me water.'

'Yes, Maluuma,' I say. But this time I do not do what Maluuma tells me to do. Why is everything always 'man' business, I think, as I turn and creep closer to the men.

Madu sees me. 'Go back to the compound now,' she shouts as she ties Salimatu to her back. When I do not move, she pushes me ahead of her. 'Go. Women and children must not look upon this one.'

I turn around though and see the main spirit that has come to take Pa Sorie to the place of the ancestors that very night. The mask is real. It is not carved from wood. It is a skull with the eye socket painted red. Fastened to its body are dead chickens and snakes, swaying to its movement. I scream and Madu slaps me.

I run crying to our compound, into the hut, to Maluuma, for comfort, but she is not in her corner with her plants, or on her sleeping mat. Maluuma is crumpled on the ground.

'Maluuma,' I shriek, throwing myself down next to her.

'I was going for water. Pass me the stick.'

She is still with us. I wrap my arms around her and feel her bones sharp through skin once the colour of ebony, black as the night, now grey and wrinkled, like the skin of an elephant. Her head-wrap has fallen off showing a head that no longer has use of hair, shining and smooth full of knowledge and wisdom.

I help her to stand, but she sinks into me and I know that even with the stick she cannot walk. From somewhere deep inside of me I find the strength to half carry her to the sleeping mat and lay her down.

'They've come,' she says softly.

'Who, Maluuma?' I ask. But I know.

'The old ones,' she says.

'No, no, no! Not for you too, Maluuma.' I kneel beside her and wipe away the blood trickling down the side of her face. The cut is small.

'We cannot change what is. I am ready.'

I do not want to hear what she is saying. I must go get Madu. Suddenly Jabeza is by my side. She leaps on to my shoulder. I try to push her away, but she will not go. She clings to me and chatters into my ear.

'Let her be. She knows. The ancestors are here.'

I jump up and back away. 'O *Oduadua*, don't let it be this way.'

'No,' she breaths, 'don't go. Bring me water.'

Water! Something squeezes my insides so tight I feel sweat burst out all over me. This is my doing. If I had brought her water when she first asked, she would not have fallen trying to get it herself. Once again, my disobedience has brought punishment.

'*Ogun*, god of gods let the ancestors pass Maluuma by. It is me who has done wrong, not her. I am nothing.'

I scoop some water into her drinking bowl. I lift her head up. She takes a sip and speaks, the words whispering themselves out into the air and my ears catch them.

'Even when there is no cock, day dawns, you will never be alone. Give me my pouch.'

She opens it, brings out a stone, a white stone. She puts it into my hand. 'I'll always be with you,' she whispers. 'When you hold it, you will hear me in the inside of you.'

I look at the stone that can do so much. It feels cool and smooth and it cuts off my breath.

I hold Maluuma's hand and watch her chest, rise and fall to an inner rhythm. I breathe with her, as her breathing slows down. Then it goes still. Jabeza squeals and runs out. I wait, breathing in out, in out, but she does not join me. The ancestors were greedy that day. Maluuma has started her last journey and taken all that I am with her. I feel nothing, I feel everything. I am empty, I am full.

'Go, but come back,' I say into her ear.

From far away, I hear the drums beat loud and angry. It tells me that the men are at last taking Pa Sorie out of the village, to the forest of the dead. I can hear the women singing him on his way. I do not sing. I do not cry.

When the men go Madu comes into the hut. She finds me sitting by Maluuma's side, clutching the white heart-stone my grandmother had given me. Madu takes one look at her mother lying so still, so quiet on the mat and her face changes. She looks like one of the spirits.

'Is she still...?' Her question hangs in the air. I cannot speak. Something large, a stone, a coconut, blocks my mouth so there is no space inside me for words to grow and slide out.

Madu starts to keen. It is long, loud and urgent. The sound shakes the all of me. She throws herself to the ground outside and rolls in the red dust like a grieving daughter should. I do not join her, like a good grandchild should. I do not move; I have no strength.

By the time the men come back from the forest of the dead, at the break of the new day, Madu has placed blue glass over her mother's sightless eyes to light her way to the gods. The women wash Maluuma ready for her leaving the village for the last time. There is no waiting, no drums to send the messages from village to village, to cry out for all to hear that Maluuma, the great healer, has started her journey to the ancestors. The women cry out singing Maluuma to the village gateway. I still cannot cry. I find that some pain cannot be eased.

They hand Maluuma, wrapped in blue cloth, over to the men. Jaja leads the way, back to the forest of the dead, followed by Amadu and a few of the elders, those who are not yet tired out from the drinking, the eating, or the long walk with Pa Sorie.

I watch them take away my grandmother without the ceremony or ritual they had performed for Pa Sorie. She is a woman, but why should she not be helped on her journey just like him, I think. I know then what I must do. I creep into Jaja's hut, take what I am looking for and run to the furthest part of the village.

I tuck Jaja's old drum under my arm, and do what no woman should do, I squeeze the strings like Pa Sorie used to do and beat out the news to all the villages, the trees, the animals, the sky, the moon and the stars. Maluuma the great healer, mother of Isatu, grandmother of Fatmata, Amadu and Salimatu, Maluuma the wise one has started on her last journey to the ancestors. Praise be to the gods.

Only after that does the stone stuck in my throat get washed away by the tears that flow out of my eyes. Water.

'Go now, but come back, Maluuma.'

# CHAPTER 10

*Wealth gotten by vanity shall be diminished*
Proverb 13:11

## October 1850

They were getting ready to go for their daily afternoon walk when Edith came for her.

'Madam says could Miss Sarah come down now, Miss,' said Edith from the doorway. 'Lady Sheldon and Mrs Oldfield have arrived.'

'Thank you, Edith,' said Nanny Grace.

Mabel jumped up, ready to go down too.

'Madam says just Miss Sarah, Miss.'

Sarah did not know why visitors wanted to see her and not Mabel, or Emily or Anna, but they did and for once she was glad. She did not have to go for a walk in the wet and cold.

'Put your hat on so we can go for our walk Mabel,' ordered Nanny buttoning up Anna's coat. 'You heard Edith. You were not called.'

'But Jane and Bessie will be there. They always come with their Mama.'

'It is not you they want to see. If Bessie was with her Mama, she would have been sent up to the nursery to play.'

'It's not fair. Everything is about Sarah now.' said Mabel.

'Don't be mean,' said Emily who was playing with her diablo. Mabel grabbed hold of the diablo and tossed it so high Emily couldn't catch it on the string and it hit Anna on the head.

'The good lord says *envy makes the bones rot,* remember that, Mabel Forbes,' said Nanny Grace, comforting a sobbing Anna.

Nanny seemed to have a lot of discussions with the "good lord", Sarah thought. She hoped that one day he would talk to her too. There were lots of things she wanted to ask him. The first question would be, 'where is Fatmata, good Lord?'

Sarah went down the stairs, slowly. She hoped there would be a piece of the cake Cook made that morning. It would be a change from the usual nursery tea of just bread and butter. She loved Cook's cakes.

Outside the drawing room Sarah froze remembering what had happened the last time she went into the room that was full of paintings, chairs, occasional tables. There were also many things, called 'statuettes' and 'bric-a-brac' by Nanny Grace, which could be damaged by careless hands. Although Sarah knew that the children were not allowed in there without supervision, she had persuaded Emily to creep in with her to see what the room looked like with the drapes open. They were pulling at the drapes when Mabel came in.

'What are you doing?' she cried. 'I am going to tell Nanny.'

'No,' pleaded Emily, 'please don't tell.'

'You would never have done this without her, Emily,' said Mabel glaring at Sarah before pushing past Sarah who stumbled backwards. She fell against one of the tables and trying to save herself, grabbed at the tablecloth. All three gasped as a small statue rocked, smashed on to the floor.

Mabel ran to the door and screamed, 'Naaanny.'

Mama had been very cross, Papa said he was disappointed in

all of them for being disobedient and Nanny sent them to bed early without any supper.

'It's not fair,' said Mabel later. 'I don't see why I'm being punished. It's your fault, you should not have gone in there.'

'You shouldn't have pushed me.'

'Well, I wish Papa would send you away.'

'Don't say that,' said Emily, 'where would she go?'

'To the workhouse. Miss Byles says that is where naughty children are sent when they have nowhere else to go. Papa will get tired of her soon and then she will be sent away, and I don't care.'

✷✷✷

Now Sarah took a deep breath as Edith pushed the door open. Today the heavy drapes were open and there was a blazing fire in fireplace.

'Miss Sarah,' Edith announced at the doorway.

'Come in Sarah,' said Mama Forbes. 'Say good afternoon to Lady Sheldon, her daughter Miss Jane Sheldon and Mrs Oldfield. Edith, go bring the hot water.'

Sarah stepped forward, gave a quick curtsey, but said nothing.

Mrs Oldfield beckoned her closer. She took a very small step forward then stopped, afraid of stepping on the woman's purple silk skirt that was spread out like a shimmering sea. Lady Sheldon, her dark hair scraped back so tight her face looked pinched, just sniffed. Miss Jane Sheldon, who was only a few years older than Sarah smiled and nodded. She was round, her hair falling in ringlets to her shoulders brushed against the collar of her pale green dress which matched her eyes.

'Does she speak English Mrs Forbes?' Miss Sheldon asked

Before Mama Forbes could answer, however, Lady Sheldon said, 'I doubt whether she would be speaking the Queen's English, Jane. Coloureds can't. They're not very intelligent.'

'Oh, Mother,' Jane muttered looking down. Her mother glared at her.

'In fact, she speaks beautifully, Lavinia,' said Mama Forbes, putting her arm around Sarah's shoulder. Her grip was painful, and Sarah winced but remained silent. She could see that Mama Forbes was cross for some reason. Had she done something wrong? Maybe she should have told Lady Sheldon that she had learned many new English words.

'In the five months she has picked up the language astonishingly well,' said Mrs Forbes letting go off Sarah's shoulder. 'She is bright, very good tempered and we have all grown rather fond of her. Maybe you would like to hear her recite something, later?'

Mrs Oldfield gave a big sigh and leaned forward. 'Oh yes, please. I love poetry.'

Mama Forbes inclined her head and sat down by the table covered with white linen, that had intricate lace decorating the edge. Sarah stared at the many tea things on the table but what caught her interest was the three-tiered serving tray full of sandwiches, chocolate cake, scones, shortbread cookies and various small tarts.

Mama Forbes rinsed the teapot with the boiling water and emptied it into the slop bowl. This was a ritual understood by the others, no one spoke. Sarah too watched as Mary Forbes took a small key from the key chain pinned to her dress, opened the tea caddy and carefully measure out loose leaf tea into the newly rinsed teapot before pouring some water over it. This was steeped for a minute or two before she added more water.

'How do you like your tea Violet?' Mama Forbes asked, pouring the first cup of tea. 'With lemon or Milk?'

'Lemon? Oh no, milk and sugar, please.'

Sarah saw Lady Shelton look at the tray and raise her eyebrows. 'Really Mary, you still use sugar?

Mama Forbes took a deep breath. 'Yes, Lavinia. We do not, however, use sugar produced by slaves on West Indian plantations.'

'Like everyone else I did stop taking sugar years ago,' said Violet Oldfield, 'but I must admit that I have a sweet tooth and it was such a relief when they started selling sugar brought from the East Indies. Of course, I did use the tea-set that had the slogan *East India Sugar. Not made by slaves all over.*'

'I would not put such crockery on my table. Not for all the tea in China,' sniffed Lady Shelton. 'They're so ugly.'

'Don't get on your high horse Lavinia, they were put away a long time ago, although I do still use the nippers on the sugar-loaves. And I did wear the Wedgwood *"Am I Not a Woman and A Sister"* brooch after I went to a Female Society for Birmingham group meeting.'

'Stuff and nonsense,' said Lady Shelton sitting up even straighter. 'Some slaves might be women, but they are certainly not my sisters.'

Violet responded, 'some of the abolitionist leaflets were quite explicit about the indecencies women slaves endured. Horrible, horrible.'

Before anything more could be said Mama Forbes stepped in. 'Sarah, why don't you recite the poem you have been studying with Miss Byles now, while we have our tea.'

Sarah felt her hand go damp. She did not dare wipe her hands on her dress though. Standing straight and lifting her chin up just as Miss Byles had taught her, she took a deep breath and recited.

> 'My mother bore me in the southern wild,
> And I am black, but O my soul is white;
> White as an angel is the English child:
> But I am black as if bereav'd of light'

'Oh, oh, oh' cried Lady Sheldon, dabbing her temples with a little lace handkerchief. Sarah stopped and looked at Mama who waved to her to sit down.

'What is wrong, Lavinia?' asked Mama Forbes.

'Comparing herself with an English child, it's not natural.'

'Mother, please,' said Jane, 'it is just a poem by Mr Blake.'

'You must admit, you've not met a Negro who spoke so well,' said Violet Oldfield.

'I have seen what they're like. I warn you; she'll get above herself if you treat her like one of us,' said Lady Sheldon staring hard at Sarah.

'Oh, Lavinia,' said Mrs Oldfield, 'she's only a child.'

Sarah said nothing trying to work out why Lady Sheldon did not like her. Had she, broken another unknown rule? She had learned a long time ago from Fatmata that if you sat quietly people soon forgot you were there and that way you learned a lot of things. So now she sat still and listened.

'Yes, and they grow up,' continued Lady Sheldon ignoring Mrs Oldfield. 'We lost a lot of property in Barbados when they were emancipated, you know. None of them are to be trusted. First, they joined the rebellion in '16 then in '34 they all said they would stay. Father said he would pay them but within the month every single one of them had left and there was no one to work the plantation. We lost everything. The government never compensated us properly. Father used to say that William Wilberforce and his abolitionist cronies should have been whipped.'

'Lavinia,' said Mary Forbes, 'your family-owned slaves? I never knew.'

'You never asked.'

'Well, Sarah is not a slave. She is free.'

'The African Princess, that's what the newspapers are calling her,' said Mrs Oldfield leaning forward. 'And here she is, right here in front of me.'

Jane smiled and passed Sarah a slice of cake. 'I'm having tea with a princess.'

'Please do not be silly, Jane,' said her mother. 'Princess indeed! She should be in the kitchen scrubbing pots or cleaning shoes.'

'Lavinia!' said Mary Forbes.

'Is it true what the papers say,' interrupted Mrs Oldfield her eyes wide and inquisitive. 'Is it true that their king was going to sacrifice her, but Captain Forbes made him change his mind and she was sent as a gift to our queen?'

'Yes, Violet, according to Frederick.'

'What's to happen to her now?' asked Mrs Oldfield.

'You're not going to keep her,' interrupted Lady Sheldon. 'This is England. She will never fit into polite society.'

'It is not for us to decide what is to become of her, Lavinia,' said Mary Forbes using her napkin to dab at the drop of tea she had spilt on the table. 'She belongs to Queen Victoria.'

Sarah bit into her slice of cake. She noticed Mama Forbes' hand was shaking.

✿✿✿

*Wednesday, 30th October 1850, Winkfield Place*

> *Today I found out too things. Furst is I am called a prinses. That is what Mama says. Lily ran round me calling me Prinses Sarah. She laffed and laffed but Mabel did not laff. I wish she was like Fatmata. Also, Mama sed I belong to Queen Victoria not Papa Forbes. Why? What is to happen to me? I wish I was back home in Talaremba with Fatmata too*

# SALIMATU

# CHAPTER 11

*Above all else, guard your heart, for everything you do flows from it*
Proverbs 4:23

## November 1850

As soon as the letter arrived commanding Papa Forbes to *present Sarah Forbes Bonetta at Windsor Castle 11 a.m. on Saturday 9th November 1850*, there was intense discussion about what she should wear.

'I had no idea that Her Majesty would ask to see her,' said Mama Forbes, as Nanny Grace laid out not only all of Sarah's but also Mabel's best dresses for inspection. 'There's nothing suitable for her to wear. We've less than a week. Sarah and I will go to town and stay with my sister, Lady Melton. She will take us to her London seamstress.'

'Mama, can I come to London too for a new dress? I am the oldest.'

'Now, Mabel please do not be difficult. We will go to London after Christmas as usual.'

That night there was a wet flannel in Sarah's bed and she had to sleep on damp sheets. She coughed all night and kept Mabel awake.

All Sarah could remember of the two days she spent in London with Mama Forbes and Lady Melton was rushing from place to place, for hat, shoes and coat. She spent a lot of time at the seamstress' standing still to be measured while materials and colours were discussed.

'A white dress would look very good with her dark skin, don't you think? She's quite a pretty little thing in a Negro kind of way. Pity about the marks on her face. So disfiguring.'

'Shh, Josephine,' said Mary Forbes. 'There's nothing we can do about them. You're right about a white dress, though.'

And Salimatu was there again. She pinched and poked Sara, squeezing her heart, whispering 'you must stop them. We cannot go anywhere near a queen wearing a white dress. It is the clothing of those going to be sacrificed. Remember King Gezo.'

'Mama, please not white, not white.' Sarah burst into tears.

Remembering what the Captain had said about Sarah's rescue, Mary Forbes shook her head at her sister and gathered the sobbing Sarah into her arms.

'I will never make you wear white Sarah. Shall we go for the blue? The light blue will look just as pretty.'

✿✿✿

*Saturday 9th November 1850, Winkfield place*
 *Today I go to visit Queen Victoria. Is she like a king? Does*
 *she make sacrifices too? I am afraid, but no one would under-*
 *stand except for Salimatu. She is here.*

✿✿✿

The day had arrived, and Sarah wished she could refuse to go. Salimatu had brought the nightmares back, like shadows drifting in and out of her dreams, all night whispering, 'we must be careful. Remember King Gezo embraced us, told us we were safe, yet he was going to sacrifice us on his ancestors' grave.'

'Why do you cry in your sleep,' asked Emily in the morning.

'I have dreams.'

'They must be bad ones if they make you so sad.'

'I don't want to talk about them.'

Emily asked no more questions. Instead, she gave Sarah her favourite doll. 'You can play with Arabella.'

'Thank you, Lily.'

Still thinking about meeting the Queen, Sarah pushed her bowl of porridge away, got up from the table and went to the window, stroking the *gri-gri* hanging around her neck. It did not comfort her.

When she had first arrived at Winkfield Place her *gri-gri* had been put away by Nanny Grace, but one night after yet another nightmare, Sarah had taken her *gri-gri* pouch from the drawer. Just holding it had soothed her and she had put it on once more.

'What's that?' Edith asked the first time she saw Sarah wearing it.

'My *gri-gri*.'

'What is a *gri-gri*?' said Mabel.

Sarah frowned. Surely, they knew what it was? Every child had one, didn't they? 'You know, your pouch where you put special things that keep you safe.'

'What things? Let me see,' said Mabel, reaching out to grab it.

'No, you can't,' Sarah said backing away. Fatmata had told her, 'inside your *gri-gri* pouch is all of who you are. Never give another person a sight of the inside you.' She held the pouch so tight she could feel her *ala* that had brought her safely across the ocean and the blue stone that was protecting her from evil. After that day, to keep it safe, away from Mabel, Sarah only took her *gri-gri* off at bath-time.

Sarah stared out of the window. She longed for some sun, some brightness. It seemed very cold out there. She frowned. She had never seen the garden look like that before. Everything was white and glistening. The tree branches stretched out; searching for some leaves to keep them warm. But they were covered in white, like salt. She saw a maid rushing by, head down, pushing against the wind, clutching her flapping shawl. Although she was indoors Sarah pulled her wrap tighter around her shoulders.

'Edith, where did all this salt come from?'

'Salt? What salt?' asked Mabel, leaving the breakfast table and rushing over to the window. She looked out and burst out laughing. 'That's not salt. It is frost. Edith, she thinks frost is salt, isn't that silly.'

'Leave her alone Miss Mabel. They don't have frost or snow where she comes from in Africa.'

'What is frost?'

'Frost is cold,' said Emily, 'like ice.'

'We have frost at the beginning of winter when it starts to get really cold. It is like ice. When the day warms up it'll melts away,' said Edith. 'Later we will have snow.'

Frost? Ice? Snow? Salimatu/Sarah shivered. She remembered the first time she had seen ice it had not looked like the frost out there. She had been in the kitchen when Mrs Dixon, called for Edith.

'The ice-man is here,' she said, 'go get the ice-box.'

'What is ice?' Sarah asked the cook as she watched the ice-man use his ice pick to break off a block of ice and put it in the wooden ice box before going off on his horse and cart.

'What is ice? My you do ask some funny questions. Ice keeps fresh food, meat, butter, milk cool so that they don't go off. Davy brings me fresh ice once a week. Now out of the way Miss Sarah, I've got to get on.'

When no one was looking she had gone into the pantry, shut the door and opened the box to see the ice. She had been surprised to see smoke, but it was cold. She wanted to know what it felt like, so she touched it and almost immediately her hand was stuck to the block. No matter how hard she pulled she could not get it off. She screamed and Edith had to pour some water on her hand to get it off. It was numb and she could feel nothing for ages. She had to warm it in front of the fire then it felt as if a thousand red ants were stinging her hand. She was the talk of the house for some time after that, people commenting or asking how she was until she grew weary and simply stopped listening to the talk or responding. Slowly life resumed as normal.

The cold from the outside seemed to seep through the window to wrap around her heart. She wondered whether she too would turn into ice, hard and cold. Maybe her heart would freeze, maybe she would stop feeling so afraid of going to see the Queen at the castle.

'Sally,' said Emily, popping her last piece of bread and butter into her mouth, 'what are you going to say to Her Majesty?'

Sarah liked it when Emily and Freddie called her Sally. They were the only ones who did. It reminded her of the sailors on *The Bonetta* and her Salimatu self, her old life when there was Fatu and Sali.

'Mama says that I must just curtsey and say nothing.'

'She only said that you should not speak first,' said Mabel. 'If the Queen asks you a question, you do have to say something. It would be very rude not to answer. And don't fall over when you curtsey like you did yesterday. And just after Mama said how graceful you were!' She laughed, spluttering milk all over the table.

'Of course, she won't,' said Emily, glaring at her sister. 'Her curtsey is much better than yours or mine.'

Miss Byles had taught Sarah exactly how to bend the knees outward, back held straight, sweeping one foot behind, while holding skirt out from her body. She had practised the curtsey again and again but after Mama praised Sarah's curtsey, falling over had seemed the only way to stop Mabel's pout and bad temper. She was glad that no one had realized that it had been deliberate. Sarah did not understand why she could not just lie down flat on the ground and kiss the Queen's feet as she had to in Africa. That was so much easier.

She did not want to think about what Her Majesty might ask of her. Was Queen Victoria going to send her away? How was she ever going to find Fatmata?

'What if Her Majesty asks you about Africa?' said Mabel.

'I've told you before, I cannot remember anything,' Sarah said, turning away from Mabel. She knew that it was naughty to tell untruths, but she let them all, even Papa Forbes, believe that she could not remember anything. She was afraid sharing her good memories would make them disappear, leaving just the nightmares. How could she find the words to tell them about the big fire, the guns, the killing of her mother and father, the long walk, the raid on Talaremba and Okeadon or her life in Abomey? Would they understand what it felt like to be dragged from Fatmata by Santigie, carried away on a big horse, sold several times, then kept alive for the right time to be sacrificed, dressed in white? She shook her head.

'Not even about that king who held you captive?' asked Mabel, moving closer.

Sarah blinked and stepped back. 'What do you mean?' she said, wondering how Mabel knew about that? What else did she know? She felt for her *gri-gri* once more.

'I heard Nanny Grace telling Edith about you.'

'Miss Mabel, you know Nanny was only reading out what was in the newspaper,' said Edith quickly before turning to Sarah. 'You're all over the newspapers, Miss Sarah.'

Sarah stared at Edith. 'Me? In the newspaper? Why?'

'You're famous Miss. Everyone wants to know about you.'

'I do not know why. Miss Byles says that there are many

Negroes in England, even if we do not see them here in Windsor,' said Mabel, going back to the table.

'There are?' said Emily.

'Yes, I asked her. She says they come off the ships; students, servants and sometimes those who have escaped slavery in the United States of America. Therefore, I don't see why Sarah is so special.'

London? Was that where she would find Fatmata? Why had she not thought of that before? She had to get back to London. 'I didn't see any Negroes when Mama Forbes took me to London for my new dress.'

'Well, you wouldn't Miss, not where Lady Melton lives,' said Edith with a laugh. 'You might see one or two servants who are Negroes around there but not people like you. Nanny says the blacks in London sweep the streets or beg to make enough to live. You're different. The African Princess. There's not a week goes by without something about you in the paper.'

'See, everyone wants to know,' said Mabel. 'If you don't tell Queen Victoria, she might just order your head to be cut off, Princess.'

Sarah's eyes widened. She bit the corner of her mouth hard to stop her from screaming as Salimatu whispered, 'I told you to be careful.'

'Oh Sally,' cried Emily, running over to hug Sarah, 'don't listen to Mabel. The Queen would not let anyone cut off your head after Papa saved you from that horrible king.'

'Cut off your head?' said Freddie who came into the nursery just then. 'It would bounce all the way down the hall. But don't worry, my little Sally, I'll be waiting to catch it and stick it back on your shoulders, I promise.' He put his arm around her shoulder and gave her a squeeze.

Emily giggled. 'You're funny Freddie.'

Sarah stopped shaking and leaned against his shoulder. At fourteen, Freddie was almost as tall as his father. His eyes were as blue as the sky on a sunny day. He spoke slowly, always smiling, looking as though he had something special to tell just you. From the start he had been kind to Sarah. He talked, teased, played with her, just as he did with Mabel, Emily and Anna. Freddie came home from Eton every weekend and always came up to the nursery to see them. She felt safe when he was around. She wished he was her brother. She did not remember much about her own brothers. Amadu and Lansana were just names, part of her fading memories.

Nanny Grace came bustling in. 'Come on Miss Sarah. Madame is waiting. Your things are laid out in her room. She is going to oversee you getting ready.'

Sarah stepped back pleating and un-pleating the edge of her shawl.

'What's the matter?' asked Freddie.

'I don't want to go and see the Queen,' Sarah whispered.

'Don't be scared, Sally. Papa will look after you,' he said, tweaking her nose.

'No time to be difficult Miss Sarah,' said Nanny Grace, ushering her out of the nursery.

In Mama's room Sarah stood still while Nanny slipped the pale blue dress over her head and tied the navy blue sash in a big bow at the back. Sarah winced as Edith struggled to do up the little pearl buttons on stiff new black ankle boots. She still hated wearing shoes.

'Your bonnet is lovely too,' said Emily stroking the blue and white flowers on it.

'It sits beautifully on her head now I've cut her hair short, doesn't it, Madame?' said Nanny tying the ribbon under Sarah's chin.

Sarah was glad Nanny had cut her hair. She wished she could

change her hair. It did not look like Mabel's or Emily's or anyone else she had seen in England. No matter how hard Nanny pulled and pulled, until tears ran down Sarah's face, it stuck out bouncy and thick. After reading the story of Naughty Nancy, who played with matches and burned all her hair off, Sarah decided to do the same. Mabel told on her. Papa had made her promise never to play with matches again and now her hair was very short. Lily said that it was like a black cap.

'Yes Nanny, she looks very smart.'

When Sarah came downstairs everyone in household was waiting in the hall. Even Miss Byles had come over, although it was not a school day.

'O, don't you look a picture!' said Mrs Dixon.

Mama took the dark blue woollen cape from Nanny, put it around Sarah's shoulders, bent down and kissed her cheek.

Sarah's lips quivered. She had never been kissed like that before. She flung her arms around Mama Forbes' waist and clung on.

'Now, now, you'll be fine,' she said giving Sarah a little push towards the door. 'You be a big girl and remember to curtsey like Miss Byles taught you.'

'Ah, you're ready,' said Papa Forbes, with a smile. 'Come, Davy has got the carriage at the door. Better not keep the horses waiting.'

He took Sarah's hand, led her outside, helped her into the carriage and tucked the blanket around her knees. When Sarah turned around, she saw that even though it was cold Mama was still by the door, holding on to Anna, while Miss Byles, Nanny and Cook kept on waving. Mabel, had gone back upstairs and was staring out of one the window. She did not wave.

# CHAPTER 12

*Wisdom restest in the heart of him that hath understanding*
Proverbs 14: 33

## November 1850

O n the ride to the castle, Sarah sat up straight, her hands clasped on her lap just as Mama had taught her but her fingernails were biting into her palm. The frost had disappeared and in the grey foggy morning Windsor Park was full of shadows. It reminded Sarah of walking through the forests after she and Fatmata were captured and her heart beat faster. She was sure that at any moment hidden devils would come through the trees to surround them and only the noise of the horses' hooves kept them away.

When at last she saw the castle high on the hill with its surrounding wall, Sarah caught her breath, shut her eyes tight and clutched the Captain's arm. The last time she was at a palace it too had been encircled by walls, six gates, a deep ditch filled with acacia thorn trees and two cannons on either side of the road. Those walls had been topped with skulls and more piles of skulls, humans and animals, lay for effect at the gates, to show the power of the king and the fierceness of his people. In the years that she had been held captive within the walls of King Gezo's palace she had seen many skulls added to the top of the wall.

Salimatu was screaming inside her head, 'I told you, I told you, Ayee! We are dead. We are dead. A ti kú.'

'What's the matter child?' asked Papa Forbes.

'I don't want to see the chopped-off heads stuck on the wall like at King Gezo's palace,' said Sarah gripping his arm even tighter.

'Open your eyes and look, there're no heads. Look! Queen Victoria does not cut off her enemies' heads.'

Sarah opened her eyes just a slit. There were no heads. 'Then what does she do?' whispered Salimatu. Sarah shook her head, sat up straight again and let go off Papa Forbes's arm until the carriage came to a stop in front of the great big wooden doors of the castle. She could not move. Papa Forbes had to help her out of the carriage and guide her through the door.

Inside Windsor Castle a courtier bowed and informed them that Lady Margaret Phipps who supervised the day-to-day affairs of the Queen would meet them in the Long Corridor. Sarah's eyes darted from side to side as they were hurried along, still frightened of what might be around the corner.

They turned the corner and there was the long corridor, bright with a red patterned carpet that seemed to go on way into the distance. Many paintings, in golden frames, of the royal family, of palaces, castles, and many-sailed ships, papered the walls, fighting for space amongst long red and cream heavy curtains. Set in the many alcoves were large ornate gilt chairs, stools and benches, while lined along the corridor magnificent objects fought for space secured in exquisitely carved and decorated rich wood encasements.

'Queen Victoria has a lot of things, hasn't she Papa?' whispered Sarah.

'These are treasures from all over the world given to her Majesty as gifts.'

Sarah caught her breath. I am a gift too, she thought. Wasn't that what Papa Forbes had said. Did that mean she would be left in a room for people to come and stare at forever? Her hands felt hot and wet in her gloves. She had had enough of people doing that, or wanting to touch her face, her hair.

It was the many heads, white as though the flesh had fallen of leaving just their bones, that pulled her to a stop as her whole body shook. So, here the cut-off heads were not stuck on the wall outside as in King Gezo's place. No, here they brought the heads inside, and placed them on marble pillars almost as tall as a man. This was what she had feared, this was *djudju* indeed. Salimatu screamed inside of her, 'we are dead, a ti kú. run, run, şişe, şişe.'

Sarah covered her eyes; she did not want to look at any of them.

'Sarah? What's wrong,' Papa Forbes asked, taking her hands away from her face.

'The heads,' she said pulling away, ready to run back to the carriage. 'Look at the heads. Their eyes are empty, but they watch me, waiting to drag me away.'

'No, they're not, Sarah,' said Captain Forbes. He put his arm around her and pulled her close. 'They're not real; they're busts carved out of marble.'

There was a sudden burst of gun fire. She recognised that sound, the signal at King Gezo's that someone was about to be sacrificed. She heard steps behind her and turned and froze. A woman in black, accompanied by a man, his bright red jacket covered with gold braids, and wearing a sword, strode down the long corridor towards them. Salimatu screamed inside her, 'he cut head off, O ge ori kuro.' Sarah moaned and hid behind Papa Forbes.

'What is it? What is it this time?' said the Captain.

'Let's go home, Papa,' cried Sarah, tugging at him. 'Look, the Queen is coming with her soldier to cut off our heads!'

'Listen, listen, she's not the Queen. That is Lady Phipps and I've told you; these soldiers do not cut heads off.' Captain Forbes picked Sarah up and held her in his arms. 'Come child you are safe. He will not hurt you; I promise.'

Sarah struggled in his arms. Lady Phipps hurried over.

'Has something happened?' she asked.

'No, no, Lady Phipps. She's just frightened of the soldier and his sword.'

'He cut off head, cut off head, I heard the signal, the guns,' cried Sarah again and again, running her hand fast across her throat in a cutting motion.

'Now, stop it Sarah,' said Captain Forbes, setting her down.

'Ssh, child. Nothing is going to happen to you,' added Lady Phipps. 'That was the "feu de joie". The soldiers were firing the guns in honour of the Prince of Wales' birthday.'

But Sarah, convinced that she had been brought all this way to meet her end, could not stop shaking and crying. None of them saw Queen Victoria come down the long corridor to stand behind them.

'Is the child hurt?' asked Queen Victoria. Lady Margaret spun around and tried to curtsey and stumbled, Captain stood up straight and bowed. Sarah stopped mid-cry to gaze at the woman in front of her. Was this really the Queen? Where was her crown? Mabel had said that the Queen wore her crown and jewels all the time. This woman was small, not much taller than Sarah. Her green dress, with tartan cuffs and collar had a very wide skirt and made her seem even smaller. Dark hair drawn back into a bun and covered with a little lace cap made her brown eyes seem very large in the round, smiling face. This queen did not look as though she would let anyone's head be chopped off.

'Well, is she hurt? Why was she crying?'

Captain Forbes recovering from the surprise of the Queen's sudden appearance bowed again before replying. 'Your Majesty, she's not hurt, just frightened.'

'Of me?' she said with a smile, handing her cape and bonnet to her lady-in-waiting.

There was a laugh and only then did Sarah notice several children standing just behind Her Majesty.

'Oh no, Ma'am,' said Captain Forbes. 'It's the sword and the gunfire. I think it reminds her of the horrid scenes she witnessed in Dahomey.'

'Ah, indeed.' Turning to the courtier standing behind her Queen Victoria said, 'Sir Charles, send the soldiers away please. Make sure that there is never anyone wearing a sword near the child. Dry your tears, you are quite safe here,' she said to Sarah, handing her handkerchief to Sarah. 'Come, Captain Forbes, Prince Albert is in the Crimson Drawing Room. We want to hear about your journey into Africa before our guests arrive for the Prince of Wales' birthday luncheon.'

She waved her hand around and without thinking Sarah took it. Queen Victoria looked down at Sarah. Her lips twitched. She gave Sarah a little smile and a quick squeeze of her fingers. Neither said anything but together, hand in hand, they walked down the long corridor past more statues, busts and portraits. Sarah did not look at them instead she concentrated on the small gloveless hand holding hers and for some reason she did feel safe.

'Ah, there you are,' said Prince Albert standing up as they came into the drawing room, followed by the royal children, Lady Phipps, and several other members of the household. 'Is this the child we've heard so much about?'

'Yes,' said Queen Victoria, 'this is Sarah.'

Only then did Sarah realise that she had not greeted Her Majesty in the correct manner. Slowly she gave the deepest of curtseys, first to Queen Victoria and then to the Prince Consort. Mama would have been proud of her for she did not fall over or even wobble.

Nodding at the three children Queen Victoria said, 'Sarah, meet Princesses Victoria and Alice and Prince Alfred. Where is Bertie?'

The Prince of Wales came running in, holding a golden bird cage up high. Inside it was a small bird. It fluttered its wings but stayed on its perch.

'I'm here Mama. I went to get Gimpel,' he said.

'Gimpel?' said Prince Albert.

'Yes Papa. My birthday gift. It is German for bullfinch.'

'I do know that,' said Prince Albert laughing. Everyone joined in. Sarah saw the Prince of Wales go red. Quickly she took from the pocket of her cape the gift she and Mama had bought for him in London.

'Happy birthday, Prince Albert,' she said.

'Thank you,' he said smiling and shaking her hand before ripping of the paper to unwrap a wooden soldier with moving arms and legs.

'Papa, she is afraid of swords,' said six-year-old Alfred, running over to his father. 'I like swords. I'm going to wear one when I'm older.'

'That's enough Affie,' said Queen Victoria. 'Sit down and be quiet or you can go join the little ones in the nursery.'

Affie hung his head and immediately sat on the floor at his father's feet. Sarah saw Prince Albert bend down and pat Alfie's head and he smiled.

'Do sit, Captain,' Queen Victoria said, waving to a chair. 'So, this is my gift.'

Sarah did not know what she was supposed to do, sit, stand, stay with the royal children? Papa Forbes called her to his side.

'Yes Ma'am. That is what Gezo said, a gift from the "King of the Blacks to the Queen of the Whites" in honour of his treaty of friendship with Britain. I had to bring her with me. To have left her would have been to sign her immediate death-warrant.'

On hearing the name of the King, Sarah held her breath. Was Her Majesty going to send her back to the King to wait with the women to be used or sacrificed?

Queen Victoria's lips tightened. 'You were right to remove her from such horror, Captain.' She turned to her Secretary to the Admiralty, Admiral William Baillie-Hamilton. 'What are we doing about the treaty for the suppression of slave trade in his dominion?'

'King Gezo refused to agree like some of the other nations, Ma'am. He does not want to give up his unenviable notoriety as the largest purveyor of slave in the world in exchange for the production of palm oil which he fears is not as profitable.'

'This disgraceful illegal trade has gone on long enough,' said Prince Albert. 'As I have said before, I deeply regret that the benevolent and persevering exertions of England to abolish the atrocious traffic in human beings have not yet led to any satisfactory conclusion. It is the blackest stain upon civilised Europe. It has to be stopped.'

'Now that the West African Squadron have better vessels, we are gaining the upper hand, Sir,' said Captain Forbes. 'We seized the slave ships and their equipment then liberated the newly captured slaves at Freetown. Patrolling that area of the coast is arduous, unpleasant and frustrating, but we're slowly shutting down most of the slave trade routes.'

Queen Victoria sighed. 'The crusade against slave trade is a holy one. Although the missionaries are doing some good work, coercion alone will not stop it. We are pleased that Lord Russell has been able to rally enough votes to beat back Mr Hutt's motion, however, his attempt to introduce a parliamentary resolution for our government has failed. We will certainly not withdraw from any treaty. We must continue patrolling the coast of West Africa to stop this horrible trade even if it requires the use of force to do so.'

'Yes Ma'am.'

'And the child, what does she remember?' asked Prince Albert.

'She has only a confused idea, Sir. As far as I can gather her parents were killed. She knows not the fate of her brothers, but she was captured with her older sister, Fatmata. Later they were sold separately. The King's Amazon warriors captured her during the Okeadon war that spread all over that area of Egbado.'

'The women warriors?' asked Prince Albert.

'Yes Sir. The Minos. Some call them Amazons. They're ferocious.'

The Queen nodded and beckoned Sarah closer, 'Are you well, child?'

Sarah gave a quick bob before answering, 'Yes Ma'am. I am well. Mama and Papa Forbes say I am like one of their daughters.'

Queen Victoria turned to Captain Forbes, 'Thank you Captain Forbes.'

'She is very amiable, Ma'am. She has won the affections, with few exceptions, of all who know her.'

'Her English is very good. Does she speak any other languages?' said Queen Victoria.

'*Oui Madame, Je suis en train d'apprendre le francais,*' Sarah said, before the Captain could reply.

'*Tres bon,*' said Queen Victoria smiling. 'She speaks French?'

'My wife, Ma'am. She teaches our girls French and Sarah has picked up some of it. She is very intelligent and quick.'

'Until children are five or six years old, they are too little for real instruction,' said Prince Albert, 'but they should be taught their language and the two principal foreign languages, French & German for at least an hour each day. Children at this age have the greatest facility in acquiring languages, you know.'

'Indeed,' said Queen Victoria. 'She should be taught German as well, Captain Forbes. How old is she?'

'According to what she has told me it seems that she is eight years old, Ma'am. She would be nine around twenty seventh April. She is far advanced for her age, in aptness of learning and strength of mind. She does well at her lessons and shows a great talent for music.'

'Ah,' said Prince Albert, 'she might be sharp and intelligent now, but is it not generally supposed, that after a certain age the intellect becomes impaired, and the pursuit of knowledge impossible? The Negro child may be clever, but the adult will be dull and stupid.'

'That is what is said, Sir, but it is an erroneous belief. I have met many sharp and intelligent adult Negroes throughout my journeys in Africa.'

'Well, God grant she may be taught to consider her duty, leading her to rescue those who have not had the advantage of education from the mysterious ways of their ancestors,' said Queen Victoria.

Sarah played with her bonnet ribbon, rolling and unrolling it around her finger round and round until it got as tangled up as her thoughts. She wished she knew what was going to happen to her, she pulled at the ribbon and her bonnet fell off and landed at Queen Victoria's feet. She stood bare headed in front of the Queen.

'She would be quite a pretty child with her black woolly head if she did not have those awful marks on her face,' said Queen Victoria.

'What is wrong with the marks on our face?' growled Salimatu in Sarah's ear. 'Didn't all the women and girls, even in Abomey, have tribal marks? Why did this Queen and the Princesses not have any marks to show their status? Our face is not bare and ugly like the women of England. How do they know who kin is, or who is an enemy?' Sarah wanted to tell her to go away, but she knew that Salimatu was a part of her, the keeper of her memories.

'Apparently the marks on her face are a symbol of her status, her royal blood, Ma'am,' explained Captain Forbes. 'It is what saved her from being sacrificed as soon as she was captured. She was confined in King Gezo's palace for over three years waiting for a special occasion when she could be offered up at one of the "watering of the grave" ceremonies to bring even greater honour to the King's ancestors.'

'Barbaric custom,' said Prince Albert.

'We are very pleased to know that this is not the way we show status in this country,' said Queen Victoria.

'Look at her head,' said Prince Albert suddenly. 'We must have her head measured; don't you think? It is an outstanding phrenological specimen.'

Queen Victoria nodded in agreement and turned to Sir Charles Phipps, 'Please instruct Mr Pistrucci to take a cast of her head.'

'Mr Pistrucci, Ma'am?' said Captain Forbes before he could stop himself.

'Yes,' said the Queen, 'the medallist of the mint. He will make a bust of her head. We have decided that you and your wife may raise the child, but she will be under our care and we will pay all her expenses. Sir Charles will make all necessary arrangements and Lady Phipps will oversee Sarah's care.'

'Thank you, Ma'am. We have all grown very fond of her.'

'And you changed her name?'

'Yes, Ma'am. I was advised to give her an English name. Sarah after my mother and Bonetta after the ship, if you approve, Ma'am.'

'Has she been christened?'

'No Ma'am, but she does attend church with the family and receives the elements of religious instruction with my children.

'Her mind must receive good moral impression. I am quite clear that she should be taught to have great reverence for God and religion. Get her christened and I will be her godmother. Christenings are such a happy family time. I know. She may keep the names Sarah Forbes Bonetta.'

Listening to all this, Sarah wondered why no one asked her what she thought.

✿✿✿

*Sunday 10th November 1850, Winkfield Place*

*Yesterday I met Queen Victoria. She is very kind. She sent the man with the sord away. Bertie likes his toy soldiers. He had many gifts and a bullfinch he calls Gimpel. I do not want a bird in a cage. Prince Albert took us to the pond, and we fished some goldfish out. Bertie says they will be put in the stream in the slopes.*

*Mabel sed my new blue dress did not soot me, but I think she was telling an untruth becos everyone, even Princess Victoria and Princess Alice, sed it was pretty. They all wanted to torch my hair. Vicky sed it felt like a cushen. Affie wanted to no if I could scrub off my black skin. I said no. But I have not tried. It wood hurt inside and out.*

*Salimatu kept talking to me but I pushed her away. I wish she wood leave me alone now.*

*I am to be chrisend as Sarah not Salimatu or Aina, but no one has sed that name into my ears. No one has told the ancestors that I am Sarah. I am now two peple in one.*

# CHAPTER 13

A kì í fini joyè àwòdì ká má lè gbádìẹ
*One cannot have the title 'eagle' and yet be incapable of snatching chickens*

## 1846

I stand outside the cooking-hut where the women and the other girls are cutting, scraping, grinding, peeling and pounding food preparing for the Chiefs and *alagbas*. So many have come from the neighbouring villages for the *palaver* talk. I watch them sitting on stools and mats on the raised gathering platform in the centre clearing. I long to be out there, among the boys and men, with the breeze tickling my skin. I am hot and tired from helping with the cooking. It isn't that I do not want to cook, make baskets, wear beads around my waist or dance, it's just that I want more. I want to also hunt and climb trees and be free.

'Hey, you Fatmata. Get in here at once and do some work,' Madu calls. I do not answer, and she comes up and grabs my arm to bring me back to the present. 'Didn't you hear me call?'

'I'm only looking, Madu,' I say.

Madu shoves a cooking spoon in my hand and pushes me into the kitchen. Ma Ramatu is watching. 'She needs training,' she says and shakes her head. 'She's seen almost fourteen planting seasons and she should be ready by now to become a woman.'

Ready? For what? I wanted to shout. To have a new walk, slow, sliding, shuffling, shifting the red earth so that it rises and falls like a sigh, taking a long time to pass water, crying in pain every time you get your moon cycle. Have they forgotten what happened to Binta at *zadeji*. Once, about three harvest seasons past I heard Soji and Daria whispering about it.

'What about Binta?' I kept asking, refusing to leave the older girls alone.

They looked at each and shook their heads. 'You don't want to know,' said Soji.

'If you don't tell me I will ask Madu,' I had warned.

'You'll find out when your time comes,' Soji said.

'Binta was afraid,' said Daria.

'Why?' I asked, looking from one to the other.

'Enough,' said Soji. 'You know what Ma Ramatu said.'

Daria sucked her teeth, she no longer cared what anyone thought as before the next moon cycle she would be married and living in her husband's compound in Bantumi.

'She should know. I wish someone had warned me, or Binta. She was afraid of Ramatu,' Daria said, ignoring Soji. 'You see, it's Ma Ramatu who always sharpens the stones to a thin cutting edge before slicing away the remains of maleness, the 'unclean' parts of girls so that they can finally become a woman.'

'No,' I said my eyes wide with the thought. Was this really true?

'Yes,' said Daria, leaning forward so that she was almost whispering into my ear. 'After the cutting she feeds the bits to the birds so that they can take it far, far away.'

'But, but...' I stuttered. Was this what every girl went through to become a woman?

'Binta would not lie still,' said Daria shaking head, 'so they tied her down and Ramatu cut but then they could not stop Binta's blood flowing, so she journeyed to the ancestors.'

'I can still hear her howling like a trapped dog,' said Soji rocking. 'Ayee.'

✿✿✿✿

No, I am not ready to go into training and give Ramatu the chance to send me to meet the ancestors. I avoid looking at Ma Ramatu and stir the pot of cassava leaves.

When the drums start thumping and throbbing, we know this is the call to say the men talking was over for now.

'Come on, come on, we can't keep them waiting. Soji, Adjoa and you,' Ma Ramatu says, pointing at me for she never says my name, 'put some water in the small calabashes and take it to the men so that they can wash their hands.'

The food is brought into the yard in wooden bowls, on large, tightly-plaited trays and long-brewed palm wine is served in enormous gourds.

As chief of the village, Jaja is served first. He tastes a little of everything before crying out loud and clear, 'It is good. *Oloroun*, god of all, we praise you, we thank you. Now eat. Eat, my brothers.'

Only then do we girls move forward, to kneel in front of the men and offer them the food. The men are hungry and shove great handfuls into their mouths, smacking their lips and licking their fingers.

'Can I get you anymore, Ke-mo?' I ask each man as I kneel before them offering the trays of food without looking into their faces. They scoop what they want on to large banana leaves and ignore me.

For the first time I see Sisi Jamilla, Jaja's second wife, busy. Every time I look, she seems to be serving just one person. It is the tall man wearing the funny clothes. He is unable to squat down like the other men because he is wearing what Khadijatu says is called 'boots, trousers and coat'. The black 'boots' on his feet are covered in the red earth of Talaremba. How can he feel he is part of Mother Earth with his poor feet imprisoned so?

Hurrying back from the cooking-hut with more food I am grabbed by Santigie.

'What, no food for me?' he says, tightening his grip. I try to pull away because he is hurting me.

'Are you ignoring me now?' He pushes me down and I fall at his feet, almost spilling the food all over the ground. I do not answer but stare at his boots. 'Ha! You watched me before, so look at me now.'

He had been drinking a lot of palm wine, maybe too much.

'I beg forgiveness, Ke-mo.' I say, giving him the title of an older man, you did not know. I look up at him, something a girl must never do to a man. His broad nose seems to have overtaken his long thin face, his eyes are half shut, his open mouth full of wide, yellow, teeth.

'What's your name?'

'I'm Fatmata, Ke-mo.'

He bends down and stares into my eyes 'Dauda's daughter?' he says and squeezes my arm. I bite my lip and nod. He laughs then, with his mouth but not with his eyes. The sound sends a feeling of ants crawling up and down my back, making me wriggle and itch.

I pull myself up to a kneeling position and lift the tray of food to him. He takes a large handful of *plantains* and *akara* and put it all into his mouth at once so that his cheeks push out like Jabeza's when she wants to save her food for later. I get up and back away refusing to look into his eyes again.

Madu grabbed my arm as I hurry by. 'What did Santigie say to you?' she asks sharply.

'He asked my name.'

'Don't go near him again, you hear me? He's a dangerous man. Go back to the others and wait at the cook-hut.'

So that was Santigie, I thought, the man who should have married Sisi-Jamilla before her father gave her to Jaja to make peace between Talaremba and the village of Kocumba. I'd heard the story.

✧✧✧✧

The drums had beat loud and strong on the day of their marriage and the other girls, their backs and stomachs painted with camwood, nodded their heads decorated with elaborate hairstyles in time to the drums. They shook their *jigida* waist beads, stamped their bare feet hard and fast to make Mother Earth's dust rise up and join, twisting and turning, in the dance. At the end of the dance, Dauda handed the palm-wine gourd to his bride-to-be, a sign of acceptance, but Jamilla, her body covered in coconut oil, so she shone in the sunlight, shook her head and threw herself down at Chief Lamin's feet.

'Please, my Jaja, don't send me away,' she begged, 'you know I'm already betrothed to my cousin, Santigie. Send Samia, she's prettier.'

The whole gathering whispered like a hive of disturbed bees. The Kocumbers could not hide their shame at having a child who would argue with her father about whom she should marry. The Talarembans kept their faces clear, stared straight ahead. They were not sorry to see their one-time enemy made uncomfortable.

'Be quiet, girl,' Lamin ordered, his voice loud, like thunder cracking. 'How dare you shame our village with this display? You're my oldest daughter, anything less will be an insult to Chief Dauda and the people of Talaremba. Go get ready for your marriage. It happens today.'

'It is great to see a young girl so faithful to her people that she loathes leaving their loving arms,' Pa Sorie had said. 'We are grateful that you would even consider parting with such a jewel. We thank you.'

The drumming, dancing, eating and singing had gone on far into the night. Jamilla, somehow, escaped from the women guarding her, desperate as she was to have a last farewell meeting with Santigie. But she was seen and Chief Dauda cut short the celebrations and brought his new bride to Talaremba that very night. The marriage did seal the peace between the two tribes but Talarembans never forgot that Jamilla had first rejected their chief.

☆☆☆☆

And now here is Santigie at our village. I look back to find him staring at Madu and I. He is not laughing but once again those ants dance on my back. Madu takes the tray from me and pushes me in front of her.

When the men finish eating, they go back to their palaver talk. This time I escape from the women, run to the back of the huts and hide in the bushes behind Jaja's hut, where I could see and hear them.

'We've talked enough,' I heard Jaja say. 'We can wait no longer.'

'But, as I said before, how do we know for sure that these white devils are responsible for these disappearances?' A Gambilli villager asks, his eyes bright and hard.

White devils? My heart pushes against my chest as if trying to break through and run away. Had Khadijatu and Adebola, the Kocumba boy she has been meeting secretly, been right after all? I remember now just what she had said only that morning while several of us were at the waterhole.

'So, what did Adebola say?' Soji had asked, eager to get any news form outside our village.

As usual pleased to be the centre of attention, Khadijatu, pushes out her large breasts, puts her hands on her hips and puffs out like a plump bird. 'Adebola says the council of war is about white *ngafas*, the white devils. They're coming this way!'

'White devils?' I laugh glad that she is making a fool of herself. 'There's no such thing as white devils. Don't you know that is just something our mothers say to scare us? How can you believe a stupid Kocumba boy?'

'If that's how you feel I won't tell you anything else,' says Khadijatu sitting down and wiping the small waterfall of sweat dripping down her round, flat face.

'Come on Khadijatu,' Soji says, flicking her with some of the water. 'Tell us, otherwise we'll tell your mother that you've been seeing that boy.'

'You wouldn't,' says Khadijatu wrapping her arms around herself and swaying. 'She'd kill me.' But one glance at our faces and she decides to tell us all she knows. 'He said that there are "white devils", whiter even than *osu*. They come from a long way away, where the water is as blue and as wide as the sky.'

'Is there any place that big,' asks Gashida.

'Shh,' says Soji, 'let her talk.' She sits down next to Kadijatu. 'White devils? Has he seen them? What do they look like, then?'

'He said they are men, but they look like *osus*, white and raw. In the sun they go red like cooked meat and they have a nasty smell.'

'O, *Olorun* protect us,' says Gashida. 'I would fall into the arms of the ancestors at once if I met one. They must all be so ugly.' She shudders at the thought.

'The white devil-men carry long iron hot-sticks, which makes noise like thunder,' adds Khadijatu, sure that she has everyone's full attention now.

'They walk around with iron-sticks?' asks Hawa. 'Why?'

'It blows out little iron stones.' Khadijatu's voice grows soft so that we have to lean forward to hear her. 'If those hit you, they have the power to send you on your last journey to the ancestors.' She sighs and adds, 'Adebola said that they use the sticks to take young boys and girls away from their villages, from the fields or even when they go to get water.' Khadijatu's eyes are wide as she says almost in a whisper, 'They're worse than the Moors. They do not just take *akishas* or even *crus*, they take whole villages, anyone they can capture,' says Khadijatu, nodding her head.

I had laughed but now I creep closer and wait. Jaja will tell them all that there are no such thing as white devils.

'You heard what has been said,' Jaja says, 'the white devils have been seen around here. Action must be taken.'

I start to shake. Jaja believes these people are nearby. How can this be so?

'They're responsible for the wells and rivers drying up, the animals dying, the crops failing. It was not *djudju*,' says another man whose face I could not see. 'So, all our sacrifices, all the rituals, libations and gifts were useless.'

'But how could these white devils have done all that?' says the Gambillian man. 'How could we not have seen them before?'

'They must be working with clansmen,' interrupts Jaja. 'I say that any man who carries our blood and betrays us should be captured and sent to answer the ancestors and the gods they no longer respect. This is my word.' He bangs his chief's staff down three times on the ground in front of him and the red earth swirled up as if winging the promise up to the gods.

All the men beat the earth and howl their agreement. Well almost all. I notice that Santigie does not join in.

'I've heard,' says someone else, 'they come by boats from over the big water, carrying iron-sticks that shoot out fire and sharp stones.' Fear darkens his eyes to the colour of new coal.

'They call the iron-sticks, guns,' says Santigie bringing out a small knife with a shiny white handle to cut off the fleshy top of a coconut.

I could feel my heart thumping. That is what Khadija had called them iron-sticks. Ayee!

'How do you know of this?' says one of the other Chiefs leaning forward.

'Chief,' replies Santigie, with that same smile that sends shivers of fear through me. 'I know this because I have seen and spoken to the white men in the big towns way past Bantumani. They're not skin-less, devils or evil spirits.'

The other men shout and beat the ground. 'What are they then?' asks someone. 'You who know so much, tell us.' I look at the men and their faces are hard.

'They're just men who are also traders of slaves, *akisha* or *cru* or anyone in the wrong place at the wrong time. They do not come up-river. It is the warriors from the coast. The tribes who make war on each other and sell those they capture. It is they you must fear.'

'Why haven't you told us this before?' Jaja asks. The lion is in his voice, deep and as thick as the air on a night full of storm. I dread the breaking of that storm.

Santigie takes a long drink of coconut-juice, wipes his mouth on the back of his hand before answering. 'Weak men who can't defend themselves, men who would never be able to lead or protect their people, men and woman who are no good to us, are captured. Then they are sold to the white men who take them far away in big ships.'

His words are like liquid poison, and although he does not say it, the echo of a forbidden name floats in the air and all fall silent. The men nearest him shifted away as if they did not want to be touched by his words. The drums beat harder and louder.

I could see the lines on Jaja's face deepen as he gets up from his stool. Hot in his monkey-pelt cloak, his bare chest covered in a film of sweat, like a shiny second skin. He and Santigie held each other's gaze, two lions about to spring.

'What are you saying, cousin of my wife,' said Jaja. By addressing Santigie in that way, claiming family relationship, everyone knew the chief was warning the other man to be careful of his words.

Santigie smiles. 'Some say that maybe your lost son, Lansana was sold to the white man because he was not warrior enough to fight,' he says, before turning away.

Lansansa! The name rings in my ears and makes me dizzy. 'No, no, no,' every part of me screams silently. The thought of my brother dragged away from his people stitches my tears to my soul. Lansana would have fought even if the white devils had iron-sticks, wouldn't he?

'Who dares say such a thing?' says Jaja raising his spear. He points it at Santigie. All the men jump up, as spears were only aimed at enemies. Some of the Kocumba men step between the two men.

'Stop,' cries the chief of Kocumba. 'This is not the way nor the time to settle old wars.'

Lansana, my brother, captured? A slave, maafa? That's why he never returned from *Obogani*. I knew he had not run away. I never want to think of that day, but it is always there. In the centre of the noise and celebration, Jaja standing still, tall and straight, a mighty man-tree rooted to the spot. He too, like me, waiting, waiting, while the drums got louder and faster. No wind, but the feathers on Jaja's chief's headdress shake and tremble like the branches of palm trees in strong *harmattan* breeze. His spear, shining and sharp, points towards the sky. It catches the dying sun sending shafts of light up to the heavens to blind the jealous gods and turn them away from his son. As the sun moves behind the trees to hide its face in shame, and the words of the Kocumba chief, still hang faintly in the air, Jaja, Chief Dauda of Talaremba, gestures for the ceremony to begin.

The people move to obey Jaja's silent command, their voices beginning to rise with the sound of the drums. 'Maybe he's been eaten by wild animals,' I remember hearing one of the women from Gambilli say, as I left the dancing and singing.

'They say he's run away because he was not man enough to

survive the trials,' said another. 'Whatever it is, his initiation is not complete and therefore he is not fit to be the next Talaremba chief.'

Now I'm learning the truth and it is too much. I must get away from the throbbing, beating, banging drums, away from the village. More than ever I need Maluuma. If I can get to our spirit-tree, where she taught me about plants, medicines and healings maybe her being would enter me there and speak to me, from beyond time.

'What does the spirit-tree do?' I had asked her the first time we went there.

'Whatever you ask of the gods when you come here goes straight to them. So you must always be careful what you ask for.'

# CHAPTER 14

*If thou seekest her as silver, and searchest for her as hidden treasures;*
*then shalt thou understand the fear of the LORD*
Proverbs 2.4

## November 1850

*Thursday 15th November 1850, Winkfield Place*
> *I am happy that Nanny kept me in today. It is very, very*
> *cold. I do not like going for walks in the cold. It is good to be*
> *without the others sometimes, especially Mabel.*

✧✧✧

When Sarah started coughing Nanny stopped her from going for
that day's walk.

'Coat off. The others can go with their Aunts Caroline and
Laura. We don't want this cough settling on your chest. You have
to be well for the christening.'

'What are you doing?' Sarah asked later when Nanny sat down
with the blue dress and the sewing basket.

'This is what you will wear on Sunday. Madam thinks that the
sash and the buttons should be white so I'm changing them.'

White? I feel another cough welling up inside of me and I cannot
speak, I cannot say to Nanny that white always means that death
is near. I hate white.

'You may work on your Christmas gifts until the others come back.'

They had all been working hard on making Christmas presents. Every afternoon, Miss Byles brought out the materials; silks, threads, needles, scissors, paper, ink, old magazines. Mabel, Emily and Sarah drew, cut and pasted and stitched while Miss Byles read Charles Dickens' *A Christmas Story* to them. The story fascinated and worried Sarah. She feared that if sent away before finding her sister she would end up in the streets, like the children in the story, alone, starving and helpless. Then what would happen to her? Until now she had not known that there were ghosts and spirits in England too. Bad spirits, like *djudju* that could come and take you, with dragging chains, to the place below.

Sarah picked up the handkerchief, with initials, she was making for Papa Forbes. She had finished embroidering the first initial. Now she spread it out and pulled the blue silk through to start working on the second intertwined letter F. She tried not to prick her finger and leave a red spot on the white cotton. It was going to be the best gift Papa had ever had.

There was still almost four weeks to Christmas. With the help of Nanny and Miss Byles she had made pen-wipes for Miss Byles and Freddie, a book marker for Mama, a very small quilt for Anna's doll. She still had to make a needle-case for Nanny, paste a picture collage for Mabel's scrap book, cut up some soft chamois leather square to give to Cook and sorted out some of her ribbons for Edith. After she finished Papa's handkerchiefs, she was going to make a *gri-gri* pouch for Emily. But without an *ala*, birth-string or blue glass, what was she to put in it that would keep Emily safe?

If only Fatmata was there, she would know. The thought of how she had got the blue glass, the noise of the fire, the screaming, echoed in her head and started her coughing again. The more she tried not to think about it, the tighter her chest felt, the more she coughed, and gasped for breath. Nanny Grace went to her room and got the bottle of Godfrey's Cordial.

'Here child, here,' she said, pulling the cork out of the small blue bottle, 'drink some of this. It will ease the coughing and calm you down.'

Sarah drank the teaspoonful of sweet, sticky dark brown liquid without hesitation. She liked the medicine. In fact, all the children liked it. Nanny gave it to them if they coughed, had a cold, a head-ache, stomach pains or were teething. To Nanny Grace Godfrey's Cordial was good for every ailment.

'There,' said Nanny when Sarah stopped coughing and could breathe again. 'I'd better take this with me on Sunday. Can't have you coughing like that during your christening, can we?'

'Nanny, why do I have to be christened?' Sarah asked. 'Is it so that Queen Victoria can become my mother by God?'

'What a question. You read the Bible everyday with Miss Byles,' Nanny said, shaking her head and going back to her sewing.

Sarah did not tell her that she found the Bible hard to under-stand. How could there be only one God in England when there were so many different gods in Africa? Was the English god greater than those gods?

'Miss Byles did not read that bit.'

'Jesus loves you and your christening shows that you have taken him to your heart.'

'But how can he love me? He does not know me.'

'He loves us all. The Bible tells us so. Now let me see your stitching.' Nanny smoothed out the handkerchief and nodded. 'Your sewing is getting very good,' Nanny said, then continued with her sewing.

Sarah watched Nanny Grace's rapid needle go in and out. She opened her mouth a couple of times but did not speak. Eventually she blurted out, 'are you christened Nanny?'

'Yes,' said Nanny Grace before licking the end of the cotton and trying to push it through the eye of the needle. 'Everyone in this house has been christened. In two days, you will be too, then Reverend Byles will write your name in the parish church register just as he did for Freddie, Mabel, Emily and Anna.'

'Nanny Grace, who is going to be at my christening?'

'We'll all be there and most of your godparents too. You've met Captain's sisters, Miss Caroline and Miss Laura. They've come all the way from Dundee to stand as your godmothers.'

Sarah nodded. Caroline and Laura were tall although not quite as tall as Papa Forbes. They looked very alike with brown eyes, wide smiles and light brown hair plaited and wound into a bun at the nape of their neck. The only difference was that Caroline, the elder, wore a brown silk dress trimmed with pale yellow, whereas Laura's was dark green trimmed with red. Sarah was not sure that she could tell them apart if they changed their clothes.

'And there's Her Majesty too.' Sarah wriggled in her chair with excitement. 'I am going to have many mothers now.'

'You're a very lucky girl to have Queen Victoria as your godmother, but she'll not be attending. Neither will Lieutenant George, Captain's brother, he's still at sea. You remember Lieutenant Heard from *The Bonetta?*'

'Is he coming, Nanny?' asked Sarah, putting down her sewing.

'Yes. He's standing as your godfather with The Captain.'

Sarah clapped her hands and wriggled even more. 'Lieutenant Heard used to laugh at the faces I made every morning when Papa made me suck half a lemon to keep the sickness away. But the lemons didn't stop my cough though, did they, Nanny?'

'No, it didn't so we have to make sure you are well on the day.'

'Jesus will be at the church too?'

'Yes, Sarah, he'll be there to see you saved.' Nanny said, nodding her head.

'Saved? From what?'

'From being a heathen. That is what you were in Africa, the missionaries say.'

Sarah gave a little sigh. The more she heard about Jesus the more confused she became. There were so many things about him that were difficult to understand. Why couldn't Jesus save her while she was still in Africa? Why did she have to come to England to be saved? What about Fatmata, would she be saved too?

'You see,' said Nanny Grace, before Sarah could say anything, 'God so loved the world he sent us his only son. He was born…'

'In a stable at Christmas,' interrupted Sarah. She knew this bit about Jesus. 'Miss Byles read us that story.' She picked up her needle ready to sew again.

'Yes, he was born in a stable in Bethlehem and…'

'The wise men came and gave him gifts, gold, frankincense and myrrh. That is why we too give gifts on his birthday,' said Sarah, eager to show that she remembered all that Miss Byles had told them about the Nativity.

'And then he died on the cross.'

'Died?' said Sarah. Her mouth felt dry. She didn't remember Miss Byles saying anything about Jesus dying.

Salimatu, was there in her head again, whispering, 'he went to join the ancestors. Maybe if we make some sacrifice, he will talk to those who have gone before to bring Fatmata to us.'

The word sacrifices made her stomach twist and turn. What could they offer as a sacrifice? They had no goat, or sheep or even chicken. She did not want to think what else she had seen offered up as sacrifice.

'Yes, he died at Easter time,' she heard Nanny Grace say, her needle flying in and out.

Sarah could feel her heart beating 'Why do we give presents for his birth if he has died?'

'Now, Sarah, you did not think that Jesus was alive, did you? He was buried, then on the third day he rose again, so that we might all be saved.'

'Jesus rose again?'

'He rose from the dead to sit at the right hand of God with the Holy Spirit.'

Sarah's eyes widened, her hands suddenly wet. Holy Spirit? Inside her Salimatu cried, 'ayee, only *djudju* come back from the other side as a spirit. He is not a god, he's a spirit, a *djudju*. He'll not help us. We must have nothing to do with their Jesus Christ.'

'Save me from the devil,' Sarah cried, jumping up.

'Be calm child. Jesus will save you from the devil and hellfire,' said Nanny. 'That is why you are being christened.'

Sarah clasped her hands and pricked her finger with the needle she was still holding. She watched the blood bead, grow, burst and run down her finger.

'Be careful, Sarah,' said Nanny sharply, snatching the handker-chief away but not before a tiny drop of blood had landed on it.

She sobbed loudly then.

'Not to worry,' said Nanny, 'it's only a little speck. Luckily, we can cover it up with the embroidery. Stop the crying now or you'll start coughing again.'

# SALIMATU/SARAH

# CHAPTER 15

*The blueness of a wound cleanseth away evil*
Proverbs 20:30

## November 1850

H olding on to her *gri-gri* did not work that night. Sarah tossed and turned and coughed and thought about the christening. Through the open bedroom door, she could see light flickering in the day nursery from the lamp that burned through the night because Emily was frightened of the dark. Afraid of waking Mabel up again, Sarah got out of bed and went into the other room. She saw her blue dress hanging in the half-light. Nanny must have been working on it late into the night. She stroked it, the beautiful blue dress; blue to keep her safe.

'But it won't, it won't,' whispered Salimatu. 'That blue dress is not going to save us from Jesus who rose from the dead to become a spirit. He will come after us to take us down to the world below. We must stay away from him. You must not be christened.'

Sarah sank to the floor. She did not know what to do, what to think anymore.

'If you have no dress you could not be christened, could you?' said Salimatu.

But how could she get rid of it? thought Sarah looking around. The nursery cupboard! That was it, that was where everything was kept out of sight. If she pushed it right to back no one would think of looking there for a dress. She took the sewing basket out to make room for the dress. A pair of scissors lying amongst the threads and silks fell out and stuck in the dress. She pulled it out and the dress ripped. She gasped; she had not meant to do that at all.

Salimatu's voice came loud and clear. 'cut it up, get rid of it.'

Sarah cut off one end of the long white satin sash. It fell on her bare feet and slithered off like a white snake. She wriggled her toes and kicked the material away afraid that someone would see what she had done.

But no one came and suddenly she felt free of fear. Why did she have to wear these clothes, and shoes and hats and gloves? Why could she not just be Salimatu? After that it was easy. With Salimatu's voice in her ear ordering and pushing, Sarah cut and slashed. The scissors became her warrior spear, the dress that would capture her body and deliver her to the enemy had to be destroyed. She stabbed the dress, the beautiful; no, the ugly, stupid dress that could not save her. Why had she ever thought it was pretty? When at last she stopped, her breath came in short sharp gasps; her was face wet. She gathered the torn dress in her arms, curled up on the floor and slept. She was no longer coughing.

✭✭✭✭

It was Mabel's scream that woke Sarah up. At first, she could not work out why she was lying on the ground in the schoolroom. Then she saw a sea of blue around her, and her heart started to beat fast. Last night was not a dream. Last night Salimatu had taken over. What had she been thinking? Had she not promised Papa Forbes that she would be good.

'Nanny, Nanny, come quick, come and see what Sarah has done,' cried Mabel practically dancing with glee.

Sarah crawled under the table in the centre of the room and lay there trying not to breathe, wishing she could disappear.

'Come out of there this instance Sarah Forbes Bonetta,' said Nanny. 'What is the meaning of this?' She held up the tattered blue dress that Sarah had been so pleased to wear just a week ago. The great slashes were like gaping wounds.

'Did you do this, did you?' Nanny's face was bright red, her breathing was loud.

Sarah crept out from under the table. She opened her mouth to explain but Nanny looked so angry the words seemed all knotted up inside her mouth.

'Oh, you bad girl. You bad, ungrateful girl. What are you going to wear tomorrow now? I must show Madam this, immediately,' said Nanny Grace, hurrying out of the room.

Emily ran over and hugged Sarah. 'Oh Sally,' she said, 'didn't you know that you would get into trouble? Papa will punish you.'

'You've done it this time,' said Mabel.

✦✦✦✦

Both Papa Forbes and Mama Forbes came up to the nursery. None of them had ever seen Papa look so serious. There were no smiles, no running into open arms.

Papa took the torn dress from Mama Forbes and said, 'Sarah, did you cut up the dress?'

Sarah did not answer. Now it was morning she did not know how to explain what she had felt last night. Sarah glanced at Mama Forbes but knew that she could not tell her either. Her eyes were no longer bright blue but dark as the sky before a storm.

'Answer me,' Papa Forbes said, his voice louder than before.

'I thought you liked the dress,' said Mama Forbes. 'Just look at it. How could you?'

Sarah opened her mouth but shut it as Salimatu ordered her, 'don't speak. They'll never understand about their god and *djudju*,'.

'Sarah, I'm waiting,' said Papa Forbes leaning forward.

'I did not want to wear it anymore, sir,' Sarah muttered at last, her head hanging down not daring to look at him.

She could hear Nanny tut-tut behind her and saw Mabel's mouth fall open.

'Oh dear,' said Mama Forbes, sitting down quickly as if her legs had suddenly given way under the weight of Sarah's defiance.

'You do not decide what you will or will not wear. Mama and I are most disappointed that you could do such a thing,' said Papa Forbes shaking the cut-up dress at her. 'For this wanton damage you will stay apart for the others for the rest of the day and write out one hundred times in your best handwriting, *I have done wrong and I am truly sorry*. You are, are you not?'

Sarah chewed at her lips, said nothing and backed away.

'Come on, you are sorry, surely,' said Mrs Forbes reaching over and taking hold of Sarah's hands. But Sarah pulled away sharply and Mary Forbes' hand hit the table hard. She cried out and the Captain grabbed hold of Sarah. From deep within her came a memory of being held tight. She could not say where or when but the feeling of a hand holding her tight, tugging, yanking her along, made her heart pound. She struggled against Papa Forbes' hold, scratching and kicking. Then she bit him.

'Is this the way you repay our kindness, with insolence and violence? Kicking and scratching, biting?'

Sarah and Salimatu together screamed and fought harder, hitting out at Mama Forbes and Nanny Grace too. Emily cried and Mabel stared open-mouthed.

'This will not do. You must be taught a lesson. Nanny the cane, please,' Papa Forbes said in a quiet but deep voice.

The cane! Sarah stopped fighting and shook. It had last been used on Freddie when he was nine. Mabel had told her once.

'He tied a stone to the cat and threw it into the pond to see how many lives it had left. Freddie could not sit down for two days.'

'Oh, Frederick, no, not that,' cried Mama Forbes, jumping up. 'Remember she belongs to the Queen. Punish her, yes but not the cane.'

Emily sobbed louder. Mabel looked at the floor.

'Her Majesty would not thank us if we allowed our charge to remain savage, wilful and violent. Take the other children to the parlour.'

'But the cane, Frederick? Isn't that being violent too? What will your sisters say?'

'Go please, Mary. This has nothing to do with anyone else.'

Mama Forbes face went red. She pressed her lips together, took Anna and Emily by the hand and hurried them out of the room, Mabel following.

✿✿✿✿

The first hit took Sarah's breathe away. She felt the pain travel from her right hand to her wrist, up through her arm, her shoulders and into her chest. The next lash pushed the hurt through her throat, into her mouth. Salimatu let out a scream that flew past the whistle of the cane as it came down for the third cut. The pain rushed into every part of her, a torrent, searching then bursting to stream out of her eyes and nose. She had never been hit like this before, not even as a slave in King Gezo's palace. *'Aba Yaa! Ma ko pa mi. Don't kill me,'*

Sarah cried as she fell to the floor and curled up into a ball. She waited for more strokes. Salimatu kept on screaming. But there were no more because Mabel came rushing into the nursery to stand in front of her.

'No Papa, no more. Please Papa. She's sorry I'm sure.'

From far away she thought she heard Freddie's voice. 'Father, that is enough.'

❉❉❉

Later, Mabel brought a wet washcloth and laid it on Sarah's hands, while Emily knelt by her side, crying still.

'He'll never hit you again, I promise,' said Freddie before striding out of the nursery, taking the cane with him.

Sarah sat there, her face blank, her eyes open but unseeing.

Her hand throbbed. She knew that she would never forget the pain. Everything had changed, and she did not know what to do. Inside her head she heard Salimatu whisper, 'no matter how long we stay here we will never be part of them. We must get to Fatmata and go back home.' And where is that, thought Sarah.

# CHAPTER 16

*When pride comes, then comes disgrace, but with humility comes wisdom*
Proverbs 11:2

## November 1850

Later in the day of the caning, when Sarah slid into the kitchen, Edith was peeling potatoes and Mrs Dixon was checking the joint of beef in the range. The kitchen was her most favourite place in the whole house and she would creep down the many stairs from her room into its warmth whenever she had a chance.

'Young ladies do not spend time in the kitchen,' Nanny had said when she found Sarah there not so long ago. 'When you have your own home, the Cook will come to you every morning for the day's orders.'

Mrs Dixon reminded Sarah of Peg-leg Zed although they were not at all alike. Mrs Dixon was much shorter, rounder and in possession of both of her legs. She too, however, rushed around throwing things into pots, chopping, stirring, tasting and talking, always talking, asking questions. Sarah did not mind her questions. She liked telling Mrs Dixon about Peg-leg and Amos and the ship. It made her feel close to the sailors and especially Papa Forbes. Not this one with the cane, the other one, the Papa Forbes who held her close and said she was safe.

'Well I never,' Mrs Dixon would say with a laugh, when Sarah told her about life on *The Bonetta*. 'You're just a bit of a thing and you've seen all that. And the way you can talk! If I close my eyes, I would think it was a lady speaking, not a darkie, my o my.' Then she would give Sarah a piece of cake before sending her away.

✹✹✹✹

When Edith saw Sarah standing in the doorway, she ran to her. 'O Miss Sarah. Go back to the nursery or you'll be punished again.'

'Mind you own business Edith,' said Mrs Dixon. 'Go get some coal and see to the fireplaces upstairs. She'll be fine. Sit down child. You've had quite a day of it, haven't you?'

Sarah sank into the chair and burst into tears.

'Why did you do it, child? Such a beautiful dress too. I saw you when you were going to the castle and you looked like a princess. Black but still a princess.'

'I don't want to be christened,' cried Sarah.

'Why ever not? Things are all arranged. And after the service many are coming here for luncheon. I've been baking and cooking and all for you. What is wrong with that?'

'Nanny says Jesus rose from the dead as a spirit. I know spirits come from the devil. It is *djudju*. I don't want Jesus to get me and drag me down to hell fire.'

'Oh, lawkes, you think it's like where you come from? You've got that wrong my dearie. Things like that don't happen here.'

'I don't want to join the ancestors. I just want to go back home.'

'It's not that easy. I don't think they'll let you go back to where you come from dearie, not with all that is still going on over there.'

'What?' asked Sarah, frowning.

'Buying and selling you people, as if you were animals. Not everyone in England agreed with the slavers taking you darkies.'

This was not anything Sarah had thought about before. 'So

why did they not just stop it?' she said blowing her nose on her handkerchief.

'Some people did. The papers called them abolitionist.'

Sarah leaned forward. 'But it hasn't stopped. I got taken during a raid.'

'I know lovey. Even after we got the laws changed to stop it, some who were making money from it wanted it to go on. Some of the other countries are worse, 'cause they still haven't passed any law against buying and selling people as if they were cattle. And some darkies are just as greedy, you know. They sell their own people for guns and trinkets. They don't care that the slavers take their own people far away to the Indies to be sold again for rum and sugar and tobacco,' said Mrs Dixon, shaking her head. 'My Harry used to say that's why ships like the Captain's still going up and down that area, waiting to catch them slavers.'

Sarah caught her breath. Memories pushed way back into dark corners of her mind stirred. People running, crying, caught, held, dragged, horses, hooves pounding. That was what had happened to Fatmata and herself, captured by Santigie and sold, again and again.

'Captain had to get you away, otherwise God knows what would've happened to you. From what I've read you would be a gonner by now.'

They had not seen Edith come back. She crept forward. 'How do you know all this Mrs Dixon,' she asked.

'Harry, my husband, was a sailor, man and boy. Later he was with the Captain on patroller ships. Service on the West African Squadron, as it is called, is thankless, full of risk and violence from seas and slavers. He said they had to fight against all kinds of diseases. Sometimes when he left to go to sea it would be almost a year before I saw him again. But after a while he could not stomach it.'

'Why?' asked Edith.

'Oh, the things he used to tell me. The way the darkies were treated on those slave ships, tied up below deck as if in a coffin, with little food or water, the beatings, the smell. Dreadful it was. Sometimes when they were in danger of being caught some captains ordered the slaves to be thrown overboard to reduce the fines.'

'Oh, Mrs Dixon, how terrible,' cried Edith. 'To not even have a grave to visit.'

Mrs Dixon nodded her head and blew her nose. 'And to think that there were clever darkies like you who were just taken away and sold.'

Sarah sat back trying to understand all that Mrs Dixon had just told her. In those few minutes she had learned a lot. Indies, America? She had no idea how far away these places were, but did the patrollers bring those they rescued to England with them, like Papa Forbes had brought her?

'Mrs Dixon,' said Sarah leaning forward, 'did your Harry bring Fatmata to England?'

'Fatmata?'

'My sister. They took me away from her. I must find her.'

'Oh, I don't think he did, child. Harry died years ago. Anyway, they didn't catch all the slave ships. Those that got away sold the slaves in many different places, Barbados, Jamaica, some to Brazil or America. Don't know where those countries are, just heard the names. The ones they rescued, Harry said, were taken off the ships in Africa, somewhere called Freetown.'

'Then how will I ever get back to her?' said Sarah.

'If she is in England, she is free, 'cause there are no slaves here. Maybe she's looking for you too. What does she look like?'

Sarah opened her mouth and then shut it. Fatmata's face was not there. She could not describe her sister. She shut her eyes, but still there was nothing, just a dark space that seemed to get bigger.

'I can't see her. I can't see her face anymore. She's gone,' Sarah cried, rocking and moaning, the stinging tears running down her face.

Mrs Dixon clasped Sarah to her chest. 'Shh, shh, child.'

'Will I never find Fatmata?'

'Listen to me. God knows what has happened to her or could have happened to you, for that matter, if the Captain had not rescued you and brought you home with him. There is nowhere else for you to go. Tell the Captain you are sorry, wear whatever you are given, get christened in a couple of days and soon everyone will forget all about this.'

'If I don't will Papa send me away?'

'I don't know, lovey.' She took Sarah's hand in hers, and Sarah winced. Mrs Dixon saw that it was red and swollen. 'O lawd,' she said, 'The Captain do that?'

Sarah nodded.

Mrs Dixon shook her head and sighed. 'Let me tell you something, princess or no, Her Majesty's godchild or no, you got to learn to look after yourself, understand? You'll not always be a child but you will always be a darkie. Learn something for the future, teach, play the piano, anything.' She looked at Sarah's hand again. 'I'll get you some ointment to soothe that.'

✿✿✿✿

*Friday 15th November 1850, Winkfield Place,*

> *This afternoon I wrote a hundred times <u>I have done wrong and I am truly sorry.</u> Mabel said she would write half of them for me. She said Papa will not know. But I said no. We will know. I must do it on my own. She drew the lines on the paper for me. Why is Mabel being friendly? Am I going to be sent away to the workhouse? I tried very hard to do my best*

*handwriting. Papa did not say anything when I gave him the
lines. My hand still hurts.*

✪✪✪✪

Mrs Newbury, the local seamstress, her spectacles perched on the
end of her nose, her mouth full of pins, worked with Nanny on
another dress for Sarah to wear to the christening the next day.
Sarah did not dare fidget while they measured and pinned, cut
and sewed. She was not allowed to speak, to ask questions and
certainly not to comment on the dress that was being made from
one of Mama's old grey silk dresses. There was no time to get more
suitable material. In the end, even Miss Caroline and Miss Laura
came into the nursery to help Nanny with the trimmings, dark blue
ribbons and the old blue satin sash.

Sarah hardly slept, still afraid of what was to come. On Sunday
she was up and without any help put on the grey silk dress. With
her blue cloak on Papa and Mama would not see the grey dress;
they would not be reminded of the ruined blue one. When she came
down the hall. Mama and Papa were waiting. They said nothing to
Sarah.

'Good. Everyone ready?' said Papa. 'We had better be on our
way. Mustn't be late. The others will meet us at the Church.' At the
front door he stopped. 'Where is Freddie? Where's the boy?'

'Here, Father,' called Freddie as he thumped down the stairs.
'I'm here.'

This was the second time Freddie had said Father instead of
Papa, Sarah noticed. She took the arm he held out to her and
they smiled at each other. She felt that nothing bad could possibly
happen to her with Freddie there.

'Come on Mabel,' said Freddie.

Sarah looked back to see Mabel standing alone on the steps.

'Walk with us,' said Sarah.

Mabel ran down the steps. She took Sarah's hand and gave it a squeeze, but it was not like the old squeeze, this was different, this was friendly. Sarah was glad she had not taken her other hand though. That still hurt.

By the time they had walked the short distance to the church, there was quite a crowd.

'Here she is, here's the African Princess,' shouted someone.

'Never thought I'd see the day when savages would be praying in our church. What do darkies know about God?'

Someone else shouted, 'is Her Majesty coming 'ere, or the Princesses?'

'Here?' said another. 'Not bloomin' likely, is it?' They all laughed.

Sarah, wanting to turn and run, stood firm knowing she had nowhere to run to. Mabel held her hand and Freddie hurried them past the crowd, into the church.

Later, Sarah could remember little of the service except for Reverend Byles saying, *'to follow Christ means dying to sin and rising to new life with him.'* She shook then. This was it. Jesus was coming to take her and there was nothing she could do. She shut her eyes and from far away she heard him say, *'do you reject the devil and all rebellion against God.'*

She opened her eyes wide and shouted, 'I reject the devil, I reject the devil, I reject him.' None of the congregation knew that even as she promised to repent her sins, submit to Christ, she was also clutching her *gri-gri*.

At the font Mama Forbes took off Sarah's bonnet and Reverend Byles poured holy water on her head. The water soaked into her thick, curly hair before running, down her neck like a cold ghostly finger. She bit her lip to stop herself from crying out as he made the sign of the cross on her forehead, and through it all she prayed to the old gods of her ancestors, gods that she did not know, to save and protect her.

On the walk back to Winkfield Place, Papa walked by her side. 'Good girl,' he said. 'Mama and I are pleased with you.'

✲✲✲✲

*Sunday 17<sup>th</sup> November 1850, Winkfield Place*
   *I am christened, and I am still here. Jesus did not get me.*

# CHAPTER 17

*Abanij n ba ara rè jé*
*He who destroys others destroys himself*

## 1846

Lansana, Lansana, the name pounds in my heart. I have to get away. Without thinking I run to the village's big closed wooden gates. The armed guards are not there. I lift the heavy latch but before I can pull at the gate it is pushed wide open from outside, knocking me over. I lay on the ground and look up at a horse.

Fear grabs hold of my inside and twists. I've done wrong again. I shut my eyes and curl up waiting to be crushed by the horse's feet. But it jumps over me. The earth trembles as hooves pound on past me.

They had been waiting outside, quiet and ready. Now they are everywhere, climbing over the high mud wall surrounding the village. Men on foot carrying weapons rush past me. I must let Jaja and the other villages know.

'Arabs, Moors, Moors,' I scream, struggling up. They are the only people I know who had horses. I reach for the sling and stone always tucked in the folds of my *lappa* and pull. The stone flies into the air hitting the man running ahead of me on the side of his head. By the time he falls to the ground I have another stone in my sling. I do not look at him or the blood spreading around his head. I pick up his short spear and run.

Then something strikes the back of my head. I fall again, and all goes black. When I come to, I am being dragged along through grass. My head hurts, my side hurts. I cannot breathe. I groan and the pulling stopped.

'Fatmata, Fatmata,'

'Taimu?'

'Yes. I thought you were dead,' he sobs.

The drums that had been throbbing and pounding in the air since before sunrise have stopped but inside of me the remnants of their sound filled my ears. Grey clouds blot out the sky above. I breathe in the smell of smoke; the village is on fire. Tears of pain and fear flow from my eyes.

I try to stand up but all of me is in pain. 'My head.' I touch the back of my head and feel a lump the size of a chicken egg and there is blood.

'One of them hit you with his stick. I dragged you here.'

Screams and shouts fill the air. The sound of hooves pounding the packed earth, racing past us, towards the gate told us that at least some of the attackers are leaving our village. We peep through the bushes and I cover my mouth to stop me screaming. The attackers are not Moors as I had thought, they are not white devils, they are our own people and many of them are women. How can that be? Women Warriors! We see friends and neighbours bound and being dragged out of the village by viciously armed men.

'I must go find Madu and Jaja.'

'No,' Taimu whispers, 'they'll take us too.'

I cannot tell how long we hid there in the bushes, waiting for the many feet to stop running, walking, dragging, past us. But at last, as the shadows get longer, it grows quiet. The silence is even scarier than the noise.

'Come,' I say, even though I'm trembling, 'we must go see if our mothers are safe.'

With every step I think my head will burst open. We must be careful, for we do not know whether all the raiders have gone. As we get closer to the huts, I see that in less time than it takes to kill and cook a goat, everything has changed. All the huts are on fire; smoke pushes through cracks in the mud walls and wanders away, black streams fading into grey nothingness. On the roofs the dried palm leaves burn fast, sending angry sparks into the air only to fall, devouring more. Dead men, their bodies littered with arrow and spear wounds, are piled by burnt down gathering hut. I fall to my knees and bring up what little I have eaten that day. These are the men I had been listening to, the men that had been planning war against the white devils, not knowing that their attackers, our own people, were close at hand.

'*Ogun* save my father,' I cry as I search among the dead. He's not there but I have no time to send thanks to the gods for wailing fills the air now that the raiders have gone. Fear thick and heavy, spreads from person to person, from belly to bowels. Fear of the raiders coming back; fear of what we might find or worse, of what we might not find. Already vultures are circling everywhere, their shrill calls an argument over the spoils of the day. I choke on the smell of death spreading fast over everything. It is a smell as sharp as tooth pain and solid enough to chew.

The huts in our compound are smouldering, burnt shells, and there is no one there. I am paralysed, fearing to leave, fearing to stay in case the killers return. Over the pounding of my own heart as I stand rooted to the spot, I hear a cry from behind the carcass of our hut. My immediate reaction is to move and I run towards the voice, which rises and fades fast. As I reach the back of the hut I fall to my knees. I don't want to believe it and I am awash with emotions, joy, relief and terror. It is my mother.

'Madu, Madu.' I scream, crawling to her. She has heard me, she's alive. As I reach her, I grab her arm. As if she knows I am beside her she tries to lift her hand, to take mine but there is no strength left in the hands that once moved mountains. Tears leak from her eyes, making snail trails down her ashy face. I put my arms around her and hold her so close, we are like two halves of a peanut. I am not going to let her go.

She opens her mouth and a sound like water tumbling over stones comes out, 'Aina.'

'Madu,' I say, 'where is Salimatu?'

Her face twists but before she could say anything she slumps in my arms. Her eyes are open but staring into nothingness for her spirit is already journeying.

'No, no. *Oduadu*, mother of all, do not take Madu away,' I bawl, shaking her.

She is gone. I close Madu's eyes, my tears fall on her face, following the track of her tears, and when I take my hands away, they are red with the blood of my mother. My cries rise high, into that day of sorrow, pushing through the smoky air to join the laments of the other villagers. I shower myself with red earth turned black and mark my face with Madu's blood.

I reach over for the blue woven 'country cloth' to put over Madu. It is the first cloth I made by myself and I had given it to Madu. Now it is blackened by smoke. I pick it up and find myself looking into the blank, vacant eyes of Chief Dauda, my Jaja. I yell, 'not him too, not Jaja.' It is a sight I do not want to witness, but I must look. I see a small knife with a white shiny handle stuck in Jaja's neck. I know that knife. I have seen the knife that very day. It is Santige's. It is the same knife he had used to cut meat, and now to kill my father.

Raw, unexpected, unimagined grief, has my tongue twisted. I cannot speak, I cannot shout, a boulder of anger and fear lodges itself in my throat. I roll into a ball, wanting to disappear, to take root and go down, down, down to Maluuma. She has a healing balm for this pain. She must.

I do not know how long I am like this but at last I gather myself together. There is something I must do first. I cannot leave that knife in my father's neck dishonouring him. How many times have I said that I am as good as any boy, how many times have I said I am a Talaremba warrior? Well, here was my first test. If my brother Lansana was here, he would not hesitate, but he is not, so I must do it. The thought of him makes me strong. Taking a deep breath, with a shaking hand, I close Jaja's eyes before I pull the knife out of his neck. His blood spurts out, covers my hand and drips into the earth. I back away from the cut, open and tender and I hear the voices of my ancestors say, 'yes you are your father's warrior.' I look at the knife and swear that I will never part with it until I have plunged it into its owner's flesh. Without stopping to think I use the knife to carve out on my thigh the warriors monkey tattoo that all boys of our tribe are marked with at their initiation. Tears flow from my eyes as my Jaja's blood and mine mingle and became one. The pain is good.

And then I remember Salimatu. Where is she? Has she too gone to the ancestors? Is she captured or wandering around the village, lost? I must find my sister,

'Fatmata,' calls Taimu, running into the compound. 'My mother is alive.' He stops when he sees the bodies at my feet.

Saying nothing I hide the knife with my sling and before I can make sense of it, I see Tenneh hurrying up carrying Salimatu in her arms.

'Odudua, god of all women, praise be,' I say crying and shaking. I grab Salimatu from Tenneh and holding her tight whisper to her that she is safe now. She does not speak. She who had words flowing from her mouth before she had two harvest seasons is now silent.

'Sali, did you see the men?' I ask.

She stares at me, unblinking, her eyes big and black and full of tears and nods.

'Did they do anything to you?'

She shakes her head.

'Sali' I say, 'talk to me.' Her silence scares me.

'Madu says I must not cry or talk. I must just hold this tight.' she whispered.

I touch her closed hand. It is bleeding. She opens it to show she has been clutching eight small pieces of blue glass. I know then that amid fear and death Madu has not forgotten to try to protect at least one of her children. She made Salimatu hold on to those pieces of the blue glass to keep the evil spirits away. I put her down, take them from her, open her *gri-gri* and without looking, put two inside. The rest I place in my pouch.

Seeing Madu and Jaja, Tenneh shakes her head.

'Come now Fatmata,' she says, 'we have to leave. The raiders might come back under cover of night.'

'Sisi Tenneh,' I say, 'Chief Dauda has started on his journey to the ancestors and taken Isatu with him. I don't know what to do.'

'Child, there are many lying in the village this day who will have no ceremony to send them on their journey. I've just left the bodies of my husband and my mother. May the gods help them.' She wipes her eyes with the end of her *lappa*. 'Come, everyone is going. They will leave us behind.' Tenneh hurries away, to join the other villagers going, though none of them know where to, leaving their dead and dying.

I know we must go. Still, I cannot leave Madu and Jaja without some ceremony. I cannot leave their spirits to roam forever, unable to find the path that will lead them to the ancestors. There is no Pa Sorie, no man, to sing their praises, no one to beat the drums to tell the people that Dauda, Chief of Talaremba and Isatu, his third wife have started on their journey to the other world. There is only me. I must do something.

Then I remember what Madu did for Maluuma when her spirit went beyond us.

I open my amulet and take out four pieces of glass and place them over Madu and Jaja eyes that can longer see this world.

'Maluuma,' I cry, 'with the light from this glass lead your daughter, my mother Isatu, my father Dauda, safely to the other side. I bring no water, no kola-nuts, no sacrifices but I beg all the ancestors to forgive me. Accept my mother and my father; do not let them become evil spirits roaming forever.' My voice echoes the sounds from the exploding blue bottles. I hear the spirits searching, searching, searching, for the way home.

I pick Salimatu up, bring her wet face close to mine and wonder what would happen to us from now on. I lick her tears and swallow her pain. I touch the marks on her face and thank the gods that like me she has them. Wherever we go our faces will show we are the daughters of a Talaremba chief, part of Isatu and Dauda, and joined to the ancestors for all time.

I tie her to my back with Madu's blue cloth and run to catch up with Taimu and Tenneh. I never reach them. Grabbed from behind, my wrists pinned to my side, I cannot get to my sling. I twist and scream, and when a hand tries to cover my mouth, I clamp my teeth over a fat finger. I feel a warm spurt of blood in my mouth before I hear his cry and feel a thump on the back of my head, right where I had been hit before. It brings me to my knees.

'I'll teach you to fight with Bureh,' he says and slaps me across the face.

My head snaps back, and my scream is sucked in. I can feel side of my face swelling. I squint up at him. Bureh? From the sound of his voice, I know this is a Kocumba man. Salimatu clings to my neck screaming and he pulls her off my back.

'Here, Momoh, take the child. I'll deal with this one. We can have our pay right here and now,' he says, pushing me down. He grabs hold of my lappa and tries to rip it off but Momoh yanks him off me.

'We don't have time,' he says. 'This is the one he wants. Tie her up. He'll be waiting.'

Although I cannot understand everything they are saying, I know enough to understand that they have come back to find me, and I wonder why.

# CHAPTER 18

*Discretion shall preserve thee, understanding shall keep thee*
**Proverbs 2:11**

## November 1850

Two days later they came down to say goodbye to the Captain's sisters who were going back to Dundee that morning. Sarah stood by the door, unsure of her future within the family.

'Come and sit by me Sarah,' said Mama Forbes, smiling and holding out her hand. Sarah gave s sigh of relief and hurried to her. From now on she thought, I'll be good, do everything I'm told to do. I want to stay here.

Captain Forbes hurried into the parlour waving a letter. 'Mary, guess what's just arrived. You have a letter from the castle.'

'Windsor Castle? Me?'

'Yes, I have one too, from Sir Charles Phipps setting out the arrangements for Sarah.'

Mama Forbes opened her letter and frowned. 'Mine is from Lady Phipps. She wants to see me too. There is also an invitation for Sarah.'

'Oh,' cried Laura, 'to the castle?'

Mama Forbes nodded and read out:

*'Her Majesty, Queen Victoria, would like to see Sarah on Thursday, 21ˢᵗ November 1850, 3 p.m. at Windsor Castle. Sarah will be staying on to partake of Princess Victoria's tenth birthday party.'*

'Is she going alone, Mama?' asked Mabel.

Sarah glanced at Mabel who although was not smiling was not frowning either.

'No. Papa and I will go to the castle with Sarah then we can work out the arrangement for her with Sir Charles while she sees Queen Victoria.'

Captain Forbes' reaction to the letter is one of pride and bemusement. 'I did not think that Her Majesty would take such interest in Sarah,' he said with a smile. 'I was right to bring her home.'

✲✲✲✲

Sarah sat between Mama and Papa Forbes trying hard not to slide off the seat as the carriage rocked and shook through Windsor Park. Was it only twelve days ago that she and Papa had ridden up this very road? This time she took no notice of the swaying trees or the wall that surrounded the castle. She knew that her head would not be cut off, she knew that there were no spirits hiding behind the trees ready to jump out and get her, for after all the spirit of Jesus had already entered her soul. That was what Reverend Byles had said. It must have worked for here she was, still alive. Jesus had not dragged her down to that other world, to the ancestors.

Inside the castle they followed the courtier down the Grand Corridor towards the Kings Tower and the Queen's private sitting room. Sarah was no longer bothered by the eyes on the paintings, or those of the busts and statues. Wasn't she the African Princess, looked after by Jesus on one side and her *gri-gri* on the other? Double protection.

The courtier knocked on the door, opened it and announced, 'Captain Forbes, Mrs Forbes and Miss Sarah Forbes Bonetta.'

Sarah rushed forward, hardly noticing Sir Charles and Lady Phipps sitting by the fireplace and did a rather unsteady curtsey. Queen Victoria reached out quickly and took hold of Sarah's hand to steady her. Sarah was thankful her gloves were hiding her still reddened hand. She did not want to explain.

'*Guten tag*, Your Majesty,' Sarah said. She stood with her hands behind her back.

Queen Victoria smiled. '*Das ist sehr gut*, Sarah.'

'*Ich danke sehr*, Ma'am,' said Sarah then added, 'that is all I know so far, but I have been practising.'

Queen Victoria looked past Sarah to Captain Forbes who bowed. 'Your Majesty, may I present my wife, Mrs Forbes,' he said. Mama Forbes gave a deep curtsey.

'Good afternoon, Your Majesty.'

Queen Victoria gave a nod and smiled. 'Mrs Forbes. Do either of you speak German?'

'No Ma'am,' said Mama Forbes. 'I speak French. Our governess has a little German.'

'I see.' Queen Victoria studied Sarah for a moment then said 'Sarah may join the princesses for their German lessons once a week in the new year. Lady Phipps will you arrange it with Frau Schreiber.'

'Yes Ma'am,' said Lady Phipps.

'I hear that the christening went well, Mrs Forbes. I'm sure that Sarah will be able to tell me all about it while Sir Charles goes over the arrangements to be made for the child.'

'Ma'am,' said Mrs Forbes curtsying again.

'The Phipps and Seymour children are coming for Vicky's

birthday tea party too. In fact, Sarah will stay the night and be taken home tomorrow. The band is playing later and there is a dance in the Servants hall in Vicky's honour.'

'Ma'am,' said Captain Forbes bowing.

Sarah watched Papa and Mama Forbes back out of the room, followed by the Phipps.

For a moment, left alone with the Queen, Sarah felt afraid. She had not known that she was to stay the night. What if she never goes back to Winkfield place? She felt like running after the others, but she dared not.

When Queen Victoria went to the fireplace and pulled at a bell, Sarah looked around the huge room which was even more crowded than Mama Forbes parlour. There was a large mirror over mantel; on the left of the fireplace was a table, with a bust of Prince Albert. The walls were red with gold patterns, draped curtains over two long windows, the carpets and upholstered settee and chairs had flowers all over them and there was a huge candelabra hanging in the centre of the ceiling.

'Take your cloak and bonnet off and sit down,' ordered Queen Victoria. 'The children will be down soon. Now tell me about the christening?'

Sarah licked her lips. Where should she start? She could not speak about the dress, or about her whipping. She could not tell the Queen about her fear that Jesus would drag her down into the world of spirits and death.

'I rejected the devil,' she said at last sitting on the stool next to Queen Victoria. The words floated in the air, searching for a place of truth to rest.

Sarah was relieved when Vicky came rushing into the room. She would not have to say anything more about the christening. Alice and Bertie followed closely; they all bobbed a curtsey before Vicky launched into complaints about Bertie.

'Mama, Bertie, is not at all grateful that Mr Birch has let him off lessons today because it's my birthday,' said Vicky. 'He's been quite horrid. He kicked me and tried to pull my hair because I said that Alice could read better than him.'

'She started it, Mama, Vicky is just being bossy as usual,' said Bertie making a lunge for Vicky but she side stepped him. 'Ask Alice. Didn't she Alice?'

Alice stood between them, eyes wide, biting her lip. Sarah could see that she was not sure whom she should support.

'Now stop it at once or I will box your ears,' said Queen Victoria. 'I will not have you behave like savages in front of Sarah. Vicky, calm down and Bertie, apologise to your sister.'

Only then did the prince and princess see Sarah.

'Good afternoon, Prince Albert' she said.

'Good afternoon Sarah,' he said, the fight with his sister forgotten. 'Call me Bertie, everyone does. It is Papa who is Prince Albert.'

Sarah smiled and turned to the two Princesses. 'Good afternoon Princess Victoria, Princess Alice.'

The two girls returned her greetings, but Vicky kept an eye on Bertie.

'Where is Lady Lyttleton?' asked Queen Victoria

'We left Laddle in the schoolroom,' said Alice.

'Now Alice, it is Lady Lyttleton, not Laddle.'

'She doesn't mind us calling her that Mama,' said Bertie flopping down at his mother's feet. 'We all have other names.'

'Be that is it may, you must always be polite. I think you two need some fresh air. I'm sure Miss Hildyard …'

'You mean Tilla, Mama?' said Bertie with a grin.

'Do not interrupt, please, Bertie. I'm sure Miss Hildyard,' said Queen Victoria with emphasis, 'will take you all for a walk as there are no lessons today. I will see you at tea time.'

Sarah picked up her cloak and remembered the present she had for Vicky. She dug into the pocket and brought out a parcel. 'Happy birthday,' she said.

'Oh, thank you.' Vicky pulled at the ribbon and ripping the paper. Inside the parcel in a simple wooden frame was a water-colour painting of a red hibiscus flower.

'It's beautiful,' she cried and showed it to her mother.

'Did you paint this?' Queen Victoria asked.

'Yes, Ma'am.'

'It is very good. I must show this to Mr Leitch when he comes for my next lesson.'

Sarah smiled, happy that the Queen liked her painting. It had taken her such a long time to decide what to paint once Emily had suggested it as a birthday gift.

'What about a plant or flower?' Mabel had said. 'You are good at those.'

Sarah had liked that idea but which one. She tried to remember the flowers and plant from home, but the memories were shrinking away from her.

'What is the flower you like the most?'

'Hibiscus.'

Sarah frowned. Why had she said hibiscus? She had not thought of it for a long time.

'What does it look like?' asked Emily

Now Sarah remembered the large bush covered with flowers near a hut. A woman picking the flowers. She could not see her face, but she could see her hands, long dark brown fingers, picking, plucking, putting the flowers in hot water, leaving it for a while before pouring it into a calabash. She'd swirl it around to cool it down. '*Gbaw*, drink,' she would say. Was that Madu, or someone else, Sarah could not tell.

'It's big and red and you can make tea with it,' she said, remembering.

'Let's see if we can find a picture of it in Miss Byles botany book,' said Mabel. 'Then you can draw it for her.'

They had found a picture and Sarah had spent the whole of that day painting the five big petals with the long stamen and yellow pollen.

'I know what it is,' said Vicky. 'It's a hibiscus.'

Sarah was surprised that Vicky knew the flower and wanted to say so, but she started to cough instead.

'That is a nasty cough. Have you been given anything for it?' said the Queen.

'Yes Ma'am,' said Sarah between coughs. 'Godfrey's Cordial. Papa says that it is the change of weather and I will stop when it gets warmer.'

'Hmm, we must keep an eye on it. Now, all of you, go find Miss Hildyard. Get some fresh air and no arguments.'

Once they left the Queen's presence, Bertie raced down the Grand Corridor shouting 'hurry, hurry, let's get Tilla to take us to see Dot and her puppies in the kennels.'

'The puppies are ever so sweet,' said Alice walking fast.

Sarah tried to keep up with her. She kept her eyes straight ahead so that she could not notice the busts. 'How many puppies?'

'Five, but there are lots of other dogs here and at Buckingham Palace. I think that there are almost fifty dogs. Mama loves all kinds of dogs, but she does have her favourites.'

Fifty? Sarah could not believe that there could be so many dogs in one place, belonging to one family. All the dogs she had seen before were the ones fighting over food in the slave women's compound in Abomey. Those dogs had been nasty, biting and snarling at everyone. They were not pets.

'The puppies are kept from the other dogs,' said Alice. 'Dot does not mind if we pick them up gently, you'll see.'

They ran up the stairs, Sarah struggling to carry her hat coat and shawl.

'Stop,' said Vicky. 'You know we are not to run up here.'

Alice and Bertie stopped immediately so that Sarah bumped into them and dropped everything. They all waited for a moment before taking another step. Alice saw Sarah's puzzled looked and explained as she helped her with the shawl.

'Mama says she hates noisy children. If we are, she gets very cross, and we are punished.'

'Yes,' said Vicky, 'and Bertie gets punished the most because he is the noisiest and the most annoying.'

'The thing is,' added Alice, 'our rooms are above Mama's sitting room. Sometimes she has visitors, and they can hear us if we run.'

Vicky opened the door next to them, 'This is the nursery for Lenchen, Louise and Arthur. They will stay in the nursery until they are six,' she said. 'They are babies. They will not come to my tea party.'

There were three cots side by side with hinged cane-work sides and upholstered pads to protect the babies from hurting themselves against the cane sides. Sarah stroked the pads. Anna did not have one in her cot. Maybe if she did, she would stop tearing and eating the new green wallpaper when she was alone. It made Nanny very cross.

Next door, in the schoolroom, Sarah saw that each child had their own individual high-backed chair topped with a shield and inlaid with its royal owner's initial. There was still plenty of room for toys, rocking horses, dolls house and clockwork mechanical toys.

'Tilla, I mean Miss Hildyard, teaches us in here and our rooms are through that door,' said Alice, pointing across the room. 'I share with Vicky, Bertie shares with Affie. Although now that Mama has had Buckingham Palace renovated Bertie has his own suite of rooms with his tutor nearby when we are there.'

Betty the nursemaid came in with the princesses' coats. Alice reached out and stroked Sarah's grey dress.

'You have on another pretty dress,' she said.

Sarah wondered what they would say if they knew about why her dress was grey.

'Vicky and I share some of our dresses. Do you have to share yours?'

Sarah gave a little smile remembering Mabel's anger when one of her dresses had been given to Sarah to wear on her arrival at Winkfield Place. 'No, not now. Mabel does not like sharing. Emily would but her dresses are too small for me. She is only seven.'

'Are Mabel and Emily your sisters?'

Sarah swallowed, and the cough came back. Was it hers or was it Salimatu's cough? Sarah could not tell; all she knew was that it had come back. She did not know what to say. She had promised not to speak of Fatmata again, to forget; but, how could she?

'Ssh, Alice,' said Vicky. 'Remember her story?'

'Mabel, Emily and Anna are not my sisters, they are Mama and Papa Forbes' children. They look after me. My sister is Fatmata. I don't know where she is. I look for her everywhere, but she is never there.'

Alice's lips trembled. She grabbed hold of Sarah's sore hand. 'I'm so sorry Sarah, I should not have asked. One day you'll find her, I'm sure. Maybe Mama could help. We'll ask her, won't we Vicky.'

*Friday, 22ⁿᵈ November 1850. Winkfield Place*

*Went to Princess Victoria's (Vicky, her family name) birthday party yesterday. The royal children have 'family' names too. Albert is Bertie, Alfred is Affie, Helen is Lenchen. Alice is sometimes called Fatima. It sounds a like Fatmata. I have a family name too, 'Sally' not Sali, not Salimatu.*

*Maria, Harriet and Charles Phipps and Augusta, Arthur, Leopold and Alfred Seymour were at the party too. We had bread and butter, bread and jam, little cakes and jelly. I do not like jelly it wobbles in my mouth. I drank tea today for the first time. There was also raspberry lemonaid. We played games, look-about, beggar my naybor and blind-man's bluff. A band played in the garden. They were very loud. We saw the servants dancing in their butiful hall. Alice / Fatima missed everything becos she was unwell. Poor Fatima. I am to go play at the castle again. Next time I hope I can take Mabel and Emily. They will like it there. I like it there.*

# CHAPTER 19

*Even in laughter the heart is sorrowful*
Proverbs 14:13

## December 1850

2
0ᵗʰ *December 1850, Winkfield Place*

*Anna has been ill. Edith found her covered in Nanny's cordial, the blue bottle broken. Anna could not wake up and the Doctor came. He says Anna is sick from eating the green wallpaper. It has arsenic. I think that is poison. All the wallpaper is gone from the nursery now. Papa and Mama were very worried. Mabel says it is because two baby brothers died before Anna. I wonder if my two brothers are dead too. Why do people die? If I don't stop coughing will I die? I have put a piece of the broken blue bottle in the gri-gri I made for Emily. Inside it is also some of my hair tied in one her ribbons. She likes my hair. I do not. She must not show what is inside of her gri-gri to anyone.*

❈❈❈

When Edith came running into the schoolroom, banging into the table and knocking over several books to the floor, they all jumped.

'Madam says to say sorry to interrupt your lesson, but could you please send the girls down to the drawing room?'

'Now?' asked Miss Byles.

'Yes Miss. All three. Now. There are some visitors.'

Sarah hurried after Edith with Mabel and Emily clattering behind. She was relieved that Mama had sent for all of them. She was tired of Mama's visitors. It was not as if they spoke to her. They only wanted to stare or sometimes touch her as if to prove she was real. And she was, she was no different to Mabel or Emily, except for her skin. Why did that matter so much?

Outside the drawing room Edith checked that they were indeed presentable. Mabel pushed her away, opened the door and stopped. Over her shoulder Sarah saw the visitors. She gave a little squeal for there, right in front of her, were Princesses Victoria and Alice. It was almost a month since the tea party at Windsor Castle and not a word since the note from Vicky.

*Dear Sarah,*

*Thank you very much for my painting. It was very kind of you to go to so much effort. I will always treasure it. We all hope that you will come over to play soon.*

*Princess Victoria (Vicky)*

Alice smiled broadly. 'We wanted to surprise you.'

'I am so happy to see you,' said Sarah. 'Mabel, Emily and I talk about you all the time.' She looked round at Mabel and Emily still standing by the door, their mouths wide open.

'Lady Lyttleton, these are my girls, Mabel, Emily and Sarah,' said Mama Forbes to the lady sitting on the sofa by the fireplace.

Sarah eyes widened. Was she one of Mama Forbes' girls then?

'Good morning, Lady Lyttelton,' the three of them chorused.

'We did not know you were coming to see us,' Sarah added in a soft voice.

'Laddle did send a note,' said Vicky.

'But we begged Mrs Forbes to keep it a secret,' added Alice clapping her hands. 'We wanted to surprise you.'

'You did,' said Sarah grinning widely. She pulled Mabel and Emily forward. 'Princess Victoria, Princess Alice, I would like to present my...' She stopped and looked at the other two girls. She did not know what to call them, how to present them now. So instead, she simply said, 'I want you to meet Mabel and Lily, I mean Emily.'

'We've heard a lot about you,' said Vicky, 'and we wanted to meet you too.'

Sarah looked at all of them and something inside felt good. She let out a deep breath. 'Mama Forbes,' she said, 'may we take the princesses up to the schoolroom?'

'There's no time. Maybe another day.'

'Did Her Majesty send you?' asked Emily.

'You have not come to take Sarah away, have you? She lives with us. She likes it here,' said Mabel, frowning at the princesses.

'Mabel!' said Mama Forbes. 'They have come to take you all for a drive and then to the castle.'

'Oh,' cried Emily, 'really? Thank you, thank you,' she bounced up and down so hard Mabel had to grab her before she fell off the chair.

They all laughed at her excitement.

'Mama and Papa went to London yesterday to look at the building for the Great Exhibition in Hyde Park,' said Vicky, 'but they'll be back later today.'

'Papa says that when the building is finished there will not be anything as grand in the whole world,' said Alice, as the hats and coats Edith had returned with were put on.

When they left, there was a crowd waiting outside the gate. Some waved, some trotted alongside the carriage. A woman called out, 'there they are the black and white princesses.'

'How did they know you were here,' asked Emily.

'We're always followed,' said Vicky.

Not everyone was happy to see them though. A man, his face twisted and ugly, yelled out something and shook his fist as they went past. All Sarah could make out was the word German. Mabel and Emily shrank back into the leather seats. Vicky sat up straight and looked ahead. Alice hung her head.

'Look up, Alice,' said Vicky, 'remember what Papa said. We must never show fear.'

'Well, I am a little afraid when they get so close and stare.'

'Mama says people will always stare. That is what happens when you're a princess. You are different, or they think you are. Just ignore them,' said Vicky.

'I can't. You have not had a mad Irishman fire a gun at you.'

Emily gave a little squeal and moved closer to Sarah.

'Someone fired at you?' said Sarah searching Alice's face to see if she was joking.

'He fired at Mama. Luckily the gun had only blanks in it. Affie, Lenchen and I were in the carriage with Mama.'

'Why would anyone want to hurt the Queen?' asked Mabel, frowning.

'I don't know why, but some people do.' Vicky said. 'It wasn't the first time either.'

'That was the fourth time,' said Alice with a catch in her voice. 'Mama is sometimes very cross with us but not with them, so I don't know why someone would want to hurt her.'

'The fifth time was a few months ago,' said Vicky. 'Mama had no escort except for Lady Fanny, her lady in waiting. That time Bertie was also in the carriage with Mama, Affie, and Alice. Papa was riding in the park,'

'The man hit Mama on the head with his stick. He crushed her bonnet. Lady Fanny burst into tears and kept saying "they've got the man",' said Alice, her lips trembling. 'Mama was very brave. She staggered to her feet in the carriage and calmed the people around telling them that she was not hurt. But she was, for her head was bleeding. Lady Fanny said that it was only the deep brim of Mama's bonnet that stopped her being more seriously hurt. That is the second time I have seen Mama attacked.'

'Maybe Mama should not travel with you in her carriage, Alice' said Vicky trying to make the others smile.

'It's not my fault,' said Alice unable to keep the tears at bay anymore.

'Girls, enough' said Lady Lyttleton. 'Those things happened in London and you were in the open carriage. No one can get to you here.'

'But what happened to the men?' asked Sarah. 'Were their heads cut off and stuck on a pole for all to see?'

'Oh, dear me, no. We don't do that sort of thing here. We are not savages. They were taken to court, found guilty and transported to Australia, a long way away, as punishment.'

Sarah's eyes widened. 'Were they too sold as slaves?'

'No, no, no. They were white, not black. They were sent away for seven years. They can come back after that period. They very rarely do though, criminals.'

The chatter of the others faded into the background as Sarah thought about what she had just been told. Someone who had tried to kill the Queen could be sent away for seven years and then come back to his town, his people. Why then could someone be captured in her village, sold many times over never to return home, never able to find her sister, never be free again, because they were black? Why? There was no one to ask.

At the castle, the carriage had hardly stopped before Bertie and Affie came running down the stone stairs to pull open the carriage door.

'Where have you been?' Bertie cried. 'We've been waiting for you all day.'

'Stop exaggerating, we've only been gone for two hours,' said Vicky.

'We went to get Sarah,' added Alice. 'Here she is, with Mabel and Emily Forbes.'

'Hello Sarah. Come on everyone we want to start. Mama and Papa are back, but Papa says that we must wait for you.' He turned and raced up the stairs.

Start what? Sarah wondered. Was this another surprise? She would not ask; she liked the princesses' surprises. She rushed after the princesses. At the top of the steps, she realised that Mabel and Emily, still standing by the carriage had not moved.

Sarah smiled at the look on their faces, their mouths were wide open, eyes darting everywhere trying to take in everything at once, the wide steps leading up to the huge open door, the garden with its green grass, tall trees with gently swaying branches, the castle with its may windows like sightless eyes watching.

'I was afraid too, the first time I came with Papa, but it's fine.'

'There is just so much, and everything is so large,' said Mabel.

'Will we see the Queen?' whispered Emily.

'I don't know, but if we do,' said Sarah, giving Mabel a nudge, 'don't forget to curtsey, or your head will be cut off.'

They laughed remembering what Mabel had told Sarah when she had been to meet the Queen. Was that only six weeks ago? Sarah thought.

'All of you, close your eyes,' ordered Alice, 'We will lead you into the dining room.'

Mabel, Emily and Sarah did as they were told, held hands and allowed themselves to be guided into the room.

'Open your eyes now.'

Sarah and the other two did and gasped. Like all the other rooms it was large with high ceilings except that this was the round Octagon Dining Room. Large as it was though, the room seemed full to overflowing. There were big boxes and small boxes, all full of things that shone and glittered. Two very tall ladders were in the centre of the room and from the ceiling grew a tree. Sarah spun around and saw that there were many other trees in the room, big and small on tables. Trees inside a house? She had never seen the like before. She stood transfixed. There were so many people hurrying here, there and everywhere, aides, butlers, courtiers, all with jackets off, sleeves rolled up and busy.

Vicky and Alice hugged each other with glee and spun each other around. 'it worked, it worked,' cried Alice, 'the surprise worked, Papa.'

Only then did she see that both the Queen and Prince Albert were in the room.

'There you are, ladies,' said Prince Albert. 'You've come to help us decorate our trees, have you? *Gut, gut.*'

His voice still sounded strange to Sarah, but she understood what he said. Quickly she did a curtsey first to Queen Victoria and then to Prince Albert. The other two followed her lead.

'*Guten morgen*, Your Majesty, *guten morgen* Prince Albert,' said Sarah.

'*Sprechen sie Deutsch?*' he said.

Queen Victoria laughed and put her arm around Sarah's shoulder. 'She's learning.'

'*Ah, wir sprechen uns Spater.*' He looked over their shoulder and said 'Excuse me, my dear, I must get them to change that. It is all wrong.'

They watched him hurry off to the other side of the room.

'Come on,' said Bertie, 'Let's start decorating our Christmas trees. Mine's going to be the best.'

'No, it's not,' said Vickie, chasing after him.

'Sit with me for a moment,' Queen Victoria said to Sarah, before she too could run off with the others. 'Those two, always they argue and fight. They don't know how lucky they are. How I longed for a brother or sister when I was their age.'

Sarah watched the other children as they pulled long coloured paper chains and what seemed like paper flowers, out of big boxes. She wished she could join them, but the Queen was speaking to her and she had to stay.

'You've never seen so many Christmas trees before, have you?'

'No Ma'am. I have never seen trees growing down from the ceiling before. Do they only grow at Christmas?

'No,' said the Queen with a little laugh, 'they are cut down from the forest and brought indoors to be decorated at Christmas time. I thought that you might like to do that with our children.'

'I would. Thank you very much Ma'am.' Sarah did not know what made her do it, but she leant across and kissed Queen Victoria's cheek. The Queen blinked and touched the spot. Sarah sat back and lowered her eyes. Had she done wrong? Would Her Majesty have her punished? Then she remembered the man that had hit the Queen and wondered whether that spot was where the cane had hit her.

Queen Victoria smiled. 'You sweet thing,' she said, patting Sarah's cheek. Her fingers touched the three tribal marks on Sarah's face. She traced the scars and said, 'did it hurt.'

'I don't remember, Ma'am. I was a baby.'

'Yes, you must have been. Do you remember anything of your village, your parents?'

Sarah shook her head, then changed her mind and nodded.

For some reason she felt that she could be honest with the Queen.

'Sometimes I do, but it is never very clear. In the night I dream, bad dreams and they scare me. '

'You poor thing. I used to have bad dreams too when I was little.'

'I used to remember my sister Fatmata, but now I have lost her face. I wish I could find her.' Sarah stopped talking because she was afraid that she would start crying and she must not.

'So much, so young,' said Queen Victoria, almost to herself. She stood up. 'Come let's go join the others and decorate the trees.'

Besides the Christmas tree hanging from the middle of the ceiling there was a very large tree, almost as tall as the room, at one end of the room. There were ladders leaning against the trees as courtiers got ready to attach candles all the way to the very top. Sarah wondered how long it would take to light all those candles every day.

Sarah counted seven tables covered with white clothes at the other end room. On each table was a Christmas tree, the branches reaching out as if each wanting to stay in touch with the other. The table trees were each fastened to a flat board covered with moss for grass so that they could have an outdoor scene with a mirror to look like a pond. Wooden animals, sheep, horses and dogs taken from a box brought down from the nursery were placed around the tree. Vicky and Bertie were at their tables already decorating their trees from a jumble of paperchains at their feet.

'Help me decorate mine,' called Alice. 'We all do our own tree and on Christmas eve, in three days' time, when we are all asleep Mama and Papa come and put our presents on our gift table. If any is too big for the table, they will put it under the big tree over there. Is that what you do?'

Sarah frowned and suddenly felt outside of it all. 'I don't know. I've never celebrated Christmas before. Ask Mabel. She'll know.'

'It doesn't matter. Let's do it now. I'll show you. Mabel is helping Vicky and Emily is doing it with Helena. Mama says she will decorate Louise and Arthur's and when the Phipps' arrive, we will all do the big tree.'

Soon they had put up string garlands of popcorn and cranberries, made chains of paper flowers and long tinted paper loops to be fastened to the top of the tree and allowed to drop down in rows. The trees were decorated with coloured garlands wrapped tightly around the trees as though they were giant parcels There were candied fruits, gingerbread men, soft marzipan cookies, and sweets wrapped in paper to add to the trees. Men up the ladders decorated the bigger trees with the many candles before the little toys, pinecones, paper fans, dried fruits, nuts, berries were hung on the trees.

Bertie and Affie had a fight when they both wanted the same wooden man for their table. Bertie was scolded by his mother when he hit Affie who sobbed while Bertie sulked. Louise ran around fell over and screamed loudly.

'Take her away please, nurse,' said Queen Victoria, walking away. 'Such a noisy child.'

Soon the trees were bright and colourful. But the best thing of all was the angel that was put at top the tall trees. It had wings of glass, a crinkled golden skirt, and a smiling wax face white with blue eyes and red cheeks. Sarah wondered if all angels looked like that, all pink and shiny. Were there angels liked looked like her?

Lenchen came over, stood in front of Sarah, took her thumb out of her mouth and said, 'why are you brown?'

Alice said, 'You do not ask questions like that.'

'I don't know,' said Sarah. 'God made me this way I suppose.'

'Now, Lenchen,' said Queen Victoria, taking her by the hand, 'God makes us all different, some have blue eyes like baby Arthur, while others like you have brown eyes. Same way, some people are white and other are black.'

'She's not black, Mama. She's brown,' said Lenchen. She took Sarah's hand and held it out. 'See,'

'Enough now,' said Queen Victoria, leading Lenchen away. Sarah heard her say. 'All Negroes are black.'

Sarah was no longer thinking about the Christmas trees as they left the Octagon room. Why was she black? Was she and Fatmata and all the others captured and sold only because they were black? Could she change and become white? A passing courtier bowed to her and walked on. Sarah stopped. If she turned white, she would no longer be the 'Black Princess', different, special. No, she did not want to be white, to look like everyone else, she decided. She liked being special, she liked being black. And she wanted to go home

✾✾✾✾

*26th December 1850, Winkfield Place*

*Yesterday I had my first English Christmas. We too had a big tree to decorate. On Christmas eve we all put the gifts we made under the tree. I had many gifts, including a cut-out picture for a scrapbook from Mama Forbes and a beautiful woollen shawl in red and green from Queen Victoria. Mama says it will keep me warm and stop me coughing. I will paint a picture for Her Majesty to say thank you. Everyone liked the gifts I made them. We ate in the dining room with Mama and Papa. There was a lot to eat. The roast turkey was very big. When I said it was bigger than any chicken at home, Mama said that this was my home now. I like Christmas pudding. I found the silver coin and it is the first time I have any money. Mama says that is good luck. Maybe I will spend it with Fatmata when we are together again.*

# CHAPTER 20

*Ẹyẹ ò sọ fún ẹyẹ pé òkò m̀bọ̀*
*A bird does not tell a bird that a stone is on its way*

# 1846

We are dragged away to the edge of Kwa-le forest where the shadowy shapes of others wait in the dark.

'Did you get them?' calls the man sitting by a glowing fire.

I know that voice. It is the voice of the owner of the knife with the shiny handle, Santigie, the cousin of Jamilla, my father's killer. My insides squeeze tight.

'Yes. This one is plenty trouble,' Bureh says, pushing me to the ground.

I face Santigie as he stands up, light from the fire falling on his smiling face. He turns to the woman behind him and says, 'So we've got them all.'

Salimatu struggles out of Momoh's arms and runs to me.

'Jaja, Jaja, Jaja,' she cries. And I know that she saw this man kill our father.

The woman moves into the light and my insides tumble over. It is Jamilla, my father's second wife.

I know that she does not like us but still I plead with her. 'Jamilla, help us,' I say. 'Tell him who we are. Tell him that Salimatu and I are your daughters, daughters of your husband.'

'You stupid child,' she sneers. 'He knows. That's why he took you.'

'Dauda took what was mine when he married Jamilla, now I have taken what is his,' says Santige pulling her to him. 'Soon your brother will join you,'

'Amadu?' I cry. 'You have Amadu too? Ayee. Ayee.'

'Before too many moons you'll all be sold as *akisha*. Just like the other one. He was so easy to capture,' a cruel laugh bursts from Santigie, 'no fight in that boy. He would never have made chief.'

His low laugh rumbles inside my aching head. Lansana. Now, I know everything. It was Santigie who took my brother away. He must have planned this raid for many, many moons and all along Jamilla has helped him.

'Tie them with the other women,' he says to Bureh, stretching. 'I want a good price for this load.'

Jamilla smiles. I have never seen her smile like that before. A deep anger rises scattering any fear away and without thinking I break from Bureh's hold and rush at Santigie.

'You killed my father,' I yell, grabbing his coat and kicking.

He pushes me away, pulls out a short black iron-stick from inside his coat but before he could do anything, I feel a stinging pain race down my back and wrap around my waist. It makes me stagger like one who has drunk a whole gourd of palm wine. I scream and grab hold of the thing around my waist. It is a long-plaited leather whip, the kind I saw the Moors use on their horses. This time it is Jamilla using it. She pulls at the whip and I scream again as it rips at my hand, my waist, my back, stinging and throbbing as though a whole hive of bees has landed on my back. I sink to the ground twitching and crying. Salimatu runs to me. The next lash gets both of us and Salimatu's screams join mine.

'Give me,' says Santigie. He takes the whip from Jamilla, swings it above his head and there is a cracking sound that makes me curl up and wait for new pain to land on me. It does not. Instead, the whip hits the ground in front of me scattering dirt, leaves and twigs into my face. I look up, tears streaming down my face.

'You see that tree over there?' he says, 'watch it.' He raises his arm again and pointed his iron-stick at the tree. There is a loud bang, a flash of fire, the bushes shake, and leaves fall, the women and girls tied up under the tree scream, a big hole appears on the tree.

Santigie grabs my arm and pulls me up to face him. I sway with the pain.

'If any of you try to attack me or run away,' he says, including all who are tied to the trees, 'I'll shoot you with my gun and leave your body for the vultures. Hear me.'

Bureh pushes us towards the other women. I sink down and Salimatu creeps onto my lap. I look at her thigh where the whip caught her. It is bleeding. I attempt to clean it with my spit and bits of grass I have managed to scrape up. With the blood cleared, I see three cuts that look like our traditional monkey tattoo. Without knowing it my father's treacherous wife has marked his youngest daughter as a Talaremban warrior. With a deep sigh, I thank the ancestors.

The light from the new day had barely started to roll over the dark sky when Bureh approached us.

'Come,' he says to the woman next to me, 'we go get water.'

She gets up fast and stands with her eyes fixed on the ground. I cannot see her face, but I know she is not from Talaremba. Bureh shoves Salimatu off my lap, and tugs at my rope.

'You come too,' he says to me. I bite my lip to stop a cry of pain. The way he smiles remind me of when he and Momoh caught us the day before. He had thrown me to the ground and tried to rip of my *lappa*. I am afraid of what he could do to me. He ties the woman and I together with a long rope, gives us a gourd each, picks up a whip and leads us away. I can hear Salimatu crying 'Fatmata, Fatu,' but I do not turn around. I do not want her to see the fear in my eyes.

'Move, quick, quick. We must leave this place as soon as we have water. We have far to go before night falls on us.'

'Where are we going?' I ask, hoping that if he is talking, he would not try to force himself on me again. 'Is it far?'

He laughs. 'Far? Of course, it is far. We'll be walking for more than a moon cycle to get to the waterside where the big, big canoes wait.' He moves ahead of us.

'Waterside? Ayee. *Odudua*, save us.'

Every step hurt, I can feel the wounds cut across my back and around my side where the whip landed. I need herbs and ointment. I search the bushes for the right healing plants as we walk, thanking the gods that Maluuma taught me about their medicinal values and how to use them.

I started helping Maluuma on my fifth harvest season. Although almost blind, her eyes covered by a thin layer, the colour of watery goat's milk, Maluuma, showed me what to look for, the shape and size of the leaves and bushes.

'Fatmata,' she would say, chopping and boiling, stirring and tasting, before storing the balms in little clay pots, 'even if you don't know the names, remember the smell, shape, taste and colour, they will tell you all you need to know. Watch the birds, watch the animals, if they eat it, you can use it.'

Maluuma taught me that Osain ruled over all wild herbs but that lesser gods influenced their own particular herbs.

'Remember, Yemoja is in charge of Buchu, the one that smells like crushed ants but is good for fever and for stopping bleeding. The *Oshun* is the force, the power within a woman. She governs Wild Yam Root, Plantain, Ursi, all healing for women problems.

Obatala controls the Kola-nut and Fo-ti. Look how this plant has leaves like little hairy hearts, proud, slender stalks with wings like birds of heaven. They are good for wounds, broken bones, or calming the pains of old people.'

I listened, I learned, I remember.

Maluuma, however, showed me no plants for a heart that was broken.

✿✿✿

We are moving down the small slope towards the stream when I see one of the plants I have been looking for and I stop. The woman walking behind me slips in the mud and falls dragging me down with her. Still holding on to our gourds we roll into the stream. It is only ankle deep; I will not drown in that, so I close my eyes and lie there as the water cools my sore back.

'Hurry and fill them up,' shouts Bureh, pulling at the rope before tying it to a tree. 'Santigie is waiting.'

I open my eyes remembering I am in the forest tied to a woman I do not know, on the way to be sold as a slave, by the wife of my father. Ayee, the gods have indeed turned their faces away from me.

The woman stands up and reaches out. I look at her for the first time. She is taller than me and has maybe ten more harvest seasons. Her eyes are big and round, her mouth small but full. Her *lappa* is tied around her waist and from the way her breasts hang I know that she has given her milk to at least two young ones. I take her hand and she pulls me up. We nod without speaking and bend down to fill the gourds.

I do not fill mine. Instead, I dig into the earth and yank out some of the plants at the water's edge. I know this plant, with its little white flowers that hang their heads as if bowing to the water that keeps them alive. I picked them many times with Maluuma.

'Boil the roots, mash it up, lay it over the wound, and wrap it with leaves or cloth,' she had taught me. 'Or grind the leaves, mix it with a little water then spread it so it sticks to the wound. It will ease the pain, take the swelling down and bring the wound together.'

Although I cannot boil the roots, still I can use the leaves. I pluck them, quick but careful, for although the top of the leaves is smooth, the undersides are prickly. I wrap as many of the plants as I can into the folds of my *lappa* and re-tie it. We feel a tug on the rope and see Bureh checking that the rope is tight around the tree before he moves away. Hearing Bureh relieving himself I know I have time. I rush to pick more leaves, then between two stones, I crush the leaves, and scooping water from the stream I make some paste. I lift my *lappa* and spread the paste on my monkey tattoo which hasn't fully healed and the cuts on my sides. The woman watches me, and as I try to rub the mixture on the stinging cuts on my back she waves her hands gesturing for me to turn around. She squats down behind me, the rope, thick and heavy, coiled between us, raises my top and covers my back with the paste. The instant calming of the throbbing wounds feels good, and we remain in that position, her hands a salve on my aching back until our captor returns. The woman treats me as her child and my eyes burn with unshed tears as I wrap the rest of the paste in some leaves. I can take some back to put on Salimatu's cuts later.

By the time Bureh returns the big gourds are full and heavy. He lifts them on to our heads and we begin our walk back. My pain has eased a little and not just from the paste. We make good time and much sooner than it seems it took us when we left, we are back with the group. Salimatu sees me immediately and jumps up.

'Fatu,' she cries holding tight.

Her little body is hot to the touch and I know she is bearing much pain. I sit down, lay her on to my lap and retrieving the remaining paste from my lappa, I rub the paste on her skin.

'Shhh, take the pain,' I whisper when she cries. 'These marks are your tattoo. They show you're a little warrior.'

Momo brings us cold boiled cassava. I take a bite, it has no taste in my mouth, but I chew and swallow. I do not know when next we will eat. I take another bite and almost choke. I spit it out and stand up in shock, for there in front of me is Taimu and Sisi Tenneh. I thought they had got away. Taimu will not look at me.

'Sisi Tenneh,' I say, 'I'm sorry to see you here.'

She glares at me and turns away.

'Sisi Tenneh?'

'I warned you. If you had come when I called, we would not be here now. Ramatu was right; your mother has not trained you well.'

The mention of my mother brings tears to my eyes. I sink to the ground and hold Salimatu to me.

'And there is Khadijatu, tied to Delu. Two more from Talaremba. How many more?' I look past them to see three other women I do not know. Where are the men? I saw them take many men for the village so where were they now?

Khadijatu tries to walk over to me but the rope joining her to Delu is not long enough.

'Here,' said Momo, holding out her piece of cassava. Khadijatu snatches it, as if afraid that he might give her share to someone else.

'Fatmata, you too? We thought that you'd got away,' she says, stuffing a whole piece in her mouth. 'I didn't think that they'd catch a warrior. Isn't that what you told us you were?'

Khadijatu always has bad things to say to me. I look at her, with her mouth full of half chewed cassava and think, she'll lose some of that fat by the time we have walked for two moon cycles, then I will show her who is a warrior when I get Salimatu and myself away from Santigie and she is the one sold as a slave.

As more people are fed, an uneasy calm settles over us. Salimatu sleeps fitfully on my lap. The blistering heat of the day is slowly subsiding, and the long night ahead fills me with trepidation. It was clear preparations were being made as the men and women who captured us moved about the camp with renewed but silent urgency. Then as the sky turned darker, I heard Santigie says just before he and Jamilla took leave, 'Get them to Sahwama town by the set of sun.'

Bureh and Momo stuff their large animal skin pouches with what food is left and fill the water bags. Then we are all re-tied together in twos around the waist, and then tied to the person in front by our ankles. In my small group two girls I did not know were in front of Taimu and Tenneh, behind them were Khadijatu and Delu. The woman and I are last. Momo walked in front of all with a cutlass to cut a path but I see that he also had a gun. Bureh is behind us, with his whip.

I must find a way to mark this path, I say to myself holding Salimatu's hand, as we walk on and on through a forest that gets darker as the trees get closer together. Whenever Bureh is not looking I bend twigs to mark my way. The woman, tied to me says nothing, she has been crying nonstop, but her whole body is in unison with me, making my attempts to forge an escape route back to our home feel a little less futile that it was. Later I pick up a long stick, that functions as a walking staff and use it to draw our monkey tattoo in the earth. With each line I prayed that it would sink down into the centre of Mother Earth. Even if the marks are scattered and sent up into the air by the wind or other shuffling feet, the earth will take pity. She will show our ancestors the way our feet have travelled so that we would not be apart from them to the end of time.

At last, spent and weary, the woman I am tied to stops crying. I glance sideways at her and nod.

'Minata,' she says, pointing to herself. Before I could say anything, she points to me, 'You Fatmata?'

'Yes,' I answer. I guess she has heard Tenneh and Khadijatu say my name. I touch my sister's head and said, 'Salimatu.'

'Salimatu,' she repeats and nods.

'The mother of my husband was from Talaremba.' Minata says. 'She called your Maluuma to come catch my third child, Yema. We had lost two before.'

'Maluuma helped you with your third child? When?'

'Five harvest seasons past. We came to Talaremba three moons later, when we knew that Yema had come to stay. We brought cowrie shells for Maluuma. I saw you, helping her.'

'I don't remember.'

'Salimatu, makes me think of Yema and Afua,'

'You have another?' I ask pleased that I had been right when I first looked at her.

'Yes, Afua. She came after Yema. She has seen four harvest seasons. The raiders caught me because I could not leave her. She had the shakes. They hit her with a stick and sent her to the ancestors, saying they had no use for little children. Too much trouble. Then they bound me and took me. I don't know what happened to Yema.' She starts to cry again.

Now I am afraid for Salmatu and when she whimpers, I pick her up. She must not be trouble. I cannot carry her on my back which is full of pain, even with the paste spread over the cuts. I put her on my hip and walk on. Minata seeing that I am in pain takes Salimatu from me.

'How many seasons in Salimatu?' she asks.

'Four.'

'Like Afua.' She ties Salimatu to her back and her step is firm.

We walk on and on, through short grass and long grass, through brambles and bushes that cover us with scratches. Mosquitoes bite us everywhere, arms, legs, face, even our heads. Dragging and shuffling our bleeding feet, we still must be careful, keeping a lookout for snakes and scorpions. The ropes rub our bound ankles raw so that we always have flies buzzing around us. When we stop in the darkness of the night, I make more paste to put on our cuts and give some to Minata. Then I shut my eyes, not to sleep but to see what is behind them.

# CHAPTER 21

*Even a child is known by his doing, whether his work is pure and whether it is right*
Proverbs 20:11

## January 1851

2nd *January 1851, At home.*
> *My first writing in 1851. A new year. Twelve new moons to come. In 1850 I had six moons in Abomey as a slave and six as a princess in England. I wonder what will happen to me in the next twelve months.*

> *We go to London tomorrow. I will look for Fatmata. Papa says he will take us to see the strange animals in a zoo. We are also going to have a daguerreotype (Miss Byles spelt it for me) done before he returns to sea. He wants to take our portrait with him. But it is a copy of us. How many Sarah Forbes Bonetta are there? What about Salimatu? Does he take her too? When he returns, we will be different? I do not know.*

☆☆☆☆

It was wet, foggy and cold when they arrived in London. Lady Melton's carriage was waiting for them at the station however, they had so much luggage Papa Forbes had to hire a cab.

'5 Wimpole Street,' he said to the cab driver before climbing into the carriage.

Sarah's eyes could not take everything in. There was so much to see; elegantly dressed women riding by in their carriages, and those struggling along, wrapped in shawls to keep out the cold damp air. Many of the men walking by in their tall black hats had beards like Papa. The newspaper boys waved damp copies, shouting news she could not hear. Everywhere she looked people hurried along but those who caught sight of her in the carriage suddenly stopped to stare. She saw some black faces but none of them was Fatmata.

As soon as the carriage stopped outside Lady Melton's, the front door opened, and they hurried up the steps before they got wet. Sarah stopped short when saw the man in the hall. They stared at each other. Who was he? He licked his lips and opened his mouth as though he was about to say something and then he shut it again.

'Mama, is he Sarah's Papa?' asked Anna, in a whisper that echoed in the hall.

Sarah's heart began to pound. Her chest felt so tight she found it hard to breathe. Was this tall, very black man, with teeth so white and tongue so red, hair so grey, was he her Jaja? She could not tell; she could no longer remember anyone's face. Was that why she had been brought to London? Did she have to leave Papa and the others now? She stepped closer to Papa Forbes.

Everyone was speaking at once and all she could hear were words, jumbled up. No, papa, same colour, brown, black, servant, princess, me, him. No.

A sharp voice broke through it all. 'Ah, Mary, Frederick, you've arrived. Good. Do come into the drawing room and I'll ring for tea. Fanny can take the children up to the nursery. She'll look after them until Nanny Grace arrives tomorrow.'

'Hello Josephine,' said Mama Forbes giving her sister a kiss. 'Is Charles joining us?'

'No. He's still at the Houses of Parliament. Some bill or another. I never listen when he talks about politics. He will be here for dinner though.'

'I see there are changes since Sarah and I were here a couple of months ago,' said Mama Forbes as she took off her cloak and waited for the butler to take it from her.

'Oh, do you mean Daniel?' Josephine said, waving at the man to take the cloak. 'Yes, I got him from Lady Carlyle. She wanted a younger man. I remembered our conversation about helping to get these people off the streets, so I took him on. He's well trained, and usually does his job well. Not today I see, standing there like an ebony statue. Daniel, coats and cloaks, now? See Frederick, I'm doing my bit too. We all are nowadays, following Her Majesty's example although we can't all have a princess to parade.'

✿✿✿✿

The next morning, they set off for the daguerreotypist. Unlike the day before Sarah did not watch the people as they rode by. Her mind was occupied with the thought of having her face and maybe even her soul captured in a box.

The carriage came to an abrupt stop and they all fell against each other. Emily and Anna squealed, Freddie and Mabel laughed. Papa did not find it amusing as two omnibus squeezed past, each driver trying to outdo the other, shouting out their routes in loud, hoarse voices.

'These omnibus drivers! Chasing each other to get to the passengers first. And the cab drivers are no better,' said Papa Forbes, glaring at a hansom cab driver trying to push past their waiting carriage. 'One day they will cause a terrible accident. The men sitting at the top of the omnibus would have no chance if they fell off.'

'Oh no, oh dear,' cried Mama Forbes, staring out of the carriage window.

'What is it Mama?' asked Mabel trying to lean across.

'That's the workhouse by St Martin-in-the-Fields. Look at those people pushing and fighting outside, all hoping that maybe today they would be taken in, given food and shelter.'

The workhouse? Was this it? Was Papa going to leave her there? Sarah shrank back. The noise inside her head was so loud if she opened her mouth, she would deafen everyone with the sound. She glanced at Papa, but he was still watching the traffic. Sarah sat still, hardly daring to breathe, waiting, waiting, waiting.

'Oh, Frederick, look at that woman, trying to hand over her baby,' said Mama Forbes her voice a little trembly. 'If they take it, she'll never see that child again. Why do they have to separate husband from wife, mothers from children, even brothers from sisters, never to be seen again.'

Mama Forbes has tears in her eyes, I frown and think, but what about us, captured as slaves, separated from brothers and sisters, mothers and fathers, don't we matter? I bite my lip.

'Why is she giving it up?' asked Emily. 'I wouldn't give my baby up, ever.'

'Dear child.' Mama patted Emily's cheek. 'She has no choice. She can no longer look after herself or her child.'

'London is too crowded,' said Papa. 'Even these workhouses cannot cope with the number of people needing help. They should clear out the disease-ridden slums, move the people to new housing, clean the streets and bad drains to get rid of the smell.'

'Everywhere does smell in London,' said Freddie.

'May I have a sniff of your nosegay, Mama, before I pass out with the smell?' said Mabel, pretending to swoon. 'I love the smell of the lavender in it.'

Mama smiled and handed it to Mabel who buried her nose into the little bunch of flowers and sneezed.

'Me too?' said Anna, reaching over to get it from Mabel and almost sliding off Mama's lap as the coach moved forward.

'And me,' said Emily. 'I want to have a sniff too.'

Mama turned to Sarah. 'What about you? Do you want to smell the lavender?'

Sarah shook her head. She could not speak. So that was a work-house? The place she would be sent if she they got tired of her. She was never going to be naughty again.

✿✿✿

'Here we are,' said Papa Forbes reading the sign by the door. 'John Jabez Edwin Mayall, Daguerreotypist, 433 West Strand, London.'

Before he could pull on the doorbell, Mama Forbes touched his arm and stopped him.

'Are you sure about this Frederick? Mrs Cameron said that there was such a bang when she had hers done, she was prostrate for two days after, from the fright.'

'Mama, we can't turn back now,' said Freddie. 'I want to see the camera. I want to see how it's done.'

Sarah smiled, much happier now they had left 'that place' behind. Ever since Papa had told them they were going to have a daguerreotype done, Freddie could talk of nothing else. He had tried to explain how it worked, the copper plates that were covered in silver, washed in iodine, before being put it in the camera to capture their image. It is really called photograph from the Greek, phos meaning 'light' and graphe meaning 'drawing or writing'. See? Sarah, Mabel and Emily did not 'see' nor did they care to.

'That's because you're girls. You cannot appreciate these things' he had said crossly.

'Don't be silly, Freddie. We just do not care to know about such things,' Mabel had replied, giving him a little push.

Sarah thought it was strange that people seemed so ready to capture any part of themselves forever. Still, she was getting used to seeing portraits and paintings of people she knew. Now there will be a portrait of her too.

'I am sure it will be fine,' Papa said, ringing the bell. 'After all it was Her Majesty herself who suggested we use Mr Mayall. She has had several of them done of herself, the Prince Consort, and the royal children. She would not be such a great supporter if it was dangerous. Her Majesty wants one done of Sarah, so we must and while we are here, we can do one of our family too.'

'Good Morning Captain, Madam,' said the young man who opened the door. 'My father is waiting for you upstairs. I'm Edwin. Please follow me. I'm sorry for the long climb but we need the glass roof to get as much light as possible.'

The room was large, much brighter than the stairway and quite empty, except for a few chairs, velvet drapes and two small pedestals, four large windows set into the roof letting in what little light could squeeze past the grey fog. Sarah longed for bright blue skies and sun. It was hard for her to breathe in the smelly, foggy, smoky London air.

Mama sat on one of the straight-backed chairs and pulled Anna to her. Mabel and Freddie wandered around the room looking at "Portraits of Eminent Men" in carved frames on the walls.

'Sarah, look, a portrait of Mr Dickens,' said Mabel, pointing to the photograph of a man with a beard, holding a quill, his eyes fixed on the blank paper in front of him. Sarah gazed at the man who had written A Christmas Carol, the man's whose story of ghosts had so frightened her. She found it strange that he did not seem any different to other men.

'What a fine family,' said Mr Mayall rushing in, wringing his hands and smiling, 'very fine indeed, Captain.' He shook Papa Forbes' hand and bowed to Mama Forbes.

'Where do you want us to sit?' asked Papa.

'Ah, let me explain what will happen while Edwin prepares the plates in the dark room. Capturing the daguerreotype image is a very delicate procedure. With light, it takes only a few minutes, however, you must all remain perfectly still throughout as the slightest movement will ruin the image. It is sometimes difficult for the little ones, to hold their positions, so if you do not mind, I will arrange you, either sitting or standing, in front of the drape and then we can begin. Could you ladies please remove your bonnets? They'll cast shadows on your faces.'

Once the camera was set up and Mr Mayall had positioned them, he threw a black cloth over his head and peered through the lens. He ordered his son to fix a drape there, change the angle of Freddie's head and move the lamps.

'Hold it,' Mr Mayall said. They all stiffened. He counted, and they waited and waited, getting hotter and hotter. The camera and Mr Mayall under the cloth grew bigger, became one, an animal, black and frightening to Sarah. She felt her legs shaking with the effort of standing still. Just as she could bear it no longer, feeling she would have to speak or move, Mr Mayall threw back the cloth.

'Finished,' he said and handed the camera over to Edwin who rushed into the dark room. They all breathed out. Papa Forbes hugged Sarah who was standing next to him and she leaned into him. It was a long time since they had been that close.

'Good family photo,' said Mr Mayall. 'Your children were very good. No fidgets at all. We should have a very good image.'

Sarah smiled. A good family photo, a good family. Her good family.

SALIMATU/SARAH

# CHAPTER 22

*She is more precious than rubies: and all the things thou canst desire*
*are not to be compared unto her*
Proverbs 3:15

## January 1851

4th *January 1851, Wimpole Street, London*
>    *Today we go to the Zoo. After leaving the studio, yesterday,*
>    *Mama took us to the milliner. We all got new hats to match*
>    *our coats. Mabel chose a green one with ribbons. Lily's is pink*
>    *with little grey and white flowers. I had dark red one with*
>    *navy blue ribbons. Outside people surrounded us. I heard*
>    *whispers of 'Black Princess'. Someone pulled at my hair. 'It's*
>    *just like a cushion,' she said, and everyone laughed. I lost my*
>    *new hat. Sometimes it is not nice being a 'Black Princess'.*

✥✥✥

On the way to the zoo Sarah turned her head from left to right looking, searching, hoping, to see what?

'Josephine says that the gardens are among the chief sights of London, especially in the summer and almost as popular as the zoo since it opened three years ago,' said Mama, as the horses clip-clopped along.

The greatest attractions were the elephant houses, the snake room, the seal pond and the monkey houses. The buildings were crowed and noisy, divided into compartments with the day cages in front and sleeping dens were at the back. The outer cages were enclosed on three sides with walls and on the fourth side with strong iron railings through which the animals could be seen. Sarah moved closer to Papa Forbes. The smells of animals and people made Mama Forbes put her handkerchief to her nose.

'Hurry everyone,' called Emily running ahead, squeezing past people, laughing, clapping her hands, squealing at the size of the hippopotamus. The crowd watched the animal plunge into his bath, splashing all those close by. He lay down on the sand, gave a wide yawn before curling up like a huge India rubber lump and going to sleep.

'I thought they said it was like a sea-horse,' grumbled one lady poking her umbrella into the hippopotamus' side. 'It looks more like a hog. Paying all that money to come look at a hog. I ask you.' She gave it another poke then disgruntled, hobbled away.

Others walked slowly past cages on either side of the walkway, looking, reading the cards with the animals' names and countries of origin. Anna covered her eyes when she saw the spiders and clung to Mama when she saw the crocodiles.

The more she saw of the zoo, the more upset Sarah became. She wanted to turn back, run away. She stopped walking.

'What's the matter?' asked Freddie, who came back when he realised that Sarah was lagging behind.

'Why are the animals brought here from all over the world?'

'So that we can learn about them. It's scientific.'

'But they are not even outside, not free to go where they want.'

'These tropical animals would not survive outside in the cold weather.'

'There are so many people, everywhere, just looking at them. It is not like that in the jungle. There they hardly see people.'

'It is Sunday afternoon, the only time some people can come to a place like this.'

'I hate people staring and pointing. Do you think the animals hate it too?'

'I'm sure they do not. They do not have feelings like we do. Come on, or we'll lose the others. There are still so many things to see.'

She went with him, but kept her eyes down, would not look, would not stare at the animals.

'I see the lions over there,' cried Emily, turning to Sarah. 'Are they like the one your Papa killed?'

Sarah bit her lips. Why had she ever said that to Emily?

'You did not tell me about a lion?' Papa said.

'Really? How?' said Freddie. 'He must have been very brave.'

'You just made that up,' was Mabel's contribution.

'Do you remember that?' asked Mama.

Sarah shook her head. How could she tell them that it was not Jaja but Fatmata who had told her about their father's fight with the lion? She had been frightened by the noises at night during their march through the forest, a long time ago. Fatmata said that she would kill any lion that attacked them just as Jaja had done when he was a boy. But did Fatmata tell her or had she imagined it?

Emily squeezed her hand. 'I'm sorry, I should not have told.'

When the lion roared and walked towards them many people screamed and ran away, but Sarah stayed. So that was what a lion looked like? She had never seen one. She shut her eyes and was back with Fatmata, listening to the many sounds of the forest, the cicadas, the frogs, snuffling in the grass, snakes gliding by, insects biting. She trembled, and tears trickled out of her shut eyes. She felt her sister's arms around her. She opened her eyes. It wasn't Fatmata, it was Mabel.

'Let us get away from here,' was all she said, leading Sarah away.

They were almost at the exit when Sarah saw them, the monkeys, leaping from branch to branch, chattering, calling. One peeled away from the others and leapt at the wire fencing, screaming its call, his eyes never leaving Sarah's. As if in a trance she walked towards the monkey, her heart beating fast, from deep within a name burst out.

'Jabeza, Jabeza,' she said and pushed her hand through the wire fence.

'No,' said Mama, trying to pull her back. 'He'll bite you.'

Sarah did not hear her or see all the people who had gathered around them as she stroked the monkey's green fur through the fence while he chattered into her ear. The other monkeys in the enclosure jumped and squealed a welcome.

'*Ekaro*, Jabeza, *Ekaro*. Hello,' sobbed Sarah.

Papa led her away and the others hurried after them. Sarah sobs did not die dow and she struggled to go back to the cage. 'That's Jabeza, she knew me. That's Fatmata's monkey. She must be here. Let me go get her, please Papa, please,'

'Stop it Sarah. It is not your sister's monkey. She is not here. Stop making a scene.'

Sarah clutched hold of her *gri-gri*. She knew that for a moment she had been able to go back to her village, to Fatmata. She rubbed her thigh. She had her monkey tattoo. She too was a warrior.

✿✿✿

Creeping downstairs early next morning, Sarah hoped Daniel would be in the hall. He was a Negro in London and the only person she had met so far who might be able to tell her where she was likely to find Fatmata.

'*Ekaro*, Daniel.' Sarah called as he crossed the hall. He stopped and looked up at her. She did not know why she had used that word. Then she realised that Salimatu was back.

'Miss Sarah?'

'Ask him to help us,' said Salimatu. 'He's from Africa.'

Sarah's heartbeat fast. '*Joworan mi lowo.*'

'Sorry, Miss Sarah, what you say?'

Her lips trembled. He didn't understand the 'please help me.' How could she have been so stupid? Why would he know Yoruba?

'Is something wrong?' he said, crossing over to her.

'Daniel, are you not from Africa too?' she said, running down the last few steps.

'Africa? Oh, no miss. No, I from Barbados.'

'Where's that?'

'That's the Indies. There I was born on a sugar plantation. Later they sold me off and I was taken to South Carolina.'

Sarah's eyes widened. 'You're a slave?' she whispered.

'Not now. From there I run way and work me on a ship. In London, when I land, I become a freeman, no slave in England you see, slavery done'. Daniel settled into his story as if he had just been waiting for someone to ask. 'Took me a while to get me a job but at last I got took on to work in the kitchen at Lord Carlyle's. I rose up, I surely did. Twelve years there and then I gets too old, or so Lady Carlyle say and they let me go. After that I comes here, but all the time I work hard with many others to help free my people. It ain't no slavery here in England, but my people ain't exactly all free neither.'

She liked hearing him speak, in that voice that sounded as if he was singing. But she had to listen carefully for she could not really recognize all the words he said.

'Daniel, where are all the Negroes?' she asked, standing directly in front of him to see his eyes. 'Mabel said that there are many in London, but I've only seen one other coloured man. He was sweeping the streets. He had one leg like Peg-leg Jed but his was not painted with flowers.'

Daniel's forehead creased into deep furrows. 'They're plenty around, near the markets, the docks and so on. All kinds o' we kind', he said with a smile. 'Some sell fruits and vegetables, some are beggars, others are street singers but they ain't no better dan a beggar really, 'cause things be hard for them. You'll not find them around here no way.'

'Then where will I find them?'

'Now, why would a fine young lady like you want to know such a thing?'

Sarah sighed deeply, 'Fatmata might be with them.'

'Who?' A flutter of unexpressed laughter traces Daniel's face. Sarah feels suddenly self-conscious, wondering if she looks funny, all dressed up and fancy, or if her voice is strange, but she continues, buoyed by their easy exchanges.

'Fatmata. My sister. We were taken together from our village but then we were separated and sold. She must be in London because Jabeza is here at the zoo. Fatmata must be waiting for me. I've got to go to her.'

Daniel stepped back. 'No, no, no' he said, bending down so that he could look into her eyes which held an odd mixture of mirth and deep concern. 'No. You can't do that. That part of London, where they lives, is not for the likes of you. Nor your sister. Your sister wouldn't be there, for sure.'

'How do you know?' Sarah said, rushing to door. 'I must go, I have to search for her.' Daniel came up behind her and, taking her firmly by the shoulders, turned her around. 'Stop child. Stop. You must leave me now and go back upstairs.'

✿✿✿✿

Sarah waited until Daniel had disappeared before she tiptoed back downstairs and made her way to the front of the house. She stood in the quiet, semi-dark main hall. Then reached for the handle on the front door. The front door was big and heavy, but she pushed it open, just wide enough for her to slip out into the sleepy street. The cold hit her throat and she gave a little cough. Shivering under her coat, she hesitated for a second, not sure what to do or where to go now that she was outside. Daniel's soft admonishing eyes appeared in her mind, but she shook the image off and began to make her way down the steps into the street, where she took off, stiffly, half-running, half walking as if this would make her less conspicuous to anyone she might meet. Her mind raced the further she drew from the house. Did Mabel see her leave the nursery with her coat and hat? How long before she was missed? I must get to the zoo, thought Sarah. She was sure that if she waited long enough by the monkeys' enclosure, Fatmata would come and get her. But was it left or right to the zoo?

She picked up her pace, only stopping for a moment when from one of the mews where the horses were stabled, a carriage came out unexpectedly. The sound of the pair of gleaming horses' hooves had been deadened by the small gravel stones laid down on the street. Sarah shrank back into the shadows as the carriage rolled by, the driver so still and staring straight ahead he might have been asleep. Only the puffs of white smoke from the horse's noses and the muffled clatter of their hooves broke the night air.

As they disappeared, she continued on her way. At the cross-road she stopped still not sure which way to go. Sarah realised that for the first time in her life there was no one to tell her where to go or what to do. She felt free, unafraid. She would find the zoo and her sister all by herself. Taking a deep breath, her mind racing with excitement, she stepped into the road. The sudden squeal of a cab's wheels and thunder of horses' hooves rattling and clacking on the now cobbled streets made her jump back and in doing so she landed with one foot into a pile of horse dung which wedged between her heel and the sole of her boot and would not budge no matter how many times she scraped she boot against the ground. This smell of London followed her with every step.

She walked on her mind now more focused on the lodged dung and its putrid aroma than anything else. When the shoe-black boy sitting on the cold, damp pavement, clutching a package wrapped in filthy cloth, offered to clean her boots she went over to him happily. She put one foot on the box he laid in front of her and then the other for him to shine. Unperturbed by anything about her, not her fine clothes, her dark skin, nor the unbecoming nature of the sole of her boots, the boy set to work, twisting and turning his filthy cloths, after a cursory dislodging of the bulk of the dung from beneath her boot. He eventually finished with a final swipe and then extended a dirty, hard, hand toward her. 'That be a fadge,' he said.

Sarah frowned and shook her head.

'You owe me a farthing.'

'Farthing? I don't have a farthing.'

'What? You think I clean boots for noffing? Gimme the money,' he said reaching out to grab her.

Sarah stepped back and shrugging off his grip ran with no idea of direction or place. A farthing? She had no money. She'd never had to think about money, never had to pay for anything. Did one have to pay for everything in London? Turning around from time to time to check that the boy was no longer following her, she bumped into a man wearing a wooden signboard, front and back, like a topcoat. The boards were so large all she could see were his shoes at the bottom and his eyes and his tall hat above the sign.

'Why don't you watch where you going?' he growled, trying to straighten the boards that had gone lopsided and threatening to topple him over.

Two men standing outside the pub holding mugs of beer and

smoking their pipes burst out laughing. 'You'll need to grow almost as big as that hippo you are advertising to go far with those boards,' said one of the men. The other spat and Sarah had to do a little jump for his spittle not to land on her newly cleaned boot. She looked at the board then. There was a drawing of a very large animal, with small ears and eyes and a huge mouth, spread out as if to dry on a stone slab. Slowly she read the writing below it.

*Come see* OBAYSCH
*the first Hippopotamus in England*
*since pre-historic times.*
*London Zoo at Regent's Park.*

Sarah's heartbeat fast. An advert for the zoo. Was this a sign? Maybe he could take her there. She pulled at his sleeve.

'What you want? First you try to knock me over, now you pull at me.'

'Will you take me to the zoo with you, please? I've lost the way.'

'Do I look like a map? I don't go to the zoo; I just tell people about the place.'

Sarah's bit her lips. How was she ever going to get to the zoo and to Fatmata? This was much harder than she had thought it would be. With her head down, she walked down the street, coughing.

# CHAPTER 23

*The wicked flee when no man pursueth: but the righteous are bold as a lion*
Proverbs 28:1

## January 1851

The running, the smoke, the soot and dirt had all brought on her cough again. Sarah leant against a wall and tried to get her breathe back.

'That's a nasty cough, you got there, little lady. I've got just the thing for that,' said a man standing by her side. 'I'm the street doctor you know.'

Sarah examined him. He stood lop-sided, one leg longer than the other, the sole of the right boot twice the height of the other. His coat was long and stained, his beard and short moustache untrimmed, his eyes dark and sad looking. Could he really stop her cough? She was tired of it. He did not look like Doctor Spencer who came to Winkfield place when Anna was ill but then that was the only doctor she had ever seen. This man could be a doctor too, how was she to know.

He pointed to his stand and a tray off goods. His sign board read,

*Prevention better than cure*
*Try our new Cough Preventative.*
*Cough lozenges and Peppermints*

I must pay for that too, she thought and shook her head. He picked up a peppermint, 'have one,' he said.

'No money,' Sarah whispered, between coughs.

'Never mind,' he said, 'take it.'

Sarah took the peppermint and sucked hard on it.

'You should not be out in this fog and cold. Not good for the chest. This weather's bad for you people. I know. Used to be a sailor. What are you doing around here anyway?'

'Looking for my sister's place,' Sarah said, relieved that the cough had eased a little.

'You won't find her round here,' he laughed, pressing another peppermint into her hand. 'Although some of you darkies do live past the market, back of Oxford Street not too far if you know where to go.'

She popped the other sweet into her mouth, closed her eyes, sucked hard and a tear slid out and rolled down her cheek. She began to walk away her mind racing with conflicting thoughts and emotions. She soon lost track of where she was walking and for how long, as the streets became more populous and brighter. She soon heard the faint strains of music and looking around saw that she had arrived at an alehouse in front of which was a group singing a rowdy song. The crowd swelled quickly as people tried desperately to see who they were as they began to move forward down the street.

All around her the crowd jostled and people talked over one another, laughing and some were even joining in with the songs. She struggled to see over the growing crowd and found herself shouting to be heard. 'What is it? Who are they? What's happening?' into the backs of the wall of onlookers.

Eventually, a tall thin man in front of her, turning to see who was making such a racket looked down at her. He tapped her shoulder and said, 'listen, can you hear the music? Look. Down the street, The Serenaders. They go everywhere. Maybe they know where she is.'

'The Serenaders?'

'The blackface street singers. There many of them around. These are "The Strand Serenaders". They come here regular but moved on by the peelers, though.'

Black face? Negroes. They would know where other coloured people lived. She ran down the street, the music getting louder all the while. By the time she got to The Serenaders there was a small crowd and all she could see was the backs of the four men dancing and singing. She pushed through the crowd and her mouth fell open. She wondered where in Africa they came from for they were four of the blackest people she had ever seen, with big red lips that took up half of their faces. They looked strange with coat collars right up to their ears, black hats with white bands perched, like blackbirds, on tight curly black hair.

It wasn't music she had heard before, yet it was familiar, it made her want to dance too. She watched the fiddler's fingers fly over the strings while the second man plucked at the banjo. The two men in the centre of the circle shook their tambourines and danced. The shorter man breathed heavily and shuffled around, but the taller one's long legs twisted and flicked. He walked and danced, feet taping out the rhythm, while singing a song about 'Jimmy Crack Corn'.

The music reminded her of home, well her old home, her African home. There had always been music. Even in King Gezo's slave compound there had been music. Without thinking, just as she had on HMS Bonetta, she danced with abandonment. It was only when the music stopped, and she heard the clapping that she was brought back to the reality of a cold London street. Her hat hung down her back by its ribbons, her coat was open, she had lost her gloves and Salimatu was back.

'Keep on dancing,' she said. 'They'll take us to Fatmata.'

'What you think you're doing, you skilamink?' said the shuffler, glaring at her. 'This is our pitch. Go away.'

'She's good,' shouted a man in the crowd. 'Ain't she one of yours?'

'Yes,' said Mr Longlegs, staring hard at her. 'We training her up.'

'All darkies can dance anyhow. What she need training for?' said a woman. Sarah did not know why everyone laughed but she laughed too. Fiddler-man burst into 'Come Back Steben' before anymore could be said. Two barefooted boys came pushing through the crowd, bumping into people.

A man cuffed the ears of one of them, 'you thieving scumbag,' he said, snatching his wallet back before it could be passed to the other boy.

Suddenly there was a cry of 'bluebottles, bluebottles. The peelers are coming.'

Sarah turned and there was a policeman in his long tailcoat, with big shining brass buttons done up to his neck, the wide leather belt tight across his ample stomach. His wooden truncheon raised, he shouted, 'move on, move on.'

One of the boys threw something and knocked the policeman's tall leather hat off before running away, laughing. The policeman picked up his hat, shook his rattle and chased after them but they were already lost in the mass of people.

'Let's leg it before that peeler comes back,' said the banjo-player,

They gathered their instruments and hurried away. They were half-way down the next street before they realised that Sarah was still behind them.

'Why you following us? Hook it,' said banjo man.

'I'm looking for my sister.'

'What's that to do with us?'

'Can't you take me to her? You must know where she is.'

'Us? We don't know your sister, child. Get lost, we're going home.'

The four men walked away. She stood there biting her lips, undecided. Should she follow them and hope they lead her to Fatmata, or should she go back home. But which home?

'You've no home?' Mr Longlegs had come back and was standing in front of her.

'I don't know where it is.'

'Who taught you how to dance like that?'

'No one.'

'Well, I guess we can sort something out.'

'Where are the other men?'

'Gone to The White Lion for a drink of ale. Monday not a good day for business, especially now that it's started to rain. Come on.'

Sarah smiled took hold of Mr Longlegs gloved hand and went with him.

'See, I told you if we danced, they'd help!' whispered Salimatu. Sarah gave a little skip, partly to catch up with the purposeful strides of Mr Longlegs and partly because she was happy. Alone, without the help from anyone, not Papa Forbes or the Queen, she had found the one person who could take her to Fatmata. Her eyes darted from side to side taking in everything as they walked through the market. She tried not to wrinkle her nose but the smell of animal dung, fish guts and rotting vegetables did make her stomach churn.

It was not until Mr Longlegs stopped by a street food-seller that she realised her stomach was rumbling from hunger. The smell of baked potato mingled with the smell of different pies on the stall hit her nose and filled her mouth with spit. She had not eaten since breakfast. How long ago was that? She would give anything for a piece of pie.

'Got to buy some food if we want hot. We got nowhere to cook at home. You hungry?'

'Yes,' said Sarah and then thought, home? Her eyes widened. Did Fatmata live with Mr Longlegs? She wished the food-seller would hurry up as he wrapped the potatoes and onion pie in old newspapers. Sarah and Salimatu could not wait to see Fatmata

It was raining now, icy and sharp, stinging her face. She kept her head down and followed Mr Longlegs. They walked down many lanes, past lamp-lighters going from lamp to lamp, climbing up short ladders to light the gas street lamps, leaving pools of yellow light behind them. Sarah kept looking for black families but could see none. Maybe they were staying indoors, out of the freezing rain.

Sarah pressed against the damp wall of a house when a man, his long coat flapping behind him, black hat pulled low, long hair and beard, stringy and wet, rushed past pushing a cart piled high with clothes.

'The skilmalink. Better hold on to your coat,' said Mr Longlegs, spitting after the man. 'These Jews are everywhere nowadays. Rip the clothes off you and sell it before you can say Whitechapel. I've seen one strip a body and sell the clothes on before the dead man was cold.'

They went past dark holes for gateways with children running in and out, their bare feet splashing through icy puddles and dirty grey water that spilled out of the gutters. The alleyways got narrower and narrower, smelling even worse than the market. The houses on either side seemed to lean towards each other so that neighbours, huddled in shawls, could talk, whisper, shout at each other from the windows of their rented rooms.

Wet and cold she could no longer feel her feet. Her gloveless hands would have been just as bad except that Mr Longlegs had given her two hot potatoes to hold. She hoped they would get to wherever they were going soon, before the rain cooled the potato.

At last, they reached Mr Longlegs home. This was one large room with red sand covering the wooden floor and tattered curtains at one end, separating the sleeping area and its two beds from the rest of the room. The windowpane was broken and stuffed with rags, the one lamp threw long shadows around the room. Sarah could immediately see that Fatmata was not there, instead there were three small children staring at her, mouths open like birds waiting to be fed. The youngest sitting on the floor, stuck his thumb back in his mouth and sucked loudly. The two girls, pale and thin, not much older than Anna, said nothing but their eyes followed their father, and the pie he was holding.

'Take you coat off, make yourself at home,' said Mr Longlegs.

A tiny woman, with a tiny mouth, large grey eyes and a head full of curly blond hair took the still warm potatoes from Sarah.

'Who's this then Jim?' she said.

He looked at Sarah and shrugged his shoulders. 'Don't know, Maggie, forgot to ask.'

'You mean you just pick up any darkie you see in the street and bring her back here? What for?' asked Maggie, unwrapping the layers of newspaper around the potatoes. 'Can she even speak English? What's her name?'

'I'm Sarah. Where's Fatmata?'

'What? Who?'

'He said he was bringing me to her.'

'I never said that, Maggie,' shouted Jim his face shiny in the flickering lamplight 'She said she was lost, no home and so I brought her back to you.'

'To do what, you glocky man. We can't keep her. There's not even enough room or food for us and the children.'

Sarah wished now that she had not come to Mr Longleg's one-room home. Fatmata was not there. She shivered, wishing she'd not taken her coat and hat off. There was only a small fire that threw out very little heat. She sank down into the rickety armchair, tired and afraid.

'Listen, Maggie, I had an idea,' said Jim pulling his black curly wig and his gloves off before pouring some water into a bowl. 'We can start a nigger school.'

Sarah sat up and her throat went dry. How could he take his hair off like that?

'You coot, what you thinking?'

'All the groups are doing it now, so why can't we start one?' said Jim washing his face while he spoke. 'She can be our first. And they don't have a true darkie. People will like that. Look at Juba, the only darkie with the Ethopian Serenaders. They make more money because of him. We'll get other darkies later and be better than even the Westminster school or the St Giles lot. There are many blackface groups around, but we'll have an advantage. Once we've taught them a few songs and dances we can go do busking at pubs or street corners and get more money.'

When he turned around Sarah eyes widened, heart beat fast and her breathe came in short gasps. The water in the bowl was black and Jim's face and hands had turned white.

'Ayee,' screamed Salimatu in her ear, 'he is *djudju*, a black man who can turn white. We must get out of here before they drag us down.' Sarah jumped up and pulled her wet coat around her so that no part of her body would touch anything in the room.

'You're not black?' she shrieked and burst into tears. 'You're not from Africa?'

Jim laughed and wiped his face, leaving streaks, like zebra markings across his cheeks. 'Me African? That's burnt coke and shoe polish. We just dress up to sing the songs. Me black? Ha, ha, ha.'

'You are *djudju*,' whimpered Sarah. 'I want to go home.'

'You have no home. You stay here,' said Jim, taking Sarah's coat off her.

'Jim, she can't,' said Maggie. 'Look at her, look at the things she wearing. She look like a child who don't have a home? I bet they're searching for her right now. You want the peelers to come here? Want them to find out we've done a midnight flit from the last two places?'

'Shut your tatur-trap. This is different.'

'Yes. We can be done for taking her,' shouted Maggie.

'Now, don't kick up a shine. They'll never find this place.'

Maggie was no longer listening to Jim. She picked up her heavy plaid shawl and threw it over her shoulders. 'I'm taking her away from here. Come, where you living?'

'I think Papa said Wimpole Street?'

Maggie stared at Sarah. 'Wimpole Street,' she repeated backing away so quickly she stumbled over the baby who yelled but was ignored by them all. She wrung her hands muttering, 'O Mary Mother of God.'

'You work there Sarah and you've run away. Is that it?' asked Jim, cutting a piece of pie. 'They'll soon find another darkie.'

'You prannock,' cried Maggie. 'Don't you get it? The 'Black Princess'. The newspaper boys been shouting about her the past two days.'

'What? Bring the lamp,' he ordered. Jim grabbed the potatoes newspaper wrappings. Spreading them out, he searched the columns, then stopped and pointed to a heading.

*AFRICAN PRINCESS IN LONDON. Yesterday, Sarah Forbes Bonetta, the goddaughter of Her Majesty, Queen Victoria arrived in London from Windsor. The Princess lives with the family of Captain Forbes, who saved her from a sacrificial death. She is staying with Lord and Lady Melton at their home in Wimpole Street.*

Maggie did not wait for Jim to finish reading the article before she was dragging Sarah out of the room and down the stairs, without her hat or coat. They walked for a long time, Maggie avoiding streets that were lit. When she saw a policeman on his beat, she pulled Sarah into a doorway and signalled for her to be quiet. Then suddenly she disappeared leaving Sarah all alone cold and wet.

It was Daniel who found her shivering and alone at the end of Wimpole Street.

*Tuesday 7th January 1851, London*

*Nanny has kept me in bed all today because of my cough. Papa says that I have punished myself enough and learned my lesson. Mama cried when she saw me last night. She held me tight and said that they all love me. Papa was out all afternoon searching for me. He made me promise that I will never run away again. I made him promise to never send me to the workhouse. Mabel is cross that I did not take her with me. She and Emily have been with me all day. I have lost my coat and another hat. Maybe Mr Longlegs will sell it to the jewman. Nanny says it is by the grace of God that I have been saved. We go home to Winkfield Place tomorrow, without Papa. He leaves for Chatham and his new ship. Is he taking Salimatu with him? Is Fatmata gone?*

FATMATA

# CHAPTER 24

Dúkìa tí a fi èrú kójọ kò mú ká dolówó
*The treasure one gathers by foul means will not make one rich*

## 1846

We journey through the forest for many, many suns, moving as soon as the sun starts to peel back the dark of night and stop when darkness creeps over the sky. Bureh and Momo tie us to the trees and start the fire, to boil cassava, yams or make a thin rice pap. Most of the time there is not enough food, so as we walk along, we look for berries and fruits.

The forest is a place to be feared. It is always alive for there are the animals that come out with the light and those that creep out in the dark. One night a big bush rat bites Salimatu, I take out my sling, throw the stone and knock the rat out. Bureh skins and cook it. There is meat with our rice then. After that I am the hunter for extra food.

Every night the men take it in turns to stay awake, to keep the fire going. Usually Khadijatu snores loudly, Minata cries in her sleep for her children while I hold Salimatu tight and listen to the cicadas, the laughter of the hyenas, the stumping of the elephants. The distant roaring of lions reminds me of Jaja. Above my head, the chatter of monkeys, makes me long for the time when I was free and climbing trees with Jabeza. Then I fall asleep.

✿✿✿

I dream that I return to Talaremba. I reach the entrance of the village dragging the lion I have killed with my sling; the gate is flung open by Jaja on a big horse. He bends down and lifts me up shouting 'Ayee, my child is back, my warrior child has returned. Look at the lion she has killed and brought as meat for us.'

Then Madu, and Amadu and Salimatu had come running, singing my praises.

Jamilla offers me a bowl of cassava stew, a live monkey sitting in it. I do not take it.

'To learn the way, you must first get lost,' Maluuma says, walking slowly towards me. 'You have done well, my daughter.'

Then even as I reach out to them, they disappear, one by one. I tried to run after them but could not move.

'Take me with you,' I call after them, again and again, but none of them turn around.

I am crying, shaking, shaking, crying.

'Fatmata, open your eyes, come back.'

I open my eyes. I am not in Talaremba but in a forest with Minata and Salimatu.

'You were dreaming,' Minata said.

'Don't leave me, Fatu,' said Salimatu.

'I'll not leave you Sali,' I say, wiping away my tears and lying down next to her.

'I hope that is the end of your noise,' calls Khadijatu.

'Leave her,' says Delu. 'We all dream.'

Maluuma always said that dreaming was a message from the ancestors. The message is not always clear, so you have to find the meaning. So, while we march through the forest, the sun following us, peeping through the leaves and branches, I work out the message. The people had come to tell me to escape with Salimatu and be with them.

We come out of the forest and though we pass many villages, we never stop. Always people come out to watch us go by. The first time, we shout to them for help. They stare at us but do nothing. Momo fires the gun and the people scream and run. One old woman, however, hobbles over with water. Bureh tries to stop her but she gives him such a look he let her be.

'May the gods go with you,' she says. We drink thirstily and she presses a small orange into Salimatu's hand. When we stop for the night, I peel it and we share it with Minata.

We've been walking for almost a whole moon cycle and Sisi Tenneh speaks to no one, not even to Taimu. Sometimes she talks to herself in whispers and other times laughs and laughs at nothing. Taimu follows me with his eyes. Whenever he tries to speak to me, his mother gets angry and hits him or take away his food. Delu talks all the time but no one listens. We are all hurting. Khadijatu is the only one getting fatter. There is never enough to eat but as we walk she eats as much as she can of any berries or fruit we find, before anyone else has any. Khadijatu stops often to take breath and cries for her mother. Bureh hits her with the whip, but not as hard as he hits others.

Then one day when we stop at the heat of the day, Khadijatu sits down and I see that she is full with child.

'How many more moons before you drop the child,' I whisper later, in the darkness of the night.

'Three.'

'Three? You do not show much.'

'Sometimes being big helps,' she says and cries then. The more she tries not to, the more she shakes.

'Does Sisi Jiani know?'

'Yes. Just before the fire take her.'

'What about Adebola?'

'All this time he was working for Santigie, making me tell him things about the village. I thought we were bethrothed.' She sobs even harder as she rocks and rocks. 'Now he says what is in my stomach is not his and gives me to Santigie as a slave.'

'Who else knows?'

'Bureh knows about Adebola but not that my belly is full. That is why he is after me. He comes to me in the dark.'

'I will help you if I can,' I say, 'but you must try to walk and not make trouble. Tie your lappa around your neck to cover your stomach.'

Although we do not get on, she is Talaremban and in times of trouble we help each other. If Santigie finds out she is carrying a child, he will either kill her or sell her to the Moors. But I do not tell her this.

Santigie comes back to us again and again, riding on huge horses, bringing more captured women. I fear them. Their hooves are big and hard and when one steps on Bureh's foot, he screams and jumps up and down like a dancer without music. Bureh cannot walk for one whole circle of the sun and we have to stay hidden in the forest. By the time we have been walking for over a moon cycle, there are over twenty of us.

The day he comes riding up with an Arab and three other men we are all afraid. Salimatu runs back to me screaming. The noise frightens Santigie's horse and it throws him to the ground. The Arab laughs. Santigie gets up and slaps Salimatu's face. I pull her to me and without thinking I spit in Santigie's face. He stares at me as he wipes his face. I feel the ants crawl up and down my back and I know that I will have to pay for this later.

We are lined up. I keep my head down and try not to shake when the Arab stands in front of me. He reaches out and I move back thinking that he is going to touch me, but he touches Salimatu instead. He turns and says something to Santigie. I do not understand their speak and I hold on tight to Salimatu. The Arab shakes his head and walks away. When the Arab leaves he takes Delu, two other women and Taimu with him. Santigie has sold them. Taimu struggles and fights. A rope is put around his neck. Momo and one of the other men hold their guns.

Long after the sound of the horses and the cries of Delu and Taimu have died down, Tenneh stands on the same spot, watching and waiting. It gets so dark not even the moon can send down enough light to see the person tied next to you and it looks as if she has taken root.

Then the rain comes, pouring down as if the sky has opened to let the tears of our ancestors fall upon us. Lightning flashes across the sky sending down fingers of light that lead us nowhere. The night is angry. I raise my face to the gods and pray that they can see us in that dark, damp forest and save us. But all that comes is thunder that leaps from mountain to mountain, roaring repeatedly like angry lions. Salimatu trembles and covers her ears. I pull her close, but the sound does not frighten me, instead it reminds me of Jaja. I remember his story of how he fought and killed a lion and it gives me strength, so I tell Salimatu about it. We fall asleep and I dream again about escaping.

I know that something is wrong as soon as I open my eyes. There's a different kind of quiet after the noisy night. The rain has stopped, everything is wet and muddy. There is a strong smell of rotting leaves. As I remember Delu, Taimu and the other two women my eyes fill up. Minata is awake but she doesn't speak. I turn to wake Salimatu but she's not here. Maybe she has gone to relieve herself. I take a twig and start to chew on it.

'Minata, did Sali go empty herself?' I ask. I know that she has heard me but there is no answer her mouth just opens and shuts. I can tell there's something she cannot say. I jump up and look around. All are awake, all are silent. Something twists inside of me.

'Salimatu,' I scream. 'Salimatuuuu, Sali, where are you? Come back.'

The sound goes and comes back without an answer. Minata is crying now. And then I see them, Santigie riding away with Salimatu tied up lying across the horse, her head bumping up and down, as if she is nodding.

I scream again and try to run after them, but the rope tied to the tree would not let me go and I fall to my knees. Again, and again I scream for Salimatu. Her name races around and shakes the trees, the leaves, the bushes, racing to reach her ears. It flies up to the sky and calls to the gods, it pushes deep into Mother Earth but still no answer came back. Minata crawls over and puts her arms around me.

'Santigie came and took her,' she says, through her sobs.

'Where's he taking her? What's he going to do to her?' I cry.

Bureh comes over, grabs hold of my hands and shakes me. 'The Arab wanted her. Santigie says this is better than whipping you. Now take the food. We have to go.'

I give a cry that comes from deep inside of me. It is long and never ending. This is my fault. My actions have resulted in first Lansana, now Salimatu, being taken away by Santigie. I cannot move, my legs are as heavy as tree trunks. Bureh hits my legs with his whip until I have to move my feet. Minata holds me up. I do not know how, but I walk because I have to, I walk because there is nothing else for me to do. There are no words to ease the pain that wraps around me. Each step beats out my sister's name so that my whole being is the name.

'Sali–matu, Sali–matu, Sali–matu, on and on and on.

# CHAPTER 25

*The light of the eyes rejoiceth the heart: and a good report maketh the
bones fat*
Proverbs 15:30

## January 1851

Three days after returning to Winkfield Place, Sarah woke up
early. Restless, she got up and wandered into the school room
and gasped. Out of the schoolroom window she saw that everything
had turned white, like foam on the sea.

'Mabel, Lily, come and see,' she called clapping her hands.

The girls rushed to the window. 'O it snowed while we were
asleep,' said Mabel pressing her face to the windowpane.

'Hope it doesn't melt away. We can make a snowman,' said
Emily, jumping up and down before grabbing Sarah.

'A snowman?'

'Yes, make a man from snow,' said Mabel. 'It's great fun.'

'Can we? When?' asked Sarah, eager to go out straight away.
'Oh please, I've never made a snowman.' She stopped talking and
coughed instead.

'We can't. We'll get into a lot of trouble. You still have your
cough, Sarah.'

'I'm fine. I always have a cough.'

Mabel looked thoughtful for a second, nodded and said, 'It's still snowing, we can make a small snowman and get be back before Nanny or Edith come for us.'

Grabbing shawls but still in their slippers, they crept downstairs, opened the front door and stepped out. Sarah hesitated. It was cold, and her breath came in short gasps. Maybe this was not such a great idea after all. She looked at the wide spread of snow, white and smooth, glistening in the wintery sunshine. Remembering the white sacrificing cloths she had seen spread out to dry in Abomey she wanted to shout, 'no, don't step on it' but she pushed all those thoughts and memories away.

'Have you ever made snow angels?' asked Emily.

Sarah shook her head. She was not even sure that she knew what angels were. She had heard about them in church, but Reverend Byles said they were up in heaven with God so how could children make angels?

'Lily,' said Mabel giving her sister a gentle push 'Sarah has never seen snow before, remember? Come on, let's show her.' They ran to the side garden, their feet sinking into the snow, turning their slippers into white boots. Sarah watched Mabel and Emily fall to the ground and lie flat on their backs, flapping their arms up and down, giggling all the while.

'You must lie down too,' said Mabel.

'Come on,' called Emily, 'make your angel wings. See. Look at mine.' She stood up and where she had lain Sarah could see the shape of a person, but instead of arms and hands the shape had wings like a bird ready to fly.

Sarah, her feet already frozen, trembled but lay down. The cold went through her shawl and flannel nightgown. She flapped her arms, pushing the soft, powdery snow away. Was this how God made angels too? Would she become one when she died? Were there black angels like black princesses?

'What do you think you are doing? You naughty, naughty girls?'

Sarah looked up to see Nanny without even a shawl, standing there. 'Sneaking out of the house like that? Look at all of you, soaking wet. Lord preserve us, what would madam say if she heard of this?'

'Sorry Nanny,' said Emily, trying to brush off the snow that clung to her.

'Nanny Grace,' said Sarah jumping up, 'Please don't be angry. I touched snow for the first time and Mabel and Lily showed me how to make snow angels. Look, look at my angel.'

'Be that as it may, you'll all catch your death,' said Nanny Grace not bothering to look but ushering them towards the front door. 'Go in at once and get out of those wet clothes.'

The girls ran up the stairs their slippers squelching and leaving puddles of water. In the nursery Nanny grabbed hold of Mabel and gave her a shake. 'I'm surprised at you, Mabel Forbes. I thought that you were sensible. As the eldest you should have stopped your sisters from being so foolish. Now go and get dressed. It's true what the good lord says, *the devil makes work for idle hands.* You will not be idle today. I will deal with you all later.'

✿✿✿✿

*Saturday, 11ᵗʰ January 1851, Winkfield Place*
  *Nanny called us sisters today. Is that what I am to Mabel, Lily and Anna? Is Freddie my brother then? I do not know. There are so many things I cannot ask. I'm glad I have sisters here now, even if it is only pretend. Still, I want Fatmata.*

  *Today I touched snow and go for my first German lesson with Vicky and Alice at Windsor Castle. I have learnt some more words. Ich bin glücklich. I am happy.*

✿✿✿✿

By the time the carriage from Windsor Castle came for her, Sarah was ready and waiting in the hall.

'She should not be going out in this weather Madam,' Nanny said to Mrs Forbes.

Sarah held her breathe. Was Nanny going to tell about the morning adventure? Although it had taken her a long time to get warm, but she did not care. It was the most fun she'd had since Captain Forbes brought her to England.

'We've no choice, Nanny. Her Majesty has commanded that Sarah should learn German with the Princesses. Unless she's at death's door, I cannot refuse to send her.'

'You'd better take this,' Nanny said, placing the plaid shawl, Queen Victoria's Christmas present, around Sarah's shoulder. 'I'm sure it's draughty in that castle.'

'Thank you, Nanny Grace.'

They both knew that she was thanking Nanny for more than just the shawl.

It was the first time Sarah had gone anywhere alone. The carriage rolled along hushed streets, as though it was the middle of the night. Everything was ghostlike, the roof tops covered in white, the railings like thin sticks stripped of their bark, pointing to the sky, while the lamp-posts wore night-gowns of white wool.

People, half trotting, rushed past, their heads down, hands stuffed in pockets or muffs, necks bound with thick scarves, looking like black ink blobs on white paper.

The few carriages out drove in ruts made by other carriages; horses struggled where trodden ground had caked into slipperiness. By the time they got to the long climb up to the castle, the horses breath rushed out of their nostrils like fine mist. The driver had to get down and holding on to the reins, lead the horses up to the castle entrance.

This time the footman did not take her down the long corridor but through a big door and up a winding staircase towards the school room.

'Ah, there you are,' said a lady Sarah had never seen before. She was not very tall, her dark hair was in two plaits wound around her head and covered with a cap, her brown dress was covered by a lace shawl around her shoulders. 'You must be Sarah. I'm Lady Barrington, the new supervisor of the Royal Nursery.'

'Good morning Ma'am,' said Sarah with a quick bob and a smile but there was no smile back.

'Come I'll take you to the schoolroom. The princesses are waiting.' The lady turned and hurried down the corridor, her dress spreading out and rustling. She reminded Sarah of a cockroach scuttling around. She half ran to keep up with her.

'Here she is,' said at the schoolroom doorway.

'Thank you, Lady Barrington,' said Miss Hildyard, beckoning Sarah to the big table in the centre of the room.

'Good morning, Miss Hildyard,' said Sarah giving a little bob.

'I'll leave her with you,' said Lady Barrington. 'Frau Schreiber will be here later.' They all waited for her to leave and then both Alice and Vicky cried 'Sarah' and ran around the table to grab a hand, each trying to pull her in the opposite direction.

'Let go girls,' Miss Hildyard said. 'You are about to pull poor Sarah apart.'

'And we thought you were never going to get here,' said Alice, her eyes crinkling into slits with her smile.

'Where's Lady Lyttleton?' said Sarah taking her outer garments off.

'She left last week to go look after her now motherless grand-children,' said Miss Hildyard. 'Now, do sit down and let us continue our lesson. Lady Barrington will not be pleased if she returns and you are not getting on with your lessons.'

'Yes Tilla,' said Alice sitting down next to Sarah.

'Lady B is not at all like Laddle,' whispered Vicky. 'She writes down everything we do and tells if we have been naughty. Then Mama gets very cross and punishes us. Papa doesn't. Laddle used to only report about what we ate and our health. We were all very sad when she left. Even the nurses and maids were in tears'

'She did like to give us castor oil every week, though,' said Alice making a face. Sarah did not know what castor oil she was, still she could tell that it was not nice. She did not understand why so many things that were not nice were supposed to be good.

Tilla lifted the big globe off the shelf and placed it on the table. 'We will continue our lesson until Frau Schreiber arrives.'

Sarah smiled, she liked geography lessons. It reminded her of evenings on *The Bonetta* with Papa Forbes. Sometimes he would bring out his globe, 'this is the world, our world,' he explained spinning it around to point out the places he had visited, telling her about the countries, the lakes, mountains, rivers, the peoples.

Sarah could not understand how the whole world could be squeezed around a spinning ball that size.

'How big is the world?' she had asked Papa Forbes.

'It is very big. If we started now to go all the way around in this ship it would take us over one hundred and eighty days, six months to get back to this point.'

'Sarah,' said Miss Hildyard, 'Can you find me the United Kingdom of Great Britain?'

'That's easy,' said Sarah pointing. 'There. It's an island shaped like a big, fat, funny shaped letter L.'

Both Vicky and Alice laughed.

'I never thought of it like that,' said Miss Hildyard, with a smile. 'Very good.'

'Miss Byles says that a lot of the world is coloured pink on maps, to show the countries that belong to Queen Victoria and Great Britain,' Sarah said.

'They all belong to Mama?' asked Alice.

'And when Mama dies, they will belong to Bertie,' said Vicky.

'To Bertie? All of it? Why him, you are older Vicky? Why can't we share?' said Alice staring at the globe.

'I thought you knew all this Alice,' said Miss Hildyard. 'Bertie is a boy. Everything goes to the boys, even if he is younger, before you girls.'

'Even baby Arthur?' asks Alice, frowning.

'Yes.'

'But why? Mama is girl and she is Queen.'

'Mama has no brothers,' said Vicky, shrugging her shoulders.

'But that is not fair,' said Sarah. 'What are the girls supposed to do then?

'They marry,' said Vicky.

'Or become companions and governesses,' said Tilla, putting the globe away.

Sarah shook her head. Were not girls as good as boys? Her thoughts were stopped by the tap, tap, tapping of a walking stick.

'Good morning Frau Schreiber,' said Miss Hildyard, gathering her books together.

'These stairs will be the death of me,' Frau Schreiber said, taking off layers of clothing. Her greying hair was pulled into a tight little bun at the nape of her neck. She was round and small and looked hot. Her cheeks were so red that even after half an hour in the cold schoolroom they never lost their colour. When she spoke, she reminded Sarah of Prince Albert, the words coming from the back of her throat, deep and round.

Once Tilla left the schoolroom, Frau Schreiber started the German class. She worked hard with Sarah going over the alphabet and numbers again and again, listening carefully

'*Gut, gut,* you have the ear.'

Even though Vicky and Alice were far more advanced and

could speak in full sentences, Frau Schreiber said that Sarah, after only one lesson, had a much better accent. Sarah stiffened, glancing quickly at the princesses. Were they cross hearing such praise for Sarah? She gave a sigh of relief when Vicky smiled and said, 'well done, Sarah.'

They all jumped up with the arrival of their next visitor and gave quick bobs.

Frau Schreiber struggled to get out of her chair 'Your Majesty,' she said, giving a rather wobbly bob.

'Do sit down Frau Schreiber,' said Queen Victoria walking across the room to sit in the armchair by the window. 'So how did my goddaughter do?'

'She is intelligent, Ma'am and very quick. Already her accent is coming along.'

'And the princesses?'

'Princess Victoria is a very *gut* student of German, learner of words and their meanings but she must train her ear to hear. Princess Alice also, she tries hard. Now I have too another good pupil.'

'Thank you, Frau Schreiber,' said the Queen before beckoning to Sarah. 'Come here child. Lady Phipps has shown me your other work, beautiful handwriting. It is arranged, you are to come once a week for German lessons when we are in residence.'

Sarah smiled. Alice clapped her hands. 'Now we will see you often.'

'That is settled,' said Queen Victoria before turning to Frau Schreiber. 'When do you start rehearsals for the play?'

'What is a play?' whispered Sarah to Alice.

'Have you never seen a play before, Sarah?' asked Queen Victoria.

'No, Ma'am.'

'The children are always doing charades and little plays. Last

Thursday they performed a little comédie, *Le Ballot* written by Madame Rollande.'

'It was a long piece, almost an hour, but *gut* they were,' said Frau Schrieber nodding.

'Yes, they were,' agreed Queen Victoria. 'I'm sure that you'll all be just as good in Herr von Kotzebue's *Das Hahnenschlag.'*

'Mama, can Sarah be in the play too?' asked Vicky. 'She has a month to learn it.'

'Oh yes, Mama, please,' said Alice, her face lighting up. 'It would be such fun.'

'Frau Schreiber?' said Queen Victoria, 'What do you say?'

'I do not see why not, Ma'am. The Phipps and Seymour children, they're going to be in it and they have no German. We will rehearse every week after our lesson. The time, it is enough.'

'Well, Sarah,' said Queen Victoria with a smile, 'each year the children and their friends put on a little play to celebrate Prince Albert and my wedding anniversary. Would you like to be in this year's play?'

Although not sure what a play was Sarah said, 'I would like to very much, thank you Mama Queen,' and threw her arms around Queen Victoria.

Vicky and Alice gasped, and stiffened. Vicky shook her head and Sarah stepped back quickly. Had she done something wrong? She had seen both Mabel and Emily do that to Mama Forbes when they were happy.

'Mama Queen? Is that what I am? I like it.' Queen Victoria got up and gave Sarah a pat on the head. 'Mama Queen. Hmm. I must tell Albert'

Alice whispered to Vicky, 'she hugged Mama and Mama was not cross?'

'Mama likes her,' said Vicky

'More than she likes us?' asked Alice in a quiet voice.

'No. I think it is just that Sarah is different.'

'I could never just hug Mama like that,' said Alice her voice giving a little wobble.

They watched Queen Victoria walk towards the door then she stopped. 'Mr Kean's company is bringing another one of Mr Shakespeare's plays, to amuse us, at the end of the month. This time it is the comedy, *As You Like It*. The older children plus the Phipps and Seymour children will be there too, Sarah. You must join us. Lady Phipps will arrange it. Theatrical performances are an important part of a child's education.'

'Will Mr Shakespeare come too?' asked Sarah.

Queen Victoria laughed, giving her cap, another shaking. 'I hope not. He has been dead for a very long time. Maybe his ghost will be there. He did write a lot about ghosts.'

'There's one in Hamlet is there not, Mama,' said Vicky quickly.

'Yes. Mrs Kean acted Ophelia's mad scene most touchingly, in the greatest perfection.'

'I did not like the ghost,' said Alice to Sarah. 'I covered my eyes.'

Ghosts? Sarah felt a cough rise into her throat and turned away trying to stop it spluttering out of her. She trembled with the effort.

'Hmm, that cough has been going on for too long. We must do something about it,' said Queen Victoria. 'It is stuffy indoors even though we do not paste the windows from September until May as they do in Russia. We must have fresh air. We'll walk to Frogmore to see my Mama after luncheon. If the ice on the pond is good, we might go ice-skating. Maybe Papa will join us if he's back from London.'

# Chapter 26

*He that loveth pureness of heart, For the grace of his lips the king shall be his friend*
Proverbs 22:11

## January 1851

Two days later Sarah was back at the castle for her first rehearsal. Vicky and Alice rushed over to her side as soon as she entered the music room.

'We must wait for the others. They'll come with their governess,' said Alice pulling a face. 'Miss Staithe is very strict. She scares me.'

'Leopold told me that if they're very naughty, she whips the boys with a cane,' said Bertie, joining them. 'We're punished but never caned.' Then he laughed loudly and added, 'once Vicky had her hands tied, and was kept in 'solitary confinement' for a whole afternoon.'

'Why? What did she do?' asked Sarah, worried that this too might be her fate if she did anything else wrong.

'Told a deliberate untruth,' said Bertie. 'She told our French governess, Madmoiselle Charrier, that Laddle had said she could wear her pink bonnet, but she was found out.'

'My hands were not tied tightly. Anyway, I stayed in my room and read,' said Vicky going to the pianoforte and played loudly.

Sarah shuddered and moved away not wanting to hear any more. She still had nightmares about caning, feeling every stroke, hearing every crack. Sometimes it was Papa Forbes holding the cane but then it would change to King Gezo. Sometimes it was a man with no face. She stood by the window and concentrated on the falling rain, pressing her lips shut to stop the cough that was trying to push itself out of her mouth. Her eyes felt prickly. She blinked and watched the rain run down the windowpanes.

Once everyone had arrived, Frau Schreiber tapped the floor with her stick. 'Vicky, the music-making, you must stop now,' she said. 'This year, the play it is set in a small German village. You all, villagers you will be, on a special festival day.'

'That does not sound like fun,' said Arthur his mouth set in a stubborn line. 'I thought that this year there'd be some fighting.'

'You wouldn't say that if your governess was here,' said Maria Phipps.

Frau Schreiber tapped her stick once more. 'Come, the rehearsal we must start, so please listen. Prince Alfred you will be Peter Lorch, a rich farmer, Princess Vicky, you are his wife Margarethe.'

'Why is Affie being the rich farmer?' stuttered Bertie, something he still did when he was angry. He threw a cushion at his brother but Affie ducked and the cushion hit Charles. 'I should be the farmer. I am older.'

'Stop being so horrid Bertie,' said Vicky. 'You can't always be first.'

'I am first.'

'No, you are not. I am first.'

'But I will be king,' stuttered Bertie, jumping up, his hands clenched.

They all held their breath for when Bertie was displeased, he could behave very badly. Sarah had been shocked the first time she saw him in a rage over mutton broth. He'd refused to eat the meal of mutton broth because, he said, it was fatty with too little meat. When he was given nothing else to eat, he screamed and stamped his foot, kicked and scratched. In case he hurt himself or one of the younger children Lady Barrington had called for a footman to hold him down, until tired out, as ordered by the Queen. He lay down panting, for almost an hour. Later, when Dr Clark arrived, he ordered red meat to be cut out of meals for a week because, he said, it was dangerous and overheated the blood.

Frau Schreiber spoke quickly now. 'For you, Prince Bertie, there is something special. You will be Fritz, a poor peasant boy who must sell his only possession, a cock-bird, to provide food for his starving mother. You see this way your bird can sing not only for the villagers in the play but also to the guests of your Mama and Papa. They will see how clever you are to train the bird so *gut*.'

Bertie smiled, jumped up and spun around shouting 'Gimpel, will sing, Gimpel will sing. I'll go and fetch him. He must be here.' He dashed off.

'Come back,' said Vicky, but he was gone. She flopped back down. 'He is so annoying.'

'He will be back,' said Frau Schreiber. 'The rest of you are the other villagers. It is more than just a *tableau vivant*. You will all do the dancing and the singing of some German songs.' She waved some sheet music at them. 'Her Majesty and Prince Albert, they like the music of Mr Mendelssohn so his *Leider ohne worte* we will have.'

Sarah frowned. What was a *tableau vivant*? Before she could ask though, Vicky took the music sheets and ran over to the piano-forte and started to play. The music was light and fast. Although always in trouble with Mrs Anderson because she disliked practicing her scales or five-finger exercises, Vicky was a good pianist. Sarah wished she could play as well as her.

'Is Vicky doing the music?' asked Helena.

'How can she? She's in the play as Margarethe,' said Alice. 'Sarah could play it, Frau Schreiber. I'm sure she can.'

'Sarah is not going to be a villager and Dr Barker will be playing the music,' said Prince Albert from the doorway.

Everyone jumped up and there was a lot of curtseying and bowing with a jumble of 'Your highness' and 'Papa, Papa.'

'Mama, said that Sarah was going to be in it,' said Alice, taking hold of Sarah's hand.

'We can't leave her out, Papa,' said Vicky coming to stand on the other side of Sarah.

Although she'd never been in a play, the thought of not being in this one brought back the feeling of being on the outside. Sarah bit her lip and looked down, not wanting to catch anyone's eyes and see their pitying looks.

Prince Albert smiled, 'Do not worry. Sarah will be part of the show. Frau Schreiber and I have made some changes to the story. Sarah will not be a villager but a visitor to be entertained at the festival. She sees Fritz and his bird. It reminds her of when she was a captive, so she gives Fritz some money for the bird and releases it. The villagers sing and dance. She joins in, happy that she had been able to set the bird free. She does not know that its wings have been clipped. Later she finds the bird, broken and dead and she is devastated.'

'Oh Papa, that is a lovely, but such a sad story,' said Alice with a sniff.

'Why does the bird have to die?' whispered Sarah.

✩✩✩

*Thursday 31ˢᵗ January 1851, Winkfield Place*

> *I go to Windsor Castle every afternoon to rehearse. I know all my words starting with 'Oh, die arme Junge'. Frau Schreiber says that I speak it very well. Mama Queen will be pleased. Next week we will learn the dances and the songs. Today there*

*is no rehearsing, Tonight I see my first play, 'As You like It'.*
*I hope I like it. I have a new pink silk dress. Queen Victoria*
*ordered I should have it. Mama says that although I live with*
*them it is Her Majesty who is my guardian and provides for*
*me. I will thank her, my mother, my Mama Queen.*

✿✿✿✿

That evening the Rubens Room looked very different from the last time Sarah had been there. Many chairs had been brought in and arranged in rows facing the temporary stage set up at one end of the room. The clock with the organ that played beautiful music had been moved to a shelf too high for her to reach. She liked its wooden case with carvings of the sea both rough and calm that reminded her of *The Bonetta*.

Sarah sat with the other children, on low stools at the front and spread out her new dress, glad that she was not wearing white like the princesses. It was the first time Sarah had been in a room with so many people. Her eyes darted around, wanting to take it all in. She had to remember everything, so she could tell Mabel and Lily later. She wished they could have been there too, but they had not been invited.

*As You Like It* might have been a comedy play to the others but to Sarah it was soon more than a play. Although she didn't understand a lot of the words, she recognised the actions, rhythms and emotions. She was quickly drawn in and leaned forward to watch the story unfold. She did not laugh with the others. For her the forest had not brought protection but fear. How could Oliver be so horrible to his brother Orlando? When Rosalind and her cousin Celia left court to find refuge in the forest, they became Fatmata and herself.

Suddenly Salimatu was back. 'Stop them,' she shouted in

Sarah's ear. 'Tell them that even if she dresses as a boy, they're still not safe.'

Sarah shook her head. No, no, no. She wanted Salimatu gone. She did not want her at the castle, this was Sarah's place.

But Salimatu was right. When Oliver came on stage to tell of Orlando's bravery and his fight with the lioness, Sarah felt her heart pounding. Once again, she was in the forest, held close by Fatmata, listening to the roar of lions, waiting to be attacked. When Rosalind collapsed at the news of the lioness tearing at Orlando's arm, Sarah jumped up and ran to her.

'*Awọn kiniun yio pa wa,*' Salimatu screamed through Sarah. 'Quick, we must go before the lion gets here.'

But no one moved. Instead, they burst out laughing. Were they not afraid?

'There are no lions here, Sarah' said Lady Barrington, leading her off the stage area.

'But there is. It has attacked Orlando,' said Sarah struggling to get away. 'It's just out there. We must leave this place.'

'It's a play, Sarah,' said Alice, taking her hand. 'It's not real.'

Sarah blinked and looked around her. She was back in the Rubens Room. The stage was there, the people were there, the fire was blazing in the fireplace. Now she wished she could run away from the staring eyes of the Queen and all her guests.

'Lions? The poor thing. She thinks she's back in Africa, Ma'am,' said one of the ladies-in-waiting.

'I do not suppose you can get the bush out of them no matter how much you change their outward appearance,' said a gentleman sitting near the Queen, his white moustache fluttering as though waving the words out of his mouth. 'You must have a painting done of her before she becomes a proper little English girl, if that is possible. Octavius Oakley is extremely good at painting gypsies, and those kinds of people.'

'Well, Lord Carlisle, we will show you,' said Her Majesty, gesturing for Sarah to come and sit at her feet, 'My ward is personable, intelligent and quick to learn. We are sure that she will use the education she is gaining to help change the ways of her people.' She patted Sarah's head and Sarah who had seen the Queen pat her dogs just like that, tried not to flinch from the touch. She was not a pet and was tired of people feeling they could touch and comment on her 'springy' hair. How would they like it if she was forever commenting on their sharp nose or crooked teeth?

'We cannot relax our efforts against slavery, until we have forever, put an end to a state of things so repugnant to the spirit of Christianity, and the best feelings of our nature,' said Prince Albert.

It was only when Queen Victoria said, 'shall we carry on with the play, my dear?' that they all realised that the actors were still standing on stage, frozen in their last position. She nodded to the players and the play continued. Sarah did not look up. She and Salimatu did not want to see what else was going to happen in the forest. In the darkened room she did not bother to wipe away the tears, as the others laughed at the songs, the dances, the happy ending. She knew that it had come to an end when she heard clapping muffled by gloves.

'Mr Wigan was perfect, the Keanes excellent and the Keeleys quite delightful,' said Queen Victoria.

'Very well acted, with but two exceptions,' said Prince Albert.

'Still as an evening of entertainment I thought it rather heavy, with all its interruptions,' said the Duchess of Kent, glancing at Sarah.

'Oh, Mama,' said Queen Victoria, 'she's never been to a play before. She will learn.'

What? What else do I have to learn, thought Sarah. Will it never end?

# CHAPTER 27

Idà kì í lọ kídà má bọ
*The sword never departs without returning*

# 1846

The sound in my head becomes a drum beat that seems to lift me up, up, up, to the top of the tallest tree and I look down on all of us walking to we know not where. If only I could reach up and part the sky and let the gods see our plight. I must find a way. I begin to hum a lament, a plea that Maluuma used to sing.

'What's that you are humming,' asks Minata.

'It's a funeral song,' says Khadijatu who is now tied to Tenneh. 'Why are you humming that? Are you saying we're all going to meet our ancestors soon?'

I do not answer; instead I sing. It is the only way I can make one step in front of the other. As the song washes over her Khadijatu, in a low voice, begins to sing too. Minata joins in too even though doesn't know the words.

In the fading light, we come to a big clearing, a compound. There are several huts and two circular pens made with sticks so tall they would have pushed past the roof of Jaja's hut. The men open the gate and push us into the empty pen. On the other side of the clearing is a larger pen, full of many boys and men.

The women shout and scream, calling out the names of

husbands, sons, brothers and fathers. A few hear the voices of their men even if they cannot see them in the dark of the night. I call for Amadu again and again until no sound can leave my mouth but there is no answer. Far into the night there are shouts and calls, crying and wailing, but I am silent. I have sung my way to under-standing. No Salimatu to look after now, no sister to carry on my back, so this is it, I am going to escape. I will flee into forest, and although the marks I made as we journeyed will be gone by now, the gods will lead me to find my sister and my brother and return home.

In the dark, while Minata sleeps I bring out the white handle knife still hidden in my wrap, the knife that had killed my father. I cut at the rope that ties me to Minata, and to Santigie.

The rope is tough and the knife small. My pulling and tugging wakes Minata.

'What are you doing?' she whispers

'I have to go. This is my chance. Look, the gate is not locked. It will open if I push it. There are no guards near us. If I can get away before first light has pushed away the darkness, I can hide until you all leave here. The men won't search for me too long.'

'We're not leaving here at sunrise. We wait here until Santigie says we can go on. Only the gods know when or where they'll take us after that. There are guards around even if we can't see them.'

'Well, if I can't go tonight,' I say putting the knife away, 'I won't cut the rope all the way tonight, but from now on, every night I will cut it a little. When I see another chance, I will break off and run back into the forest.'

By first light, before the sun is awake, many people are moving in the pen. Then I see it and I gasp. Water. Water so far out that to try to see the other side hurts my eyes. It is clear and bright and many different shades of blue. The water moves and shifts all at the same time, never stopping, never still. Where it rolls on to the sand the water foams up just like the dog that had run wild in the village barking and snapping because evil spirits had entered it.

'Minata, look,' I call trying not to pull at the rope. 'Come quick.'

In the middle of all that water is the biggest canoe I have ever seen. It is almost as big as a mountain and the sticks pushing up in the middle, with cloths hanging off them, are taller than any tree in Kwa-le forest. The canoe rocks, moving up and down, but it goes nowhere. It lies there waiting, waiting.

'The white man's ship has come,' the men in the other pen shout. 'They'll be taking us away soon.'

The wailing and crying from the women rise higher and louder as they watch many men carrying food and other goods in baskets to the water's edge, get into smaller canoes and row out to the big canoe. We know now that soon we will all be sold and taken away from our land and our people.

'The time has come,' I say to Minata. 'I'm not going in the white devil's canoe. I have to escape today.'

'Fatmata, Fatu, Fatu.'

I hear my name and turn around and there running across the clearing is Amadu, the water he is carrying in a gourd splashes all over him and onto the ground.

'Amadu, Amadu my brother, you're here,' I scream, pushing my hands through the gap between the sticks to grab at my brother. '*Odudua*, I praise you, I thank you. My eyes can once more look upon my brother. Ayee!' I hold him tight and our tears wash other's faces. 'I called and called your name when we got here but you did not answer,' I sob. 'I thought that you must have journeyed to the ancestors like Madu and Jaja.'

'Ayee,' says Amadu, sinking to the ground. 'Madu and Jaja have journeyed? Ayee, Ayee.' He gathers a handful of dust and covers his head with it. He reaches out and takes hold of my hand. 'And our sister, Salimatu, she is well?'

I bow my head and cry, 'Santigie sold her to the Moors. We can't let the white devils take us away.' I pull him close and whisper. 'I have a knife. I'm cutting my rope. When I tell you to run, do it.'

Amadu shakes his head, 'You won't be able to get away. Santigie has many guards here in the compound, near the forest and down by the water's edge. We've been here many sun circles. I've seen them.'

'I'll find a way, don't I always?'

Just then one of the guards cracks his whip and pulls Amadu away from the fence. I sink down to the ground but jump up when Santigie and Jamilla come out of one of the huts, wearing the white devil's clothes.

'Soon you all will be on your way and I on mine,' he says, rubbing his hands.

As he speaks a *wasi-ngafa*, a white devil, comes towards us. I feel a watery sickness in my bowels; numbness spreads over me and stops my feet. I am face to face with a white devil. Many of the women cover their face or turn away. They do not want to look on the face of a devil. I stare at him though. He is not white, not like the clouds in the sky, he is more like a pig, before it rolls in dirt. He is almost as tall as Jaja and looks strong. His thin stand-up nose is ugly, not flattened with wide nostrils like ours, his lips thin and straight pulls back to show teeth that are not orange from chewing kola-nut but black. He has long hair on his head and hair on his face. His smell is strong as he passes by me. But most frightening are his eyes, green as grass. Devils have grass coloured eyes. That's what Madu used to say. I make sure that I do not look into his devil eyes.

The white devil said something in a strange voice.

'Yes, this is all,' says Santigie.

The men who came with the white devil put down the boxes and baskets they are carrying and Jamilla immediately opens them.

I can't see what is in every one of them, but I can see that one is full of cowrie shells, the other with guns.

The white devil says something else to Santigie who says, 'stand up so he can have a good look at you all.'

'Just tell me how much you want,' says the white devil in bad Kocumber talk, then he changes to his tongue and I cannot understand what he is saying.

One man seems to speak the white man's talk and shouts out to him. The white man turns and listens and then he laughs.

'Leye, what did you say?' the other men ask.

'I told him that I'm a free man and he should let me go. I was captured when I was a child, taken away across the big sea, got my freedom, came back to my people and now I'm tied up again. I know what waits for me where we are going.'

Bureh cracks his whip and shouts, 'stand, stand up.'

I hang on to my almost cut rope, the time is not right yet. The white devil looks in our mouths, touches our bodies in a way no man has ever touched me before. I want to scream or bite his hand, but I do nothing, waiting for the right moment to escape.

There is shouting from above and three men come running down the hill, their guns at the ready.

'Patrollers,' shouts one of Santigie's men. 'The patrollers are coming.'

'Where?' asks Santigie, snatching the gun from one of the men. 'How far away?'

'Their ship is coming fast round the bend.'

The white devil-man knows what is happening because he makes a sign to his men. They quickly open the other boxes and Jamila checks them.

'We've got to get out of here,' says Santigie. 'No time for bargaining. Give me what we agreed and take them away before the patrollers stop you.' Then he shouts to the guards, 'yoke them up.'

The guards come running with long sticks and ropes. They put the men one behind the other and yoke them around the neck. Everyone is screaming, crying and when I see them grab Amadu to yoke him I know that the time has come. There is confusion all around and without being seen, I get out the knife and hack at the almost cut rope.

The rope snaps. I am free. I run.

'Now, Amadu, run, run.' I scream. He does not wait for me to repeat my command, he runs. The man holding Amadu turns around and tries to grab hold of me but I bend low and keep on running.

Santigie sees what is happening and shouts, 'Stop, stop them.'

The white devil is shouting, 'They are mine. Catch them.'

We keep running. Others also are trying to use the confusion to get away. The guards don't know who to go for first. Santigie fires his gun but he hits the tree to my right. He fires again and this time I feel a sting. I look at my arm and it is bleeding. I hear him scream, I look back to see Tenneh attacking him with his knife that I had dropped in my escape. He knocks her off, points his gun and Tenneh drops like a coconut.

'Tenneh,' I scream and without thinking, I run back and try to lift her up.

'Chief Dauda,' she says, closes her eyes and starts her journey to the ancestors. Jamilla grabs me by my arm that is still bleeding and pulls. The shock and pain knock me to the ground. I writhe in pain. Even as they tie me up, I scream and fight. Momo pushes some cloth into my mouth to shut me up. My tears flow from silenced cries.

✦✦✦✦

Trees line the narrow path to the water. I am yoked and my arms are tied. I can't struggle even if I had the strength to do so. The guards push us on to the sand that moves under my feet, pushing between my toes. I drag and slide my feet, leaving my marks on the sand. I look behind me and can see the trees sway and the leaves shake. I see some monkeys screeching, jumping from branch to branch. My heart beats fast. Is that Jabeza come to say goodbye? My eyes let the tears fall for I know where I have been even if I do not know where I am going.

The water's evil spirit foams and rushes forward to wash away any marks that could show I have been there. At the water's edge our yokes are removed and tied by the legs we are thrown into the canoes.

The men pull at the oars and we are rowed out fast to the white devil's boat in the middle of the water. The canoes full of slaves jump and smash around in the water as if laughing at us, playing, happy. Water splashes on my face. I lick my lips and spit for it is salty. How can anyone drink that?

The white devil's boat is like some huge animal rocking and shaking, hungry waiting to be fed, to swallow us. It would need a lot of people to fill it up. The nearer we get to the canoe, the bigger it becomes. The smell coming from the boat is so bad it hit me in the face and almost stops my breathing. The nearer we got the stronger the smell. It is like the stench behind the huts, when Madu was collecting piss in big pots for dyeing the cloths. But this is worse, many times worse. This stink is not just of piss but also of emptied bowels by all the people of more than ten villages.

I stare into every canoe searching for Amadu but cannot see him. Did he get away? Has Amadu been sent to meet his ancestors? My tears, mixed with salty water, sting my eyes. There is no chance of escaping now. The pain inside fills every part of me. I have no space left to feel the outside pain.

# CHAPTER 28

*So that thou incline thine ear unto wisdom, and apply thine heart to understanding*
Proverbs 2:2

## February 1851

*Saturday, 2nd February 1851, Winkfield Place*
*I will not think of As You Like It, or devils, or ghosts or forests and all they hold. I do not belong there. So many names, so many me. Why can't I be new? No more, Aina, or Salimatu or Slave, or Captive. I want to leave them all behind. I am Sarah Forbes Bonetta now. Isn't that enough?*

The morning was bitterly cold. It had snowed through the night, but by the time Sarah arrived at the castle it had stopped, and a pale sun was out. Vicky came running down the stairs followed by Alice.

'Frau Schreiber is waiting for us in the music room,' said Alice. 'The costumes have arrived.'

'See,' said Frau Schreiber, 'our traditional Bavarian *tracht* costumes, for the girls and for the boys, *lederhosen* and *hosenträger*. You will all look very handsome, very German. Very *gut*. Later we try them on.'

She held up a full skirt trimmed with ribbons over its many petticoats and shook it so hard it seemed to dance. Vicky and Alice pounced on the pile of skirts, giggling and pushing wanting the best for themselves.

'Which one is mine?' asked Sarah, imagining the skirt of her costume flaring out.

'Miss Sarah yours is not here. Prince Albert wants you to wear your African costume. Mr Oakley has been called to make of you this watercolour in it.'

Sarah frowned. Did she have a costume in Africa? What was it?

'Alice and I are going down to Frogmore to the ice,' said Vicky.

'And when Vicky is having her lesson in ice-skating, Mama and I will have a drive in one of the ice chairs,' added Alice.

Sarah's eyes widened. Why was she not going with them? She would have loved to learn how to skate on the ice. She remembered the fun she had had with Mabel and Emily when she learned to make snow angels.

'I'm going to learn to skate?'

'Oh no,' said Lady Phipps who had just entered. 'Mr Oakely is going to paint you now. I'll take you to him.'

'Maybe next time,' Alice called out, hurrying after Vicky.

'Maybe next time,' repeated Sarah, her lips trembling.

❁❁❁

When Sarah and Lady Phipps arrived at the room where Her Majesty had her painting class with Mr Landseer, the windows and the door to the garden were wide open, and Sarah shivered. A man in a long white coat, stood in front of an easel. His grey hair stuck out in every direction; his wiry, unkempt beard fluttered as he spoke.

'Ah ha, my subject.' His hand was soft and cold as he took Sarah's face firmly in his hand and twisted it to the right and left. 'Humph, good bone structure.'

'I will send down one of the maids,' said Lady Phipps as she left.

Mr Oakley waved at the wooden screen in one corner. 'Get changed over there then I can put you into the frame.'

Sarah hurried behind the screen eager to see what her costume looked like. Would it be red or blue or even green? How wide was the skirt? She stopped short, for there were but two lengths of cloth. One rough woven in white and dark red strips, the other pure white like a burial cloth. Sarah backed away.

'Don't touch it,' screamed Salimatu, there once more.

'The costume is not there,' Sarah said to Mr Oakley, busy flicking paint at the canvas.

He looked up and frowned. 'It's there. Wrap the cloths around you. Is not that what you do? Quick, quick I need the light.'

Slowly Sarah stepped behind the screen smoothed down her grey and black woollen dress before wrapping just the stripped cloth around herself and stepped out. Mr Oakley looked up, dropped his paint brush and strode across the room.

'For goodness sakes,' he said pulling at the cloth so that Sarah spun round like a top, 'you must take your clothes off. How can I paint a Dahomean captive in a woollen dress?' He threw the piece of material at Betty, the nursery maid, who had just entered, and barked, 'get her into this.'

'Yes sir.' She bobbed a quick curtsy. 'Come, Miss Sarah.'

They scuttled behind the screen. Sarah stood still while she was stripped of dress, petticoat, hose, shoes, even pantaloons. Betty wrapped the white piece around Sarah's waist and tried to cover her legs. It was not wide enough. White. Sarah's body shrank from it.

'Take it off before he kills us,' cried Salimatu.

Betty threw the other material over Sarah's right shoulder and pulled it across her body.

'Is this how you wear it over there?' she asked, shaking her head. 'I don't know why he wants you to wear this, in this weather.'

Sarah stepped from behind the screen and stood still, head hanging. Mr Oakley pulled and tugged at the materials fussing with this fold and that, before passing some brass bangles, two bead necklaces and a pair of drop earrings to the maid.

'Put those on her.'

Sarah had worn earrings before but never like these, long and delicate like iron lace. Betty tried but could not get the earrings through the blocked holes on Sarah's earlobes.

'Try again,' said Mr Oakley

Betty nodded and pushed one, then the other through quickly. Sarah yelped.

'There, it's over,' Mr Oakley said, dabbed at the spot of blood that trickled down her neck, with his paint rag but did not notice her tears.

He stepped back and eyed her. 'That will have to do,' he said before turning to Betty, 'You may go now. I'll ring the bell if I need anything else.'

Sarah wanted to beg Betty to take her away or at least to stay but the words did not slide out of her dry mouth.

'Come,' said Mr Oakley. 'Sit here.' He perched her on a high stool. In her left hand he put a large broom made from palm tree spines. She had last used such a broom to sweep the yard in the slave quarters of Abomey. Next to her on a low stool was a small woven basket, the kind Fatmata had once told her their mother made. Then he knelt at her feet. She heard him mutter himself, 'this should do it.' The cold iron manacles he put around her ankles rested on old scars.

'Ayee,' screamed Salimatu in Sarah's ear. 'I told you don't trust them.'

Sarah's heart pounded so loud she was surprised that the painter man did not hear it. She coughed. He glared. She tried to stop but the cough burst out of her, again and again, so that her body rocked.

'Please stay still,' he ordered. 'I have to catch the light before it goes completely.'

The wintery sun faded, the snow darkened with the shadows of the trees, Mr Oakley's brushes raced across the canvas changing white to many colours. Sarah grew tired and hungry and cold, very cold. She tried to sit still but could feel herself swaying.

✧✧✧

Sarah opened her eyes. She was in bed but not in the room she shared with Mabel and Emily. This room was large with white and gold walls, long golden yellow curtains, a roaring fire, ornaments on the mantelpiece.

'Can you hear me Sarah? I'm Doctor Clark.'

She tried to sit up. Her head felt as heavy as a coconut. She lay back coughing. It hurt to breathe. How long had she been lying in bed, five minutes, five hours, five days? Sarah did not know. She looked at the doctor. He was tall and everything about him was long and sharp, his face, sunken cheeks, eyes, his thin drooping waxed moustache.

'Betty, give her some water,' he said.

The water filled her mouth and trickled down her throat, cool and soothing.

'Now, stick your tongue out for me.' His voice was gruff, and it hurt her ear. He bent down and looked into her mouth, nodded his head, checked his pocket watch, twirled it around, pulled the gold chain across his round stomach and tucked it back into his waist coat pocket. 'Good, good. She can get out of bed for a while and receive visitors,' he said, and left.

'Where am I?' Sarah asked Betty. The words hurt her throat.

'You're in the yellow bedroom, near Her Majesty's sitting room. She wanted you close. It's been three days since you fell off the painter man's stool and hit your head. I'm sorry I left you Miss. He should never had made you stand in the cold for over six hours with no food! But don't worry, you'll be fine. You just need to take it slowly,' the maid said, putting a tartan rug around Sarah's shoulder before leading her to the armchair by the fire. 'Rest here, I'll be back.'

Although she was hot sitting by the fire, Sarah pulled the rug close to cover her white nightgown. She did not want to see the whiteness on her body. The fire drew Sarah in, and she stared at the flames flickering from yellows to mauves and blue with touches of red. It grew brighter, stronger, hotter as she looked right into its centre and saw things from the past, things that she did not know she knew. Fire surrounded everything, palm-roofed huts, trees, bushes, men, women, children, everything. And there, in the centre of a small black circle, a blackness deeper than the centre of night. Sarah saw herself, her other-self, mouth opened as in a scream.

'Salimatu?' she whispered shrinking away.

'You stared too long,' said Salimatu

'But you stared back.' Sarah felt she could not breathe and clutched her *gri-gri* now around her neck again. She had heard Salimatu's whisper in her ear many times but now she could see her. Sarah became lost in the silence of the space between them.

'You look like me,' Sarah said at last.

'No, you look like me. Remember I was first. Aina, child born with a cord around her neck, a veil over her face, who became Salimatu, who became you, Sarah.'

'What do you want?' Sarah asked, her voice trembling.

'You. The time has come. We must go. They're waiting.'

They? The ancestors? Was this what Salimatu had come for? Sarah wanted to jump away from herself, but she seemed stuck in the chair.

'We do not belong here,' said Salimatu stretching out her hand.

'I do. I'm the "Black Princess",' said Sarah. Her voice, louder than she had intended, seem to bounce around the room. 'I'm not going back with you.'

'I cannot go without you. I've waited too long.'

'I'm not going into the fire,' cried Sarah, shrinking further into the chair. She could still smell the smoke and the burning. Everything was now a sea of darkness with nothing beyond.

❖❖❖❖

Sarah was back in bed when Her Majesty came to visit. Betty almost dropped the bottle of medicine she was holding and gave a curtsey. Sarah discovered that one cannot curtsy if you are lying in bed. She nodded instead and pulled herself up into a sitting position. 'Good morning, Mama Queen,'

'Your Majesty,' said Betty and quickly brought a chair to the bedside.

'Thank you. Betty. You may go and fetch the doctor. And please shut the door.'

'Yes Ma'am.' Betty gave a bob and backed her way out.

'Good morning Sarah. Dr Clark says you are much better and able to have visitors now,' said Queen Victoria. 'I see that my children got here before me.'

'Yes, Ma'am, the Princesses brought me Mr Lear's Book of Nonsense to cheer me up,' she said, picking the book up from the side table.

'Ah, Mr Lear. Prince Albert used to read the rhymes to Vicky when she was little. She loved them.'

'I like this one best,' Sarah said, turning the pages and showing it to Queen Victoria. She took the book from Sarah and read.

'*There was a Young Lady whose chin,*
*Resembled the point of a pin;*
*So she had it made sharp,*
*And purchased a harp,*
*And played several tunes with her chin.*'

'It is funny is it not your Majesty?'

'Yes, it is indeed,' said Queen Victoria laughing, her muslin cap dancing as she nodded her head in agreement. 'Mr Lear does write exceedingly funny rhymes.'

'I would not like having a nose that long. My nose is flat. It could not play anything. When I go back to the schoolroom, I am going to use the globe to find all the countries that are mentioned in the book. Maybe one day I can go to all those places.'

'Maybe you will but for now you must stay here and get better.'

Sarah opened her mouth to say something but instead a cough spluttered out. The more she tried to stop a the harder she coughed. Queen Victoria leaned over and handed her a glass of water. She watched Sarah take several sips.

'We must do something about that cough of yours,' she said frowning. 'It has gone on for quite a while, has it not?'

'Yes Ma'am,' whispered Sarah.

Queen Victoria took Sarah's hand. 'You poor thing. Standing in the freezing cold all that time. You will never have to wear something like that again. I promise.'

'Thank you, Mama Queen. But what about the play?'

'Do not worry about the play. It is not for a few days yet. If you're well enough to take part, you can wear whatever you like.'

'A Bavarian skirt with lots of petticoats?'

Queen Victoria patted Sarah's hand. 'If that is what you want.'

Sarah sighed and laid back. She glanced at Queen Victoria, opened her mouth as if to say something then shut it.

'Dr Clark informs me that when your fever was high, you were delirious. Sometimes you spoke in a different language and sounded frightened. Is your memory coming back?'

Sarah bit her lip. She did not want to tell Mama Queen any of what she had seen in the fire. 'I remember nothing,' she said.

'And what about the sister you wanted to find? You have forgotten her?'

Sarah blinked rapidly. Why was Her Majesty asking her that now? She pulled the sheet up to her chin and held it tight. 'Have you have found Fatmata, Mama Queen?'

'No child,' Queen Victoria said in a soft voice. 'I'm afraid, the Admiralty has not been able to find out anything about her. She might have been taken to the Indies or America. Or been rescued by our patrollers and living in Freetown. We will continue to make enquiries. But we may never find her. Your home is here now. I am glad that you are settled with the Forbes.'

Sarah shut her eyes so that Mama Queen would not see the tears threatening to fall as she tries to hold back Salimatu's cough.

'I see Bertie has left Gimpel with you.' Queen Victoria said pointing to the bullfinch in its golden birdcage. 'He will cheer you up.'

Almost as though it knew they were discussing him the bird lifted his head and gave a soft little song. Sarah did not look at the bird.

'It was very kind of Bertie to bring me Gimpel, but I do not like seeing it in the cage.'

'Bullfinches are bred in captivity you know. They are popular cage birds. Gimpel can be taught to imitate any bird's flute or whistle. That is amusing, is it not?'

'I suppose so, Ma'am, but isn't it sad that it has to stay in one place and cannot be free to fly everywhere?' said Sarah.

'Even if you open the cage door it will not know that it is free to go. It will fly around and come back to its cage, to what it knows. If the bird flies away it will probably be killed.' Queen Victoria's voice softened. 'The cage keeps him safe. Remember that, little Sally.'

Sarah said nothing. She could not argue with the Queen, could she? But still she thought, wouldn't birds rather fly free even if it meant they might die?

Queen Victoria patted Sarah's head. Her hand sank into the hair. 'So soft. Like wool.'

The door opened, and Doctor Clark rushed in. 'Your Majesty,' he said bending down as low as his stomach would allow.

'I see your patient is indeed much improved.'

'For the moment, Ma'am,' he said. 'She is not robust. Her chest is weak, and I do not see it improving in this weather. She needs warmer climes, I am afraid.'

Queen Victoria bowed her head, a frown knitting her brow. 'I see. Come we will discuss this in my parlour.' She got up and stared hard at Sarah. Something about the look made Sarah's stomach tighten. But all Queen Victoria said was '*Au revoir*, little Sally.'

'*Au revoir*, Your Majesty,' said Sarah.

Although they moved away, Sarah heard every word of their continued conversation.

'Other doctors may have a different opinion, but this is my belief, Ma'am. These people are not hardy; they are not used to our weather, so they wither away. This is not the place for the poor child, Ma'am.'

At the door Queen Victoria turned and gave a little smile. Sarah stroked the *gri-gri* beneath her white nightgown and pinched herself, hard.

✿✿✿✿

*Friday 7th February 1851, Winkfield Place.*

*I am back at Winkfield Place. Everyone is happy to see me, but I am sad. Mama Queen cannot find my sister. I am never going to see Fatmata again. I know that now. But am I safe here? Is this really my home? I feel like a bird in a cage. I am afraid. What is to become of me? Salimatu is no longer a part of me. I am now Sarah, the 'Black Princess'.*

# PART TWO

PART TWO

# CHAPTER 29

*Dey bless fa true, dem people wa ain hab no hope een deysef,*
*cause God da rule oba um*
Blessed are the poor in spirit:
for theirs is the kingdom of heaven
Matthew 5:3

## March 1851

My breasts hurt. They are heavy, full of milk. I know I must go back to Missy Clara's cabin and feed her baby before he starts screaming and fussing, but I stay on the top deck. The smoke has floated away, and the steamship is going forward under full sail. The smell of the sea, the touch of the wind on my face feels good. Henry-Francis is three months old and his need will ease my sore breasts, but it will not ease the want I have to hold my own baby. My Jessy is but six months old and yet they made me leave her behind with Old Rachael to be fed on pap. I learned early, that this is what it means to be a slave, our children taken away from us before they are weaned, while we are sent back to work to the fields, the kitchen, the house, with full leaky breasts.

True, I've not been put to work in the rice field, yet. I know to keep out of Lemrick's way. That overseer is even more in with the devil than the missus and that's saying something. Still can't think about the time he strings up and whip Sam-boy until the flesh hang off his back 'cause he'd tried to run away. Old Rachael put salve on him for over a week, but though his back healed it was criss-cross marked like sorrow trails. We all know that only lead to pain

249

in the soul and anger in the heart. And when Sam-boy later tried to run away again, that devil-man make us all watch him chop off the boy's foot. Then Massa sell him. Teach us all a lesson, Lemrick said, and he laughed.

It is not easy being a house slave though, the work never stops. If you in the rice fields, you have the evenings in the quarters, Sundays to look after a small vegetable plot, to visit your children, to sleep. But for us there is no day off. We still must cook and feed everyone, look after the house, the children, jump to Missus' call quick, or you get a slap, a pinch, a whipping.

And even at night there is no peace.

That first time, I call on Maluuma, Madu, the ancestors, I fight and bite and scream, but I can't get away. No one come.

When I start to swell, Missus beat me. I scream long and loud till the Massa pulls her off me. Back in the kitchen, my clothes half torn of my back, Ma Leah shakes her head and says, 'the mother is hard wood, the father is glass.' She talks like Maluuma, and says words that slip and slide, words you must peel like an onion to get the true meaning. As for Old Rachael, she says, 'Chile you don't learn? Been here a year now. I thought you know how to take care of this business.'

Where were they when I cried out and begged for mercy? Where, when he came again and again? Why did nobody stop him and say she has but fifteen years, when he tells me 'you're my property to do with as I like?' In the end, I could fight no more, and I make my body just lie there. He don't know, he don't care that I'm gone into me, to that place he can never reach.

Nine months later, who is there to stop me when my hand covers the mouth and nose, on a small face? Who sits with me that night as he flies off to the ancestors? Who knows that though they called him Anthony, I name him Amadu? Who hears me weeping, wailing deep in the inside of me, telling the ancestors I done wrong? The pain never goes away. It is stitched to my soul.

When Massa refuse to sell me down river the third time I swell, Missus Jane made him give me to Missy Clara as a wedding gift. In Talaremba they give beads, cowrie, goats, sheep, at a wedding, here they give people. But I keep my soul. Although I leave Burnham Plantation and go to Oakwood that still not enough for Missus Jane. After I birth Jessy, whom I named Jabeza, my third child, Missus want me even further away.

Missus Jane hates me and my children, Lewis, the one I call Lansana, and Jessy/Jabeza, they're proof, you see, of what her husband's doing. There be no mistaking that he my children's pappy. Nobody says anything though, not the Missus, not his white daughters, or his white sons. His friends and neighbours, they don't ask Massa William why his young slave three times birthed children all looking like his white children. They all busy doing the same, making more slaves for their own plantation. The wives shut their mouths and fill their bellies with hate.

The other slaves on the plantation, they don't say anything either. They've seen it all before. Some shake their heads, some laugh, some suck their teeth when I pass by, and some like Phibe say, 'you lucky, you work in the big house, not the rice fields where you be whipped for anything by Lemrick. You give Massa ten live children and he set you free, they say. You better be careful though for Missus will get you.'

She's right. Missus Jane's got me. I know this taking me across the water is her doing.

Missy Clara born Henry-Francis just three months after I born Jessy so I look after them two together at Oakwood Plantation. Missus Jane can't stomach the fact that the babies have the same blood 'cause one day she come visit her daughter and find both of them, my Jessy and Henry-Francis, looking almost like twins, at my breasts.

'How dare you feed your child on the breast that Henry-Francis must suck,' she says aiming a kick at my legs.

'I have plenty of milk Missus, enough for both,' I say without thinking.

That backtalk got me a slap so hard I could not hear anything clearly for the rest of the day and my face bleeds where her ring cut me.

It was after that she order Missy Clara, who still does what her mammy says, married or not, to take me to England. When Missy Clara tell me, she taking me to England, leaving my children, I fall at her feet and beg not to be parted from my Jessy.

'Don't be so ungrateful,' she says kicking me away. 'Anyway, you will have Henry-Francis to look after.'

'Who cares about what she wants,' says Missus Jane, stamping on my outstretched hand. I scream. Later I find that my little finger is broken. It heals stiff and straight. I can't bend it.

✧✧✧✧

My stomach moves with the ship, up and down, up and down just as it did five years gone. Five years. The last time, I am full of rage as the white devils take me away into slavery, into sorrow and pain. This time, I'm full of questions. I'm in the middle of the sea and it pulls me this way and that. I want to go back, not to slavery but to me children. I don't know what's going to happen, but I thank the gods that because I have to look after Henry-Francis I'm not in the bowels of the ship, that noisy hell-hole, chained up and packed in close.

No, on this journey I'm in a small cabin next to Sir Henry and Missy Clara, with enough room for me and Henry-Francis. I have a mattress, not just rough wooden boards. This time I'm not waiting for the sailors to come drag us, still in chains, up to the deck to stand blinking in the sudden light. I remember how when the stink got too bad, they'd pour water over us, crack their whips to make us jump up and down, like in a terrible dance, the chains rattling and shaking, sending out the curses we can't ourselves shout out. If the sailors saw a ship, even as a faraway dot they'd rush us back down into the devil-pit and slam the hatch shut and we are in the black, black pit once more.

All this thinking makes me want to shout out to the gods, but I let the flapping sails beat out my bottomless pain. I hear Maluuma's voice deep inside my soul. 'You must always pay your dues,' she says, '*Mamiwata* waits.' My grandmammy never leaves me. I listen now, just as I've always listened in the nine years since she journeyed to the ancestors. Her words live in the wind, in the sky, the sun, the moon, the stars, the sea. I keep her words in my being and breathe them quick into my children before they're ripped from me, new slaves for the Massa. There's no *halemo*, no Pa Sorie so I give them their true names, Amadu, Lansana, Jabeza. I take a small knife and mark them with the monkey symbol to tell the ancestors and those who know, these are Talaremba warriors, my babies, one, two, three, pulling at my sorrow chain.

Standing there on the deck I wrap my shawl tight round me. Holding my thoughts in, I stare into the blue ocean, like blue glass, blue that Maluuma told me a long time gone, keeps us safe. I think of all the slaves, men, women, children, that never made it across the ocean. Remember the ones who were sick or making too much trouble that slave-masters threw over, to go down, down deep. *Mamiwata* holds them tight as we sail over, their flesh all gone, leaving the bones sticking up, calling to us.

I pull out my *gri-gri* hanging around my neck now. Inside the pouch I feel the heart stone Maluuma gave me. There too is my caul, the *ala* that covered my face when I entered this world. It is supposed to keep me safe from being dragged down to a watery grave by *Mamiwata*. Sailors beg, steal, kill to have a piece of a caul like mine. I think of my sister Salimatu and once again I pray that her *ala* keeps her safe, that she has not joined the ancestors. I have never stopped crying in the inside of me for her. I open the pouch with care and feel around. I do not want to see the three string bracelets, white, red and green, on top of my piece of caul. They would break my spirit. I bring out one of the blue glass pieces. I run my finger along the edge, almost hoping it would draw blood so I could send part of me with it to the ancestors, to Jaja, Madu and Maluuma and the others whose blood flow in me.

Leaning forward I throw the glass into the sea. The sun turns the sky into the red, yellow and orange of a blazing fire. From deep within me I bring out the song and the tears flow.

# CHAPTER 30

*Mus be glad fa true, cause ya gwine git a whole heapa good ting dat*
*God keep fa ya een heaben*
Rejoice, and be exceedingly glad:
for great is your reward in heaven
Matthew 5:12

## March 1851

Alarge wave comes at me as if in answer to my song. I step
back, slip on the wet deck and am caught in arms so strong I
forget to be afraid of being washed away.

'You better be careful, Missy. The ocean can shake the ship like
a baby's rattle.'

I had not known that there was anyone else on deck and wet as
I am from the wave, I feel myself go hot.

'Thank you, sah,' I say, not looking at him and try to move but
he holds me firm. His black coat is soft to my hand and his waist-
coat though plain has brass not wooden buttons. My heart begins
to pound. I want no white man's embrace. I have had enough of
that. I struggle, crying 'let me go.' He did, so quick that I stagger and
am forced to grab his arm.

'Please don't be afraid,' he says, 'I mean you no harm.' His
voice is soft, and I look up at him, something I try never to do,
for once they catch your eye, they think that they catch you good.
I frown, he's not white. On the plantation, the slaves are many
shades; dark as coffee, brown sugar, honey, buttermilk all the way

to white but no matter what shade they are, they still be coloured and can be sold anytime.

Now I see that this is a Negro, but so light he could almost pass for white, like my two-year-old Lewis and little Jessy. And when Lewis is grown, he too will be like this one, just another white-black man, born of a black mother but with his pappy's colouring. I fear for him and Jessy too. 'They be neither fish nor fowl,' says Old Rachael. 'They can't be in the white man's world but the black world going be hard for them too. It always hard when your pappy be your Massa, hard to see the things your white brothers and sister get while you are treated like a dog. Hard to hold your head up high.'

✲✲✲

I come back into myself on the ship when I hear the man ask, 'is that African you were singing?'

Something about the ways he says it stop me from walking away.

'African?'

'Yes. You can talk African?'

I smile. So, it is not just on the plantation most of the coloureds think that Africa is one big place, with one language, like America. 'Africa has many countries, each country has many tribes and they all speak different languages, like Yoruba or Fon,' I say to him.

I stop, hearing me sound just like Missus Halston, who teach the big house children.

He looks at me as if I'm telling him the most amazing story. 'Is that a fact?' he says, and I nod at him.

'And you speak all these languages?' he asks, his eyes big and round.

The way he's smiling at me I see that he's teasing me. I forget that he a stranger. I throw back my head and laugh like Maluuma used to laugh. Then he too laughs, deep and long and the sound pleases me. I didn't know until now that I can make a man sound like that. I swing a good look at him. He is fine. His eyes are pale as honey gold, full of light. He stands strong and tall with no hat on. A feeling I never have had before passes through me. I want to reach out and touch his thick, black, wavy hair that is sleeked back with a sweet-smelling oil.

'I don't think anyone can talk all of the different tongues of Africa,' I say, 'but I used to know three or four.'

'Well goodness me. You can speak three or four different languages. You're an educated woman.'

The thought of me being an educated woman warms me. I step back and say, 'I am not a woman of learning, Mistah.' I start to walk away but he steps in front of me.

'So how come you know these different African words then? Your Mammy teach you?'

'I was not born slave. I come from a village called Talaremba near Okeadon.'

He takes my two hands and hold them tight. 'You from Africa? You made the crossing? You? How long ago?'

I look up at him. He stares back at me, waiting for the answer. His eyes darken almost to black and for some reason mine fill up with tears.

'Five years ago,' I say. 'My Jaja, was the chief. I was sold by Jamilla, his second wife and her cousin.' I stop, surprised I have said even that much to this person I have just met.

He looks at my wrist and sees the deep ridges. I do not have to tell him that they are the marks left from being tied up tight and dragged to another world. These are the marks, the signs of my failed fight to be free. He drops my hands as if the scars of my slavery burn him. His hand bunches into a fist and his mouth tightens as though to keep the words he wants to say inside himself. I step back a little afraid.

'I am sorry,' he says. The look on his face makes my heart shake. I take in a sharp breath. He turns away, his head up high and looks across the sea into the faraway. 'A law has been passed against the capture and selling of our people from Africa, but we are still fighting for our emancipation. The triangle, the chain, must be broken.' He turns and leans against the ropes. 'My Grandpappy was free-born in America, my Pappy was born free, my brothers, sisters, my twin and I, we are all free blacks.'

I catch my breath and tighten my grip on the ropes. A twin? This man is a twin and grown, not left in the forest to die.

'My twin, Tamar is not with us anymore. She died giving birth, almost a year ago. The baby got stuck. There was no birther and the white doctor would not come out,' he says, shaking his head.

I can feel his anger and his sadness wrap around him. I touch his arm. 'I'm sorry,' I say, and I truly mean it.

'We've never been slaves but still it is hard for us coloureds,' he says, staring out across the water. 'That is why one day, soon, I will go back home to Africa.'

I smile at him calling Africa home when he has never been there.

'Pappy said his Grandpappy Omara, the one we call "The Old One", was captured in Africa, sold as a slave and eventually brought to Massachusetts.' He takes my hand and gently rubs his thumbs along my scars. 'One day we will all be free, and we will get to the promised land, the land of our ancestors.'

'Amen,' I say before I could stop myself.

He smiles, the sweetest smile I ever did see from a man and I smile right back at him. 'What is that song you were singing?' he asks. 'You have a mighty fine voice.'

His words warm me. I frown as I try to translate it and hum the tune a little first.

> *Everyone come together, let us work hard;*
> *the grave not yet finished; let his heart be at peace.*
> *Everyone come together, let us work hard:*
> *the grave not yet done; let his heart be at peace at once.*

'That is powerful. Why do you sing it now?'

'It is a song to send the dead on their way. I sing it for all those who did not make it across the water. For those who jumped or were thrown into the arms of *Mamiwata*, those whose bones now lie scattered on the seabed.'

He nods and stands as if carved out of the darkening sky, his silhouette strong, firm and lifting his eyes to the heavens, he opens his mouth and sings out,

> *Get away to Jordan, get away to Jordan*
> *There's one more river to cross*
> *And that's the stream that flows*
> *Thru Bethlehem call the Jordan*

His voice is beautiful and strong. As he sings he seems to reach inside and grab my heart. I do not know as I listen to him that tears are running down my face until he takes a handkerchief out of his pocket and tries to wipe my cheek. I take it from him and step away. A coloured man with a handkerchief. What next, I wonder, but I feel special. 'It is the sea spray,' I say.

He smiles.

Cool air on my chest reveals that my breasts are leaking milk. Henry-Francis will be screaming by now. I've been away too long. Although she's not as bad as her mother, Missy Clara knows how to slap and pinch if I do not do all that she asks and quickly.

'I must go,' I say. Pulling my shawl tight to cover the tell-tale stains on my bodice. I rush away.

He calls after me 'Absalom Brown.'

I stop, not understanding what he has said.

'My name. I'm Absalom Brown.'

The name rings in my ear and I stand like a fool, a silly smile on my face. I hear him say from a long way away, 'Yours? Your name?'

'Faith,' I say, before turning and hurrying away.

'Faith,' he says after me and I hear it as though for the first time. Faith.

# FAITH

# CHAPTER 31

*Dey bless fa true, dem wa saaful now, cause God gwine courage um*
Blessed are they that mourn:
for they shall be comforted
Matthew 5:4

## March 1851

I never allow thoughts of men to enter my mind but somehow this one, this Absalom, has slipped through. I like the picture he seems to have of me—a strong, educated woman, with a fine voice. I could have told him that he has a mighty fine voice too.

I've been looking for him two days now, and not just to return his handkerchief. I know Absalom is not a first-class passenger and not in third class either, so he must be in second class which I pass every time I go down to steerage for water. I walk past slow searching for him. I see the cramped cabins, their doors opening straight into the main saloon space all the passengers mix and eat together. He must be here, somewhere, for he's not a slave. I am not allowed to sit there, for I am a slave.

Not that I would be welcome in the third-class steerage either. It is different from first or second class. Here they're packed in with no private space at all and no way to get away from each other. It is smelly, dirty, damp, dark, always noisy and too hot, for the steam engine rooms are close by. Still, they are not chained together.

It is worse in the evenings when the hatches are battened down leaving the people with just a few lamps, no candles, for fear of

261

fire and very little air. Many arguments and fights break out over simple things, especially stolen rations, or whose turn it is to use the small galley where they cook their skimpy meals.

But I know that no matter how bad things are for them most of them agree that someone like me has no place among them and some of them let me know this every time I go down there for water.

I look at no one as I walk past but one of the women, Lil, who has a young child clinging to her skirt, stands in front of me. She pushes the little boy away without even looking at him. 'We should not have to mix with darkies, whether they be slave or no, should we?'

I look around for support but there are no Negroes, men or women in steerage and none of the whites will help me if I'm attacked. I step back and hold my water pail tight in front of me. I'm scared but I will not let them see it. Once more I hear Maluuma telling me, *'face fear and it will disappear.'* The fear may not disappear but remembering Maluuma helps me feel strong. I hold the pail tighter ready to swing it against anyone who tries to attack me. For a moment I wish I had my old sling and some shots. I would fling one at Lil and knock her out, knock all of them out after all I am still an Talaremban warrior, wasn't I?

'Let her be Lil,' a man says from the other side of the saloon. 'What's the matter with the lot of yous. They'll come after all of us if anything happen to her. Them up there protect their property and that is what she is, a talking, eating, farting, shitting piece of property.'

Lil moves and I go quickly to the galley though my legs are shaking. A pregnant girl, younger than me, holds on to the water butt swaying as if she's going to fall so I help her sit down, scoop some water and give it to her. She drinks some and splashes her face with the rest.

'I felt sick. It's the movement of ship,' she says.

'You'll feel much better once the child comes.' I look at her and add, 'in three days.'

'Three days? How do you know that?'

I smile.

I don't tell her that after I'd helped Maluuma bring my sister Salimatu into this world, she let me help her at many other birthing. I can look at any woman and tell when her baby will come, almost to the hour. Old Rachael, the plantation birther until her hands got twisted and useless, says I have a gift. I smile at the girl leaning against the water butt now and nod, 'yes, three days.'

'It's my first. I wish my mother was here.' Her eyes fill up.

'Where's she?' I ask.

'She's dead. That's why we're going back; to look after my three little brothers and sisters. John and me, we don't want them in the workhouse. Ma make me promise.'

'She'll be with you when the time comes,' I say.

'What they call you?' she asks.

'Faith, Missy.'

The girl laughed. 'I'm not a Missy,' she says, 'me ma named me Ada.'

A young man came rushing. 'You been sick again?' he says and put his arm around her waist. I look away for all I see is Absalom's arm around me and I feel shame for thinking so.

'I'm fine, John. Faith here help me. She say this all over in three days. That good, no? She a birther.'

He looks at me straight and nods but says nothing.

'Don't worry, you'll be fine,' I say and, picking up my filled water pail, hurry through the steerage. I keep away from Lil. We have many more days before we arrive in Liverpool.

✦✦✦✦

That night I lie thinking of Absalom when Henry-Francis wakes and whimpers. To quiet him I open my bodice and his mouth finds my breast. I close my eyes and pretend that it is Jessy or maybe Lewis sucking, and I am comforted a little. When Henry-Francis falls asleep in the middle of his feeding, I lay him back down.

Then I hear voices and I stiffen. It is Missy Clara. I hear her every night, pleading, crying, 'no Henry, not again. It's too soon. I'm still sick.'

Usually their voices are low, and I go back to sleep. Tonight, however, Sir Henry who has been drinking all day, is angry and loud. Tonight, I hear his words clearly and my heart pounds loud and fast.

'Dammit, if you won't do your wifely duty then I'm warning you, I will find someone else who will. And I won't have to look too far either. Will I?'

'You wouldn't Henry!'

'A man has his needs. How long should I wait?'

'No, Henry, no. You're not like Papa and the others.'

'How do you know that?'

Although he does not say it, I fear that he means me. Not him too. Don't they never think of anything else? Oh, lord, O *Oduadua*, save me. I thought I had left that trouble behind in America. I need fresh air. I creep up the steps to the upper deck. It is cold, dark, full of shadows and the wind sings my old name, Fatmata, Fatmata. I pull my shawl tight across my chest and lift my eyes to the sky to call to the gods but there is nothing there only the stars. I search the sky and soon I find *Arewa*, the North Star.

'Maluuma, talk to the ancestors. Jaja, help me,' I call out.

'Faith?'

The voice squeezes my inside. Jaja? I turn. It is not my father though, it is Absalom. I burst into tears. He rushes over and puts his arm around my shoulder. I bury my face in his chest and sob. He says nothing, just holds me.

# SARAH

# CHAPTER 32

*New thoughts and hopes were whirling through my mind,*
*and all the colours of my life were changing.*
*—David Copperfield* by Charles Dickens

## March 1851

*Wednesday, 13th March, 1851, Winkfield Place*
*I am now truly Sarah. My Salimatu-self has stayed away for*
*ages and I am glad. No more confusion. Tomorrow Mama*
*Forbes and I go to Lady Melton in London. Mama says she is*
*only going to stay for a couple of days.*

*On Saturday, I, however, am to travel with Sir Charles*
*and Lady Phipps to stay with the Royal family at Osborne*
*House. Miss Byles says that the house is on an island, the Isle*
*of Wight. I wish Mabel and Lily were coming but I do not*
*know if the house will be big enough for all of us.*

*Mama Queen says that I need the sea air after my illness. It*
*is a month since I came back from Windsor Castle and I do*
*not cough so much anymore. Nanny Grace has not once had*
*to give me Godfrey's Cordial.*

*Dr Clark says the English weather does not suit me. What*
*does that mean?*

✦✦✦✦

Sarah, Mabel and Emily sat on Sarah's bed watching Edith put another garment into the case.

'Why can't we go to the seaside too?' said Mabel.'

'Her Majesty has invited only Sarah,' said Nanny Grace, adding handkerchiefs and stockings into the case.

'Why does she need so many things, Nanny?' Emily said cradling her doll, Arabella. 'We thought she was only going away for a week.'

'Her Majesty has provided these things for Sarah. She will want to see that Sarah is wearing them, don't you think?' said Nanny.

'And because she's not coming back. She prefers to stay with the Princesses, so who cares,' said Mabel, jumping off the bed and running to the schoolroom.

Sarah caught her breath. Was Mabel being horrible again? Was she wishing that Sarah would disappear? Were they not sisters, now? Although she liked the Princesses, and Mama Queen, she did not really like going to Windsor Castle or Buckingham Palace. They were always full of people. She never knew what the right thing was to say or do. She would much rather stay at Winkfield Place.

'Don't be silly, Mabel,' Emily called after her. 'This is Sally's home. Isn't it, Nanny?'

'How can it be your home when you're hardly ever here?' said Mabel, sitting at the table in the middle of the room. She jabbed a knitting needle into the table again and again. She sounded angry but Sarah saw Mabel's lips tremble. Confused, Sarah put her hand in her pocket and held on to Aina her wooden doll. Did Mabel hate her or not? Sometimes she was so nice and other times she was truly horrid.

'Yes, it is her home,' said Nanny. 'Remember, what the good Lord says, Mabel, *envy is the littleness of soul*. Be kind. You know Sarah stayed at the Castle so long because she was ill. Now, out of here all of you. Edith and I will finish the packing without interruption.'

'Will you get us some more shells?' asked Emily, laying Arabella down before bringing over a box half covered in shells to the table. 'Mabel collected them when we went to the seaside last summer, but we did not have enough cover the whole box. We need some more to finish it for Mama.'

'I'll get us some shells, Lily. I promise. A whole bagful. I love shells.'

'Oh, good.'

'I'm only going for ten days, Mabel,' Sarah said. 'Then I'll come back to my sisters and my brother.'

She reached for Mabel's hand. Mabel held on and squeezed, hard. Sarah did not mind. They smiled at each other.

***

Nanny got Sarah up early the next morning and without waking the others got her dressed in layers of clothing although it was going to be quite warm; stockings, vest and shimmies, heavy linen green dress, before hurrying her downstairs.

'But Nanny Grace,' said Sarah, pulling away, 'I haven't said goodbye to Lily or Mabel. I want to give Anna a kiss before I go.'

'Now, Sarah, you be a good girl, the girls are asleep and you know that Anna is still unwell. Madame says we must be in the hall on time. We cannot keep the horses waiting.'

Sarah walked down the stairs with her head bowed so that Nanny could not see that her eyes were wet. Maybe Mabel was right, maybe she was never coming back, no one wanted to see her anymore. Was she really going to the Isle of Wight? Why did she not travel with the Princesses when they went last week? That would have been so much more fun. Instead she had to do the long journey with Sir Charles and Lady Phipps. She pinched her hand hard to stop herself from crying. That pain took away other bigger pains she had found out when she lay ill in the yellow room at Windsor Castle. If she pinched herself hard, it stopped her from thinking about Salimatu or Fatmata. Pictures of fire and chains faded away, back into her memory box. Now she pinched herself to stop thinking about being taken away.

'Madam will be down in a moment,' said Nanny. She helped Sarah into a dark red coat and a black bonnet. She tied the matching dark red ribbons into a large bow. 'Here, we'll button you up, so you'll be warm and snug the whole journey.' She picked up a red and green shawl and held it out to Sarah.

'Do I need to, Nanny Grace?' said Sarah, wriggling under the weight of all her garments. 'I'm quite warm.'

'We don't want you to catch a chill, do we? And this,' she said, trying to put it around Sarah's shoulder, 'was your Christmas gift from Her Majesty herself.'

Sarah pinched harder. She wished she had her sewing needle or the pin of her brooch with her. She used them sometimes when no one was around. Pin pricks. Little pricks that hurt and drew little drops of blood.

'You are quite right Nanny, but it is getting warmer,' said Mama Forbes who had heard the conversation as she came down the stairs. 'Maybe Sarah could take it with her, instead of wearing it just now?' She put her arms around Sarah. 'It will be a long journey, tomorrow, my dear, you have a train and a boat crossing. It could get chilly.'

'Yes, Mama Forbes,' said Sarah and took the shawl from Nanny Grace. 'Thank you, Nanny Grace.'

The thumping, crashing noise made Sarah look up to see Emily and Mabel, still in their white nightdresses and barefooted, running down the stairs. Sarah blinked and took a step closer to Mama Forbes, afraid for a moment of the figures in white hurtling down the stairs. They shook her memory box, girls in white garments carried to their death. Their screams in her head turned into Emily and Mabel's voices calling her name and then the box banged shut again.

'Girls, please,' said Mama Forbes. 'What is the meaning of this?'

'We wanted to see Sarah before you left,' said Emily, breathing heavily from running down so fast. 'I've got something for you,' said Emily.

'Lily, it's Arabella!' said Sarah when she saw what was being held out to her. 'She's your favourite doll. I can't take her.'

'I want you to take her, because Aina might get lonely while you were busy with the Princesses. But it's just a loan. That way you will have to come back to return her, see? Goodbye.'

Sarah smiled. Although she had much nicer dolls now and no longer played with the stick doll Abe had made for her so long ago, she always took Aina with her when she went away. 'Thank you, Lily,' said Sarah, hugging Arabella and knocking its bonnet off so that its yellow wool hair tickled her nose.

'Goodbye,' said Mabel, pressing something into Sarah's hand.

They were almost at the train station when Sarah remembered that she had not looked at what Mabel had given her. She was still clutching it so she opened her hand. It was a tiny shell, wrapped in a small blue ribbon. The tag said, *to my sister, bring some more home.* A sob escaped before Sarah could swallow it. Mabel did like her.

'Are you feeling unwell?' said Mama Forbes, reaching out to pat Sarah's hand.

Sarah shook her head; she could not speak. If she tried to, either a cough or a sob would escape, and that would not do. She slipped the shell wrapped in blue, into her pocket. The little shell made her think of all the things that were special to her, safe in her *gri-gri* pouch; the blue stones, her caul, the piece of blue cloth Fatmata gave to Salimatu a long time ago. Not that she wore the *gri-gri* around her neck anymore. What was the point, she had thought, as she lay ill in Windsor Castle? It did not work. It had not helped her to find Fatmata. She had put it away with her hand-kerchiefs, on returning to Winkfield Place. Still, she could not leave it behind and last night after Nanny Grace and Edith had finished her packing, she had opened one of the bags and slipped her *gri-gri* in next to Aina. Just in case. Now she had something else to put inside the pouch. Something for Sarah and nothing to do with Salimatu.

✵✵✵✵

Trains no longer frightened Sarah. She had been in quite a few now and knew that the rumbling noise and black smoke was not *djudju* coming to drag her to the ancestors. She walked close to Mama Forbes, however, as they searched for a carriage.

'Mary,' called a lady who was already seated by the window of a half-empty carriage. 'Do come and join us.'

Mama Forbes stopped and waved. 'Good morning Lavinia. Are you going up to town for a few days?' said Mama Forbes, moving past the other two people in the carriage to sit down quickly before the train jerked into action. The whistle blew her words away.

Sarah recognised Mrs Oldfield, the lady who had asked so many questions on her visit to Winkfeld Place. She just knew that there were going to be lots more questions.

'This is Mrs Fletton-Jones,' said Mrs Oldfield. 'I don't think you two have met before, she's just returned from India. Her husband is in the Bengal Army. Olivia, Mrs Mary Forbes.'

'How do you do?' said Mama Forbes, sitting down.

Once they were all settled, Mrs Oldfield said so loudly the other people in the carriage stopped their conversation to listen to her. 'And this is Sarah, the African Princess. You must have heard about her. Always in the papers.'

'So, this is her?' Mrs Fletton-Jones said, but she did not look at Sarah.

'She is Her Majesty's ward although she lives with the Forbes.'

'She does?' Mrs Fletton-Jones said to Mama Forbes who was facing her. 'As part of your family?'

Sarah felt Mama Forbes stiffen. There was a beat before she replied. 'She is very much part of my family. The children see her as their sister.'

Mrs Oldfield's mouth dropped open. 'Mary, is that wise?' she said, then seemed to realise what she had said, for she leaned forward and added, 'I mean, I know she's a princess, but she can't stay with you forever. What will she be trained for? A governess I suppose, or a companion but who will hire her?'

'Violet, please. It's not for us to decide what is to become of Sarah, but Her Majesty. Anyway, she is still a child. We do not have to discuss her future just yet.'

'I see,' said Mrs Oldfield, smoothing out her skirt. She sat back, and all was quiet.

Until now Sarah had not thought about her future. Something else to worry about. She was sure that Mabel or Emily, the Princesses and the other children she had met did not have to worry about what was to become of them. Why did she have to? No matter how hard she tried, she was always different. She pinched her arm, hard. She had found out when she lay ill in the yellow room at Windsor Castle that small pains took away other bigger pains. When she pinched herself, it had stopped her thinking about Salimatu or Fatmata, and the pictures of fire and chains faded away, pushed back into her memory box. Now she pinched herself to stop thinking about what was to become of her.

Mrs Oldfield leaned forward, and Sarah knew there would be more questions.

'Are you going to stay with your sister, Mary? I hear the Melton's have a Negro butler. How interesting.'

'In India, we have servants, of course but we never entertain the natives in our homes,' said Mrs Fletton-Jones. 'Not done. Complicated caste system. In the army there, if we absolutely must associate with them, we do so at the Mess. Much better that way.'

'Well, my husband is in the British Navy, different system, I suppose,' said Mama Forbes without looking at Mrs Fletton-Jones, who tutted and stared hard at Sarah.

There was a silence which Mrs Oldfield immediately filled with, 'and Sarah? Will she be staying at Lady Melton's too?' asked Mrs Oldfield.

'Only overnight.' said Mama Forbes. 'She travels to the Isle of Wight in the morning.'

'Isle of Wight?' said Mrs Fletton-Jones, eyeing Sarah.

'Yes, she has been invited to stay at Osbourne House. Her Majesty is fond of Sarah.' Mama Forbes smiled at Sarah.

'I see,' said Mrs Fletton-Jones diving into her purse. She brought out a small lace handkerchief and dabbed her cheeks with it. 'Surprisingly warm for March, though not as hot as in India.'

Mama Forbes took the plaid shawl Queen Victoria gave Sarah for Christmas and wrapped it around her shoulder. 'Are you warm enough, Sarah?' she said.

Sarah was far too hot and had thought she could unbutton her coat, but not now. 'I am, thank you, Mama,' she said, and they smiled at each other.

✵✵✵✵

Later that afternoon, Sarah saw Daniel open a door at the end of the hall and disappear. She looked around quickly and hurried after him. She needed to talk to him, to hear his voice. It did not sound like any other voice around her. She wanted to see his face with its creases and folds, shining through its blackness, familiar and yet disturbing, pulling at memories that flitted in and out, too slippery to hold on to for more than a second.

Sarah found him in the pantry, sitting with a tray of cutlery on a table in front of him. He looked up and she stepped into the room. Now she was there, with him, she did not know what to say.

'You still here? No more running off, like you did last time, you hear me?' said Daniel, picking up a fork and polishing it with a soft white cloth.

Sarah refused to meet Daniel's eye. 'That was three months ago. I don't want to run away anymore.'

'Glad to see you finish with all that foolishness. Sometimes it best not to go searching and looking. Best leave well alone.'

Sarah bit her lip and shuffled from foot to foot.

'You a princess, you different from the likes of us,' said Daniel, still polishing. Then he stopped. Sarah looked at him then walked over and sat on the other end of the bench.

'They treat you well?'

'Oh, yes,' said Sarah, swinging her legs back and forth, making the bench creak. 'Even Mabel. We're friends now, sisters. I have Mama Forbes, Papa Forbes, Mama Queen and many other people. Everyone is very good to me.'

'That Queen lady be a good woman. She doing her best to free all of we, they say. God bless her. I thank the Lord that she taken at least one of our childrun and put her up high.'

Daniel picked up a knife and polished it, his hand slow and sure. Sarah stared at his bent head, hair still thick, black flecked with white patches as though unmelted snow had fallen on his head and stayed. She wished she could touch it, instead she asked, 'You got any children, Daniel?'

He stopped polishing and looked up.

'You the first person in this house who ever ask me that question, you know. Nobody else care to know what I had before or what I might have lost.'

Sarah slid along the bench, until she was close and touched his hand. She waited.

'Yes, little lady, once upon a time I had me childrun, three of them, two boys and a pretty little girl like you.'

Sarah's eyes widened. 'Like me?' she said wriggling with excitement. 'Are they here with you? Will I meet them?'

Daniel smiled but his eyes were misty. 'No, you won't meet them, Miss Sarah. They be all grown now, maybe with childrun of their own, if they be still alive. I ain't seen them in a mighty long time 'cause they got sold on by my old Massa, when they were real small. Later he sell me too.'

She squeezed his hand. She did not know what else to do. She had been sold too, torn away from everything she knew, and that other life had faded away. Were all black people always sold? Why?

Daniel patted her face with his white-gloved hand. 'They do that to your pretty face? Them that catch you? Lord, it bad enough they mark our backs, our bodies, but to do that to a chile?' He shook his head. 'That must have felt like the devil himself be attacking your face.'

'I don't remember. It was done before I was sold to King Gezo. Papa Forbes says that these marks show that I am a princess.'

'Now is that so?' said Daniel. They both sat in silence, Daniel frowning, then he said, 'If the markings on your face tell them where you from, why they not send you back to your people?'

It was Sarah's turn to frown. She had never thought of that and the question brought Salimatu to her side once more. Sarah jumped up and shook her head as if to shake an answer into her dry mouth.

'Yes, why has your Mama Queen not sent us back to our village?' whispers Salimatu. 'Why do they keep us here? We must find Fatmata and go back.'

Sarah stamps her foot. 'No, no, no,' she said, 'this is my home now.'

'Is it?' said Salimatu in her ear. Sarah chewed at her lip. She wished Salimatu would go away and not make her feel so confused.

Daniel stood up, slowly like a tree growing strong and straight in front of her. He put his hands on her shoulder and for a moment it was as if he was going to hug her and Sarah felt a loss when he did not. Instead, he bent down and stared into her eyes.

'Is it?' Daniel said softly.

Sarah's lips trembled. 'I must go.' She turned, running down the hall. Halfway up the stairs to the nursery she stopped, overcome by the return of her cough, of Salimatu's cough. Sarah sat down on the stair and coughed until tears rolled down her face. She was tired of the struggle between her and Salimatu, the keeper of a past life she no longer wants. She tapped her chest reaching for her *gri-gri*, then she remembered that she had not put it on. It was in her case. Sarah ran up the rest of the stairs. She must put it on. She needed it. Her *ala* was in it, her protection against *Mamiwata*. Tomorrow she was crossing water again. Tomorrow Salimatu was going with her to Osbourne House after all.

# CHAPTER 33

*Dey bless fa true, dem wa ain tink dey mo den wa dey da,*
*cause all de whole wol gwine blongst ta um*
Blessed *are* the meek: for they shall inherit the earth
Matthew 5:5

## March 1851

I try not to be near Sir Henry. He has done nothing yet, but I keep away from him. Missy Clara is afraid of what might happen. We both know he never wanted me to come with them in the first place. I heard him say so to Missy Clara, just before we left Oakwood Plantation.

✿✿✿

Missy Clara sits high up on the bed. 'So how am I to look after Henry-Francis if she does not travel with us?'

'No, Clara, I've told you before, she cannot come to England with us. Send her back to your father.'

'Faith feeds him her milk. I can't send her back,' she tells him, her voice rising in anger.

I pray that Sir Henry will stand strong and make me stay behind so I can be with my children. Then Missy Clara burst into loud crying and wailing. She makes more noise than the baby. She knows what she's doing for sure, as Sir Henry gives in, as he does every time, trying to please her.

'Fine, fine, stop crying.' He comes around the bed and kisses her on the head. 'We'll say she is your maid. I do not want the word slave mentioned near my mother or the rest of the family. We do not have slaves in England.'

When I hear that I stop. A place where there is no slave? I am shaking as I listen.

'Mother has very strong views about slavery. She's gone to meetings, signed petitions, including the one sent to Queen Victoria in '38.'

'Petitions for what?' asks Missy.

I wonder what is a 'petition.'

'End of slavery. Mother is so serious about it that though she loves sweet things, she joined the boycott of sugar.' Sir Henry laughs but I don't know what is funny. 'She even wore the Wedgewood anti-slavery broach. It was an ugly thing, but mother wore it to show her support of other anti-slavery society ladies, like Lady Byron and Mrs Lucy Townsend.'

'Why did she if she hated the broach?' asked Missy shaking her head.

I was sure Missy Clara would not have done so because she always wants her way.

'Mother didn't want them to know that there was still a slave-owner in the family. You do understand Clara, don't you? No talk of slaves.'

'Yes Henry,' she says her eyes dry, 'but can we wait a little longer before we leave? I'm not ready to meet your family yet.'

'Sorry Clara, but I've stayed far longer than I intended. I was supposed to get rid of Great Uncle Matthew's plantation and return to England. The exhibition at Hyde Park is in two months and we are showing some of the new machines from the mill. I must be there.'

'My trousseau is not finished.'

'We can buy you anything you need when we get to London.' He pinches her cheek. 'Just think of all the shopping you could do. You would be able to get all the latest things from Paris too, ready for the start of the season when you can be presented to the Queen. You will be the belle of every ball.'

Well, that make Missy change her mind.

'Oh, Henry, you are right,' she says clapping her hands like a child. 'The season and meeting the Queen! I shall get the rest of my trousseau in London.'

Then when Sir Henry goes, she looks at me and says, 'no matter what they call you in England, you better remember under my roof you still my slave.'

✫✫✫✫

Four nights now, I wait until it is quiet next door, Missy sleeping, Sir Henry gone drinking, then I creep up to the deck. When I hear a noise, I push my fist into my mouth to stop me shouting, afeared that I have been followed by my master.

'Faith.'

Absalom. A cry burst out of me. Without thinking I run to him. He opens his arms and gathers me.

'Why you scared?' he says soft.

'I was afeared the Massa follow me. I keep away but his eyes are always on me.'

'Oh, Lord!' he says stepping back from me. 'That he would ever put his hand on you!' He kicks at the jollyboat and I jump. Did anyone hear the noise above the sea and the wind?

'I'm sorry. I will go back. I should not be here.'

'Don't go. I should not be here either.' He stopped and gave me a look. 'I come at night when no one can see me, that is no one but you.' He gives a little laugh, 'I come to smell fresh air, feel the sea on my face, look up at the sky and feel close to those who have gone.'

He pulls me down to sit. We lean our backs against the jollyboat that is on deck ready to take people to the shore when needed. I look at the stars and for the moment I am at peace.

'*Arewa,*' I say.

'*Arewa?*' he says

'North Star. It shows you the way.'

'Polaris? Where?'

'There, can you see it?' He is not looking at the stars but at me, so I take his hand and point to the star.

'I see the star.' He winds his fingers around mine and smiles, his teeth gleam in the dark. My hand lies quiet in his while my heart sings and dance. We stay like this for a long while and when he takes his hand away it feels as if he takes a part of me with him. I pull my shawl tight to hold me in me.

'You're cold,' he says and wraps his arms around me. Were the stars so bright before? I rest my head against his shoulder, and it is as if it has always found a place there.

'How come you know about Polaris?'

'From Jaja, my father. He's with the ancestors, but I do not forget the things he taught me. They are deep inside of me and holds my pieces together.'

I swallow hard remembering the night we stood outside his hut and he told me about the stars, which he called *irawos*.

'All the peoples from beginning of time have looked to the *irawos* for direction at night,' Jaja had said. 'If you know how to find *Arewa*, the bright star that never moves, you will not get lost in the wilderness.'

'But how can anyone find it. The sky is full of them.'

'The *irawos* move and turn around. Only *Arewa*, North Star, stays in the same place. That is why we look for it. From that star we can work out which way to go.'

✧✧✧✧

Absalom squeezes my shoulder and I know that he understands. 'My Father has taught me many things too,' he says. 'He's still showing me the way. Did your father tell you about all the stars?'

'No, I learn the others by myself.' I stop and pull away. I have almost uttered the secret I have kept for a long time and I am afeard.

'You learn the others, how?'

I stand up. I must get away. He jumps up and stand in front of me.

'Oh, Lord. You can read?' he whispers, as if the very words will knock us down.

I do not answer, I just shake. He lifts my head up. The moon shining bright on his face. He gives me a smile that slips into me and makes me feel as if I'm hot from the inside out. I nod. He touches my face, tracing the marks that say I am the child of a chief, and it feels as if a little bird with a soft feather has just brushed my cheek.

'How did you learn? Who teach you?' he asks, fast, fast.

I know what he is thinking. He fears for me. Massa can brand, sell, even kill me for learning to read. I catch my breath and look around. What if anybody hear that? But there is no one there.

'Mrs Halston teaches me, but she don't know she's doing it. I look after Elise while Mrs Halston teach the older children. Nobody pays me any mind, but I listen and learn. I practice all the time. Every place I go, I read, sound out the letters so they touch every part of me mouth without coming out. One day I going to read a whole book.'

'You will,' he says and pulls me into him. 'The Bible says, whatever you ask for in prayer, believe that you have received it, and it will be yours.'

He kisses me, on the mouth. No one has ever done this before and I cling to him because I am falling, falling, falling. He kisses me again and our tongues dance in my mouth. My legs cannot hold me up, so I sink down. I am lost. When he sits down next to me, we kiss again, tongues dancing. The wind seems louder, making the sails sing a song I never heard before, but my heart knows it. I give a soft laugh and it wraps us together.

'So, what you read?'

'I read the children's schoolbooks,' I whisper. 'When I go dust the library, I read anything Massa leaves open; his books, letters, the old newspapers which we use to light the kitchen fires. If no one is looking, I tear a bit off and hide it to read later.'

'You like playing with fire,' says Absalom with a laugh.

'I find a tin, put the papers in it, I dig a hole way back, under the porch and hide it there. I know it is a safe place to hide my papers because I find snakeskin there. Maluuma used to say that healers are like snakes, their eyes are always open, so they see everything, but beware, some have *djujdu* inside them. They can attack without warning and their bite can send you down to the ancestors. I tell the others a big snake lives there, but it is never going to bite me because I come from Africa and know how to talk to snakes. None of them go under the porch after that. But I do and slowly, slowly I read what I have in the tin and I learn a lot. I learn where I be and what happening way out in the world, then I write it down.'

'You can write too?' He looks as if I've done something wonderful and I nod.

'I practice writing on anything I can, bits of the newspaper, dirt, stone. I use whatever I can find, pen, charcoal, sticks and then I wipe it away. Never leave it where anybody find it.'

'I have never met woman like you,' he says, before he takes my hand and slowly spells out FAITH in my palm. I shiver. I want to write his name too, but it is long and I'm not sure how to spell it. I take his hand. It is big and strong but not rough. This hand has not worked in the fields. I open his hand flat. I don't look at it as I write STAR and look into his eyes that are black, black, black.

He hugs me tight. 'My grandpappy, Moses, started a school with his wife Martha, for any child who wants to learn; black, white or brown. She too could read and write. Her father treated all his light-skinnned slave children same as his true borne. We're Quakers. Slavery is a sin against God and a crime against mankind. That's our belief. The elders say we go back to Africa and we'll be free. That's why as a young man, Pappy sailed to Africa with Mr Cuffe, to see if it could be done.'

'Your father has been to Africa and come back, a free man?' I ask. 'He was not captured? Not sold as a slave?' I remember Leye who had screamed that he was a free man returned to his fatherland. That had not stopped Santigie selling him as a slave. Sudden tears stinging my eyes.

'My father went to Sierra Leone twice, first in 1811. Four years after the Parliament of the United Kingdom prohibited the slave trade in the British Empire making it illegal to purchase slaves directly from the African continent.'

'It was stopped that long ago in England?'

'Unfortunately, no, that did not stop the practice. Long before then many people, Quakers, Anglicans, joined together with a group called the Sons of Africa made up of Africans, including Ottobah Cugoano and Olaudah Equiano. These were people who had escaped or had been freed from slavery and living in London, all were campaigning hard for the end of slavery.'

'If they had been able to stop it, I wouldn't be here now,' I say grabbing hold of his hand. 'I would have still been in my village with Madu and Jaja, with Amadu and Salimatu.' That thought made me want to howl like a dog in pain.

'The British Navy established the West Africa Squadron whose task was to destroy the Atlantic slave trade by patrolling the coast of West Africa. That's why Mr Cuffe thought that it would be safe to set up a colony in Freetown. They left some people there to start one, but it did not last. They were going back to set up another colony but before they could, the 1812 war between England and America happened. They went again to Sierra Leone in 1815 you know. Some stayed, but Pappy came back to his family.'

'The others still there?'

'That colony too failed,' says Absalom. 'Another law was eventually passed ordering not only the trade but slavery itself must end, although it did not come until twenty-six years later with the help of people like Mr William Wilberforce, Mr Granville Sharp and Mr Thomas Clarkson.'

'But it is still going on.'

'We are still fighting. Change has to come, and we opponents of slavery still believe that coloured people should be free and should be able to go back safely to Africa. That's why I'm going to England, to meet some Quakers who have been collecting money at talks and lectures to send people out to Sierra Leone once more. My Pappy can't do that journey anymore, but I can. I plan to go with them to Africa, as a missionary.'

I hear something in his voice that is different. In the moonlight I can see his face is set. I touch his face. He kisses my palm. I feel the warmth of his breath in my hand and lift my face up to his.

Then bang. The noise brings us back. We both know if anyone finds us here, we will b be in trouble. Me for leaving Henry-Francis and him for being there at all.

I pull away and run before he can say anything more. My heart races faster than my feet, my mouth spread wide with the laugh that wants to burst out of me. I hold it in, slip quickly into my cabin and lie down. I clutch my *gri-gri* as I twist and turn. I'm hot, I'm cold and in between all that I see is Absalom Brown and I wish that he was there next to me.

# CHAPTER 34

*Dey bless for true, dem wa hungry and tosty fa wa right,*
*cause dey gwine git sattify*
Blessed are they who do hunger and thirst after
righteousness: for they shall be filled
Matthew 5:6

## March 1851

Missy Clara been sick in the stomach, I mix some herbs I bring with me and make a drink for her but when she is better, she still tells Sir Henry she is bad. I know why she says that, I say nothing, but I use it. I give her a different drink at night, and she sleep. Although Sir Henry has not come near me, I make some for him too, I even put a few drops in Henry-Francis mouth, and they all sleep through the night. I know that if anyone finds out what I am doing I will be whupped into the arms of the ancestors. I am willing to take that chance though, for now each night I go on deck, without the fear of my Massa or Missus coming after me.

Absalom is already there. He reaches out and I walk slow, slow towards him. When he takes my hand, I know that I want to walk like this to the end of time.

'Come,' he says, and takes me to the jolly-boat. He has pulled back part of the canvas cover so that there is space to sit under it. 'See, no one will find us here. If we hear anyone, we pull the canvas down.' He smiles, his head to one side waiting to hear what I think.

I clap my hands, like a child. 'Yes, yes, this is good.' I say.

Under the canvas, we talk now, low, low. I want to know about this man, who he is in the inside of him.

'I've got something for you,' he says.

I laugh, happy that he wants to give me something, anything. He reaches into his pocket, brings out a small book. It is too dark to read it, but I know it is a Bible. I swallow hard. I cannot tell him that it is just a book to me. Although I go to the chapel on the plantation when the Reverend comes through, the Bible holds no truth for me. If God loves us so much, why does he not come and save us. When I said that in the kitchen Ma Leah say, 'what wrong with you, chile? Chapel de only time we get to stop. Say dat so missus hear and yuh work til yuh broke. You best know to keep wat yuh tink to yuhself.'

Absalom puts the Bible in my hand and says, 'in Isaiah, God says, "*When thou passest through the waters, I will be with thee; and through the rivers, they shall not overflow thee: when thou walkest through the fire, thou shalt not be burned; neither shall the flame kindle upon thee.*"'

I nod but there is nothing I can say. How can I believe that his God will be with me? He has not so far. But sadly my old gods and the ancestors have not either.

'As I said before, Omara, my great-grandpappy, did the crossing like you, but my father says he never talked about it, never said how he was captured, never spoke about his journey.'

I feel a tremble run through me. I know why Omara never told anyone about his life in Africa or about the journey either. I have never talked about it. Those who have not been through it can never understand. Most of the slaves on Burnham Plantation were born there, some of them, their mother and father born there too. What do they know about seeing their village burn down, their people killed, or be dragged for many moons through the forest to be sold and shipped in dirty stinking ship to the land of the white devils? They don't want to know because it scares them. I don't want to remember but it won't let me go.

'It is hard to talk about,' I say.

He takes my hand and lays a kiss along the scars on my wrist. And his lips are cool like a balm. He pulls me to him. I lean back, and he supports my weight. I know now I can tell.

✵✵✵

'After the long walk through the forest, losing all that I hold in the inside of me, Jaja, Madu, my two brothers, Lansana and Amadu, my sister, Saliamtu,' I say, 'I called to the ancestors, to all those who had gone before to save me but none came, not any of the gods, not *Oduadu*, not *Olorun*, or *Ogun*. I get put in that boat. I didn't think I could last the journey in that pit of hell, chained to the living and the dead. Khadijatu from my village, died birthing her child too early. I could not help her, but I took her baby, Khadi. She lay between us for two days before sailors dragged us all up on deck and unchained us. I watched them throw Khadijatu overboard. I put Khadi under my *lappa* and what little food I had I chewed up and spit into her mouth like I used to do with my monkey, Jabeza.

Others jumped or were thrown overboard, like Leye. He told us what would happen to us. He had been sold to the white devils before but he came back to his village a free man. One day as he walked in the street, right by the big cotton tree of freedom, two men attacked him and captured him again. Santigie sold him back into slavery with the white devils. When he could not take any more on that slave ship, Leye cried "I not going back, I a free man," and rushed at one of the sailors. Big noise comes from a gun that blast him straight to the ancestors. Three sailors picked him up and threw him over. It took a long time before I hear the splash and a bird flew up high. I think it led his spirit to the ancestors while *Mamiwata* took his body down. I prayed then for the ancestors to take me too. Then I heard Maluuma, my grandmother's voice once more. "Live," she said, "*You have got to live the life that Leye, Khadijatu and all the others thrown overboard can't live, otherwise what is the reason to be at all.*"'

I stop for breath. Only then do I notice that Absalom has his arms around me and is rocking me, both of us have tears running down our face. I have never seen a man cry before. I look at him and I know that he is the strongest, truest man, I will ever know.

'No more, no more, you do not have to think about it no more,' he says and bends down to give me a kiss. I put my hand on his chest and push him away gently. I have no handkerchief, so I wipe his tears with my fingers.

'No, Absalom, do no stop me now. I have to tell someone.'

✿✿✿✿

'The ship stopped once before we reached America, South Carolina, Charleston, we heard them say. They cleaned us, rubbed oil on our skin, put clothes on our back, check to see if we sick, line us up with some other longtime slaves and sell us, quick, quick. When Massa first see me with Khadi tied to my back, he thinks she's mine. Old Rachael says that's why he brought us to his plantation on the Gullah Island. Massa William wanted a woman full of milk 'cause Missus had no milk to feed her three-week-old sick baby. Massa mad as hell when he found out that I have no milk either, because Khadi not mine. I was but fourteen and had not born any babies then.

They take Khadi away from me and the Missus put me to looking after baby and the other children, cleaning house, helping Ma Leah in the kitchen. I cannot understand anything they say to me. Nobody wants me to speak "Afric" around the plantation. Those who used to know even a few words have forgotten them, or so they say. Ma Leah, the cook for the family and all the slaves, she tells me this on my second day, when she put a bowl of stew in my hands and I said, "*Bi sieh.*"

"What dat you say?"

I only have a few words in this new tongue. The other slaves, stop eating, their eyes fasten on me. "*Bi sieh?*" I repeat. Leah shakes her head. I try saying thank you in different African tongues but nothing. I look round. With all these black people there must be at least one person who could understand me. But no matter which one I tried, *ablo, Mumo, e dupe,* none of it meant anything to any of them, until I try "*tenki.*"

"*Tenki?* She talking Gullah now. She thanking you, Ma Leah." said one of the women and they all laughed.

"Well you keep to Gullah or English," Ma Leah say. "We not from Afric, we American and we don't have no Afric talk in this plantation. We all is born and bred right here or thereabouts. The Massa, him don't like to hear that Afric talk round here. It bring troubles on you and on the family, you hear me. And if'n Mr Lemrick hear you, it be the whip he'll lay on yuh back."

But later I find out that most of the black plantations folks know words from different African talk and they mix Gullah talk with it. They never been pulled away from the Gullah Sea Islands, from their blood. They not sold again and again like some slaves in other part of the country. They stay put. They never say the words that they drink in with their Mama's milk, where the white man, woman or child will hear them. These are words that pass from mother to child, down, down.

When the sun rises high and stay day after day, week after week, when the rice grow and the mosquitoes bite and suck, all the massas and the missus pack up, and go to Charleston. That is when the slaves talk Afric, that is when they tell the stories and talk about freedom, until the cool breeze start up again to make the sea grass and Spanish-moss wave and dance. The massa and the missus, the children and the house slaves come back and Afric talk is done.

So, I learn Gullah talk and fast. I learn white folks English. I learn many other things too. I learn to read and write but more than all that, I learn not to forget my tongue.'

I hear Absalom give a little laugh. 'You surely did,' he says. I laugh too.

'I see Missy Clara write in the book she call her diary, all the time. She says that she writes about the things that happen to her, good and bad. After that whenever I get any paper, I tie them together, then I have pages too. I write down the things I know and the things I want in this life. I never leave it where anybody can find it. When Massa send me to Oakwood Plantation with Missy Clara, I take all my papers and hide them with the Spanish moss stuffing inside my mattress and now I do the same in the cabin.'

'And nobody knows you can read?'

'Nobody but Old Rachael and she can keep secrets. She's been good to me. The little children are with her until they are about four years. After that, they start to work. They run errands, take water to the fields, tend to the animals, sweep the yard. When I go see my children, Rachael and me, we sit work on our quilts and talk about the things I learned from Maluuma. I tell her about some of the plants and medicines Maluuma used to help a woman push out her child. The old woman shakes her head and say, "you darkies over there know about that?" I learn from her too. She tells me about the herbs she uses, red raspberry, witch-hazel, plantain leaf and many more. Massa start renting me out as birther to other plantations, though I never see the money. Some of the women don't like it when Massa sometimes let me leave the plantation on my own.

"Why you come back?" says Thuli once. "If it be me, I just keep on running."'

'Yes, why did you not just run away?' Absalom says now, stroking my face.

'Run to where? You ever been to South Carolina, to the Gullah?' I ask him. He shakes his head. 'Well, the Gullah is many islands with many rivers to cross. We slaves are left on the plantations in the summer with water and crocodiles all around and no boat. Some of them on the plantation say it a good place to grow rice but a bad place to escape from.'

'There are people who help runaways, people from the Underground Railroad. You ever hear about them?'

'I hear of them. In the rice fields, at chapel, we sing songs like "Follow de drinking gourd" and though it sounds like we singing to Jesus, Reverend Josiah Jones say the drinking gourd is the North Star, the same star Jaja tell me about all the way in Talaremba. Reverend Jones say the song telling runaways the way they must travel to the North. I would've run if I could but my children hold me fast at Burnham Plantation. If I'm there, I know where they be.'

I stop talking. I wonder what Absalom thinks about me having children.

'How many children you got?'

I swallow hard. I don't know whether to tell just about the living, but I think, I got to name them all. It's only right. 'I got two living, Lewis and Jessy.' I stop, then I say, 'and one more, the first one, he come and go straight to the ancestors.'

'So, you have two children living,' he says.

'There is also Khadi,' I say. 'I take her as my own. She's five now. Sometimes, I see her in the yard, and she run to me, calling me mammy. Massa name her Kezia, but inside I always whisper her true name Khadi. Old Rachael says the massas always change the true names because they don't want names that remind them we come from Africa.'

Absalom nods his head and looks straight in front. I am afeared he is drawing away from me. Maybe I have told him too much, I must go. I crawl out from under the canvas. But he comes out after me. He puts his hand around my shoulder. I lean back and can feel his heart beating, making us both shake.

'Omara had his name changed to Caesar when he was brought to Massachusetts,' he says. 'When Omara was free, he chose a new name for himself—Moses Brown. He said he had been born again and he was proud to be a brown man.'

Absalom takes both my hands and he rubs his thumbs along the scars around my wrist but says nothing about my stiff finger. He does not know that it too is a sign of my bondage. He looks straight into my eyes and reach into my being. 'What is your true name?' he asks as if to bring the real me, the one before the bondage scars, into the here and now.

'Fatmata.' I say. 'Pa Sorie, the halemo, named us all after listening to the ancestors.'

Absalom hug me tight and whisper in my ear. 'Fatmata, you're a strong, brave woman.'

It is the most wonderful thing he could say to me for I am a strong Talaremba warrior. Jaja always said there were different ways to fight and win. Well, I am fighting now in my own way by learning to read and write. I am fighting for my freedom and for the freedom of my children and my children's children.

I spread my arms wide and turn my face to the sky. For the first time since I was sold as a slave, I say my name out loud, into the wind, into the waves, to the sky, to the ancestors. I am my own griot.

'I am Fatmata, daughter of Chief Dauda of Talaremba and Isatu, his third wife, sold into slavery. I am Fatmata sister to Lansana, Amadu and Salimatu. I am Fatmata, Fatu, the daughter, sister, child of Taleremba. Mother of Amadu, Jabeza and Lansana. *Oduadua*, god of all women, hear me.'

Absalom pulls me to him, and we cling together.

'Come with me to Africa,' he says.

My heart stops for what feels like a long time and then it beats so fast I think it is going to burst out of my chest. Africa. To go back.

'My children,' I say. 'What would happen to them? I can't leave them on that plantation. Missus Jane, she going to make the Massa sell them away, to punish him, to punish me.'

'I will get them for you. They too will be free. Remember the Underground Railroad. They will help us. You will have your children with you in freedom, that I swear.'

I stare at him. Who is this white Negro who can help me and my children to freedom?

'Are you in the underground?' All slaves on plantations know about the underground though we never talk about it out loud. If the Massa hear about it we get sold down the river fast. We sang about it in church, about following the North Star, about the people called 'conductors' who would help you escape, using different routes, hiding you in safe houses all the way to the North and freedom.

Although we are alone, Absalom looks around. He shakes his head and puts his finger to his lips. He pulls me towards him, and my breath come in sharp bursts. I am where I was meant to be, in his arms. I want to touch him, to know him. My fingers stroke his cheek. I know it is wrong, but I must let him know how I feel. I take his hand and put it over my heart. He tries to move away, to be respectful but I keep his hand on my breast and move in, even closer so that our bodies touch. Our warmth pass from one to the other. I can feel his swelling rise between us, and we go under the canvas again, as one.

We tremble as we stretch out and lie against each other, our desires known. We do not need words for our bodies have their own language; questions asked from inside of him, answers given from the inside of me. He strokes me and kisses my eyes, my lips, my neck, my left shoulder. He stops, frozen. I hold my breath. His hand traces the raised letter S burnt into my shoulder. He tries to pull away, but I hold him close, tight, wanting, needing him to stay deep inside of me. I feel the weight of him in his stillness and then he pushes hard, and I take our pain even as I swallow the whole of him. Push and pull and push and pull, faster, harder until it is as if we were on the very ocean, riding the waves. Together we groan and moan to a swelling that rocks our bodies to another place, and we make our promises. Locked together I kiss the sweat of his face and stroke his wet hair. He groans and starts to swell again. And for the first time I know what it is to be loved by a man.

SARAH

# CHAPTER 35

*Recollect! control yourself, always control yourself!*
*—David Copperfield,* Charles Dickens

## March 1851

Another day, another train. Sarah sat next to the window,
opposite Lady Phipps and Sir Charles. She had been surprised
when Dr Clark joined them in the carriage.

'Have you been coughing much?' he asked sitting next to her.

'No, Sir,' Sarah said, although the question immediately made
her want to cough.

'You will,' he said and turned to Sir Charles. 'It's inevitable. I
tell you; our weather is fatal to her kind.'

Was that why he was travelling with them? Waiting for her to
be ill again?

'The weather's warming up though,' said Lady Phipps, smiling
at Sarah.

'Humph. Glad to see she is well wrapped up,' said the doctor,
rambling on, his droopy moustache fluttering as he spoke. 'I hope
Her Majesty is too, if she is to get over her cold. They should have
sent for me earlier.'

She must have fallen asleep for the voices seemed to be coming
from afar. She kept her eyes closed as the sounds became words.

'I sent the letter to Reverend Venn of Church Missionary

Society last month and he has made enquiries from a Miss Sass who is principal of the establishment.'

Reverend Venn? She had heard that name before. Were they talking about her? Sarah tried to keep still; they must not know that she was listening.

'Good,' said Dr Charles. 'The sooner, the better, I say.'

'It has been agreed all round. The Reverend had an audience with Her Majesty just before she left for Osborne House. She has asked me to arrange it all. We wait now for someone to be available to act as escort.'

Who was Miss Sass and why did they have to wait for an escort? Sarah opened her eyes and blinked in the pale carriage light. It was dark outside. Had she been asleep that long? When the train screeched, she squealed and reached out for Lady Phipps.

'Don't be frightened,' she said, 'we'll be out of the tunnel soon and at the Royal Clarence Yard. The Royal yacht is berthed there, waiting for us.'

'Ah here we are,' said Sir Phipps, as the train burst out of the tunnel into light, its whistle blowing, smoke and soot floating in the air. 'And there is HMY *Victoria and Albert*. The crossing will take no time at all.'

'Come, Sarah,' said Lady Phipps, 'we must get down to the steamer. Look at its twin paddles. Have you ever seen anything like that before?' She held Sarah's hand. Sarah held on to the *gri-gri* she was wearing once more.

✵✵✵

The horses raced up the avenue as though they knew they were almost home. Sarah held onto the strap inside the carriage while they rocked and shook all the way along the drive, through the double row of cedar and evergreen oak trees which lead to the entrance with its beautiful cast-iron gateway. As the drive curved sharply between evergreen hedges of laurel, she strained to see out of the window, searching for first sight of the house. Then she saw it, Osborne House, its twin towers jutting up through the trees.

House? It was huge; three sides of the building around the fore-court were sculptured and painted to look stone. The tall fountains sprayed water into the air. The two levels of terraces had balus-trades and statues of lions at the bottom of the stone steps, the gardens were a riot of colours, surrounded by urns with flowering magnolias.

This was another palace, somewhere else for her to feel lost in. Sarah shrank back into the carriage and so that she could not pinch herself she pushed her hand into the pocket of her coat, felt Aina, her wooden stick doll, the one Abe made for her on *The Bonetta*, and held on to it. The short crossing in the Royal yacht had made her long for Captain Forbes.

'Ah, we've arrived at last,' said Doctor Clark, as the horses slowed to a walk, past the front of the house, onto the entrance forecourt. 'Thomas Cubitt is doing a good job, rebuilding and extending the house. Just as he did with Buckingham Palace.'

'Most of the changes have been designed by Prince Albert,' said Sir Charles.

Out of the carriage Sarah turned around lifting her face to the sun and breathing in the different smells; flowers, trees and salt, something she had not smelt since she left *The Bonetta*. She bit her lips, hard, and stared out across the gardens to the sea below. 'Look Aina,' she said, holding up the doll with its wooden outstretched arms, 'look the sea.'

'Come on Sarah,' called Lady Phipps from the first terrace, 'we can't keep Her Majesty waiting.'

✧✧✧

15th *March 1851, Osborne House*

> *Dear Mama Forbes,*
>
> *We have arrived at Osborne House. It is not a house but a palace. The princesses were happy to see me. I have not seen Mama Queen yet. She has a cold. Dr Clark says I must not catch it. How does someone catch a cold Mama? Vicky says that we are on holiday so no lessons in the schoolroom. Please tell Mabel and Lily I will not forget the shells.*
>
> *Your loving daughter, Sally*

※※※

Sarah woke up the next day to the sound of birds and for a moment thought she was back in Africa. It brought back vague memories of hearing birds as she, Fatmata and the others were marched through the forests towards the coast. She remembered bird songs, close and yet so far away, flying free. There had been no birds singing in King Gezo's compound. That thought came from Salimatu forcing Sarah to open her eyes. She sat up and looked around

No, she wasn't in Africa, nor in Winkfield Place. She was in a bedroom at Osborne House. It was a large room with four beds. The one next to Sarah was empty. In the other two were Princess Vicky and Princess Alice. They were still asleep; the birds had not slid into their dreams. Sarah got out of bed, crept to the window and pulled back the dark green curtains. The sash window was open at the top, so she pushed the bottom one up, enough for the sound to drift in. Kneeling on the window seat, she leaned out, searching for the birds. These birds were free to fly. They were not in cages, like Gimpel.

'What are you doing, Sally?' asked Alice coming to join her at the window.

'Listening to the birds. I wish I could fly like them.'

'Me to,' said Alice. 'I would go everywhere.'

'I would fly back home.'

Alice laughed. 'Back to Winkfield Place? I would go somewhere special. Where I could meet lots of different people.'

'I would fly back to…' Sarah stopped speaking. She did not know where she would fly to after all. But Salimatu was right by her side whispering, 'we could fly everywhere until we find Fatmata. Then fly back to our village.'

'No,' said Sarah so loudly that Alice stepped back. Sarah clenched her hands into tight fists so that her nails dug into the palms of her hands.

They both turned when they heard Vicky say, 'what are you doing? Why didn't you wake me up?'

'We were listening to the birds,' said Alice, reaching out to shut the window.

'No,' said Vicky rushing across the room. 'Don't shut it. I want to see the birds. Were they gulls? Sparrowhawks?'

'We don't know,' said Alice walking away. 'I'm hungry.'

✿✿✿✿

After breakfast, Sarah ran down the corridor with Vicky and Alice, chased by Bertie and Affie, all the way to Her Majesty's sitting room. The boys pushed past at the door and fell into the room laughing. The girls walked in.

'Boys, please!' said Queen Victoria who was sitting at her desk with a pile of papers in front of her. 'You can come in while I'm working, as usual but you know you must be quiet.'

'Look, Mama, Sally is here,' said Alice forgetting to curtsey in her eagerness to bring Sarah forward.

Doctor Clark who was standing by the window with Sir Charles, put out his hand to stop Sarah but Queen Victoria waved him away.

'Ma'am,' he said. 'I have not had time to examine her yet but with her bad chest we don't want her to catch a cold.'

'Oh, nonsense,' said Queen Victoria. 'Stop fussing. My cold is gone. She's quite safe.'

'Not for long with our weather Ma'am. We know that from what has happened to other children like her.'

'Doctor Clark,' said Queen Victoria, raising her hand as though to stop him from saying another word, 'we'll discuss this later.'

He bowed his head and stepped back.

Queen Victoria stretched out her hand to Sarah. 'Come Sally,' she said.

Sarah rushed over and did a quick curtsey. 'Good morning, Mama Queen.'

Queen Victoria threw back her head and laughed. 'See, I'm Mama Queen. And not just to this child. That is why I care about all my subjects, wherever they may be. Black, brown or white, they are all of my children.' She took Sarah's chin in her hand and they stared at each other. 'And how are you now Sally? You still coughing?'

'I hardly cough now, Mama Queen,' said Sarah. 'Mama Forbes says that the fresh air here will do me good and soon I will be completely well.'

'Indeed. The fresh air does us all some good. Makes us think clearly. Is that not so Dr Clark?' said Queen Victoria. 'We will go for a walk as soon as I've finished with these papers.'

Sarah looked around the room full of people, some of whom she had never seen before. Sarah curtseyed to Prince Albert who was dandling Louise on his lap. He smiled at her.

'Sir Charles, you were about to tell me about the report from Sir Harry Smith,' said Queen Victoria, leaning forward, ignoring the children.

'Yes Ma'am. Sir Harry has sent more news from the Cape. There has been much fighting, but our troops have been victorious everywhere and only a few men have been lost. He says that the Fingoes, a race of the same kind as the Kaffirs, have behaved very well.'

'Hmm,' said Her Majesty. She spread out the papers on her desk and everyone stayed silent as she read. Sarah wondered why anyone wanted to fight with their cape. Maybe it was too big, and the wind was trying to blow it away? It did not make sense to her but then there was so much she did not understand.

'Very interesting accounts,' said Queen Victoria at last, shuffling the papers. 'A victory in South Africa, unlike my government here at home.'

'These constant defeats are very serious, my dear,' said Prince Albert as he handed Louise over to Tilly who had come to collect the little ones. 'They may lead to very dangerous consequences.'

'The government must be strengthened,' Queen Victoria said. 'Although I cannot deny the truth of young Sir Robert Peel's strong maiden speech against the Roman Catholics, I must say that it lacks prudence coming now.'

Prince Albert patted her shoulder as he walked past her. 'Unfortunately, we cannot deny the truth of his assertions against the Roman Catholics.' At the door he stopped. 'You children do not need to be indoors while Mama is busy, so I'll meet you out on the Mount Lawn in half an hour. *Schnell, schnell.*'

✿✿✿✿

Out on the mount there was no sign of the boys. Vicky and Alice jumped up and down, laughing.

'We won, we won,' said Alice running over to Prince Albert. 'We got here before the boys.'

Bertie and Affie came dashing across the terrace from the flag tower which rose five storeys high and made Sarah dizzy when she looked up. If she climbed right to the top would she be able to see everywhere, over the sea all the way to Africa? Maybe if she jumped out of one of those windows she could fly.

'As winners, you girls will have first choice of vegetables to plant,' said Prince Albert.

'We were first Papa,' Bertie screamed. 'We just went down on the lower terrace.'

'I told you to be on the Mount. You were not here.'

Sarah leaned against the stone balustrade and watched the others. Bertie scowled, his face going red and pushed Affie away muttering 'it's not fair.'

'Fair?' whispered Salimatu in Sarah's ear. 'It's not fair that we can't find our sister, is it?' Sarah squeezed her eyes tight and pinched herself to shut out pictures of flames.

'Come, we go,' said Prince Albert. 'The rest of the party will meet us there.' He ran down the steps leading down to the lower terrace and the broad walk.

Sarah shrank from the stone lions at the bottom of the steps. They looked so big. She pulled at Alice. 'Where are we going?'

'To the kitchen garden,' said Alice, skipping along. 'We all have a section of the garden to grow our own vegetables.'

'Papa pays us by the hour and then buys our vegetables when we harvest them. Isn't that great?' said Vicky.

'Pay you?'

'Yes, Mama says we must know the value of money,' said Alice.

'My vegetables are always the best,' said Vicky.

'No, they're not,' said Bertie, racing past them. 'My parsnips are going to be much bigger than yours and Papa will pay me more. You'll see.'

'They fight about everything,' said Alice, shrugging her shoulders. 'I like growing herbs.'

'Papa says we should learn everything, and I will,' said Vicky.

'No, you can't' said Bertie. 'Affie and I will do carpentry and brickwork as well as gardening, but you will have to learn about housekeeping and cookery. We do not have to do silly things like that.'

'Well, when Papa has our Swiss cottage built, it will be just for us girls. We'll make lovely cakes and you won't have any.'

'Don't be mean Vicky,' said Alice. 'You'll be invited to our tea parties. You too Sally.'

'Your own cottage?' asked Sarah her eyes wide with the thought of having a cottage built just for herself. 'How large?'

'Papa says it will have everything a cottage should and more,' said Alice, 'with space to display our fossils and other specimens.'

'We'll even have our own grocery shop!' Vicky added. 'Mama says that way we can learn the price of everyday goods.'

How will I know all those things thought Sarah? Who will teach me? Mama Forbes, Mama Queen?

'Don't care. We're going to have a fort,' said Bertie racing through the gate.

'With a drawbridge that goes up and down,' added Affie, chasing after him.

'Mama says we can keep all her dolls in the cottage too,' says Alice. 'She has many dolls. So, do we. Do you?'

Sarah nodded. 'I have some.' She did not tell her that one was Aina, a stick doll. She did not have time to think about it anymore for they had reached the walled garden. Sarah was eager to see what was behind the wall. She stopped short at the sight of all the plants, some with flowers and some without, but all green, with leaves of different shapes and sizes. When she turned around the other four, led by Bertie, were each pushing a wheelbarrow, which like their chairs, were clearly marked with their initials, P.O.W, Pss.V, Pss. A. P. A. She wished that she had a wheelbarrow like that. Would it have Pss.S on it? They had on green aprons with initials too and Sarah was sure that even the gardening gloves had names marked into them. Everything saying this is yours and you belong here. She watched them go to their plots in different parts of the garden and stand to attention.

'*Gut*, we're ready,' said Prince Albert. 'You can each do some weeding and then dig up the vegetables you think are ready for harvesting. I shall buy the best.'

Sarah watched spades and forks attack the ground. She was not sure what she was supposed to do or where she should go.

'What about Sally, Papa? Where's her garden? She must plant a garden too,' said Alice, stopping her weeding.

'You are right,' said Prince Albert putting his arm around Sarah's shoulders. 'Sally should have her bit of the garden too. Come, we will go find Thomas, the kitchen gardener. He will get you a piece of the garden so that you too can plant some vegetables.'

'My own garden? With my own wheelbarrow?' she asked her voice trembling. 'And I can plant whatever I like in it?'

'Yes, *meine kliene*, your own bit of garden, and your own wheelbarrow, just like the other children. And you can look after it, every time you come back to Osborne House. When your vegetables are harvested, I will buy them from you too. That is *gut*, no?'

'*Danke sehr*, Papa.'

Prince Albert laughed and patted Sarah's cheek. 'So, I am papa. *Gut, gut.*'

✵✵✵✵

Sarah did not wait for spade or fork. As soon as Thomas showed her the small area that was to be hers, she dropped to the ground and pushed her hand into the soft dirt. From way back somewhere, she remembered playing in the dirt with other children. They would blow the dust at each other so that it went into their eyes, their mouths, up their noses. Mixed with water into paste they would eat the earth, smear it on their faces and bodies so that they were as red as the earth. They were of the earth. They smelt of it, tasted of it, belonged to it. But this was not the dusty red earth she grew up with, this earth was black and soft and stuck to her hand. She could not blow it off, could not breathe it in. She put it to her face, smelt it, then smeared her cheeks.

It felt good and she laughed.

Then she noticed her dress. It was filthy. She stood up her heart racing. She remembered how angry Papa Forbes had been when she ruined her dress. He had caned her. Would Mama Queen have her caned or worse for getting her dress so dirty?

Bertie, who was closest to her, saw what she was doing and called to the others. 'Look at Sarah.'

'I did not mean to ruin my dress, honest,' said Sarah, her tears making streaks down her cheeks. 'Will I get punished?'

'Don't be silly. We get our cloths dirty all the time when we are here. Tilla will get them cleaned.' He took a handful of mud and laughing rubbed it into his face. 'I look like you now, Sarah.'

Alice too dug her hand into the mud and did the same. 'Me too,' she said,

'What are you doing?' said Vicky standing up. 'You'll never finish the weeding. Papa will get very cross.'

'I want to look like Sally,' said Alice plastering some mud on her face.

Affie said nothing, he just covered his face, his hair, his arms with the mud. 'I am the garden warrior,' he said dancing around Vicky.

Bertie joined him and threw a clod of mud at Vicky. 'Stop being so stuffy,' he said.

Vicky screamed and threw some mud back at him. Soon there was mud flying everywhere and plants were being trampled on. Sarah gasped. She had not expected the others to start a mud fight. Will she be blamed? She stepped away, but a handful of mud hit her on the shoulder and she staggered. She did not know who had thrown it, but it did not matter because they were all throwing mud and earth. If there was going to be any punishment it would all of them. Sarah joined in the mud fight grabbed some wet earth and hauled it. Some hit her face, she wiped it off with her hand, looked at the dark earth that was so different to the earth back in the village and wondered what it might taste like. She stuck her tongue out to lick it when Salimatu screamed inside of her.

'Stop! Do not eat their earth. You swallow it and you will become part of them. It will go into your bones, fill your soul, fill your mind, fill your mouth so that you can only think their thoughts and say their words.'

'Go away,' Sarah said to her other self.

She shut her eyes and took a deep breath put the earth in her mouth and swallowed.

# CHAPTER 36

*Dey bless fa true, dem wa hab mussy pon oda people, cause God gwine hab mussy pon dem*
Blessed *are* the merciful: for they shall obtain mercy
Matthew 5:7

## March 1851

The storm has lasted three days. It had the ship riding the waves high, the sails flapping and wailing, the wind screaming like an angry *djudju*. I did not know, until now, that one could feel so many different things at the same time, joy, fear, despair, hope, love. It is over now. My mind, my thoughts are with Absalom. I want the day to speed on to the darkness of night. I want to hold him and have him hold me. I want our heat to mingle and join us as one.

It is a long time before Missy falls asleep and I can dash up to the deck. He is not here. Did he brave the storm? Does he worry that I might have changed my mind, that I am not completely his forever? My face burns at the thought of him and me forever, doing what we did before. I crawl under the canvas to try get to that place once more. How I ache for him to be right there next to me. Then in the corner, tucked under a rope to hold it down, I see a piece of paper. I pick it up. Something is written on it, just one line. I know that it is from him, Absalom. I try to read it, but it is dark under the canvas. I hold it tight and run to my cabin.

The day breaks and light enter the cabin. I look at the paper and all it has written on it is, *1 Corinthians, 13:13*. I sound out the word. It is a message. Good or bad? Maybe it is to say that we have made a mistake. Did I not throw myself at him, being forward, showing him how much I wanted him?

I know that it is a book in the Bible. I take the Bible he gave me from its hiding place under the mattress. I open it and turn the pages fast and rough, eager to know what he wants to say to me. I search until I find it. Slowly I read it. *And now abideth faith, hope, charity, these three;* The word faith is underlined and my heart swells. Carefully I fold the paper, put in the Bible and hold the book against my chest. It smells of Absalom and I can imagine him holding it, reading it. I know that one day we will sit and read this Bible together. I cannot read all of it yet, but it is a promise, our vow between us.

I want the day to spring from morning into night. Nothing will keep me away from Absalom this night. But there is the day to live through. Swinging the water pail, I walk towards the second-class carriage, my steps light and free hoping that maybe today I will see Absalom there. Praise be to the gods, there he is, standing almost in the dark but I see him. He takes a couple of steps into the light and I stop. I cannot put one foot in front of the other with staring at the beauty of him. For the first time I see Absalom in full light, and I want to drink him in with my eyes. He looks at me and I catch myself. I move again and nod, he smiles and nods back, I smile. It happens so quick nobody notices but for us it is a whole conversation, a promise to be kept.

I move toward steerage, so happy I do not even think about Lil and the other women. Then, long before I reach them, I hear the crying and shouting.

'He should have called the doctor,' said one of the women.

'We could get to no one with the hatch down and we all locked in,' says the one they call Biddy.

'I would not let a man touch me down there. Birthing is woman's work,' says Deidre.

I get a sick feeling in my stomach. Three days. The girl, Ada. I told her three days. O God, O *Oduadu*, god of all women, not her. I move in closer. 'Is it Ada?' I say.

The women turn and stare at me as if they have never seen me before.

'What is it to you?' says Biddy.

'Is she dead?'

'No, but the baby did not make it. Lil did all she could.'

'Ada's not going to last much longer.'

'Will you shush, Deirdre. Poor John's just over there. You want him to hear that kind of talk. Give the man some hope.'

'What good is hope? We all know how it's going to end.'

I put the pail down and look around for Ada. She is at the farthest corner from the men who for once are not talking, fighting or drinking, just watching.

'Let me see if I can help,' I say. 'I'm a birther.'

'You think that we will let you put your dirty black hands on her? You think you can do better than us?' says Deirdre, standing up and getting so close I can feel her spit on my face. I did not know that John has seen all of this but before I can say anything he is there.

'Let her,' says John. 'Ada told me that she has brought many babies into this world. She can't save the child but maybe she can save the mother.'

Deirdre backs off and tuts. 'If you say so, John. She's your wife. I know that my Michael would not do that to me.'

I go to Ada. She is in a bad way. The smell is strong. I know that I must work quickly.

'How long has she been bleeding like this?' I ask.

'Since yesterday afternoon,' says Biddy.

'Did she pass everything after the baby?'

Lil looks at me for a second and shakes her head. 'Cut the cord but nothing has come since then.'

'She needs to drink lots of water. And get some water boiling.' I start to press down and rub her belly.

Lil calls out, 'bring some water.'

The women crowd around blocking the men and children out. Lil forces water into Ada's mouth until she can swallow. I press down, nothing. I know that I must do more now. My hands are small, just right for this kind of help at a birthing. I reach inside of Ada, all the time pressing and pressing until everything passes from her birthing and she is breathing well. Only then do I stop. I do not know how long I have been working on Ada, but I am tired, my arms hurt, I am covered in blood and sweat but I know that she will live.

It is Lil who helps me to stand up and Biddy who brings water to wash my hands. I leave them cleaning Ada up as best they can, making a pile of the soiled bed to be thrown overboard.

As l leave John comes over. 'Thank you,' he says. 'I wish you could've saved the child but at least I still have Ada.' He grabs hold of my hand and stops staring at our hands joined one black one white. He looks at me, his eyes wet. 'Thank you,' he says once more and lets go.

I nod, pick up my pail that someone has filled with water. Slowly I walk away. My heart is heavy for the loss of another child. Soon her little body will join the bones at the bottom of the sea. *Mamiwata* has been paid.

✧✧✧✧

Missy Clara give me a pinch for being away so long. At least she did not break my finger.

'I've had to look after Henry-Francis all the while. He has not stopped crying. Sir Henry is not pleased. Feed him.'

I do not tell her that there is a mother down in the lowest, darkest part of the ship who wished she had her baby in her arms right now, who wanted nothing more than to look after her child. I pick up Henry-Francis. He is wet through. I clean him, open my bodice and put him to my breast. I think of Ada. Missy watches me.

'Well thank God you are here,' she says as Henry-Francis falls asleep. 'Although Sir Henry did not want me to bring you with us. Mammy and I persuaded him.' She laughs. 'I would've had no one to look after Henry-Francis or me. You know what I like and that is such a relief. Come brush my hair. And don't pull like you did yesterday.'

Missy Clara has not spoken to me like this in a long while, forgetting I am her slave, wanting only to talk to someone, anyone who will agree with her. Not since she left the schoolroom and I carried her pappy's child.

'What will happen when we get to Liverpool?' I ask boldly, brushing her waist-long hair, slow and gentle, like a mother fixing her favourite child's hair.

'We go to Sir Henry's estate for a few days to recover from this horrible crossing. He says he needs to check on the mill and see if everything has gone down to London for the Great Exhibition. He also wants to find out what his brother-in-law has been up to,' says Missy, adding, 'Robert put his name but no money into the company when he married Lavinia yet he feels that he can have a say in how things should be done. Sir Henry does not trust him.'

I say nothing. I know that if I am quiet, she will keep on talking and I will learn a lot of things. Sometimes I grunt or say quiet like, 'yes Missy, no, Missy,' and let her go on, let her hear her own voice. I brush and wait. She is not done yet.

'Then we travel to his mother, Lady Fincham's place at Charles Street. That is in Mayfair, in the centre of London. Sir Henry does not have his own place in London but now we are married he says we can look for one. He has promised I can visit all the shops. I will need many things for the Season. There will be theatres, concerts, invitations to tea parties, dinners and balls. I'm to be presented to Queen Victoria and Sir Henry has ordered my dress from Worth's in Paris. His half-sister, Isabella, is being presented too. She will have everything, clothes, shoes, fan, jewelry by now.' She stops for a moment, her eyes flinty and shuttered as she describes her sister-in-law as competition. Coming out of her deep thought she says brightly, 'I'm determined to be the belle of London. Wouldn't that be wonderful? It's my dream. Mammy and Adele will be so jealous.' She gives her high-pitched laugh, pinching her cheeks to make them go red.

I'm no longer listening to her talk about seasons and queens, shops and visits, I fix her hair and think about Absalom and me in London. Though the very thought makes my heart tremble, and I want to shout out 'and I'll be free,' I know that those words can never escape from my mouth to her ears. I bury my thoughts, my dreams, inside, behind a blank face.

Freedom was just a word before but now I have a picture of freedom. I see a big tree, spreading out like the spirit-tree Maluuma used to take me too. I sit under it with Absalom, the children running around, Lewis, Jessy, Kezia and even my first born, Anthony, alive not left behind in America soil. I call them by their African names, Lansana, Jabeza, Khadi, and Amadu. On Absalom's lap is the youngest, our child Maluuma.

# CHAPTER 37

*Dey bless fa true, dem dat only wahn fa jes saab de Lawd, cause dey gwine see God*
Blessed *are* the pure in heart: for they shall see God
Matthew 5:8

## March 1851

Nothing is going to stop me being with Absalom tonight. I take the paper I had found under the canvas, fold it again and again until it is small enough to put in my *gri-gri*. And Faith, with hope and love goes to him.

He's not here but I know he will come. The spray hits my face and I shiver from the cold. Lifting the canvas, I crawl into the space under the raised jolly-boat, sit down by the opening and wait. When at last he arrives, I fall into his arms and hold on tight, as if to be sure that he is real. He gives me the lightest of kisses, our lips just touching. We pull apart and read each other's face before leaning forward and this time his kiss is slow and deep, full of a hunger that matches my own. I return to him kiss for kiss, touch for touch. When we come apart he puts his arm around me and I rest my head on his shoulder.

'I wish we could just stay like this forever,' I say.

'We will,' says Absalom. 'And later we will tell our children and our grandchildren how we broke the maafa chain and together returned to Africa.'

I hug my knees, close my eyes and see my village. I see people who look like me, talk like me, know my stories. I want to dance, sing, walk for miles, live without fear of a whipping. I want to be free.

'Absalom, are we really going to go to Africa?'

'Yes. I'm going with Faith' he says and kisses my forehead. 'And hope,' my nose gets a kiss. We smile and together say 'and love.' This kiss is a promise of things to come.

'When? Will we just walk off the boat at Liverpool and disappear? Do I go into hiding? For how long?' I throw question after question, giving him no time to answer.

He grabs hold of my hands and give them a little shake. 'Stop Faith,' I open my mouth. He puts a finger to my lips. 'Stop, Fatmata,' he says. I stop. My eyes widen, my heart beats fast. I could not have spoken even if I wanted to, for he has called me by my true name, and I am whole again.

'I'm not sure exactly when we leave for Africa. To find out our exact plans I need to meet with some of our abolitionist friends in London. They will help us.'

'There was that word again. I've heard that word before, abolitionists. Massa William did not like them. He said once, after reading the Charleston Mercury, "thank God President Taylor is gone and the new President has sense enough to go against the abolitionists and allow the Fugitive Slave Act." That's when I wrote that word down but did not know how to spell it.'

'That act is the worst thing that could have happened to us coloureds,' said Absalom. 'Although President Fillmore is against slavery, he fears some of the slave-owning states leaving the union, so they came up with this slave fugitive act last year.'

'But what does it mean?'

'Slave owners can now ask federal officer to help catch and return runaway slaves.'

Absalom's face is set; his breathing is sharp. I touch his shoulder and he relaxes a little. I can see that his thoughts are still away from me.

'It is a bad business,' he says his mouth set, determined. The worst part is these slave-catchers are handsomely rewarded, so they take anyone they like, runaway slaves, freed slaves, or free born, even those who look like me. All are sold into slavery.' He bunches his hands into fists as if ready to fight anyone who came after him or those he loved.

I cannot look at him, at his pain. Even his almost white skin would not save him.

'Many ex-slaves, like William and Ellen Craft, or Henry Box Brown have run away to England. If they return to America, they'll be caught and claimed by their old masters.'

'And that would happen to me and the children.'

'Don't worry. We're not going back to America.'

I crawl into his arms, but I'm still afraid of what lies ahead of us. I think of all the coloureds in America, slave or freeborn always looking over their shoulders, always waiting for the chain around their ankles, the yolk around their necks.

'Let me go with you as soon as we arrive. I don't want us to be parted.'

He eases himself away from me and I am afraid, for I feel a slight distance between us.

'When we reach Liverpool, the best thing would be for you to go with Missy Clara, until I have arranged everything. I will go straight to London to talk to some of our Quaker friends. I've been given names. Many of them live on Paradise Row.'

Even at such a time I could not help smiling. 'Paradise Row? So, these Quakers from Paradise Row are going to help us reach our paradise then?'

Absalom throws back his head, laughs and pulls me to him. 'Yes,' he says, you could say that. As soon as I know the travel plans, I will send you a message.'

'How long? How long will it take?'

'I don't know. A couple of weeks, a month? I cannot tell until I meet up with Reverend Thomas and Mr Hanbury. Once I have the details, I will come for you.'

I nod but I am crying. 'What if something goes wrong? What if you can't find me?'

'I will find you, wherever you may be. Sir Henry Compton, London, I will find him.'

'Missy Clara says we go to Charles Street, London.'

'I will come for you.'

'You promise?'

'I promise.' He gives me a kiss that lengthens and explores. I can feel his heat and I am shameless as I undo the buttons of my bodice. His eyes are on my breasts; he reaches behind him and pulls down the canvas over the opening and lays me down on to my back and I am lost once more.

✲✲✲

We must have fallen asleep because suddenly I can hear movements outside. I sit up to find that except for my *girgri* around my neck both Absalom and I are naked. O lord, what now? Have we slept the whole night through? My heart is thundering in my chest. Quickly, quietly I get into my dress and shake Absalom awake. I put my finger to my lips. He nods and listens, grabbing his clothes he eases into them. He lifts a corner of the canvas. It is barely light yet. The day is just breaking. We wait. Nothing happens.

'I'll go first, after a little go quickly to your cabin. If anyone stops you, say you just came up here for some fresh air because you feel sick,' he whispers in my ear. His kiss is fierce, and I cling to him for a minute and then he is gone.

I listen for a shout, a call, nothing. I pick up my shawl put it around my shoulders and walk towards the ladder. I pass a black sailor swabbing the deck. I've never seen him before. He looks at me but says nothing. My foot is on the first rung of the ladder, when I hear a shout. I stop. Is it just the sailors calling to each other? Then I hear it.

'Nigger, what you doing up here?'

'Told you the damn fool nigger up here all the time.'

'He don't know his place, so we better show him.'

Even from far down the deck, away from them, I can hear the blows and I know they are attacking Absalom. I climb back up, pick up my skirt and run.

There are four men beating Absalom, three sailors and a first-class passenger, one of Sir Henry's drinking friends, Massa Drayton watching. I looked quickly to see if Sir Henry was there, but I cannot see him. At that moment, I don't care if he is there or not, all I want is for these men to stop hitting my man.

'Stop! Stop!' I scream above the sound of the waves and wind. No one hears me, no one stops. I feel for my sling and remember I don't carry it anymore. I run. I slip and fall. A hand is on me. It is the black sailor. He is a big man. He lifts on to my feet.

'You can't stop dem, dey liking the fight too much,' he said.

'I got to stop them,' I cry. 'They'll kill him.'

'He be your man?'

'Yes, and they're killing him.'

He grabs the two sailors right of their feet and puts them down, away from Absalom, who is lying still. I fall to my knees and crawl to him. I take his head on my lap and try to wipe the blood away from his face with my shawl.

'You kill him, you dead too. That what you want?' the black sailor asks.

'He has no business up here,' says a sailor. 'He's been passing for white all this time and he nothing but a dirty nigger.'

'He never try to pass. You jes didn't know the diff'rence,' says the black sailor.

'Well, that's taught him a lesson,' says Massa Drayton as he staggers off.

'Get lost Samson, you niggers all stick together,' says the third sailor walking away.

Absalom groans when I try to sit him up. His face is swollen, his lip bleeding, one eye closing fast. His head falls forward and I know that I cannot lift him.

'Please try,' I say, as I struggle to pull him up. Samson comes over and with one hand gets Absalom to his feet. I am so grateful for his help I could have kissed him. Where has he been? I have never seen him before.

Absalom sways on his feet. His jacket is ripped, and the sleeve is hanging down.

'You better get him otta here,' Samson says. 'Ah'm sure dey goin' to get de calvary and de going be back.'

I half drag, half carry Absalom along the deck. I do not know how I managed to get him down the ladder. There is nowhere else I can take him but to my cabin. My heart is pounding hard as I ease him on to the bottom bunk. O *Oduadu* and all the god, take care of us. If we're caught, we're dead, or at least badly beaten and maybe sold down the river. Henry-Francis is still sleeping; I can hear Sir Henry snoring, but what about Missy? I open the door a little, she is asleep, her arms around Sir Henry. The tenderness between them surprises me. So, for all her talk, she sleeps like that against her man. I shut the door and go see to my man.

I wash Absalom's face; I make him a drink some of my herbs to ease the pain and put salve on his cuts. He falls asleep and I pull my patchwork quilt over his shoulders. I stroke the quilt, each square of cloth, collected and carefully sewn together over a year, sitting with Old Rachael as we talk about herbs and healings. Each section reminds me of a time, a person, a situation; pieces taken, given, found. They all have things to say, of fears and laughter, of anger and longing and now all this is wrapped about Absalom holding him. I fix his jacket, clean it and sew the sleeve back on. I wait.

He is still asleep when Missy Clara calls for me. Sir Henry is already dressed. He staggers off to the first-class dining saloon. I pray he stays there. I wash Missy, brush her hair, get her breakfast all smiling and quick. I feed and leave a quiet Henry-Francis with Missy again. Before I go for water, I move the boxes and cases around so that no one can just walk into my cabin and pray that Absalom will wake up feeling better and go to his cabin without being seen.

Remembering Ada, I wrap some of my herbs in a small piece of cloth and go down to steerage for water. Things have changed. The first person to speak to me was Lil'.

'You did good yesterday,' she says, looks me up and down and walks away.

'Ada?' I ask after her, 'she is better?'

'Yes,' says Biddie, 'but she mighty cut up about the baby. She says she want to see you when you come down.'

I nod. 'Fine.' I put my water pail down and go over to the corner where Ada is still lying. John is by her side. He moves so that I can get closer to Ada. She looks very young lying there but her colour is much better.

'I've brought you some herbs, they will help get you well. Someone will make it into a drink for you, with warm water.'

Her eyes fill up with tears and by the look of her she has done a lot of crying.

'Thank you,' Ada says. She stops looks at her husband then says softly, 'will this happen again? John and I want a family so bad.'

I squat down next to her. 'I don't know. But next time you are carrying take it easy. Drink lots of water and if the birthing does not all come out, don't wait too long. Get help.'

She nods. 'The baby was given to the water yesterday. We called her Faith.' Then she turns her head away and sobs.

When I get back to the cabin Absalom is gone.

✧✧✧✧

We have arrived at Liverpool dock. It is a very cold March day, raining, dirty and noisy. Missy is cross, Sir Henry is busy with boxes and luggage. Henry-Francis is crying. I do not care. I cannot eat, I cannot sleep. I have not seen Absalom since the fight. Every night I have tried to go up on deck and every night the hatch is closed. Is he still hurt? Alive? Dead? No, I would know if he was dead, for something inside of me would die too. But I fear for him. I fear for us.

As I walk to the gang-plank I see Samson moving some boxes. He looks around and then hurries over to me. 'Been looking out for yer,' he says. He smiles, touches my hand and was gone before I can say anything.

I have a note. I know that it is from Absalom. My heart beats fast. He is alive.

I open it quickly.

Psalm 34:18: *The Lord is nigh unto them that are of a broken heart and saveth such as be of contrite spirit.*

# CHAPTER 38

*Consider nothing impossible, then treat possibilities as probabilities.*
*—David Copperfield,* Charles Dickens

## March 1851

Standing on the upper terrace Sarah could see down the valley to Osborne Bay with its deep blue sea. The sight both excited and scared her but she could not say why. She wanted to get down to the beach though. Although the sun was shining, there was a breeze and she wished that she had a coat on or at least a shawl.

'It is fresh and bright today,' said Queen Victoria to Prince Albert. 'Let's walk down to the beach. Give us a chance to see the new plantings on the way.'

Affie immediately ran off with Bertie yelling, 'wait for me,' after him. Sarah would have liked to run down the slope with them but knew that she must stay with the girls. Princesses did not run, Tilla had said when they had been caught running in the corridor.

'Why can boys run and jump and fight but we cannot,' said Vicky. 'It's not fair.'

'Because that's the way it is, Princess Vicky, that's the way it is. There are some things men can do that even your Mama can't and she is the Queen.'

Sarah did not think that this was fair either. How could Her Majesty be the Queen, own everything and be told that there were some things she could not do because she was a woman? Sarah just did not understand. It seemed as if it was the same everywhere. Then she remembered the Minos, the fierce women soldiers, feared by men and women. Just thinking about it and those days makes her body itch. She rubbed her thigh but through her dress and petticoats she could not feel her monkey tattoo, her warrior marks. She did not feel like a warrior. She pressed her nails into her flesh.

It was a long walk down to the beach. Sarah felt the pull of the sea and held on to Alice's hand. They walked along Ring Walk, around the inner park, down High Walk on to Valley Walk with the shrubbery and early spring flowers along the edges, through the woods, full of oak and cedar trees, the road winding gradually all the way down to the sandy beach. There were daffodils every-where, in clumps, or singly, all with their heads bowing down and nodding in the slight breeze, encouraging her on. Each step seemed to make the pull tighter and the urge to run right into the water was strong. Was this pull the call from *Mamiwata*, lying there at the bottom of the sea, waiting to drag her down to the other end of the world. For a moment she wished she had worn her *gri-gri* with her caul, her protection against drowning, but she had put it away again. She was an English Princess now, was she not and they did not wear *gri-gri*. Instead around their necks they wore heart shaped lockets on a chain. English Princesses did not talk about *djudju* nor did they fear water. Sarah took a deep breath and stepped on the sand.

Affie dressed in his stripped swimwear was the first into the sea, screaming and splashing. Prince Albert jumped in from the small pier, followed by Bertie. When they all went under water Sarah squealed and took a step forward afraid that they would not come up again. Only when she could see their head bobbing up and down in the water could she go and join Vicky and Alice in the tent that had been set up for them to change into their bathing costumes.

She was surprised to see Tilla in there too, helping Lenchen into a bathing costume.

'Is Lenchen going into the water too?' Sarah asked.

'Yes, I am. Papa is teaching me,' said Lenchen, wriggling her toes in the sand and pulling at the bloomers that showed below the short skirt of her bathing costume.

'There is a costume here for you too Sarah,' says Tilla. 'You had better get changed. The others are almost done.'

'I can't swim.'

'Papa will teach you too,' said Helena. 'It's easy.'

Out on the beach once more, Sarah could see the boys still playing in the water.

'Come on,' they shouted.

Vicky took Helena's hand and gingerly they walked across the sand into the water. Alice could not resist the water and ran after them leaving Sarah standing at the water's edge, hanging on to her bathing hat that refused to stay put on her head. Their shouts and laughter made her want to run into the sea too, all thoughts of *Mamiwata* gone from her mind. She stepped into the water, the cold making her shiver. She was not sure whether it was because she was afraid or just cold. A hand on her shoulder made her squeal and as she tried to get away, she fell face down into the water. The same hand grabbed and lifted her spluttering from the shallow water. She spat out sand and rubbed her eyes that were burning from the salt water. She looked up to see that the hand belonged to Dr Clark who had come down to the beach in the charabanc.

'What do you think you are doing?' he said. 'You cannot get immersed in water with your bad chest. You will have to sit and watch the others. Please go and get dry.'

Prince Albert who had seen Sarah fall into the sea came striding out of the water. 'Oh dear,' he said. 'Come, I teach you.'

'I'm sorry sir,' said Dr Clark, his whiskers quivering, 'but I cannot agree to her getting submerged in the water.'

'It is quite safe. I designed the swimming bath myself and I have used it to teach all the children. You see the wooden grating suspended between the two pontoons over there? Well, they can be lowered or raised according to the proficiency of the swimmer.'

'Sir, I do not doubt that you could teach her to swim. However, with her bad chest, getting thoroughly wet would be detrimental to her health'

'Well, I believe that sea air and bathing give the children immunity due to the hardening effect of the salt on the constitution.'

Dr Clark blew out his cheeks and his whiskers danced fanning his face that seemed hot and red. 'Be that as it may, Your Highness, it is my professional opinion that at the moment she must not even go for a paddle.'

'Ah,' said Prince Albert, giving him a hard look. 'Maybe when she is stronger.' Sarah watched him swim away and she could have screamed or cried or both. Instead, she bit the inside of her lip until she tasted blood and went back to Tilla.

Dressed in her everyday clothes once more, Sarah sat on the beach, throwing pebbles into the sea, waiting for Queen Victoria to came out of the wooden hut called the bathing machine. Sarah had decided that as soon as the Queen was sitting on its front veranda, watching the others swimming, she was going to talk to Mama Queen about swimming. No matter what Dr Clark said, she was not ill at all and she should know. So why could she not please go swimming? Sarah had not arrived at Osborne House eager to swim but she wanted to be a proper English Princess and they swam. She did not want to be left out. She was tired of being different. She had to learn to swim.

When she saw the Queen's wooden bathing machine, rolling down into the water, she jumped up and ran screaming to Tilla,

'Mama Queen is in there. Quick, Quick.'

'Calm down child,' said Tilla, putting her arms around Sarah who was jumping up and down and pointing to the moving bathing machine. 'Listen, Her Majesty is fine. Look around no one is worried because this is how she goes swimming. See up there, the rope, winches and the footmen? When she's finished swimming, they'll winch the machine up on to the beach.'

Sarah frowned. With all the sea out there why did Mama Queen want to swim inside a hut. 'Is it not too small for swimming?'

Laughing, Tilla gave her a squeeze. 'Her Majesty will stay in the hut until it is almost in the water and then with her bathing woman, she will go down the steps and into the sea.'

'Why?' asked Sarah. Every time she thought that she understood what was happening around her something else showed her that she was still a long away from being an English Princess.

Tilla bent down and said quietly, 'Ah, your people do not know about modesty, do they? I hear they walk around with hardly any clothes on. Her Majesty does not want anyone to see her in her bathing costume.'

'Not even Prince Albert?'

'Not even him. See, there is her cap. She is safe. When she is finished swimming and ready to come out, she will get into the bathing machine and be pulled back up on to the beach. She never swims far, and she never puts her head under water.'

Sarah kicked at the sand and turned her back to the sea. She would wait.

'Shall we go get Princess Louise and help her search for shells?' said Tilla. 'There are some very pretty one around here.'

*Wednesday, 19<sup>th</sup> March 1851, Osborne House.*

> *Dear Mama Forbes,*
>
> *I want to learn to swim, like the others but Dr Clark says I will get sick if I get into the water. But I have not coughed at all. Mama Queen says we must listen to the Doctor. He watches me all the time. I wish he would go back to London. Louise was three yesterday. She had lots of presents on her birthday table and a party. Mama Queen danced with all of us.*
>
> *May I have a party for my birthday too, Mama?*
>
> *Your loving daughter, Sarah*

At Osborne House, Sarah found she had more freedom than she had ever had before. She had been too young to roam around alone in the village. In King Gezo's compound she had been in the sight of the other slaves or the King's women soldiers, big strong and ready to kill. And in England, although no longer a slave, she was still watched by nursemaids, governesses, courtiers and ladies-in-waiting.

On the third afternoon Sarah realised she was free to go wherever she liked at Osborne House. It was raining, and because they could not go spend time outdoors as usual the children decided to play hide and seek on the first floor, near their bedrooms.

'I can find you wherever you try to hide because I know all the great hiding places,' Bertie said.

'No, you won't,' said Vicky ready to argue with Bertie as always.

'Yes, I will. I shall count to fifty so that you all can go hide but I will find you in less than ten minutes. One, two, three...'

As Bertie started counting Vicky shouted 'hide' to Alice and Sarah and ran. Sarah stood for a moment not knowing what to do, where to go. Then she too ran and once around the corner found herself running down the corridor that led to the main household wings This corridor too was full of stone busts and marble statues but unlike the first time, she had seen such things Sarah was no longer afraid of them, no longer afraid of paintings. They did not trap your soul. She slowed down to a walk and looked at each statue carefully. Where they of people who had lived or maybe were still living? Vicky had told her that some of these busts and statues, carved out of stone and marble, were of gods. She searched each one to see if any of them were one of her old gods. But how would she know? How did anyone know what a god looked like?

All the thinking made Sarah's head hurt so she looked away and focused on the floor, on the different patterns of mosaic laid out in straight lines and circles, in squares and triangles. She tried to follow the patterns and so ran, twisted and spun all the way to the main house.

When she realised it was no longer raining and the sun was shining, Sarah decided she had to go outside. Just like the floor of the Grand Corridor, the many walks and drives in the garden made patterns also as they criss-crossed each other with straight borders, circular drives, large squares and trianglular flower beds, full of colour.

She walked, ran, and jumped. She smelled the fragrant flowers; heliotrope, four o'clocks, larkspur, listened to the chattering birds; magpies, swallows and finches, and felt the soft warmth of the sun on her skin. And she was alone, free. It was a long while before she thought of the others. She was afraid then. Was the whole household searching for her? She was sure that she would be scolded and punished for disappearing.

So, she was surprised to find they were all out on the Mount getting on with their own activities and not out searching for her. She was not sure whether to be happy or sad about that. Did they not care that she had been gone for so long? Her Majesty was showing some of her paintings to Sir Edwin Landseer who had arrived that afternoon, Vicky was reading, Affie, Helena and Prince Albert had taken a mechanical toy to pieces and were trying to work out how to put it together again, Bertie was throwing sticks for one of the stable dogs to fetch. Sarah did not know how long she had been away, but they barely looked up when she arrived. She put her hand into her dress pocket and held on to Aina. The wooden doll comforted her.

Only Alice, sitting by herself jumped up and ran to Sarah. 'Where have you been?' she said. 'I looked everywhere for you.' Her lips quivered.

Sarah was sorry to have upset Alice but was happy to know that someone had noticed she was not there. Still a part of her was glad to know that she could be by herself sometimes, at least while she was at Osborne House.

'I got lost; I just went too far.'

✧✧✧✧

*Monday 24<sup>th</sup> March 1851, Osborne House.*

> *Tomorrow we leave Osborne House for London. Everything is different here.*

> *I have done so many things as I learn to become an English Princess instead of an African Princess.*

> *I now have a plot of garden here, just like the others. Prince Albert says it is mine forever and I can plant whatever I like. I have planted carrots and parsnips in my vegetable bed. I*

don't know what parsnips are, but Alice says it tastes nice when roasted. When it is harvested, I can go to the kitchen and see it being cooked.

Yesterday we all went fishing again on The Fairy. Some local fishermen took us. We caught many whiting perch. I only caught two, but Mama Queen got ten. Prince Albert got eight, Affie seven, Alice five, Vicky four. Bertie only got one and he was cross.

I will be sad when we leave but I will be happy to go home to Mama Forbes, Mabel, Anna and Lily and Nanny Grace.

I have lots of shells for Lily and Mabel. Next time I come to Osborne House maybe they can come too.

# CHAPTER 39

*Dey bless fa true, dem wa da wok haad fa hep people lib peaceable
wid one noda, cause God gwine call um e chullun*
Blessed *are* the peacemakers:
for they shall be called the children of God
Matthew 5:9

## March 1851

I am cold, very cold. This England is damp and grey. It has not
stopped raining since we arrived at the docks, and I feel that the
very gods are crying for me.

'Henry, how much longer?' asks Missy Clara for the third time.
'This tossing and bumping is worse than being on the ship.'

'The roads are better than the ones in South Carolina,' says Sir
Henry, 'so stop grumbling.'

Missy Clara tucks the rug tighter around her knees. 'And it is
cold,' she says in a voice I know. 'I thought you said it would be
spring in England and warm.'

Once Missy starts complaining and fussing it goes on and on.
Sir Henry gives a sigh.

'It is spring, look out and you will see the flowers. You'll get
used to the weather.'

I wish I could see the flowers and plants, but I am trying to calm
Henry-Francis. All I can see are trees I do not know, flashing by,
backwards. Where are the giant live oaks, covered in Spanish moss,
the pines, that she had left behind in South Carolina or the palm
trees and mango trees she used to climb back in her village? Even

the grass, green and low was different. What about sweetgrass, tall and strong for weaving baskets? Everything was strange, different.

Sir Henry cannot get used to his son's crying. 'What's wrong with him?' he says. 'He is always bawling.'

'That's what babies do,' Missy Clara says. She looks at me 'Can't you stop him. Faith? You're supposed to be good at this sort of thing.'

'He's hungry Missy Clara. And wet,' I say as I shift him on my lap. His wetness has gone right through to me and the once warm patch is now cold. We are both uncomfortable.

'He's more than just wet,' Missy Clara says and puts her hand-kerchief to her nose.

'I'll push the window down a little,' says Sir Henry.

'No!' screeched Missy. 'It will get even colder. Is there nowhere we can stop, an inn or hostelry so that Faith can go change him? He smells.'

Sometimes Missy talks about Henry-Francis as if he is not her child. She wants him near her as little as possible. What I want more than anything is to be with mine.

'We are not in the city Clara. I cannot just find somewhere to stop at your convenience.'

She gives him such a look. We all can see that this is not the city. There are woods and fields, a stream flowing to our right. The houses few and far between, villages are in the distance.

'Then how long before we reach Compton Hall?'

'Another forty-five minutes or so.'

'Forty-five minutes?' cries Missy Clara. 'We have to suffer this for another forty-five minutes?'

'Fine,' says Sir Henry looking really vexed, 'I was going to leave it until you were over the journey but under the circumstances we'll stop at the mill. That is if you're not too tired, my dear. It's only a little out of our way. Then Faith can see to the child and you can get warm. The mill is always too hot and humid for me, but it must be that way, hot and humid, to keep the threads from breaking during spinning. You can have a quick look around and see what happens to the cotton from Oakwood Plantation. I'm sure the workers will want to see the new Lady Fincham.'

Missy Clara immediately stops complaining. She shakes out her skirt, re-ties the bow on her hat, pinches her cheeks and bites her lips to give them some colour.

'Once we get past the lock at the top of the canal, we will see the mill,' says Sir Henry.

He nods with his head as they move alongside a stream full of rubbish. 'Those,' he added, pointing to the long, low stone buildings, going down the street without a break, 'those are some of mill workers' cottages.'

They are dark with soot. It has many doors and few windows, like blank eyes watching us pass by.

'I thought you did not have slaves in England?' Missy says. 'It's just like our slave quarters.'

Sometimes Missy can be quite smart. Sir Henry's face goes red and I wait for him to shout as he usually does when he is angry but this time his voice is low and sharp.

'Clara, they are workers not slaves.'

'Your people, your workers are tied here, aren't they?'

'They can leave. I hope you are not going to say something like that to Mother.'

Missy just shrugs her shoulders. 'Fine,' she says.

Nothing more is said. We all watch the rain and are thankful when we reach the factory.

'Well, here we are, Compton & Davenport Mill,' says Sir Henry as the carriage turns off the road and through a big iron gate. Past it, next to the narrow canal, are some very big red brick buildings. They are three storeys high, with several tall chimneys belching out black smoke, like *djudju* breath, making the sky even greyer. Smoke, I hold onto Henry-Francis and look away. Smoke means fire and fire is terrifying.

Inside the mill, it is very noisy, hot and dusty, the air thick with cotton fluff that seems to cover everything. We walk past many rows of men and women stuck in their own rhythms, working on different machines whose parts go crashing back and forth. The workers look up but do not stop. The machines go on and on.

'It all starts here. This is the carding room,' shouts Sir Henry hurrying along. 'The raw cotton is brought to this area once the bale has been opened and the seeds and dirt been willowed out.' He pointed to one machine. 'See the cotton being teased, pulled into strands? Next it will go through the combing and drawing process over there, then on to the spinners.'

Missy is not at all interested in how cotton is made, but I am. She just wants the workers to see her and her clothes, but the workers are too busy and cannot stop to stare. He waves his hand to another huge room full of barefooted women, the floor wet, covered with water and oil from the machines. The air in this place is steamy from the heat and water. I break out in a sweat. It is hard to breathe.

'These are the spinners on the new machines. Two or three to a bay.'

Spinners. I remember Madu sitting in front of our hut, rolling and pulling balls of cotton, by hand, to make thread. Then she would go inside, sit at her loom to spin, weaving strong pieces of cloth, which always sold very well in the marketplace. I know that these big machines could not spin better or stronger thread than Madu's.

Henry-Francis is still fussing, screaming to be fed, but his noise is covered by the louder churn of the machines demanding cotton. The machines move fast, and are relentless, never stopping, while little children dart around, carrying full and empty bobbins from room to room, oiling the machines, or quickly tying broken threads to stop everything grinding to a halt.

I catch the eye of a little girl standing still, watching us. She smiles at me but before I can do anything, a man, big and strong, hurries over. He picks the child clean off the ground, gives her two hard slaps before dropping her like a bag full of cotton balls and stones, soft and hard. I cry out and step back, but the girl makes no sound.

I understand why because I reacted the same way when Missus Jane hit or pinched me, even when she broke my finger. I still remember the beatings. They came fast and often, and I barely knew why other than she felt the need to hurt something or someone and that happened to be me. I would never cry. I stayed silent knowing that Missus Jane wanted me to cry out and beg for mercy but I could not give her that power. Would not. My warrior spirit remained strong in me and soon they assumed I was too valuable to lose given my talents for healing and birthing and the beatings stopped. She found other ways to punish me, through my children. I had to bear too much and had too much to lose and she knew it.

The clattering machines' combination of a wire screens and small wire hooks pull the cotton through, while brushes continuously remove the loose cotton lint to prevent jams. I watch the child crawl under the nearest working, and with her hands clear out the lint through the bars of the closely spaced comb-like grid.

'Come, let's go to the office,' says Sir Henry, turning away. 'This area is too humid for you.'

Missy notices the child too and grabbing his arm to make him stop asks, 'what is that child doing?'

He barely stops, throwing a quick glance over his shoulder. 'That one? She's one of the scavengers. They clear out the machines. Very important to stop it getting clogged up, otherwise we'll have a fire.' He frowns as he studies the room. 'These children are good at the work. The smaller, the better. They are quick and nimble. Less likely to have an accident.' He walks away without another glance.

I hurry after Missy and Sir Henry. How many times hair, clothing or even hands have been caught in those machines? I take a deep breath, surprised at how their lives seem so much like mine. Maybe I can feel sorry for white children too.

'Ah, here is Cartwright,' says Sir Henry. He stops and shakes hand with the man, before turning to Missy and saying, 'my dear, this is Abel Cartwright, the mill manager. He knows almost as much about this business as I do. Cartwright, my wife, Lady Compton.'

Mr Cartwright is a short but tidy man, has greying ginger hair with very bushy side-burns and moustache. He pulled himself up straight and bows to Missy Clara, before he and Sir Henry hurry off, leaving us to follow them to the office.

The office is dark, and there are papers, books, and bits of machinery in every available space. In a windowless room, off the main office space I clean Henry-Francis. The room is more like a big cupboard, so I leave the door open a little for some air and light and remain there to nurse him.

'I think we need more scavengers on the floor,' I hear Sir Henry say. 'I saw quite a build-up of fluff under the machines in one of the bays. Not good.'

Mr Cartwright cleared his throat and then says. 'Lord Davenport came in and insisted I get rid of all children under ten years of age, new law and all that.'

'Damn my meddlesome brother-in-law. Get them back. I am not sending them with the machines. Only our best workers are going. I wish that he would keep his nose out and stick to his politicking. I pray he wins the blasted Parliamentary seat and stays in London.'

I stop listening, my mind is not on their talk but on the mill women. I want to see what they are doing with the cotton. I've seen it in the cotton fields; row upon row of little balls of cotton like fallen clouds, resting before continuing their journey. I've seen how at the end of the day no one can stand up straight or carry the heavy sacks to the barns. I've seen the whippings if enough cotton is not picked. None of us on the plantations knew where the cotton the field hands picked all day ended up. Had any of the slaves I know touched the cotton that is being worked on by the women spinning right now? Do these women know where the cotton comes from or how much people suffered to get it to their machines?

I have so much to tell Absalom. I must write it all down but how? Then I see, from the little light coming in, that I am sitting in a place full of paper. I feel around and gently pull the edge of one piece towards me. It is blank, no writing on it at all. My heart begins to pound. What if I take one? Two? Three? I know there will be big trouble if I am caught but I cannot stop myself. Slowly, carefully I take three pieces of paper. Quietly, hardly daring to breathe, I fold the sheets and lay them inside the basket at my feet.

Now I have paper for my diary. When we get where we are going, I will find somewhere to hide all my writings. I will put down everything; fill the papers with thoughts and feelings about my journey, about Absalom, about becoming free. Then, one day my children, and even my children's children, will read my words and know me, Fatmata, daughter of Dauda and Isatu.

# CHAPTER 40

*Ya bless fa true, wen people hole ya cheap and mek ya suffa and wen dey say all kind ob bad ting bout ya wa ain true, cause ya da folla me*
Blessed *are* you, when *men* shall revile you, and persecute *you*, and shall say all manner of evil against you falsely, for my sake
Matthew 5:11

## March 1851

At last, after two weeks we leave Compton Hall. The first evening there Mrs Nichols, the housekeeper, sends Mary, the under-maid to sit with Henry-Francis so that I can go down for my meal. I think I am to get my bowl and go find somewhere to sit but when I enter the kitchen, Mrs Nichols waves me in. The whole place is just full of eyes and all staring at me.

'This is Faith, Lady Compton's maid, come all the way from America,' she says.

The word maid makes my eyes sting with unshed tears. Yes maid, yes that what they all think I am. I wonder what they would say if they knew the truth. I do not tell them though. They will find out soon enough.

'Move over, give her some room.'

The others shift along the bench as she points and names everyone, but I cannot take in anything, partly because I cannot understand all her words and partly because I am confused. Did they want me to sit down at the table with them?

'Come sit here,' says one of the maids whose name I cannot

remember and pats the bench. I slide into the seat but am ready to jump up if I am mistaken. There are smiles and nods, questions and answers.

All was well until the day after the fire.

'Ma says the bosses treat us worse than those nigger slaves in America,' says Millie, the housemaid, brushing her hair off her face. Her mouth is small, but a lot of words pour out of it all the time. Her eyes are green and remind me of a snake. Madu used to say, 'stay away from snakes.'

I feel my inside tighten. How could anyone think that slaves have a better life than the mill workers. I stand up.

'What's the matter my dear?' asks Mrs Nichols.

'Your Ma does not know what she's talking about,' I say, before I could stop myself. Everyone goes quiet. I tremble. What is going to happen now? I would never have spoken like that back at the plantation.

'Millie is not meaning you,' says Cook. 'Why don't you sit down. Finish your food?'

I take a deep breath and was about to do just that, but Millie is not giving up. She has more to say. She stands up too.

'Huh, they are so touchy, these darkies,' says Millie smiling as if she had said something very funny. She looks around her for support but no one else is smiling. 'It's true, though. Da says, the slaves don't have to worry about nothing. They get free food, housing, clothes. We have to buy all that, don't we? And if there's no money you're done for.'

We face each other across the table. My heart is beating fast and the palms of my hands are wet. I know I should sit down and ignore her, but I cannot.

'You think we have everything for free?' I say my voice low. The words come out as if someone was squeezing it from my being.

'She is talking about the slaves they got in America, dear, not the likes of you—free blacks,' says Cook, quickly reaching out to pat my hand. I pull away.

'There are a few coloureds around these parts, you know,' says Sam, picking bits of stringy beef from his teeth with his fingernails. 'I've seen them Manchester, Bury, all over.'

I wanted to shout, yes, she is talking about me, and things she knows nothing about. I grip the edge of the table and press my lips together.

Daisy leans forward and pulls at Millie's sleeve. 'You're wrong Millie, just leave it. Last time I went to see Ma I went with her to a temperance meeting at the Lecture Hall in Warrington. This ex-slave, Frederick Douglass, he talked for over an hour about how the poor slaves are treated back in America. By the end were all crying and giving money, even Ma.'

'Why should we give them money? They can go back, be slave or free, for all I care.'

'Shh, girl,' says Mrs Nichols sharply, 'don't be so silly. Haven't we all got enough problems without you trying to stir things up? You either sit down quietly and eat or you can go clear the dining room. Which is it to be?'

Millie sat down with a thump and glared at me.

'You can walk away from a job,' I say to her. 'A slave can't. They are bought and sold like animals. The Massa's horses are treated better. We have nothing for free. We pay for it with our souls. We have no choice.' The stinging in my eyes turns into burning I can talk no more. I turn and walk away from the table, from them all before they see my tears. They watch me go; nobody stops me.

✵✵✵

Now we are in London. The fog, the smell, is overpowering not to mention the noise and busyness which is worse than the

Liverpool dockyard. Sir Henry has made sure he does not travel in the same carriage as his son. At Euston Station, it is the second carriage for luggage, Henry-Francis and me so for a moment after we disembark, we are apart, them by the first class carriage, and me an African woman with this English child in my arms. Sir Henry is searching for me and eventually we see each other across the crowded concourse. I see standing beside him Missy Clara, her eyes are raking the surroundings, no thought on her child, least of all me. It takes all my strength to walk toward them.

When we arrive outside No. 8 Charles Street, Missy Clara and Sir Henry have disappeared indoors. But where do I go now? Although Henry-Francis is sleeping in my arms I do not know whether I go up to the front door or down the stairs, from the pavement to the basement and the servants' entrance. Again, and again I am at a loss as to what I should do as a maid. As a slave, I know what I am expected to do, what I can say, where I can go. In England, it is all mixed up. I am doing and saying things for which I would be beaten on the plantation. I am learning that freedom has its own rules. Boldly, I walk up the steps to the door but before I could pull on the bell the door is opened. With my head held high I walk in.

'This way,' says the maid, waiting for me in the hall. She stares at me as if I am some strange animal. I smile at her, she goes red in the face, turns and hurries down the hall. I follow her bobbing cap. She opens a door, waves me in, gives a quick bob and goes.

I give a look around. The room is large, cold with big heavy furniture. The lamps are not yet lit and there is no fire, so the room is brightened only by the dull afternoon light coming through two big windows draped with dark green curtains. A young lady looking out of the window turns around to look at me with a smile, her blue eyes set wide apart. Her face changes and she turns away so fast, her hair, the colour of ripe corn, piled high wobbles ready to tumble down. This must be Isabella.

Sir Henry is standing by the empty fireplace; Missy Clara sits on the edge of the chair next to him, still wearing her cloak as if she is only visiting. There is a man and a woman sitting opposite her. Sir Henry's sister, Lavinia, I think for they look alike, the same grey bulging eyes. She seems very cross, staring hard at Sir Henry. The man sits with long legs stretched out, his thick black beard covered most of his face. They all look at me, then at the old woman sitting on a high, straight-backed chair, hands folded on her lap. Her walking stick by her side. She is all in black except for a white collar around her neck and white lace cap perched on top of grey hair pulled back into a tight bun. Her face is still, no smile, no frown but her eyes bore into me.

'Here he is, Mother,' says Sir Henry, rubbing his hands.

'So, this is my grandson,' she says her lips hardly moving. I step forward and hold the baby out to her, but she makes no move to take him. I do not know what to do. I look to Missy. She is twisting her fingers and seems ready to run out of the room.

'Well, my American nephew and your slave,' says Lavinia. She laughs but it is not a happy sound.

Sir Henry takes Henry-Francis from me and hands him to Missy Clara. She holds him as if he is made of glass. They are both uncomfortable and I hope that Henry-Francis is not going to start crying. I do not think that his grand-mammy would take that well at all. I go and stand behind Missy's chair ready to take the baby off her.

'Only half American, Lavinia,' says Sir Henry sharply. 'And Faith is not my slave.'

Missy glances at Sir Henry then looks down, her hold on Henry-Francis tightens so that he gives a whimper.

'Slave? Slave, Henry?' asks Lady Fincham, leaning forward on her walking stick pressing hard on the white lion's head handle. 'You know I do not hold with slavery. That has been abolished here for almost twenty years now. Even in the Indies they have let go of that barbaric system. Isn't she a free black?'

I wait to hear what Sir Henry is going to say.

Sir Henry licks his lips and says, 'she is Clara's maid, Mother, and Henry-Francis' wet-nurse.'

I look down, shocked at his lying. Missy Clara is trembling.

'It has been a great source of shame knowing that my uncle still owned a plantation with slaves, long after my father had given up his Jamaica plantation,' he added.

'Your father was well compensated by the government for his two hundred and fifty slaves, though,' says the man sitting next to Lavinia.

'That is beside the point, Robert. We did the right thing but how could I comfortably speak about emancipation of slaves with that in the background? At last, this family has divested itself of the last remnants of slave ownership.'

Robert? Lord Robert Davenport, Lavinia's husband, the man Sir Henry said was an 'interfering buffoon', the one who had stopped the smallest children from working as scavengers. Maybe if Sir Henry had not gone back to using them, the little girl would still be alive and Billy would not have been so badly burned.

'Yes,' says Robert, stroking his beard. 'But not the money, eh Henry. At least with the inheritance from your slave owning uncle, you can repair the fire damage at the mill.'

'There would have been no fire if you had not removed so many of the scavengers,' says Sir Henry, his voice deep and loud. 'The cotton fluff has to be cleared away as quickly as possible. One spark settling on it can start a fire.'

'There would have been no death or two badly burned people, if you had not allowed that little girl to go back on the floor,' says Robert, pointing a long finger at Sir Henry. 'It is against the law, Henry, to use children under ten, and you know it, but it is always money and profit with you.'

Sir Henry gives a laugh that did not sound like a true laugh. 'And what is it with you Robert? That pile of crumbling brick you call a castle or the money you get from the mill to repair it?'

Lavinia gasps and leans forward. 'Mother, can you tell Henry to stop being so nasty?'

The young woman moves away from the window, her pink dress swishing and swinging, to sit next to Missy Clara. 'Good, another family row about money.'

Lady Fincham bangs her walking stick on the floor and gives them all a look. 'Be quiet Isabella. Enough all of you. What is done is done. I will not have this crass arguing in my drawing room. Let us all be happy that Henry is home, with a new wife and baby. And that at last Uncle Clarence's plantation is sold and his slaves set free.'

Is that what she thought, that the slaves on that plantation were now free? Is that what Sir Henry was supposed to do then? Another lie. I chew on my lip to stop me saying anything.

'Cartwright will be going over in a couple of weeks to finish everything.'

'Finish what?' says Lady Fincham sharply. 'Wasn't that why you were over there so long, even though you have the mill to run.'

'He is going back to negotiate the buying of cotton now we do not own the plantation.'

'Mother, we know why he stayed there for almost a whole year,' interrupts Lavinia pointing at Missy Clara and Henry-Francis. 'While he was busy wooing, Robert was here, and he kept the mill going all that time.'

Yes, everyone knows why he remained in South Carolina for so long. Sir Henry had lost his first wife in a riding accident, and is a good twenty years older than Missy Clara but from the first moment he eyed her, though, it was an instant attraction, and he told anyone who would listen that she was the sweetest pie he ever did see and he had to have her.

✺✺✺✺

I remember that first time Sir Henry came to Burnham Plantation. There was a lot of fuss and noise in the big house, whispers and some angry exchanges behind closed doors. The day Sir Henry arrived all of us were ordered to the slave quarters except me and the cook. Massa William wasn't greeting him with any happiness and came in walking and talking fast and loud. I was so unsure of what to do I could only sit and wait outside the parlor door as the voices inside, rose and fell for hours. I could hear small parts of things. Sir Henry declared right away.

I hear him say to Massa William, 'I have come to claim my inheritance from Great Uncle Clarence but I do not intend to stay here. I have my mill to run back home in England.'

Massa William sound shocked but his replies are a jumble of sounds I can't understand. Then suddenly the door blew open and Massa William summoned me inside to serve dinner. I try to make myself small and not noticable in any way. The food is served with me and cook and sometimes the Missus helping and all is eaten in silence with only the sound of the knives scraping the china and the occasional tinkling of the crystal glasses. In the silence their breathing fills the room.

Then after the dishes are put away, Sir Henry says, 'I'm selling Oakwood Plantation, and do as my uncle has instructed, give certain slaves their freedom papers.'

Now the shock is mine. I stand still to listen, instead of pouring the wine, when he says that, even though I know I will get a slap from Missus Jane later.

Massa jumps up, puffs out his chest and bellowed, 'what? Are you one of those damn abolitionists' sir?'

'I do not want to own slaves. We English do not have slaves.'

'Then sell them sir, sell them all of them,' says Massa William. He stops talking, however, when he sees the way Sir Henry is looking at Missy Clara.

'That will all take time,' he says softly. 'Still, I might be persuaded to stay a little longer than I originally planned,' Sir Henry is smiling and nodding his head at Missy Clara. Her face is flushed red.

Within three months Sir Henry weds Clara and sells Oakwood Plantation and all the slaves to Massa William. His Great Uncle Clarence's slave wife and three slave children are not set free, as instructed in the will.

✵✵✵

Lord have mercy. He is lying to his mother again and Missy Clara, she knows but says nothing. What if I open my mouth and say to the old lady, he did not free the slaves, he sold them. I'm not a free black maid. I am a slave. What would she say? What would Sir Henry do? Throw me out? Where would I go? To Absalom? Where would I find him? What if they sell me? Send me back to the plantation? It all fine to say I'm free but free to go where? Do what? The questions all race through my mind. Questions with no answers. I keep my mouth shut.

'Henry, ring the bell for Taylor.' Lady Fincham says, pointing to the cord hanging next to the mantel piece. 'He can get the nursery maid to show the girl up to the nursery. Nanny Dot is there with Lavinia's Celia and Edwin.'

Sir Henry pulls at the cord. I hear nothing.

'She cannot be both wet-nurse to the child and maid to you Clara. You can share Bates, Lavinia's maid. She can do both of you for now until you get one of your own.'

'But Mother!' says Lavinia, jumping up. 'Why me, why can't she share with Isabella?'

Isabella rushes to Lady Fincham's side 'Mother, no. Hannah will be busy with me. I'm going to need her. I have so many functions plus the presentation and the ball.'

'You're doing far more for Isabella than you did for me, Mother. I did not get a ball, just a dance.'

They glare at each other and I know that each want to inflict pain on the other. I look at all of them and I see that they are all full of anger, fear and greed. For all that they have, they still have nothing.

'Do not argue, Lavinia,' Lady Fincham says as she uses her walking stick to help her stand up. 'Lady Whigham is sponsoring and presenting Isabella with her daughter Sophia. In exchange Sophia will share the ball I'm throwing for Isabella.'

Sir Henry holds out his arm, but Lady Fincham ignores him. He opens the door, and we all watch her walk out, leaning on her stick, Isabella following.

At the door Isabella turns. 'You had better go take some more laudanum Lavinia and calm down,' she says and runs out of the room laughing.

'Shut up,' shouts Lavinia jumping up and slamming the door shut before turning on her brother. 'You know that bringing your slave here could ruin Roberts's chances of being elected, don't you?'

'Cannot Robert speak for himself?'

Robert peels himself off the low chair. 'Come,' he says to Lavinia, 'I'm sure that as she is not our slave, sorry our maid, it will have no adverse effect on my being elected into parliament, my dear.' He bows to Missy Clara before he, and Lavinia, leave. Missy Clara looks as though she is about to cry. She hugs Henry-Francis tightly and he wriggles, stretches his arms out to me and cries loud and strong.

Sir Henry pulls hard at the bell cord once more. 'Can't you stop him crying?'

I do not know whether he is speaking to me or Missy Clara, but I reach out and take Henry-Francis from his mother.

'He's hungry,' I say.

I did not say, I'm hungry too.

# SARAH

# CHAPTER 41

*There are obstacles to be met and we must meet and crush them.*
*—David Copperfield,* Charles Dickens

## April 1851

The door opened at Winkfield Place but before Sarah could take more than a step into the hall, Emily came flying down the stairs and threw herself at Sarah, almost knocking her over.

'You're home, you're home,' she squealed.

Sarah laughed and hugged Emily. 'Yes, I am and look who brought me home,' she said stepping to one side.

'Freddie,' Emily screamed and ran at him. He picked her up and swung her around. Mabel was not far behind pulling at him wanting him to swing her around too.

'Freddie, you came too,' she said.

'What a welcome. I must stay away much more,' he said laughing. 'Where is Mama?'

Mabel stepped back and noticed Freddie's face. 'What happened to you?' she gasped.

'It's nothing.'

Sarah felt a hand on her shoulder. 'Welcome home, Sarah,' says Mama Forbes, with a quick hug. Her attention, however, was on Freddie too. 'And Freddie,' Mama Forbes stretched out her hand to him. He crossed the hall, and she took hold of his chin and moved his face from side to side. 'Oh dear, your face! Have you been fighting? You know Papa would be very disappointed. Come to the drawing room. I want to find out what has been happening at school.'

Mabel and Emily held on to his hands as Freddie followed Mama Forbes. Sarah was suddenly all alone in the hall and did not know what to do. She took a deep breath and decided to go to the drawing room too.

'What was the fight about?'

Freddie hung his head and would not look at this mother. 'Nothing, Mama.'

'Come on, no one fights over nothing. Please tell the truth. Who did you fight with?'

'George Withenshaw.'

'And why?'

Freddie straightened up and looked his mother straight in the eye. 'He called me a nigger lover. He said he did not know how we could all sit at a table with one. I told him not to use such words. But he said it again Mama and gave me a push, so I pushed him back and we fought. I could not let him say such things Mama.' Freddie's voice cracked. 'Sarah is a princess and my sister. What is fine for Her Majesty should be fine for everyone.'

'You fought because of Sally?' asked Emily, her eyes wide with admiration. 'You are so brave!'

Mama Forbes patted the seat next to her. When Freddie sat down next to her, she pulled his head down and kissed his forehead. 'I do not condone fighting but there are times when we have to stand up for what we believe and know is right. We will not talk about it anymore. Go up to Nanny Grace and get her to put some witch hazel on it.'

Freddie smiled. 'Thank you, Mama. It's better now. It was much more swollen.'

'What about George? Was his face all swollen too?' asked Mabel.

'Yes. His eye was completely closed, and he had a bleeding mouth as well.'

'That's enough Freddie. No need to relish in it,' said Mama Forbes, though she did not sound cross.

Sarah felt her eyes fill with tears. She bit her lip trying to stop herself from crying not because she was sad but because she was happy. *Freddie has been fighting because of me! ME. I have a big brother once more. I am home.*

*I have two homes, Winfield Place and Windsor Castle. At least that is what Alice says.*

✿✿✿

*Monday 14th April 1851, Winkfield Place,*

*I return to Windsor Castle today but this time on my own, going for my German lesson with Vicky and Alice. We have not had one for a few weeks. Mabel says that I will have forgotten everything, but I have not. Sie irrt sich deswegen. I think that she just wished that I have.*

✿✿✿

Lessons with Frau Schreiber were just over when Tilla came to get Sarah and the Princesses.

'We are going for a walk to the school before luncheon. Go fetch your shawls and change your shoes,' she said.

'Yes Tilla,' Vicky and Alice said, jumping up, pushing their chairs over, scattering books to the floor and hurried to get their shawls. Sarah followed them, wondering what was so special about going to a school.

'What school?' she asked, putting on her bonnet.

'The school in the park,' said Vicky, retying the bow on her bonnet. 'It's for the children from the village and those living in the workers cottages around the park.'

'But what do you do when you go there?'

'We listen to them read and sing, look at their composition writing, and their writing from dictation. The girls also do cooking and washing, while the boys are examined in History and Geography.'

'Mama visits every year to give out prizes and she takes us with her sometimes. We clap loudly when they collect their prize,' said Alice.

'It is all part of your education,' said Tilla who had returned with her bonnet on, and shawl around her shoulders. 'Our workers' children are lucky to be able to stay in school so long. Most other children, if they go to school at all, leave before they are eleven. Those who get a prize treasure it. Most times that might be the only book in their houses.'

The two-room school had one classroom for girls and another one across the hall for boys. They sat in rows, two to a desk, the youngest at the front. Mrs Heaton, the headteacher took them to the girls' section first. Most of the children in the school had seen Queen Victoria and the Princesses before, but a black girl and a princess at that, now that was different. They stared at Sarah and she stared right back at them. While Queen Victoria was with Mrs Heaton the head teacher, Vicky, Alice and Sarah walked around the classroom talking to the children, looking at the slates. Whenever Sarah came near one of them, they reached out to touch her hand or her face, then looked at their hand to see if it had changed colour. Sarah did not mind. She would have done the same.

One little girl held on to Sarah's hand and would not let go. She was no more than five, with two stumpy plaits that stuck out on either side of her face and dark brown eyes that darted from face to face trying to take everything in.

She tugged at Sarah's hand. 'Miss, Princess, can you talk? Willie says that darkies have no tongue, so you can't talk like us.'

Sarah bent down and stuck her tongue out. The little girl laughed.

'See, I have a tongue, and I can speak,' said Sarah, laughing too. 'What's your name?'

'Jane. And that's my brother, Willie,' she said pointing to the other classroom. Through the door Sarah could see into the other room. At the back was a boy of around ten years old. His bright red hair stood up as though some one had just pulled him out of a hole by his hair, his freckled face was split into a huge grin. Sarah stuck he tongue out at him and he doubled up laughing.

The other girls crowded around Sarah pulling, touching, asking her questions. She did not notice that everyone else had moved on to the other room.

'Miss, Miss. Can you read?'

'Princess, can you write?'

'Princess, look what I write on my slate. *An apple a day keeps the doctor away*. See, I can read. Mrs Heaton says it's a proverb.'

Is that possible, thought Sarah. If I eat an apple everyday would that keep Dr Clark away? Would it stop her cough?

Just then Mrs Heaton rushed back from the boys' room swishing a cane in her hand, maybe practising just how she was going to use it once the visitors had gone. 'All of you,' she said, her face red as though she had sat in the sun for a long time, 'go back to you seats at once.'

Sarah stared at the cane. She remembered how much it had hurt when Papa Forbes had hit her with one. She did not want the children, especially little Jane, to be caned later. She held on to

Jane's hand and said, 'could they stay, please? They are telling me about all the things they are learning from you.'

'I'm sorry, Princess Sarah,' said Mrs Heaton, 'but Her Majesty is ready to give out the prizes now.' She propped the cane by the door and waved Sarah ahead.

One by one, the boys and girls came up to receive their prizes from Her Majesty who shook their hands and praised them. It was Willie who came top for spelling. He grinned at Sarah as he walked past. When Queen Victoria handed him, his prize, a book about horses, he clutched it to his chest and bowed.

'Thank you, Your Majesty. I love horses.'

Queen Victoria smiled. 'I do too.'

Willie was not afraid to talk to the Queen. 'I know, Your Majesty. My pa, John, works in the palace stables. I start working there, sweeping and feeding the horses after Easter.'

'Well, I shall look out for you when I go to the stables,' said Queen Victoria.

At the end of the prize giving, Queen Victoria left with her ladies-in-waiting. Sarah was the last to leave. As she hurried past the girls' room, she picked up the cane by the door. There would be no canning that day. Outside Sarah broke the cane in two and threw the pieces away before joining the others.

'There you are, Sally,' said Queen Victoria. 'Did you like our little school?'

Sarah nodded. 'Mama Queen, will I ever go to school?' she asked

Queen Victoria gave her glance. 'Do you want to?'

Sarah nodded. 'Maybe then I can win a prize and have a book of my own.'

✿✿✿

*Friday 11th April 1851, Winkfield Place*

*This afternoon we are all going to Windsor Castle to present Mama Queen with special copies of Papa Forbes' two volume book, 'Dahomey and The Dahomans. Being the Journals of Two Missions to the King of Dahomey and Residence at His Capital in the Years 1849 and 1850.' They are based on the journals Papa's wrote during his mission to the Court of the King Gezo of Dahomey. He has written about me in it. I do not want to read the journals. I am not Salimatu anymore.*

✧✧✧✧

Sarah was not expecting the Crimson Room to be so full of people when she and the rest of the Forbes family arrived for the presentation. Not only was there Queen Victoria, Prince Albert and the Royal children there but so were Sir Charles, Lady Phipps and various other attendants.

Mama Forbes entered the Crimson room first. Behind her walked Freddie and Mabel, each carrying one volume bound in beautiful Moroccan leather, followed by Sarah and Emily.

'Ah, the whole family, Mrs Forbes,' said Queen Victoria.

They all curtseyed and bowed. 'Almost Ma'am. Anna is too young, and the Captain is still away at sea,' said Mama Forbes with a smile.

'Indeed,' said Prince Albert, moving to stand next to the Queen. 'When will he be back from this tour of duty?'

'I do not know, Sir. It could be a year or more. However, he wanted us to present the books to Her Majesty as soon as they were published and not to wait for his return. He said that he was sure you will want to read about your little African Princess in volume two. May we present you, Ma'am, with the two volumes based on Captain Forbes' journey to Dahomey.'

Freddie and Mabel passed the beautiful leather-bound books they have been carrying to Sarah and Emily. They stepped forward, curtsied again and handed over the two volumes to Queen Victoria.

'What splendid books. Thank you. I am sure that Prince Albert and I will enjoy reading all about the Captain's adventures, Mrs Forbes. You and the children must be so proud of him and the work he is doing, saving people like our Sarah here, even though it keeps him away from you for such a long time.'

'We are very proud, Ma'am.'

'And Sarah, have you read what the Captain has written about you and King Gezo?'

'No, Mama Queen.'

She did not say that just hearing King Gezo name made her insides twist and turn. Only a few months ago she was just a child slave to be sold or sacrificed, now she was a princess with a new family and important friends. No, she did not want to think about those days. She pinched herself hard. She had to stop being afraid.

# CHAPTER 42

*Oona way mo walyable den a whole heapa sparra*
Fear not therefore: ye are of more value than many
sparrows
Luke 12:5

## April 1851

Three days in London and still no word from Absalom. Almost a month now without seeing or hearing from him. He said he would be here, waiting. So, where is he? Lying sleepless in the room I now share with Nellie, the nursery-maid, I feel sick. I have not been able to eat for days. Absalom must come for me or I am lost. I kick off the thin blanket and hug my patchwork quilt. At the plantation, I slept on a pallet filled with spanish-moss, the red bugs, chiggars and spiders still hiding among the leaves. I used to lie there itching and scratching. This night I am wrapped up in the quilt that has also been around him. I hold it close and try to catch his scent.

Silently I call to Maluuma, 'O wise one, sitting there among the ancestors, talk to the Gods for me. Beg them to keep Absalom safe. Plead with them to allow him to come for me.' I hold on to my *gri-gri* and wait. Nothing.

Someone or something is shaking me. I must have fallen asleep. I open my eyes and in the half-light of morning, see a pale face, long hair the colour of straw, wearing white. I know this is *djudju*, sent by the ancestors to take me back down. Fear grips me, tight. I want to leave this place, but not to be dragged to the world below. I want to live, live with Absalom, my man. I shut my eyes, shrink against the wall and moan.

'You gotta a pain? Lor, you been groanin' and talkin' all night.'

Ancestors and *djudju* cannot talk like this. It is Nellie. I open my eyes and pull myself back into the room. She says she's nineteen years old, one less year than me, but she looks like a child, small but strong and quick, running up and down from attic to kitchen, fetching and carrying all day long. It is hard for me to understand everything she says but I get enough.

'I come to work here as kitchen maid but now I'm nursery maid,' she told me the first night. 'Nanny Dot say she too old to go up and down the stairs.'

I groan again. I don't want to talk to her, not right now. I want her to go away, to give me a few minutes on my own.

'It real bad?' asks Nellie now, hanging over me.

'I'm fine,' I say, turning to the wall. 'Go start your work before Nanny wakes up.'

'O Lor' it was that bad on the ship, huh?'

I catch my breath and turn to face her, afeared that I might have given away too much in my sleep. 'What do you mean?'

'You cryin' and sayin' over and over, "the waves, the waves, I don't want to sink in the waves,"' she says, slipping on a light grey dress.

It hangs loose from her thin shoulders. I too have a dress like that now, but mine fits much better although the cap keeps falling off my thick hair. Nanny Dot calls it a 'uniform' and says that all the maids in the house must wear it.

'I'm sorry I kept you awake. It was just a dream.' I say, relieved I have said nothing about that first journey; the chains, the smell, the people thrown overboard. Nor about Absalom.

'Some dreams be worse than the real thing.' She leans forward and whispers, as if telling me the biggest secret, 'to tell you the truth, water gives me the willies. I could never cross to America. All the time I'd be waiting for the ship to capsize.'

'Sometimes you have no choice,' I say, not looking at her.

'I won't even go on the river steamers, though they be quicker and cheaper than the omnibus. Not since *The Cricket* steamer, be blasted to bits on the river.' She wraps a big grey, work apron over her dress and pulls the belt tight.

It is the quiet way she says it that makes me sit up. 'On the river? Which river?' I ask.

'Thames. You go down to the river and you'll see many river steamers taking people from one part of London to the other, but they not safe. Ma used to say so and she was right.'

It seems as if the thought of the steamers has made Nellie's legs go weak, because she sits down on her bed suddenly. '*The Cricket* was getting ready to leave Adelphi pier for London Bridge, packed with over a hundred and fifty people, when the boiler exploded. Flames, boiling water, oil, bodies all over the place.'

She hugs herself and start to rock, just as I had seen women do in Talaremba when someone had journeyed to the ancestors.

'What happened to the people?'

She bows her head and I think that she is not going to answer, then she says, so softly I have to lean forward, 'some get blown into the air, some sprayed with boiling water, others jump into water and get trapped in mud. It was bad.' She takes a deep breath and adds, 'twenty people died right there, others later. One of them was Pa. He were the boilerman.'

I get up and sit by her side. I don't know what else to do.

'I dream about him all the time,' Nellie says. Her voice is shaky. 'Sometimes he's in the water, calling for me to come help him, other times he tell me to go get the little ones out of the workhouse.'

I do not know what a workhouse is but from the way she says it and the look on her face I can tell that it is not a good place.

'I got to put them in there,' she says, grabbing my hand and holding on tightly. 'Didn't want to. I use to help Ma look after the young 'un's but I couldn't look after the five of them on me own. No food, no home. None of the neighbours would take even baby Sam. They want paying. I had no money.'

'Was there no one to help?'

'No. Bessie already gone off, working in some bar and on the road to ruin. She be a bunter now, selling herself. Saw her one time, in Clerkenwell, dressed in feathers and fur-belows and hanging on some swell's arm. She act like she don't see me but I know she seen me, 'cause she pull at him and they rush into one of them bawd houses. I never tell it to Ma or Pa. He would've gone there, drag her out and give her his belt.' She nods and nods, sighs, then start to rock again. Tears flow down her face.

'What about your Ma?

'Soon after Pa died, Ma died too, givin' birth to Sam. They say it were the shock of seein' Pa's body. He were all burnt and swollen when they pull him out o' river after five days.'

I'm afeared to ask but I must know. 'Your sisters and brothers, they still at the workhouse?'

She gives a small cry and shook her head. 'When I go back later to see them, they gone, all of them, even little Sam. Gone. No one ready to tell me where. They give me a piece of paper, but I can't read it. They'll all be sent out working by now. Harry was always small and quick. God help us if they send him to be a chimney sweep. He scared of the dark.' She looks at me, a change in her eyes, hope-filled she says, 'Maybe he be an errand boy or somethin' like that.'

I listen as she names her lost brothers and sisters. She is like me, I soon realise. Her people torn from her. When I think of it

I feel something squeezing my inside. It is an old pain that has eased but is never gone. I try to push it away, but it stays, squeezing and twisting my insides. Salimatu, my lost sister, my brothers, my parents join the pain of leaving my children and maybe never seeing them again. Soon I join Nellie in rocking and crying our tears falling on ourselves and each other.

'Hear me telling you all m' troubles and you have yours to deal with.' She shakes her head as if to shake something loose. 'You have your terrible losses too.' Wiping her face with her apron she says, 'I'm sorry you lost your baby.'

I stop rocking and stand up. I'm too near her. 'What baby?'

She looks at me as if I have said something foolish. 'You must have at least one child and not so long ago otherwise where does your milk to feed Henry-Francis, come from?' She quickly plaits her long straw-coloured hair.

I need to move past this small room at the top of the house, get out there into the open and breathe. I walk to the window and look out. All I can see from the slanted window is the sky brightening up into new day. I can't see the stars that will lead me home one day. I can't see Maluuma, or the ancestors. I can't see Absalom.

'Yes, I had Jessy, six months ago,' I say at last. 'Missus Jane, the Massa's wife, she took my baby from me, then gave me to Missy Clara.'

'Gave you? Why?'

'So that I will have enough milk for Henry-Francis. The same thing happened with my other children, Lewis and Kezia,' I stop then, before I go too far, before I tell their Talaremba names, before I tell her about Anthony, the one I named Amadu, the one that is now with the ancestors.

'You have three children?' ask Nellie. 'Crumbs you not much older than me.'

'Yes, but when they jump you, they don't care how many years you have.'

The words rush out and wrap around my heart. The pain pushes out more words, things I've not planned to say. 'Slaves keep their babies but a month, then the women are sent back to work.' I'm sobbing.

Nellie's eyes get bigger and bigger as I talk; she licks her lips two or three times before the words come out.

'Slave? You? A slave?' She takes a step backwards, then stops. 'Nanny Dot say you a maid and wet-nurse.'

'That's what Missy Clara and Sir Henry telling everyone because his mother wants no slave in her house. But that is what I am to them, a slave. They all just lie and lie.'

I bite my lips to stop myself from saying anymore but I can't stop the tears. I've said too much. We are not the same. She is white, I am coloured. She is English, I am from Talaremba. She is free, I'm not.

'I ain't never meet a slave before,' says Nellie. 'I thought slaves be different.' She shakes her head as if trying to shake that fact away. She points at my face. 'The cuts, they show you a slave?'

'No. They show I'm the daughter of a chief.' I pull at the neck of my shimmy and show her my branding, the mark on my left shoulder, there for all times, an S, an angry snake lying under my skin.

Nellie covers her mouth as if to stop a scream. She stares at the branding but cannot look at me.

'This shows that I'm a slave and this.' I show her my right hand, the little finger sticking out. 'I can't bend it see, not since it got broke.' I do not tell her how it got broke though. How can I explain that a mistress can do whatever she likes to her slave, beat her, pinch her, break her back, break her finger, all the time trying to break her spirit?

A loud cry makes us both jump. It is Henry-Francis in the nursery next door. I have forgotten about him. How could I? Until this night he has never slept far away from me.

ANNI DOMINGO

The first two nights in this house, I sleep on the floor by his cot, in case he wakes up in the middle of the night. The third night when Nanny Dot finds me there, fast asleep, wrapped in my quilt, she shakes me awake.

'What's this?'

'I always sleep on a pallet near Henry-Francis, so if he cries in the night I am there,'

'Well, he will learn that you cannot always be by his side. We are not in America, we do not sleep on the floor in this country. Tomorrow you stay in your bed.'

Nanny Dot is small and round, with shiny black button eyes, a small mouth that forms a tight circle of surprise when she laughs. Her grey dress with its high collar and long sleeves seems to gather her in as she glides around, her feet never showing. She looks soft like a pillow, but I am sure that no one disobeys her.

'I must get to Henry-Francis and stop his cries before Nanny Dot goes to him.'

'Oh, Lor', says, Nellie, tucking her plait under her cap. 'I gotta hurry or Nanny Dot will gi' me what for and you don't want to see that. I'm sorry they took your sister and children.'

'And I'm sorry they sent your sisters and brothers away. I hope you find them,' I say as I push past her.

I rush to Henry-Francis and pick him up. He screams even louder. Henry-Francis cries all the time now. I cannot comfort him. If only I had some of my herbs, but I used the last bit before we left Compton Hall and I do not know where to get any more.

Nanny Dot watches me button up my top, 'He's still hungry.'

'I know, but he'll not feed.'

Her eyes bore into me until all I can do is lower my head. She says without accusation, 'you don't have enough milk. You're not eating enough. She grabs my arms and runs her hands down them feeling for muscle, for bones. Just like the slave auctioneers

361

when they prepare to sell people. I shrink away from her hands which fall away then from mine. 'I suppose you're not used to our food. Well, you need to eat. You need to be strong and healthy, to be able to make him strong and healthy.' She turns to leave, saying as she goes, 'good boiled or roast meat, maybe, some sago, rice, or tapioca pudding, and fresh fish, that's what you need. I'll have a word with Cook. Meanwhile I will make some food for Henry-Francis.'

Listening to her talk about food makes me want to bring up all that I have managed to eat that morning. I cannot tell her why everything I eat tastes like chaff and cannot settle in my stomach.

Nanny Dot orders Nellie to light the small stove in the box-room next to the day-nursery, before going to her room and coming back with a small blue bottle, Godfrey's Cordial. 'Not that it is something to give him at his age, but it will keep him quiet for a little while.' She measures a little of the liquid onto a spoon. When Henry-Francis opens his mouth to yell, she pours the liquid into his mouth and hands him over to me.

Nanny Dot tells Nellie 'go to Cook and ask her for biscuit and a small glass of porter. Tell her I say we have to build Faith's strength.' In the pantry Nanny Dot measures out a little wheaten flour ties it up in a cloth and boils. She takes a spoonful of the cooked flour, adds some milk, mixes it together, boils it a little more, cool it down. Pap. Nanny Dot is making pap. I remember Madu making pap for Salimatu. But she did not pour it into a bottle and put a new India-rubber teat on it, like Nanny Dot is doing. Madu lay Salimatu across her knees, pour some pap into her cupped hand and slowly, slowly drip the pap into the Salimatu's mouth. I shut my eyes to hold on to that memory, but it floats away like smoke. I open my eyes to the now.

Nanny Dot puts the rubber teat to the now quiet Henry-Francis' lips. I sit and watch as he sucks. I have nothing to do. Nellie brings me a glass of porter. It has always been me who served others. What would Old Rachael or Ma Leah say if they could see me now, as I sit and wait for a white girl to serve me?

I am no longer a maid, no longer a wet-nurse, but I am still a slave.

# CHAPTER 43

*The most important thing in life is to stop saying I wish and start saying I will.*
—*David Copperfield*, Charles Dickens

## April 1851

*Wednesday 16ᵗʰ April 1851, Winkfield Place*
*I played Fur Elise on the pianoforte for Mama Forbes. She cried. She says it is Papa Forbes' favourite music. Mama does not know when he will be back home. Mabel says she hopes he will not bring back another sister. I don't think that she was joking. We miss him. Tomorrow we all go to Windsor Castle for Easter Egg hunt.*

Sarah was excited that Mabel, Emily and Anna had also been invited to the Easter Egg hunt at Windsor Castle. None of them had been to one before.

'Will the eggs break when we get them?' Anna asked Sarah.

'I don't know,' Sarah said.

'The eggs represent new life, Jesus' new life when he is arisen from the dead,' Miss Byles said. 'The eggs are boiled hard, so they can be painted without breaking.'

Nobody could really explain Easter to Sarah though. How could Jesus die and then rise again to save people? Wasn't that what *djudju* did? Thoughts of Easter confused her. It was the story of

Easter that had made her cut up her blue dress which led to the caning from Papa Forbes. That thought made her bite thumb hard.

Besides the Seymours and Phipps children, some of the children she had met at the park school were at the castle too. Sarah was with Alice and Emily when Jane came running over.

'Princess Sarah, Princess Sarah,' she called, 'do you remember me?'

'Yes, Jane,' said Sarah, 'I remember you.'

Jane smiled. 'I told me Ma and Pa bout you. They never seen a coloured person close.'

Sarah laughed and said, 'well you have.'

'Would you like to hunt with us?' asked Alice.

Jane nodded and took Sarah's hand.

The prize for collecting the most eggs in an hour was to be bars of chocolate. They all wanted to win that. Sarah had never tasted chocolate and neither had Jane. Soon they had seven eggs and hoped that was enough to win. When they saw some of others returning to the terraces with their finds, Sarah's group of searchers decided to give up.

On their way back, however, Alice stopped suddenly. 'I forgot. Papa always hides some eggs in the stables and riding school,' she said. 'Come on, if we find them, I'm sure we'll win.'

Sarah did not know how to tell Alice that she was frightened of horses. She hesitated for a moment, then taking a deep breath ran after the others.

The stable smelled so strong it made Sarah's eyes water. She tried to hold her breathe as she walked past the horses shuffling and snuffling in their stalls. Almost immediately Alice found two green eggs.

'Sarah watch out,' Emily called, suddenly.

Sarah turned to see another horse being led into the stables by a short, bow-legged man. She jumped back but still felt the horses' breath on her face.

'Pa, this be the princess I tells you about,' said Jane pulling her father towards Sarah.

'She's scared of horses,' said Emily, stepping in front of Sarah.

'Don't worry,' said Alice, 'Bessie is so gentle. John won't let anything happen to you.'

'That'd be true. I done teach all the little 'un's to ride on Bessie,' John said. 'She won't go bolting off, that I can tell you.'

✿✿✿

*Sunday, 20th April 1851, Winkfield Place*

*I am glad Easter is over. Reverend Byles' sermon was all about Jesus rising from the dead. I want to think of nice things.*

*We have all been invited to Alice's birthday party on Friday. I have made her a picture frame from some of the shells I brought from Isle of Wight.*

*My birthday is next Sunday. I am glad it is close to Alice's. I am to have a tea party. Mama Forbes has sent invitations to Alice, Vicky, Lenchen, also to Maria and Henrietta Phipps and Augusta Seymour. I wonder what I will get for my birthday. I have asked Mama Forbes for a doll like Emily's Arabella but Aina will still be special. Mrs Dixon is baking a special cake.*

✿✿✿

The first they knew that something was wrong was when Edith came up with the water for washing. It was not hot, but the girls said nothing, they did not want to get Edith into trouble.

'Where's Nanny Grace?' asked Mabel.

'She's in the kitchen,' said Edith, her voice shaking. She would not look at any of them.

'What's wrong?' said Sarah.

'Nothing Miss,' said Edith but her lips trembled and when Sarah touched her shoulder she could feel the maid trembling.

'I must go get the breakfast.' She ran out of the room before they could ask any more questions.

Mabel, Emily and Sarah stared at each other. Something important was happening downstairs and they were being kept out of it.

'Forget breakfast,' said Mabel, 'let's go downstairs and find out what is happening.'

But before they could do so Nanny was right there. Her face blotchy, eyes red, hair falling out of her cap, her apron rumpled as if she had twisted it again and again into a knot. Sarah was sure that Nanny Grace, the wiper away of tears, had been crying,

'Sit down girls and have your breakfast when Edith brings it up.' Nanny spoke softly. They could hardly hear her. It seemed to take all her strength to say even those few words.

They were all frightened by this new Nanny Grace. What could make her look and sound like that?

'Miss Byles will be here shortly. She'll keep you occupied as I'm going to be helping downstairs. You must promise not to leave the nursery until I come for you. It is important that you obey me on this.'

Sarah frowned. Nanny Grace was never busy anywhere else but in the nursery.

'But Nanny,' said Mabel, 'Miss Byles said we were not having any lessons for two whole weeks as it's Easter.'

'Please, just do as you are told for once, Mabel,' said Nanny quietly. 'I'll go get Anna. Freddie will come and join you soon. You must all be together at a time like this.'

'At a time like this?' said Mabel, after Nanny had gone. 'What did she mean by that?'

Sarah thought hard but could not work it out.

Miss Byles arrived before breakfast was over. She hadn't been crying but she looked very sad. There were no lessons. Sarah held Aina while they listened to Miss Byles read the opening chapters of *David Copperfield: Whether I shall turn out to be the hero of my own life or whether that station will be held by anybody else, these pages must show.* Sarah hugged her knees and got lost in the story. She felt as though Mr Charles Dickens was writing about her.

Miss Byles left when Edith brought their lunch of boiled beef and carrots but none of them felt like eating.

Mabel said, 'Edith, can we start getting ready for Princess Alice's birthday party, now?'

Edith's eyes darted around the room as though trying to find a way of escape. 'I don't know, Miss Mabel,' she said.

'I'm sure Nanny will be up soon,' said Sarah. 'Why don't we just choose what we want to wear and then help each other to get dressed?'

'Yes, we can do that,' said Emily getting up from the table.

'No, Miss,' said Edith, 'don't do that. There's no point. I don't think you'll be going to the party.' She clapped her hand over her mouth as soon as she realised what she had said.

'Not go to the party?' said Sarah, her eyes widening at the thought of it.

'What do you mean, not go to the party?' Mabel said loudly.

'I should not have said that,' said Edith, clearing the table and hurrying away with plates rattling and gravy spilling over.

It was almost four in the afternoon before Nanny Grace came back to the nursery. She stopped when she saw Mabel, Sarah and Emily dressed in their silk dresses, sitting quietly at the table. They had tried to get each other dressed but the sashes were tied in untidy bows, Mabel and Emily's plaits were coming undone and Sarah's hair was in un-brushed lumps.

'I'm sorry girls, but you are not going to the party.'

'Her Majesty will be very angry,' said Emily, her lips trembling.

'No, Her Majesty will understand.'

'Alice will be upset. She won't come to my tea party on Sunday,' said Sarah and the tears that had been held at bay all day flowed now.

'You poor things,' said Nanny Grace. She picked up Anna who had been playing with her wooden dolls. 'Come girls. Your Mama wants you now. She has something to tell you.'

Sarah's stomach knotted and she held onto Aina. It stopped her from digging her nails into her arm as she usually did when she was scared.

# FAITH

# CHAPTER 44

*A Mus aks God fa bless dem wa cuss ya, an mus pray for dem wa do ya bad*
Bless them that curse you, and pray for them which
despitefully use you
Luke 6:28

## April 1851

Outside, at last. In the days since we arrived in London, I have
not left the house. I wonder how long it would have been
before I did leave if it had not been for Lady Lavinia.

She comes up to the nursery most mornings to see her two
babies, but I think it is for Nanny's special medicine. Sometimes I
hear her begging for it.

'Nanny Dotty, please I need it,'

'Now, Miss Lavinia,' says Nanny 'I've told you, it is not something to take all the time. Only when the pain is bad.'

'Well, it is,' she says, grabbing the blue bottle from Nanny and
pouring a large tablespoon.

Henry-Francis is screaming. He is hungry and wet.

'Cannot that child be quiet for once,' Lady Lavinia says to
Nanny, ignoring me.

I try to quieten him, but he wriggles on my lap and screams
even louder.

'He looks pale. He's not sickening for something is he, Nanny
Dot? I don't want the children catching something from him?'

Nanny Dot pats Lady Lavinia's arm. 'Now, do you think that I would let any harm come to Miss Celia and Master Edwin? Henry-Francis has no illness. He just needs to get out into the fresh air.'

'Haven't they been out since they arrived?' Lady Lavinia says, eyeing me up and down. 'Maybe Henry and Clara are afraid she'll run away.'

My heart skips a beat. I break out in a sweat. Does she know what I am planning or is it that she hopes I will run away. Either is dangerous.

Nanny Dot laughs, 'Run away? Miss Lavinia? Why would she want to do that?'

Lady Lavinia pats Nanny Dot's shoulder. 'Just joking Nanny.' She looks at me and adds, 'maids don't run away, only slaves try to, and sometimes they succeed.'

'It's been raining too hard Miss Lavinia. They'll all go for their constitution today.'

I bend over Henry-Francis so that she cannot see my eyes, see my thoughts.

✿✿✿✿

I take a deep breath now and look up and down the street. Is Absalom here, has he waited for me all this time? I listen for a call, footsteps running after me but there is nothing. I could cry.

'Here is Taylor. Now we can go.' Nellie says, when the footman arrives pulling with a long handle at what looks like a small black open carriage. The inside is red with a narrow leather seat at one end and a cover to keep off the rain. It has a high, shining wheel on each side and a small one in front.

'What's that?' I ask.

'It's a perambulator, a baby carriage,' said Nellie. 'Some people call it a push-along.'

Nellie lifts Edwin into it, wraps a rug around his legs and straps him in. 'Sit Henry-Francis in that.' She points to the basket that is already in the well of the carriage. Celia will walk for a little while.

I don't want to leave the street in case Absalom comes, but what can I say to Nellie, to Nanny Dot, to anyone if they ask why I refuse to move? What if he never comes?

'Where are we going?' I call after Nellie who is already walking down the street.

'To Berkeley Square. It's not far. Nanny Dot says that we must not be too long as it might rain again.'

When we stop at where the roads cross, I ask, 'we going straight on or to Queen Street?'

Nellie laughs, 'The Queen ain't no street. What are you talking about?'

'The name of the street. There,' I say pointing to the street name nailed on a wall. 'Queen Street.' The look of surprise on her face makes me laugh out loud.

'I never know the names I just know to go right or left,' she says. 'You can read. If this ain't a rum do? Never stayed long enough at the ragg'd school to learn.'

I've forgotten myself and given away my secret. My heart starts to pound. What if Missy Clara hears of this? I will be undone. I grab hold of Nellie and force her to stop walking.

'You can't tell anyone. It's a secret. A slave is not allowed to read or write. If Sir Henry or Missy finds out I will be beaten or worse.' My eyes fill with tears and I bite my lip, waiting for her reply.

'They don't know?'

'Nobody knows but you and...' I stop. Once again, I'm about to tell Nellie more than I should. I take a deep breath. 'Nobody here knows, but you.'

She shakes her head and the ribbons of her bonnet tied up in a bow under her chin shiver. 'We all have things we can't tell. I'll keep me mouth shut.'

'Thank you,' I say, and we smile at each other.

We have only gone a little way when Nellie stops. 'Sometimes, I go that way,' she says. 'Shepherd's Market be down that lane. Jack works at a stall there. He delivers fresh vegetables to the kitchen for Cook, that's how we met.'

'He sweet on you?' I smile at the look on Nellie's face.

'Yes, we walking out.' She catches her breathe and covers her mouth. 'You won't tell, will you?' she says. 'Missus don't want us maids gettin' with men. If we do she'll let us go without a character.'

'I won't tell.'

'Nanny will kill me if she know I take the children down there.'

'Then we won't tell her that either. I want to see the market,' I say. 'And Jack.'

Now Nellie has started talking about Jack, she cannot stop. She talks without waiting for an answer, which is good as there are many things going on in my head. 'We go out every other Sunday, on my day off. Sometimes we just go for walk, go to the fair, or the circus if it's in town. He taken me to the theatre to see the singing and dancing on stage, though we don't go to the penny gaff. Jack say it be too rough. Seen the black-face minstrels. They also from 'Merica. Can you sing like them? We been all the way over to Astley's at Vauxhall. We going again now that they open for the season. You can come with us. It's only a few pence.'

Me, Faith, Me, Fatmata, go to a theatre to see singing and dancing? I do not sing or dance, not anymore, not since the sailors on that hell-hole of a ship brought us up from the pits, still in chains, to make us dance for them. But I have no time to think about all these things for we are in the middle of the busy market. The noise from the men and women shouting out makes me move fast, between small girls with baskets of watercress, boys with trays of meat pies held high over their heads, a newspaper boy waving the newspaper at anyone who walks past him. I wish I could get one so that I could read about this place that I have been brought to by Missy, but I cannot stop. I bump into a man in a long black coat. He lifts his black hat sitting atop long black hair in ringlets.

'Old but good quality clothes,' he says.

I shake my head and smile.

'You can always find something to wear from these Jews but make sure you wash them first 'cause most of the time they full of lice and other things,' says Nellie, and pulls at me.

That's when I notice the books at his feet, books full of words and I open my eyes wide. The Jew man sees my face. He bends down and picks some up.

'What about a book then? Any of them for one *yennap*, one penny.'

My heart begins to beat fast. Someone is holding out a book to me. Someone not questioning whether I should read or write.

'No one buys 'em. Waste of money when you can't read, or write,' says Nellie. 'Come on, we don't have much time and I want to see Jack.'

I follow her, but I want a book now, more than ever. A book to put down all the things that I am seeing, hearing, feeling. I have run out of the paper I took from the mill.

A woman stops in front of me, her bonnet crushed by the basket of flowers on her head. She lifts the basket off and drops it onto the ground so that the flowers shake and tremble. A little girl, no bigger than Khadi, her face streaked with dirt, carries a tray of lavender. The smell stops me. I bend down and take a deep breath. Lavender, good for healing cuts, good for sleep, good for many other things. The child holds out a bunch.

'Here Missy,' she says.

I take the lavender, drop it into the corner of the perambulator, wishing that I had something to give her in return. I smile at her and walk away.

'Ma, ma,' she screams, 'the darkie ain't given me the chink.'

'Stop, you trying to half-inch that?' shouts the flower-seller after me, before turning to the child and giving her a slap. 'Don't you learn nothing yet? You take the chink first.'

'You ain't goin from here until you gi' us what you owe. Give me the half-penny,' the woman says grabbing hold of the push-along handle and shaking it so hard that all three children start to cry.

'You pay fer that, you thieving darkie,' says the man.

'I can't pay,' I say spreading out my hands. 'I've no money. She gave it to me.'

'Give it to yer! You take me fer' a mug?' says the flower-seller. 'You jus gi' me the flatch, you tea-leaf.'

I reach into the push-along and get the bunch of lavender. 'Here take it back,' I say and make my escape through the crowd. Somehow, searching for Nellie, I'm shoved, on to the narrow street among costermongers and their barrows, the brewers' drays and their yelling drivers? My arm is grabbed big a woman and I'm back on the pavement. I am shaking.

'Lor' you trying to kill yourself and them children,' she says. Her plaid shawl is pulled tight across a large chest, her skirt hitched up shows good strong boots. She is dressed like all the other sellers in the market, the same, except for one thing, her face is black though lighter than mine. I stare at her and my lips tremble. This is the first coloured person I've seen close to since I arrived in England.

'Ere, don't you start a' crying now, you safe,' she says. 'What you doing here, anyhow? This no place for children like these in their fancy push-along.'

Henry-Francis is screaming. I pick him up and rock him in my arms to quieten him. 'I came with Nellie, the nurse-maid. I've lost her, and I don't know how to go back.'

'You stay put,' says the older woman. 'She'll come find you. Eh, you shaking, sit down.' She pulls a stool from behind her pie stall.

The woman leans against her stall, takes in my black bonnet, black cloak, reaches out to touch my grey dress. 'What they call you?

'Faith.'

She laughs. 'Faith, not hope, eh? They call me Hany. Where you from? You talk different. Not like me man. He come here from Jamaica, after he be free.'

I don't know how to answer her. Where am I from? Africa, Talaremb, Okeadon, America, the Gullah? What should I tell this woman?

'It all right,' she says, 'It hard to talk about the time before you be free. When I first meet me man, James, in Liverpool, he don't say nothing of that life. We been together over two years before he tell me. Hard. Soon as he get his freedom, he left the sugar plantation and join a ship. He never going back, don't know where any of his folks be. They were all sold separate like. It different for me. I born and bred in Liverpool so never go through all that. But that don't mean we get it any easier. When it come to white man or coloured, we know coloured lose every time. A lot of them think the coloureds are coming after them now they be free. They know what they done and them afraid. That why they want to send us all back to Afric.'

I forget about finding Nellie. I want to know more about Negroes living in England.

'You were born free in England?'

'Yes. My father come from Africa. Not as a slave but as a sailor. He meet my mother, a white woman and they marry and have three of us. I marry a Jamaica ex-slave and we come down to London. He was cook on the ship. Now he go to Smithfield early in the morning, get the meat. He bake the meat pies, I make the fruit pies and I sell them in the market.'

'But don't you want to go back to Africa?'

'Africa? That backward place?' says Hany. She shakes her head. 'I never been there and I'm not going there. They still savage, begging your pardon. They not like us.'

She cannot mean what she is saying. I come close to her and say, almost in a whisper, 'but you and your ancestors come from Africa.'

'Long time 'go, child. Won't find any of us coloureds signing up to go Africa. They say there still be them out there catching people and taking them to 'Merica to be slaves, even though that all supposed to be over and done with. No, no, we aren't going there. Never meet an Afric and never want to either.'

I cannot bear to hear such words from the mouth of someone who looks like me. Hany sits on the stool she had brought out for me and mops her face with the corner of her apron.

'No, we fine here. Not one of us listen to that talk from the Quakers.'

My heart takes a jump. Maybe if I find one of them they can tell me where to find Absalom. 'Quakers? Where are they?'

'Everywhere. They always holding meetings about freeing them slaves still in 'Merica. They already free in Jamaica, Barbados, and some other places, James say. But not them in 'Merica. You must know that too. Sometimes, the Quakers, them bring along one of the slaves that done escape from slavery, to talk 'bout their time on some plantation or another. They always wanting money to help free them they've left behind.'

'Hey Hany,' a man calls, 'you sellin' today, or you jus goin sit there gabbing? I can always go to Jack's pie-stall inside the market.'

Hany jumps up and goes back behind the stall. 'Get away with you. Al's pie ain't got no meat in it. You'll be running back here faster than you can say Jack rabbit,' she says, laughing loudly, as she tears a piece of newspaper into two and wraps the pie in one half.

I pull at Hany's sleeve, once the man walks away. I cannot go until I find out about the Quakers. 'Hany, the Quakers, they ever come around here?'

'Sometimes. There be a few nobs round here who feel sorry for those that still be slaves in 'Merica. They have money to give for that, but they never think about those of us right here, just call us black poor and try to send us back to Africa. There's one of their meetings soon, next week Wednesday I think, at the Grosvenor Chapel Hall in South Audley Street. I ain't goin though. I only ever been to one meeting. Don't need to hear all that. I got a man at home that been through it. He don't need a-telling.'

I hear my name. It is Nellie. She is panting, her face red, her bonnet crooked.

'Faith, what happen to you? I turn round and you gone. Jack and me, we've been looking for you everywhere. You scare the living daylight out of me.' She turns to the boy next to her, 'Thanks Jack. Got to go now before we get into trouble with Nanny Dot.'

Jack, his face almost as red as his hair, takes his cap out of his long dirty apron pocket and puts it on.

'Right you are,' he says. 'Told you we'd find them. See you Sunday.' He nods at me and he is gone, lost in the crowd.

'Come on,' says Nellie, taking hold of the perambulator.

'You be careful,' says Hany tearing up more newspaper to wrap another pie for a woman waiting with her penny. I bend down and pick up the piece of newspaper she has dropped on the ground.

'Will you come away,' calls Nellie.

'Thanks Hany,' I say and hurry after Nellie.

'Keep away from the Quakers.' Hany's laughing voice follows me.

Nellie and I do not speak until we are back on the main road.

'So, who was that then?' she asks.

'Hany pulled me out of the way of some horses when I was trying to get away from the flower-seller.'

'What flower-seller?'

'The one who thought I was trying to steal the bunch of lavender. I have no money to pay for it. I thought the child gave it to me.'

'Dear Lor', I leave for a minute and you get into all kind of trouble. Nanny Dot can't know about any of this. You hear me? If she ask, we say we go to Berkeley Square. And don't touch anything in the market unless you got money to pay for it. Good thing it quarter day. We get pay tomorrow, last Saturday in the month.' She slows down. 'It's our day off on Sunday so Jack and me, we going to Astley's. It started again last week, on Easter Monday. You can come with us if you like.'

I am not listening, however, for I realize that I am still holding the newspaper in my hand. I see in big print, *African Princess in London.*

# CHAPTER 45

*Perseverance and strength of character will enable us to bear much*
*worse things.*
—*David Copperfield,* Charles Dickens

## April 1851

Although it was still daytime Mama Forbes' bedroom had the
gas lamps on and the curtains drawn. Sarah's hands went
wet and clammy. She saw Lady Melton in the room. When did she
arrive from London? Why was Mama in bed with Freddie standing
close? Was Mama ill? She must be because I could see Nanny blue
medicine bottle on the little table by her bed.

'My poor children,' said Mama Forbes. She pulled herself up
and opened her arms. Anna ran to her and climbed up on to the
bed. Mama hugged her.

'Are you ill, Mama?' asked Emily squeezing past Freddie to hold
Mama's hand.

'Why is Mama crying? Freddie?' said Mabel turning from one
to the other.

Freddie took a deep breath and put his arms around her
shoulder.

'It's Papa,' he said.

'Papa?' whispered Mabel staring at him.

'What do you mean it's Papa?' asked Sarah, feeling sick.
Suddenly she knew what he was going to say.

Freddie's eyes filled with tears. 'Papa's gone.'

'Gone where?' asked Emily her brow creased, trying to understand.

'Papa has passed on,' said Freddie, adding as if to make sure they understood, 'he died.'

'You liar,' screamed Mabel. 'Papa can't be dead. You're wrong. What a horrible thing to say.' She beat at his chest with her fists and wailed. Freddie held her tight.

'Papa, papa,' cried Emily and fell on Mama. 'I want Papa.'

'I want Papa too,' said Anna joining in the sobbing. Nanny picked her up and rocked her like a baby.

'The Lord says *we which are alive and remain shall be caught up together with them in the clouds to meet the Lord in the air*,' said Nanny Grace wiping away first her tears and then Anna's.

Sarah stood alone and shook. 'When?' was all she could say. She could hardly breathe. 'He died at sea off the coast of Freetown, from malaria,' said Lady Melton, sniffing into her handkerchief. 'A whole month ago. The Admiralty should have informed the family as soon as it happened. Buried at sea! There is no body to lay to rest. Dreadful.'

Hearing this Mama Forbes let out another cry, 'Oh Frederick, my dear Frederick. Who will take care of my poor fatherless children now, Josephine?'

'I'm almost grown Mama,' says Freddie. 'I can leave school and go into the Navy just as Papa did. Then I'll see that you are all taken care of.'

'No,' shouted Mabel, pushing Freddie away and staring at Sarah. 'You don't have to take care of her too. She's not our sister. If Papa had not gone over there to save her and her kind, he would be here now.'

'Mabel Elizabeth Forbes!' said Nanny Grace. 'You stop that, right now.'

Mabel's words hit Sarah like sharp pebbles flicking at her face so that she blinked and winced. Mabel ran out of the room, sobbing.

But they were her family now, one of their own, was she not? She squeezed Aina so hard a piece broke off.

✵✵✵

*Friday 25<sup>th</sup> April 1851, Home*
*Please God send Papa Forbes back like you did Jesus. I will*
*never ask for anything else. I promise. Amen.*

✵✵✵

There was little sleep for anyone that night. Sarah could hear Mabel tossing and turning, Emily crying for her Papa, Nanny in the school room, praying and praying. What good was that? When Edith came up later, Sarah heard her talking to Nanny Grace and she crept to the door to listen. Had something else happened?

'The funeral is in two days though, Nanny,' Edith said. 'I'm never going to have time to get me a black skirt.'

'Shh, girl,' said Nanny. 'you can use whatever black crepe is left over when Mrs Newbury is done, to trim your dress and bonnet. That will have to do for now.'

'Why is the service being done so quick? There'll be no one at the church.'

'There's nothing to wait for,' said Nanny Grace, blowing her nose. 'It's not a funeral. There's no body to dress, no casket, no hearse to follow. But people will come. Lady Melton has sent out the service invitations. Look how many condolences cards have been delivered today. Oh, yes there'll be many at the service, even at such short notice. Wasn't it just a few weeks ago they were writing about him and his book in all the papers?'

'I just hope that Madam will be able to cope.'

'It's the shock of it and no graveside to visit later,' said Nanny. *'But the Lord healeth the broken in heart and bindeth up their wounds.'*

Sarah sat up in bed all night, holding on to the broken Aina, staring into the dark, waiting for she did not know what.

✵✵✵✵

As soon as she could the next day, Sarah went into the garden. Tom was not there. He was busy with the horses, running errands. Everyone was busy, too busy to think. Sarah wasn't busy, but she did not want to think. She went to the far end of the garden and dug a hole, a big hole. She wished she could get into it and disappear. The rain came but still Sarah sat there, watching the hole fill up. That was where Edith found her and took her into the kitchen.

'Lawd have mercy upon my soul,' cried Mrs Dixon when she saw Sarah. 'You'll catch your death in those wet things and you with your bad chest. Edith don't just stand there, you vasey. Go get me a towel and then run upstairs and bring me a change of clothing for the child. Hurry now.'

It was when she saw her birthday cake that Sarah broke down.

'I know, lovey, instead of doing a birthday tea tomorrow, I'll be doing the funeral tea. That is not something I thought I'd be doing just yet for the Master.'

Sarah howled. Mrs Dixon sat down and cradled her.

'There, me lovey, you let it all out. He was your father in every way, no matter what Mabel says. I might be down here, but I hear everything.'

'She says it's my fault Papa has died,' Sarah gulped.

'She don't mean it, lovey. It's just that she's hurting and she's trying to find someone or something to blame. We're all hurting. Can't believe we never going to see him again. Oh, the Master.'

'Nanny Grace says Miss Sarah must come up at once,' said Edith who had returned without towel or change of clothing, but full of excitement. 'Mrs Newbury has been sewing all night and Miss Sarah's black dress is almost ready. She must get into it and go to the drawing room where Madam is waiting for her, with a visitor.'

'Drawing room?' said Mrs Dixon. 'Madame's in mourning; she'll see no one until sometime after the funeral, I mean, the service. You sure you heard Nanny, right?'

'Yes, Cook, I heard her right. Madame and Lady Melton are already in the drawing room. And Lady Melton says you must prepare your best tray of refreshments immediately,' said Edith, pushing Sarah's out of the kitchen.

Up in the nursery, Mabel and Emily were in their plain black dresses, no laces, no bows.

'Hurry, Edith get her into the dress,' Nanny Grace said taking the dress from Mrs Newbury. 'I'll try to fix her hair.'

In no time at all Sarah was in a black dress just like Mabel and Emily and hurrying downstairs. Outside the drawing room Edith checked each girl before knocking on the door, opening it and letting them go in.

The room was gloomy even though the lamps were lit. Not only were the curtains drawn but the mirrors and pictures were draped in black crepe. Mama Forbes, Lady Melton, and even Freddie, standing by the unlit fireplace, were also dressed in black.

Mabel who had stepped in first, stopped. Her mouth fell open, she looked at Lady Melton and Mama Forbes, looked back at the visitor and curtsied.

'Your Majesty,' she said.

'Your Majesty,' said Emily trying to curtsey but stumbling.

'Your Majesty?' said Sarah, curtsying. Her eyes filled with tears at the sight of the Queen sitting there. Why had no one said who was with Mama Forbes?

Queen Victoria held out her hand. 'Dear child,' she said.

Sarah ran to her and held on to her hand. 'Mama Queen, they say Papa Forbes has passed away. Is it true? Did he die on one of your ships?'

'Little Sally,' said Queen Victoria, patting Sarah's cheek. 'I'm afraid it is true.'

Sarah face twitched and though she tried to hold the cough in, her eyes watered, and the cough burst out. She coughed and coughed.

Queen Victoria raised her eyebrows and threw a glance at Mrs Forbes, who twisted her handkerchief around and around, smoothed out the black border, then twisted it all over again.

'You poor children,' said Queen Victoria. 'I know what it is like to lose a father so young. If there is anything I can do Mrs Forbes, please let Lady or Sir Phipps know.'

'Thank you, Ma'am. I am most grateful and honoured that you have come in person.'

'This is a private visit, the least I could do. Prince Albert too sends his condolences. He is extremely busy with final arrangements for the opening of the Exhibition in London. Captain Forbes was a fine man and a great sailor who helped to keep our seas free of evil. I have been reading his book that you presented to me just a few weeks ago. Dear Sally is proof of his good works. I will, of course, continue to be her guardian and provide for her.'

'Thank you, Ma'am,' said Mrs Forbes giving a small bow dabbing her eyes with the crumpled handkerchief.

Queen Victoria smiled, picked up the china cup from the table by the side of her chair and drank.

'More tea, Ma'am?' asked Lady Melton, reaching for the teapot.

'No more, thank you Lady Melton. My compliments to your cook, Mrs Forbes. Her cake was delicious.'

'I will pass on your compliments Ma'am.'

'I will not be at the service tomorrow. The children and I will be returning to Buckingham Palace after breakfast on Monday. I have to do some drawing room presentations.'

'I will be travelling to Dundee with the children on Tuesday.'

'Dundee? Whatever for?'

'My husband's father, Captain John Forbes, and his two sisters live just outside Dundee. Old Father Forbes is too frail to travel down for the service here, tomorrow. There is no grave.'

Mama Forbes tried hard not to cry but a small sob escaped from her and Lady Melton patted her hand. Freddie moved to stand behind his mother's chair and put his hand on her shoulder. Sarah glanced over at Mabel and saw that she was holding hands with Emily who sniffed and wiped her tears away with a tiny handkerchief. Mabel glared at Sarah who looked down and leaned into Queen Victoria and the cough was there again.

'Mrs Forbes,' said Queen Victoria after a sort silence. 'I see that Sally still has the cough. Even at this time of the year the weather in Scotland can be cold and unpredictable. So, she will come with us to London on Monday.'

'We're only going for a short while, Ma'am,' said Mama Forbes.

'Then she can stay with me until you return from Scotland. I will inform Lady Phipps. She will get a wardrobe together for Sarah. Not black, I think, but dark colours.'

Queen Victoria stood up. Mama Forbes and Lady Melton stood up too. There was nothing more to be said on the matter.

Sarah had not expected this. She wanted to stay with her family, wanted to stay with people who had known Papa Forbes. Sarah pulled at Queen Victoria's sleeve.

'Mama Queen,' she said, her voice trembling 'My cough is much better. I won't get sick in Scotland. Mama Forbes and Nanny Grace will take care of me.'

'No, Sally,' said Queen Victoria, running her fingers against the markings on Sarah's cheek. 'You will stay with us in London. It is better that way.' She turned to Mama Forbes, 'When you are back, Lady Phipps will acquaint you with our future plans for Sally.'

'Ma'am? I thought Sarah's future was settled. She has become very dear to us,' said Mrs Forbes, voice suddenly high pitched.

'And to us. I'm sure we all want what is best for her.'

Mrs Forbes bowed her head. 'Yes, Ma'am.'

Queen Victoria gave a nod, and walked towards the door, which Freddie hurried to open, bowing low. Mama Forbes, Lady Melton and Mabel curtsied before following the Queen out. Sarah did not curtsey. She had seen Mabel smile and knew Mabel was glad she was not going to Scotland. Emily forgot to curtsey, instead she ran over and hugged Sarah.

'I don't want to go to Scotland without you. Grandpa Forbes scares me, and he smells old. Why can't you come with us?'

'I don't know.'

No, she did not know but something about it felt scary. Once again, she was going to be moved around like a seed in a wari game. She had no choice; she was not free. She bit the inside of her mouth to hold the words in.

✾✾✾✾

Next day the church was full to overflowing, with people from everywhere, the Navy, the town, London. They sang 'Rock of Ages' and 'Abide with Me', but Sarah sat silent, refusing to join in the hymns. Reverend Byles could tell them all to pray and praise God, she could not. What good was it to talk about Captain Forbes being a great man? She wanted to scream 'that will not bring him back.' The pain inside grew, a stone inside her, weighing her down, stopping her mouth. All through the service Sarah scratched at her wrists, until she felt little beads of blood. She could cry about that pain.

*Sunday, 27ᵗʰ April 1851, Winkfield Place*

> *Today is my 9th birthday, I think. At least that is what Papa*
> *Forbes worked out from his charts. I do not care about my*
> *birthday. Today we had a service of remembrance. I did not*
> *need the service. I will always remember Papa Forbes. Will*
> *he remember me?*

Sarah stopped writing. She had an idea. She went to the bedroom opened her drawer and searched for her *gri-gri*. She wondered whether she should start wearing it again. After first checking that there was no one else around before opening the pouch, she put her fingers in and felt her dried caul. Well, that was no use to Papa Forbes now she thought, and kept searching until she found what she was looking for, a piece of blue glass. She took it out, tightened the ribbon at the neck of the pouch and went back to her journal.

> *To my ancestors, this blue glass is for my Papa Forbes. He*
> *saved me from King Gezo and now Mamiwata has him. He*
> *has no caul, nothing to protect him. If God and Jesus can't*
> *look after him, Can you? Thank you.* ~~Sarah Forbes Bonetta~~
> *Salimatu Aina.*

Sarah tore a page from the journal that Papa Forbes had given her and wrapped the blue glass in it. Before anyone could stop her, she ran down the back stairs, into the garden. The rain had stopped, and the water had soaked away leaving the hole she had dug earlier, a little muddy. She, lined the hole with some grass, put the paper in, then covered it with damp earth.

Not knowing what else to do after that, she said, 'It's from me. Sarah, I mean from Salimatu, I mean Aina. Maluuma please tell the ancestors that was my first name. Maybe that is how they know me. I don't know.'

Then Sarah heard her inside voice once more. 'It's from both of us.'

'Salimatu,' said Sarah and burst into tears.

# CHAPTER 46

*Oona bless fa true, oonawa hungry now, cause God gwine gii oona all oona wahn fa nyam. Oona bless fa true, oona wa da cry now, cause oona gwine laugh later on*
Blessed are ye that hunger: for ye shall be filled. Blessed are ye that weep now for ye shall laugh
Luke 6:21

## April 1851

I stand still. Nanny inspects my uniform, pulls down my little white cap, but it springs up again on my hair. No matter how much I try, I cannot look like the other maids in these clothes. Nanny Dot sighs, takes a pin out of her hair, pushes it into mine and says to Nellie. 'Straighten that apron and take Faith down to the morning room. Lady Fincham is waiting for you two.'

Outside the nursery, I whisper, 'Is it because we went to the market? Is that why the old lady wants to see us?'

'What you talking 'bout? Shh, nobody knows that what we done. No, we going to her to get our pay.'

Pay? I want to laugh. Does she not know that slaves are not paid? You do not pay your horse, your dog or your plough. Isn't that how our masters see us, things to buy and sell, property. Still, I follow her.

Down at the morning room Lady Lavinia is sitting by the window, working on some sewing. Lady Fincham is at a table, with a big book open in front of her.

'These are the last two Milady, from the nursery,' says Mrs Hopkins, the housekeeper. 'Good,' says Lady Fincham, 'it is almost tea time and we must change. Lady Grey and Mrs Hannah Sturge left their cards. Please send up the tea tray to the drawing room as soon as they arrive, Mrs Hopkins.'

'Yes, Milady.'

'They'll only stay the requisite fifteen minutes. Lady Dalloway left her card also and she never knows when to leave,' says Lady Lavinia.

'Be charitable Lavinia. She is old and has no family.'

'She has that wet rag of a companion. What more does she need?' laughs Lavinia.

I keep my eyes down. I do not want Lady Lavinia to notice me again for I fear what she might say.

Mrs Hopkins gives Nellie a prod forward. 'Nellie, Milady.'

'Ah yes, Nellie,' says Lady Fincham. She runs her finger down a book full of names and numbers, in front of her. 'Nellie Stokes, twelve pounds a year. You get paid three times a year so how much should you have today?'

'Four pounds, Milady,' says Nellie

'Any deductions, Mrs Hopkins?'

'No, Ma'am. There have been no complaints.'

Lady Fincham nods and takes different coins, pile them together and push it towards Mrs Hopkins.

'Right,' says Mrs Hopkins to Nellie, 'make your mark in the ledger.'

Nellie steps up to the desk, bends over and with the tip of her tongue sticking out she slowly writes her name. Mrs Hopkins bends done and to look at the page.

'When did you learn to write your name? You've always just made your mark.'

Nellie's smile was wide. 'Nanny Dot been learning me. She say everybody should know how to write their name.'

'What nonsense,' says Lady Fincham waving Nellie away from the table.

Lady Lavinia laughs, 'that is what comes from progress Mother. They all want to better themselves.'

Mrs Hopkins put her hand out and stops Nellie from backing away immediately. 'Take your money girl.'

The door bursts open, and Miss Isabella and Missy Clara enter. Nellie and I step to one side. Missy Clara does not see me, but my heart starts to beat fast.

'Mother,' says Miss Isabella, pulling off her white lacy gloves. 'We met Lord Sheldon walking at Hyde Park. He says his Mother will drop her card in tomorrow. Before I have even been presented! Isn't that wonderful? I can't wait. In just over a week, I will be presented, and I will be out in society. I can go to everything then, balls, dinners, soirees.'

'He was most attentive, Mother Fincham,' says Missy Clara. 'He is going to the debutante's ball too.' She claps her hand. She is as excited as if it had happen to her.

'I'm sure he will be there,' says Lady Lavinia, getting up. 'And, so will many other gentlemen, at the cattle market, all looking for a rich wife, no doubt.'

'Well, you know about that, do you not, Lavinia?' says Isabella with a sly smile as she takes off her bonnet and flings it on to the chair. It almost hits Lady Lavinia.

Miss Isabella is a sassy one. She is fine with me and the servants, but she and her sister are always sharp with each other. I listen to them and I think of how I would be with my sister and I fix my face quick before I cry.

'Just you be quiet Isabella!' says Lady Lavinia throwing the hat back.

It falls to the ground. Nellie picks it up and hands it to Miss Isabella with a quick bob. Mrs Hopkins waves her away and Nellie slips out leaving me in there alone.

Lady Fincham glares at her daughters. 'Will you both stop

behaving like badly brought up children.' Then she looks at me. 'Is she the last one?

'Yes Ma'am,' says Mrs Hopkins, pointing to a line in the ledger. 'Lady Lavinia told me to add her to the list of maids.'

Lady Lavinia? I glance at her and she is sitting forward and staring at Missy Clara.

Missy Clara turns and notices me for the first time. She frowns.

'What is she paid?' asks Lady Fincham before Missy Clara could say anything. 'It doesn't say here.'

Missy Clara's mouth falls open. I want to laugh at the look on her face, but it too serious for that. I look down so that none of them can see my eyes.

'Who? Faith? She's to be paid?' screeched Missy, twisting her gloves, looking as if she does not know what the word means.

'Why not,' says Lady Lavinia, her voice smooth, 'she works here, does she not?'

'Come here, girl,' says Mrs Hopkins. 'How much are you paid?'

'Nothing.' I say and catch Missy's eye.

What is she going to say now? Was she going to keep on with her lies or was she going to tell them all that I am her slave, her property, one who has never been paid, ever? I lift my head right up and wait.

'Has your maid not been paid since you left America over a month ago?' says Lavinia staring hard at Missy. 'You must learn our ways Clara. In England, our servants get paid on time. They're not slaves.'

I give Lady Lavinia a quick look. She knows Missy has lied and I am a slave. Now she wants to make trouble and I'm in the middle of it. I know that they could turn on me any moment. I hold my breath. What next. Missy looks to the left and to the right, as though searching for the answer. She licks her lips. Miss Lavinia smiles and leans back.

'Ah, I suppose you have not had time to do deal with your household requirements, so I shall pay her now. Henry can settle with me later,' says Lady Fincham. She pulls some coins from the small pile left in front of her and started to count them. 'She shall have the same as the other nursery maid.'

'Yes, Mother Fincham,' says Missy her voice high and shaky.

'Here's your money, four pounds,' Lady Fincham says to Faith, pushing a pile of coins towards her. 'Now make your mark.'

I take the pen, I bend down, I write. Without thinking I write slowly and neatly; Fa and I am about to add the 'ith' when I hear Mrs Hopkins voice.

'Oh, my goodness, she too can write her name.'

I stop. My grip on the pen tightens and I start to shake. O *Oduadua*, save me. What have I done? Now I am dead, now I am going to be sent to the ancestors by Missy Clara.

'What? Write?' Squeaks Missy. 'Faith can write?' She hurries over to the table and stands so close to me I can feel her trembling. Is she afraid too?

'Well, Clara, did you not know that your maid can write?' says Lavinia. 'People can be so secretive.'

'Faith!' says Missy. 'You write?' Her voice is sharp.

That it is not a question she thought she would ever have to ask her slave. If we were back on the plantation, after a beating, I would be sold down the river for sure. But what can she do here? Here I am not a slave, am I? Here I am a maid. I cannot look at her and I drop the pen. I try to speak but no words pass my lips.

'Nanny Dot must be teaching her to,' says Miss Isabella.

I catch her eyes. She nods. I can see that she knows that is not so, but she wants to help me. I do not know why but when she adds, 'isn't that so, Faith?'

I take a deep breath and nod.

'Yes, Miss,' I say and look Missy Clara straight in the eye, something a slave is never supposed to do. Well, they all telling lies, pretending they do not know what is, so why not me too. We all in one big lie. 'Yes Miss,' I say again. I glance at each one of them right in their face. I know that none of them going to do anything to me right then. I say slow and loud. 'I learn because I never had the chance before. Nanny Dot say if a body can read and write, even a little, then they can be free to better themselves.'

Missy Clara staggers back as if I have given her a slap. I see first fear, then anger in her eyes. She raises her hand and I know she going to give me one almighty slap but although my knees are shaking, I refuse to duck. Only when Missy hear Lady Lavinia laughing she bring herself back to where we are. Slowly her hand comes down, she is breathing hard. I turn to leave before my shaking knees go completely and I fall to the ground.

'Where are you going?' says Mrs Hopkins. 'Finish signing your name, take your money, then get back to the nursery.'

I can feel Missy's eyes on me. I'm about to give them another lie and say that is all the letters I know so far, but as I stretch my hand out to take the pen I see the scars around my wrist, I see my stiff finger and I remember the day Missus Jane broke it. I also remember Absalom saying 'Fatmata, you are a very strong and brave woman,' and I make up my mind. They can break all my fingers but that isn't going to stop me from writing. I take a deep breath bend down and in my best hand write my full name, Faith.

When I straighten up, Missy Clara is staring at me as if she seen a *djudju*. I scoop the money into my apron pocket, give a small bob and leave without looking at her. I feel her eyes on my back and I know that this is not over.

All the way up the back stairs to the nursery, I keep fingering the coins in my pocket. Mine? Yes, mine. For the first time in my life, I have money. Enough to set up home with Absalom? I stop and feel for my *gri-gri*. I must make an offering to the gods, something blue. I wish I had the blue lavender.

✿✿✿✿

'We're going to Hyde Park today,' says Nellie the next day. 'There is always much to see there. Queen Victoria and even the Princes and Princesses drive past. I've seen them. They go to see Prince Albert's Crystal Palace. It's almost done now. All London's talking about it. Queen Victoria opens it to the public next Thursday.'

The park is big, very big, with countless paths, plenty of tall trees, green grass and many people. All wanting to be seen I think, by the way they keep looking to the left and right. On the long broad road, there are those rolling by in open carriages, more men and women in fine riding clothes, the men tipping their hats to the women while the horses stamp and snort, ready to gallop away. I do not go close. I do not like horses. Sometimes, if I shut my eyes, I can still see that horse going fast, with Salimatu thrown across its back, and me not able to stop it not able to save my sister.

'That road is the grand strut,' says Nellie, adding 'but Jack say the proper name for it is Rotten Row.' She laughs and spins around.

'I don't see anything rotten about their clothes or their horses,' I say.

'You don't? I do,' she says. 'They all be rotten, through and through, the rich. That's what Pa used to say.' Her lips give a little tremble. She moves her shoulders as if to drop something hanging around her and turns away. 'Come, let's go to the Serpentine and meet some of the other nursemaids.'

I stop. My mouth falls open and I let go of the perambulator. Nellie grabs it.

'Faith, what is it? You feel sick?'

'What is that?' I ask, pointing to the huge building its dome pushing up through the trees, and all made of glass. The sun is dancing on the shining glass, sending light up into the sky and back again, to cover the building with the patterns of clouds, sky, trees. Will it send back the faces of the ancestors that are up there behind the sky? I've never seen anything like that before and it makes me afeared.

'That's the Crystal Palace.' Nellie leans forward. 'It's made of glass and built by hundreds of men for the Great Exhibition. The whole world is going to be here, to see what Nanny Dot calls "the wonders of the world."'

So, that is where Sir Henry's machines are going to be shown. It is because of that place Missy Clara had to come to England and bring me with her. It is because of the Great Exhibition that I have met Absalom.

'Can anyone go see them?'

'If you buy a ticket. They're dear when it first opens but the ticket price goes down to a shilling at the end of the month. That's when Jack and me will go. I want to see everything. You can come with us if you want.'

Someone shouts, 'the Queen. Queen Victoria is coming!' And everyone, men and women, old and young, start to run.

'Quick. If we get to edge of road, we can see the Queen close to,' says Nellie. She gathers Celia, dumps her into the perambulator, grabs the handle and pushes, racing across the grass. I pick up my skirt and run after her, my heart beating fast. I see the carriage coming, a phaeton with a pair of greys and two grooms mounted on greys, the horses going at a walk, plod, plod, plod. On both sides of the road the crowd close in, excited, waving and shouting. I do not know why, but I do too. There are five people in the carriage. The Queen is in a light green dress, with a darker green cape around her shoulders, her bonnet's brim is small and her face can be seen clearly. She waves, looking to the right and to the left. The woman sitting next to her looked straight ahead.

Nellie pulls at my arm. 'Look, look Faith, there they are, the Princesses.'

I stare. Sitting opposite the Queen are three young girls. The middle one is different. She is black, a Negro girl in a dark blue coat. I watch the carriage get closer and closer.

'Are they really the Queen's daughters?'

'Yes. Princess Victoria and Princess Alice.'

'Has Queen Victoria got a Negro daughter?' I ask, before I could stop myself.

'What?' says Nellie, but she is not looking at me, she is still waving.

'The other girl,' I say quickly. 'Is she the Queen's daughter too?'

Nellie laughs. 'No. Look at her.'

I know who she is, though. I know, from the newspaper I picked up by Hany's stall. The carriage is right in front of me. The Negro girl turns towards me, she sees me and leans forward. Without thinking I try to get closer. I slip and someone pulls me back. I shake them off. I must look at her again. She is the first black girl I have seen riding in a carriage as if she belongs there.

'Just wait till I tell Nanny Dot,' says Nellie, walking so fast I have to run to keep up with her. 'She reads everything in the newspapers about the Queen, her family and what happens in the palaces.'

'Would she know all about her too?'

Nellie knows who I am talking about. 'Yes. Nanny Dot will know all about her. She is in the newspapers all the time. She was a slave.'

Nellie throws me a quick look and bites her lip. I think that it is because she has said the word slave. When I say nothing she adds, 'but they call her "the African Princess". I never knew they had princesses there.' She leans towards me, her eyes wide. 'Jack say they all savages back there.'

I look at her and know that I can't stay in this country. There might not be slaves here but rich or poor, black or white, they all ignorant about Africa. I want to say 'I am from Africa, and I am no savage.' I open my mouth, then shut it, swallowing the words. Instead, I think of the girl in the carriage, the one I had read about from the newspaper I picked up by Hany's stall. So that was the ex-slave, Queen Victoria's ward, Sarah Forbes Bonetta, the African Princess. I think of my village and my eyes fill with tears.

# CHAPTER 47

*Wa ya kin tell we bout yasef: A de one wa da holla een de wildaness*
What sayest thou of thyself: I am the voice of one
crying in the wildereness
John 1:23

## April 1851

I stretch out on my bed. I have fed Henry-Francis and I have nothing else to do.

'It's your day off,' Nanny had said, taking Henry-Francis from me. 'I will look after him, with the other two.'

A whole day off! I have never had a whole day off to do as I please. Not even in Talaremba. Then, I had to work, pounding rice, feeding chicken or goats, fetching water, running after Amadu. I catch my breath. My eyes feel as if someone has blown smoke into them. I mustn't go back to those days, or I will start to think about my sister. Hadn't I taught myself to push it under the stone of forgetting?

But I have lifted the stone a little and my mind dances away to the plantation. Not that I want to be there either, but I want my children left behind. When I don't go back, what will happen if the Underground Railroad don't get to them?

I force myself to think instead of the money I've sewn into the hem of my coat like Nellie showed me last night. I know my pay will not be enough to buy all three children but maybe Absalom can get the Quakers to add to it. Absalom, ayee, Absalom.

✿✿✿✿

Nellie comes rushing into our room. She grabs the shawl that she had flung down on her bed after early morning church. 'Come on Faith, before Nanny Dot changes her mind. I never thought that she'd give us both our day off at the same time.'

'Where are we going?'

'Nanny Dot says I should show you how to get around, so we'll go on the omnibus.'

I smiled. Nellie has pulled me out of thinking. I want to see other parts of London, maybe see more coloured people. If the God's are good, I will find Absalom.

'So where shall we ride to?'

'I've got to go to the East End first and late afternoon we'll meet Jack and go to Astley's.'

'The East End? Where's that?'

'When I take the little 'uns to the workhouse it was to be just for a small time. I tell the workhouse master, Mr Newberry as soon as I get a job, and some money, I coming back for me brothers and sisters. But when I go back, they won't let me in and they gotta. I have the papers and the tokens.'

'What tokens?'

'Them,' she says pointing to the small bit of cloth pinned to the bottom of the paper. 'They supposed to keep it till I come back for them. They then match the tokens, he say, with mine and so they know which child you come to get, see? So, for May and Kitty, I cut a bit of me shawl and pin it.'

'What about the boys?'

She moves her shoulders as if to shift something heavy. 'I cut of the buttons from Pa's old coat before I sell it to the Jew man. He weren't wearin' it the day he drown.' She searches in her purse and brings out three strange shaped black buttons. 'See, each one different. I go every month with me papers and every month they tell me I can't go in, my papers not right and they can't find any tokens that be the same as me own. But they got to have the papers. Come with me and read it to them, I beg you. Jack went with me once but he can't read either so that was no good. They shove all these papers at me, and they know I can't make head or tail of it.'

I look at the papers. There was something not right, but I can't work out what. There was the name, Kitty Stokes, occupation blank, female, child. Been in workhouse before—no. Nearest relative—blank. That was it. They never put Nellie's name down, so she could never claim them back. I do not know how to tell her.

'Nellie, did you make your mark on his paper?'

She thinks, licks her lips and says, 'The workhouse master he write everything and give it me.'

'Your name not on any of these papers, nor your mark. If they lost the tokens there is no way they can tell which children you talking about.'

'The hornswoggler. What he done with them?' She grabs the shawl around her neck as if to choke the words out of her mouth. Shaking her head, she cries 'no, no, maybe they been there all this time and think I forget 'bout them.'

We get to Regent Street just in time to jump on the omnibus. It's a double decker bus drawn by eight horses. I don't know where to go. The upper deck has no cover and benches placed back to back. Inside are two long wooden benches, along the sides of the cabin, facing each other.

'Move in. Only the men go up top,' said the conductor. 'Where you going? This the Green line to Clapton.'

'The Swan, Clapton,' says Nellie.

'All the way, that'll be sixpence.'

'No, its not,' says Nellie. 'We're getting on now and that's almost halfway.'

I watch her give him two coins. 'Fourpence for the ride and that's it.'

Nellie had spent time explaining about the different coins and how much things cost but it is still not clear to me. All I know is that I have more money than I had ever thought I could have.

Now I count out the same as Nellie and hold out the money. The first time I ever pay for something and I feel as if I'm swelling up with the importance of it.

The conductor takes it. 'Move along then. You want to keep us here all day?'

We squeeze in. I wait for someone to say that a slave, a Negro cannot sit in the same place as them, but no one say anything. I'm surely not in America. I listen as the conductor calls out the stops, Green line, Regent Street, Great Portland Street, Euston, Kings Cross, Pentonville, Angel, Islington, Dalston, on and on. People get on and get off and we squeeze up. The further east we go the more coloured people I see but none come on the omnibus. Every time I see them, I want to jump off and go talk to them, but I stay with Nellie. Then I hear the conductor call out Stoke Newington and I feel as if my insides will climb up into my chest and spill out.

'Stoke Newington,' I shout out and jump up.

'You getting off here?' The conductor says.

East London. Stoke Newington. That was where Absalom had said most of the Quakers who could help live. Paradise Row, Stoke Newington. He was going there to see some important people. One of them must know where to find Absalom.

'No, no,' says Nellie pulling at my skirt, so I sit back down with a thump. 'We going to Clapton.'

The coach leaps forward and we are off again. I could cry. I keep my eyes down. I see Nellie's hands she is wringing them. At the

Swan, she gets off before everyone. She is in a hurry and I follow.

'You think it going to work? You filling in me name on the forms? Though Nanny Dot learning me, I still can't write good enough to fool them. You think they'll let me in?'

'I don't know. But it's worth the try.' I say the words, but I no longer care about Nellie's worry. I have my own. How to get to Stoke Newington now I know it is so near?

'You write it good. I put the pen back in the same place by Nanny Dot's chair. She won't know you used it.'

'Thanks for getting me the paper too.' I say.

Nellie nods and walks on. 'She had plenty.'

We get to a big building. On the shut iron gates is written St Peter's Workhouse. Nellie grabs hold of the gates and shakes them.

'Oi, what you think you doing?' shouts a man, trying to rush to the gates but he is very fat and can either move or speak, he cannot do both at the same time. He takes a few steps, puffs and pants and then says a few words. 'What you want that you making such a racket on God's day of rest.'

'Me sisters and brothers. I come to see them.'

'That as may be, but you got papers?'

'Yes,' says Nellie. I hold my breath as he pants over all five papers.

'This you? Nellie Stokes?'

'Yes. That's me name and them's me brothers and sisters.'

'Who is this then?' he asks, looking at me. 'Only relatives allowed.'

'She their aunty,' says Nellie.

He laughs. 'Aunty, eh, she fall in the coal bucket?' He thinks this is funny and he laughs and then can't breathe.

'Can we come in then?'

'No.' That was all he can manage to say.

Nellie grabs hold of the gate again and tries to shake it. 'Why not?'

'Get away with you.' He beats at Nellie's fingers with a stick.

She jumps back and shouts, 'you, jollocks, you gibface.'

'None of your gum. Git 'fore I call the peelers on you. They been long gone.'

'Gone?' Screams Nellie. 'Gone where?'

'How should I know? They gone that's all I know. And don't you come back no more. Go on, get away from here,' he said, tearing up the papers before walking away.

Nellie shakes the gate hard before collapsing to the ground. 'They gone, they gone.'

I put my arm around her. I don't know what to say to comfort her. In the end I say, 'we best go. No good staying here.'

'I lost them. Pa would kill me if he were not drowned.'

'We can start walking back,' I say. 'Maybe we can stop at Stoke Newington.' I stop speaking and wait. Will she do it, will she?

Nellie looks at me.

'What you know about Stoke Newington,' she says wiping her face with a corner of her shawl and I see where she has cut of bits as token for her sisters.

'Someone told me about it once.'

'Well it's on or way. It's Sunday, the next omnibus is not for an hour. We can stop there for a bit if we reach there before the bus.'

It does not take us long to walk the mile and a half to Stoke Newington.

'Why did you want to come here?' says Nellie.

'Absalom,' I say and that is the only word that can escape from my mouth that wants to open wide and scream out my need.

'Who's Absalom?'

I do not know how to name him. My husband, friend, lover? I sniff and look away.

'Oh Lor' is he your sweetheart? I tell you all about Jack and you say nothing?'

'I've not seen or heard from him for over month. I don't know where he is or if he even remembers me.'

'He lives here?'

'I don't know, but it is the only place he talked about, the Quakers on Paradise Row. If he's not here I don't know where else to go to find him.'

We keep walking and at the end of Church Street, there was Paradise Row. It was just a street with big houses.

'What now? You know a name, a number?'

I shake my head.

'Faith,' says Nellie, 'what is a Quaker? Never heard of it before.'

That makes me think. I try to remember what Absalom had said. 'Quakers belong to a kind of church and are abolitionist,' I say the word carefully.

Nellie makes a face. 'They are what?'

'Abolitionists, people who want to stop slavery in America. They get money to help slaves to buy their freedom.'

'They going to stop slavery here too?'

'Slavery here? There is no slavery in this country,' I say.

'You think so,' says Nellie. 'Show you know nothing of this place yet.'

I do not want to argue. I want to find Absalom, so I say nothing.

We walk to the end of the row passing big houses with gardens and parks. I cannot see Absalom staying in any of these houses. Back on Church Street, people hurry by us. Any of them could be a Quaker.

Nellie looks up and down the street. 'Did he say anywhere else?'

'Only about the Quaker meeting-house. I think it means the church.'

'Well, there's a church over there, St Mary's. Let's go there. See what we can find.'

The church is open but empty. We step in. Nellie makes the

sign. I do not. I look around and know that there is nothing there for me. By the door I see a board. There are leaflets and messages on it and I know what I must do. I open my purse and bring out a piece of paper. It is a piece of the paper Nellie got for me. I didn't know then why I wanted to copy out the words from Absalom's last note but maybe it was because I had opened and folded it so many times it was falling apart. Anyway, here it is, written out in my best handwriting—*The Lord is nigh unto them that are of a broken heart and saveth such as be of contrite spirit.* I stick it in the middle of the board. If Absalom comes here, he will see it, and know I came looking for him. It's a small chance, but it's a chance. I turn away holding on to my *gri-gri* hidden under my top.

FAITH

# CHAPTER 48

*Oona bless fa true, cause oona eye da see an oona yea da yeh*
Blessed are your eyes for they see: and your ears, for
they hear
Matthew 13:16

## April 1851

I planned to go alone to the Quaker meeting Hany had told me
about, but Nellie saw me putting on my hat and coat

'Where you off to?' she asks.

'It's my afternoon off,' I say. 'Nanny Dot says I must be back
by eight.'

'I know that. You going to the market?'

I shake my head. I'm not sure whether I should tell her at all.

'You not sneaking off to the park to see all the people, are you?
I thought that we were going together on Saturday.'

I smile at the look on her face. 'Eh no, Nellie. Would I do that
to you?'

Everyone in the house wants to go to the exhibition so Mrs
Hopkins says all the servants must draw lots for time off to go.
Nellie and I get Saturday. It's dear to get in but we going all the
same.

'I was only funning. You can't. The exhibition don't open 'til
tomorrow. So, where you going?'

'To the meeting about abolishing slaves in America. It's on
from five at the Baptist Grosvenor Church hall on South Audley

Street. I want to see if there are any Quakers there. I got to hurry. Missy kept me and I did not dare say anything.'

'You know where it is?'

'I'll find it. Hany said it's near here.'

'Let me come with you. I know where the hall is.'

So here we are squeezed into the back of the hall without a chair to sit on.

'I didna' think that there'd be these many people here,' whispers Nellie.

I look around but although many are white people, I'm glad to see that I am not the only black person in the room. I strain to hear what is being said by the man on the small platform. Then I hear him say, 'so, please give him a warm welcome.'

A Negro stands up and he stares out at us. He is tall and straight, though an old man, with thick white hair and a bushy white beard. Who is he?

'I thank you, Reverend Thomas,' he says, in a low but carrying voice, 'for this opportunity to talk to these good folks about my experience as a former slave, one who in the end used the Underground Railroad to get out of the clutches of slavery.'

'Thank the Lord,' shouts someone right down the front.

The Underground? Does he know Absalom? I got to talk to him. I try to go forward but there's no room to move.

The old man smiled. 'There are many folks who help us flee from slavery into freedom. Every one of you here who puts a coin into the collection is helping. Every one that speaks up and say that slavery is wrong is helping. There are many, white, brown, and black folks, all working hard to free our brothers and sister, our fathers and mothers. I thank all of you, every single one of you.'

He nods to the crowd and they clap loudly. He puts up his hand.

'There are many like me who have escaped from the chains of slavery to this your hospitable shores, to live among you and tell our stories. Some like Ignatius Sancho and Olaudah Equiano wrote about their lives, their capture, and their escape, over sixty years ago. But slavery is not over and many who look like me are still enslaved and we still asking for your help.

'But I tell you something, there's nothing like hearing it from the horses' mouth, as they say. We must tell our stories ourselves and that is why two years ago, with help, I wrote this book.' The old man holds up a book and waves it in the air. 'Yes, this is my book, *The life of Josiah Henson, Formerly a Slave, Now an Inhabitant of Canada, as Narrated by himself.*'

There is more clapping and cheering and I'm as pleased as if I had written the book.

'Not so long ago,' he says 'I hear from a lady, a teacher in Connecticut. She say she read my book and was much moved by my story. She tell me she going to base her novel on my book and some stories she heard from others escaping slavery during the time she was living in Cincinnati, Ohio. Well, I say if her book going to help our cause, good luck to Mrs Stowe, but remember, hers is a novel. Mine is already writ and I lived it. Though I can't read or write that good yet, still I can tell you my story.'

'Tell it my brother,' says Reverend Thomas, nodding and clapping. Many joined in, 'tell it, tell it.'

'Yes, my name is Josiah Henson. I was born June 15, 1789 in Charles County, Maryland. I was the youngest of six children. My mammy be the property of the Doctor but was often sent out to work for the man who owned my father. One of the first things I can remember is the beating they give my pappy one day, until he just one bloody mess because he hit a white man for messing with my mother. Pappy's right ear was cut off and stuck to a post and he got a hundred lashes as punishment and then he got sold on.'

The sound in the hall is like everyone take breath as one. It makes me shiver.

Mr Henson continue, his voice seeming to go lower, so we all lean forward. 'It was during this time I learned about God from mammy, who was always reciting the Lord's prayer. When the Doctor passed, the property was divided throughout the country. I was sold to another master, Mr Riley. I was put to small tasks and later to work in the fields.'

Unlike many of the people in the room I know exactly what he was talking about. I know how hard that work be. I seen the children working, seen the fields.

'Coming home, one day from the field, I and two other slaves were ambushed and badly beaten up. We lost the fight, and I lost the full use of my arms.'

He lifted his arms and the left one could only be raised to his chest, no higher and a sound like a wave over rough stone went around the hall.

'When Mr Riley, fall into debt he beg me, with tears in his eyes, to help him. And what was it my master want me to do? To take his eighteen slaves to Kentucky by foot. When we reach Ohio, which be a free state, the people there say that we slaves could be free. Until then I never thought of running away, I believed the only right way to get freedom was to buy myself my wife and children from my master.'

'I wouldn't go back if it was me,' Nellie whispers.

'It was then I began to plan for freedom. I worked hard, saved money from odd jobs, being loaned to plantations, but when I tried to buy my freedom, Mr Riley trick me. He was to give me my freedom papers for $450, with $350 in cash and the remainder in a note. I had enough to produce the cash, so all that was left was to pay the $100 note. But when I give him the $100 he add another zero and put the note up tenfold.'

There is a rumble of sound and I hear some people shout, 'shame on him.'

'I knew then he would try to sell me, and I began to plot escape to Canada for myself and my family. So, in 1830, twenty years ago, with the help of the Underground Railroad, we decided to escape. The Underground Railroad is not an actual railroad, my friends, it does not run on rail tracks. It is a network of many secret and dangerous routes, of people, black and white, ready to give shelter in safe house to slaves trying to reach freedom in the North or Canada.

'I mighty grateful to the Underground railroad and all them people who helped us on our way, hiding us, feeding us, pointing us in the right direction as we walked for weeks mostly at night, hide on a steamer until we made it safely over the border. Upon reaching the shore, I threw me down on the ground and rolled around in excitement.'

So that's how the Underground Railroad work, I think. That's how they're going to get my children out of slavery, walking into freedom. Not by following routes sewn into quilt patterns or singing of hymns. For a moment I remember my long walk with Salimatu into slavery and I fear for them, fear for what could happen to them if they were caught.

'Soon my eldest boy, Tom, started schooling,' continues Mr Henson. 'He learn to read and write well. Tom begin to teach me. Me and some others decide we wanted to stay put and set up our own colony to raise our own crops and food but still making trips back to Maryland and Kentucky, through the Underground Railway, to bring other slaves back to Canada. After several years I find white folks to support the idea of a black community at Dawn. We buy land and start the manual labour school, where we teach carpentry, crop growing, milling.'

There's cheering again. Those of us in the back with no seats are pushed a little forward by the press of people outside who are trying to get in somehow.

'Now many Negroes are moving from the States to join us,' says Mr Henson. 'I wrote this book to raise money for the school at Dawn Settlement. If you go to the World's Fair Industrial Exhibit, the Great Exhibition, which opens here in London tomorrow, go visit the Canadian section. There you'll see exhibits of carpentry, of high quality polished walnut boards from Dawn Settlement.'

The shouts and cheers get louder. Josiah Henson smiles and I'm glad he raises his voice because it hard to hear what he's saying above the noise.

Nellie pulls at my sleeve. 'We can see him when we go on Saturday, fancy that.'

People are pushing and calling all wanting to get to shake his hand. I want to be close to this man that make me think of Jaja. I want to touch him, smell his blackness. There are so many pressing from behind. I don't know how but I find myself right at the front. I call out, again and again 'Papa Josiah Papa Josiah, help me.'

He rose from his chair and came to the front of the platform, bent down. 'Little sister,' he says, 'you are troubled.'

Maybe it's his voice, maybe it is all that I have heard, but I burst into tears. 'My children,' I say, 'my children are left behind in South Carolina. Help me, like you've helped so many.'

'My child talk to the folks yourself. Come up here and testify. Tell them your story, in your own words.'

He takes my hand, and his strength pours into me. I find myself standing on the platform with faces all looking up at me. Mr Henson says something to Reverend Thomas. He nods, steps forward and raises his hand.

'Before we finish today, we have a little extra. This young lady is the kind of person we are working for, she's here but her little children are slaves, yes slaves, back in America. Hear her story.'

I'm hot, I can feel sweat running down my sides, down my back.

Maybe I am dreaming. But it's not a dream. From way back in time I hear Maluuma's voice.

'*Listen, my child, fear is in the eyes, in the heart, in the mind. Face your aloe-bitter fears and they will disappear. I am with you.*'

I feel for my *gri-gri* and hold it tight. I speak.

'Although here in your country my mistress tells everyone I am her maid, in truth, I am a slave, not an ex-slave, not a free Negro, but a slave.'

Some shout out. 'you're in England, you're free.' More voices join in, 'you're a free woman,' 'free,' 'freedom.'

Their words give me strength to go on.

'I was captured five years ago with my little sister. I was fourteen. We were separated and I was marched for weeks to the coast and branded, like an animal, with hot irons. And this still goes on.'

'Shame,' cried someone.

There were more shouts of 'shame,' and 'we must put an end to this barbaric trade.'

I'm no longer afraid to tell them my story. I am ready to do anything to get my children away from the plantation.

'I don't know what happened to my sister,' I say. 'I don't know whether she is alive or dead. I was transported across the ocean, chained in the smelly, dirty underbelly of the ship, given bad food and brought to the light once a day, to dance for the sailors. Many did not survive. There are many bones lying with the ancestors on the seabed. They do not sleep.'

I hear a sob. It is Nellie. Now that I have started, I cannot stop. The thought of those like Khadijatu being thrown overboard like sacks of rotten potato catch in my breath. I swallow and continue even though my voice is hoarse with my tears.

'I was sold to a plantation owner in the Gullah, to look after my master's little children. I picked up words, I picked up learning, but I could not let my master or mistress know that I could read and write, or I would have been beaten or sold down the river. One night the master came to me. I was fifteen. I have his children, three. The first is dead.'

I stop for a second. I wonder what they would say, what they would do, if I tell them just how my first baby, my little Amadu died. I take in air and tell them more.

'I was brought to England by the daughter of the plantation. I was given to her as a wedding present. You all telling me I'm free here. But what about my children back there? Because of their pappy, they as white-looking like some of you here, but they're still slaves and unless I can buy their freedom they can be sold by their own father, anytime. How can I ever be truly free if my children are still slaves?'

'You got to get your children out of there,' says someone. Everyone cheers.

'If I go back to America, back to my children, I go back into slavery. I want to get my children and take them to my people, my country, my village in Africa, to the land of their forefathers. Help me.'

I am sobbing, the tears come from deep inside of me and it is shaking my being. Mr Henson puts his arm around me, and I sob into his chest.

There are many people crying.

Above the crying, the noise, I hear Reverend Thomas say, 'this is what we are fighting for. People like this young woman. Be generous. The collection is coming around.'

I do not look up.

And then I feel another pair of hands around me, a pair of strong, young arms. It fells so right. A voice says, 'Faith.'

I look up and it is as if a lamp has been lit inside of me.

'Absalom.' I fling my arm around him and he holds me tight, tight.

'I'm here. I told you I would come for you.'

# CHAPTER 49

*It is in vain to recall the past, unless it works some influence upon the present.*
—*David Copperfield,* Charles Dickens

## April 1851

The stone inside of her grew into a boulder when Sarah went to London with Alice and Vicky instead of Scotland. Sarah did not know how to shift it. Then she dreamed of Papa Forbes. He was swimming, laughing, calling to her.

'Sarah, jump in. Swim to me.'

'I can't swim Papa. Doctor Clark won't let me.'

'Do not worry I will keep you safe.'

'Papa, take my caul. I will throw it to you.'

'No. Keep it. You may need it one day.'

'Papa, Papa, swim faster, *Mamiwata* is after you.'

'I'm safe.'

'Quick she is near you.'

'And so are the ancestors.'

And Papa Forbes disappeared.

'Papa, Papa,' Sarah screamed but he did not appear again. She woke herself, and Alice, with her screams. Vicky never woke up.

Sarah did not know if the dream meant that Papa was with the ancestors or not. Had they seen her note and the blue glass? Maybe the ancestors wanted her to know that they were looking after

Papa Forbes. That must be it, she thought and went back to sleep.

❈❈❈

*Thursday, 1ˢᵗ May, 1851. Buckingham Palace*
 *Grand opening day of the Great Exhibition but only Vicky*
 *and Bertie could take part in the procession, with Mama*
 *Queen and Prince Albert. Alice and I watched, as the nine*
 *state carriages left for Hyde Park.*

 *Mama Queen's dress was pink and silver. Her little crown*
 *covered with diamonds shone in the sun. Prince Albert was*
 *in his Field Marshal's uniform. I am not sure what a Field*
 *Marshal does or why they wear such a uniform, with gold*
 *button and braids. Vicky was in lace over white satin and*
 *wore a small wreath of pink wild roses, in her hair. Bertie*
 *had on a kilt. Alice said it is a full Highland dress, worn in*
 *Scotland. I do not want to talk about Scotland.*

❈❈❈

Once the procession had disappeared Sarah went back to the
nursery with the other children. There was nothing to do.

Looking across the courtyard all she could see were more and
more windows. Wondering what was inside all those rooms stopped
her thinking about the others in Scotland.

'Does Buckingham Palace have more rooms than Windsor
Castle?' she asked Alice,

'I think so,' said Alice with a slight frown. 'I don't know. Why?'

'We could go find out,' said Sarah in a whisper, tired of doing
nothing.

Alice smiled and nodded. Sneaking off before Tilla or Nanny

Thurston could stop them, they ran down corridors, opening doors and going into rooms large and small. All the rooms were full of things, furniture, statues, paintings, and tall windows letting in light when the red, green, or blue silk curtains, trimmed with gold, were pulled back.

'Where's everyone?' asked Sarah surprised at the many empty corridors and rooms.

'I think they've gone to see the opening of the exhibition. I wish we could have gone too,' said Alice banging the door shut.

She opened the next door and stood still not going in. 'Oh, Sally, come, come and see.'

Sarah ran down the corridor and stood behind Alice looking over her shoulder.

'Oh,' she said.

'It's you,' said Alice. 'It's the painting Mr Oakley did of you.'

It sat on an easel, facing the door as though waiting for her to walk in and view it.

Alice put her head to one side and squinted at the painting. 'It's you and it is not you.'

Sarah shook as she stared at the painting. Her legs seemed to give way under her, and she sat down on the floor suddenly. Seeing the painting brought back the feeling of cold and fear she had felt that day when Mr Oakley did the painting.

Is this what she had looked like, eyes wide, smiling. She was sure she had not smiled at all. She had been angry, cold and hungry. Had she those strings of beads around her neck? She could not remember but she did remember the long earrings. She looked at the shackles around her ankles, the slave bangles around her wrists and she felt cold all over again.

'It's not me,' Sarah said, standing up. 'It's a stupid, stupid painting. None of it is true. Look at that.' She jabbed at the background. 'Those were not in the room at the time; baskets, stools they have nothing to do with me. I was not at that place, with blue sky, sea and palm trees, I was in a cold room in Windsor Castle, with snow and ice outside and he kept me there until I almost froze.'

Alice touched Sarah's shoulder. She frowned. 'Do you think Mama likes it?'

'She must do. It's here, isn't it?'

Sarah stared at the canvas again. She read the title. *The Dahomian Captive*. Something inside of her boiled and bubbled, her hands closed into tight fists and she kicked at the easel.

'I tell you; it isn't me,' she screamed. 'He just stole a part of me. Look at the painting's name. See? I was captured and then sold to the king at Dahomey. I am not Dahomian. Why couldn't Mr Oakley get that right. He should have read Papa Forbes' book. He would know then.' She peered closely at the painting and pointed, 'see, Mr Oakley has not put my face markings. They tell who I am,' Sarah said, hitting her face again and again. 'These markings say I am a princess, an African Princess.'

Alice grabbed Sarah's hands. 'Stop, please stop,' she said, her eyes wide, looking scared. 'You're right. That isn't you. It is just a painting.'

Sarah coughed and coughed, the tears running down her face.

'I know who you are,' Alice said. She walked over to the easel, picked up a black velvet cloth by the easel and threw it over the painting.

✿✿✿✿

*Saturday, 3rd May 1851, Buckingham Palace.*

> *This afternoon we are all going to the Great Exhibition, even Louise who is only three. Mama Queen says it is something not to be missed and no matter how young she should see the great thing her Papa has done. Vicky and Bertie have not*

*stopped talking about the stalls, the music, the people from all over the world. People from Africa? I must go to Crystal Palace and find out.*

✿✿✿

On arrival at the Crystal Palace, Sarah's eyes darted from place to place, searching. She knew what she wanted to see. Then there it was, the India section a huge carved elephant next to it, right, in front of the Crystal Fountain. She rushed over with Alice, Lenchen and Tilla. They stared at the beautiful silks, bright coloured shawls, and brown men wrapped in white cloths wearing turbans, not black men. Next to it was the China section, displaying enormous vases, carpets, hanging lanterns, and frightening bronze figures, fighting dragons. Small yellow men, with eyes she could not see, hair in long plaits and dragons, embroidered on bright red and yellow silk coats, called to her. But Sarah saw no one who really looked like her, black with tribal marks and springy hair.

She could have cried as they went up to the Gallery. She was not interested in the English section with its plates, jewellery, clocks and watches, filling up almost half of one area. She wanted to find Africa.

'We can see the different sections better from up there,' Tilla said, 'and then we can decide where to go next.'

From Gallery she could see the other courts divided into sections for the various countries, Italy, Spain, Portugal, Germany and many others. She stopped at the French section when she saw a bronze head of a black woman. Sarah reached out but did not touch it. Was that what her mother had looked like? She could not remember.

'Who is she?' Sarah whispered, her eyes stinging.

Tilla bent down and read, 'African Venus—Charles Henri Cordier.'

'Come on,' called Alice. 'There's so much to see.'

Sarah turned away. And then saw them. Negroes. Black people walking arm in arm with white people, just as she walked sometimes with Emily or Alice. The people stopped in front of the United States section that had a huge bird holding a flag with stripes and stars hanging over all the American exhibits. One man standing in front started to speak. Sarah could not hear what he was saying, but those down there could because they cheered. More and more people joined the crowd, and everyone looked like they were never going to move from that spot. Sarah wanted to join them.

When the man brought out a plate, Vicky giggled. 'Is he going to eat now?' she said,

Sarah gripped the railing and leaned over.

'Shh!' said Tilla. 'That's a Wedgewood plate.'

The people down below, one by one, knelt and raise their clasped their hands as though praying. Some were crying but all were saying over and over, louder and louder, 'Am I not a man and a brother?'

'That's what's written on the plate,' said Tilla. It was on many things. I had it on a brooch. I never wore it. There were some things made with 'am I not a woman and a sister?'

A young woman stood up. Sarah thought she looked like the woman who had almost fallen under the carriage wheel the other day on South Carriage Drive on their way from the Crystal Palace. It was the first time Sarah had driven in a carriage with the Queen. When she saw the crowd on both sides of the road, men, women, children, Sarah had shrunk back. Was anyone going to attack Her Majesty that day? But everyone smiled, waved and shouted and Queen Victoria waved first to the left and then to the right.

Sarah remembered how the young Negro woman had caught her eye. They had stared at each other and the woman stepped forward almost falling into the path of the horses. Luckily, the greys were walking slowly, guided by the grooms. Sarah gasped but someone pulled the woman back. The carriage moved further and further away, while Sarah twisted round trying to see what had happened to the woman.

'Did you see that Negro woman, Mama Queen?' Sarah had said. 'She could have hurt herself badly if she had fallen under the horses' hooves.'

'More likely to have been killed,' said Queen Victoria. 'Or injure one of the horses.'

Sarah wished she could have stopped the carriage and talk to the woman. But what would she say? What would she ask her?

'She's the first black woman I've seen in England, Mama Queen,' Sarah said in a soft voice, remembering how she had gone searching for others only a few months ago. 'I thought I would see many more.'

'There are many more.'

There might be but Sarah had seen none until now. Sarah tried to catch the woman's eyes but before she could, someone else stood up. It was Daniel, Lady Melton's butler. Sarah waved and jumped up and down, laughing. Daniel was here. Daniel knew all these black people. He saw her and waved back. Sarah pulled at Tilla's hand.

'We must go downstairs,' she said.

'Yes,' said Tilla, 'it's time to go.'

# FAITH

# CHAPTER 50

*Oona bless fa true, wen people hate oona, wen dey aim wahn hab nottin fa do
wid oona an hole oona cheap wen dey say oona ebil*
Blessed are ye when men shall hate you, and when they shall
separate you from their company and shall reproach you and
cast out your name as evil
Luke 6:22

# May 1851

Nellie and I wait for Absalom at the corner of Charles and
Chester Street. He is coming to the exhibition with us. The
thought of Absalom makes me smile and I give a little wriggle. I
could dance, if I still danced.

I see him striding down Union Street, I want to run and throw
myself into his arms. When he reaches me, takes my hand and
kisses my palm, the touch of his lips is like the tip of a sharp arrow
piercing my skin to enter my being. I cling to him and drink in his
spirit.

'Good morning, Miss Nellie,' he says and tips his hat. 'Nice to
see you again.'

Nellie laughs and claps her hands like a little girl. 'Oh, lor'. I
ain't never been called Miss 'fore or have anyone lift their hat to
me.' She gave him a little bob.

We enter Hyde Park. I take a deep breath on seeing the Crystal
Palace, its round glass head poking up among the trees, shining in
the sun, like the sea in moonlight.

'Look,' says Absalom, 'the banners of all nations are floating
on top of it.'

'All nations?' I say. 'Are there any from Africa, or any from my village?'

Absalom stops and faces me. 'You are right, Fatmata. You are right.'

I go all hot because for the first time a man has treated me as equal, has listened to what I have to say and then tell me that I am right. No, more than that, it is the fact that he has called me by my true name. He sees me for the person I am, not the person I have been made into. I squeeze his arm, lean into him and we walk on.

Early though we are, there is already a long line of people, laughing, talking, pushing, waving flags. We shuffle along pressed in by the crowds. I cling on to Absalom.

And then we're inside.

I stand in the centre of the hall and stare at the fountain made of pink glass and higher than most trees. I think of Maluuma and the pouring of water to cleanse the soul. I reach over and let the water run through my fingers.

'*Odudua*, I thank you,' I say to myself.

Nellie, leans over and lets the water splash on her hand too but she says nothing. She does not hear the ancestors.

'Come,' says Absalom, 'we'll not see even the half of it today. Now we must make our way to the America area. The catalogue says it is by the North transept.'

We walk past the enormous 'Machines in Motion' hall. The complicated machines show how to turn raw cotton into finished cloth. Many people are watching in amazement as the spinning machines and power looms manufacture fabric before their eyes. I know that not one of them is thinking about where the cotton came from, who picked them, packed them in huge bales to be sent to the mills in England.

Nellie holds on to me and I hold on to Absalom and we push along, trying to see what we can between the crowds. I want to stop at the Austrian room full of fancy books and albums. The sign says 'Sent to the Queen by the Austrian Emperor', but Absalom just keeps on walking. We do stop, for a moment, in front of the funny tin figure that takes the shape and size of any person. Nellie makes a funny shape to see if the figure would copy her. It did, and everyone laughed. Nellie is good fun. Absalom is amused but eager to move on. I wonder what is on his mind for he is not saying much. We rush by little Chinese men with long plaits, fancy shawls and the India section with its metal work and fancy rugs.

'Stop.' I pull at Absalom as we go past the Canadian section. 'This is where Pa Henson has the exhibits from Dawn Settlement.'

There are many people walking round Canadian exhibition, touching the furs, lamps, furniture, the beautiful walnut boards, beautiful wooden furniture. On reading the leaflet about the settlement they ask questions and buy one of Mr Henson's book. We are seen by Mr Henson.

'Ah, little sister.' he says coming over, 'you disappeared so fast with this young man the other evening.'

'Sorry, sir,' I say. 'But I had not seen Absalom for over a month.'

'There was quite a collection after your testimonial. If you contact them, they will take up your cause. I did not get to find out your name.'

'Faith, sir.'

'Faith, a good name. And you?'

'Absalom Brown, sir.'

'And this is Nellie,' I say.

She goes red when Mr Henson shakes her hand and says, 'how you do Miss Nellie?'

She does a small a bob. 'Sir.'

'I am honoured that you have stopped to visit my exhibit.'

'You have many visitors,' I say.

'Oh yes,' he says with a laugh. 'You see as the only exhibitor of colour I'm an oddity in a place full of strange and wonderful things. I even had Queen Victoria stop to ask me whether any of the exhibits I oversee are my own work. When I answered in the affirmative, she congratulated me on the quality of my work.'

'Were the Princesses with Her Majesty?' I ask. I hold my breath.

'No, but I understand they around today.'

'Is the African Princess with them, sir?'

'So, they say. I would surely love to see the little lady.'

'So, would I.'

'Well, you keep on looking,' says Mr Henson with a smile, 'you just might.'

'Thank you for your time, sir,' says Absalom, 'but we must move on.'

'Are you off to the America section?' Mr Henson asks.

'Yes, sir,' says Absalom. 'It is almost time.'

'And so it is,' he says 'I think I can leave for a short while. Shall we?' adding 'Miss Nellie, would you be so kind as to take an old man's arm?'

Nellie gives the biggest smile ever and takes Mr Henson's arm. It's like this we walk to the American section.

Above our heads is a huge bird, larger than it was possible for any bird to be. The wings spread out holding a cloth of Stars and Stripes in its talons.

'That's never a real bird, is it?' says Nellie.

We all look up. 'No, it is paste-board,' says Mr Henson. 'That is the bald-headed eagle, the overblown symbol of America, holding the American flag.'

In the space given to America for their exhibits are some amazing things: India-rubber goods, firearms, a double grand piano with two people playing at once.

There is a crowd around a statue in white marble, in her own little red velvet tent, wearing nothing but a small piece of chain.

'I never thought that I would ever see such a thing,' says a woman covering her daughter's eyes and moving away.

I have seen worse. Women stripped naked and beaten until their black skin turns red with their blood.

'Hiram Power's statue of a Greek Slave,' says Absalom. 'This is why we're here.'

'Come,' says Old Man Henson, 'we must join the others.'

There's quite a crowd now, not only in the main space but also in the galleries above looking down. Some of us walk arm in arm around the space, a mixture of peoples, black, white, old, young. We could never have done that in America. We would've been lynched. I don't know what is to come but I am with Absalom and with Mr Henson. I'm not afeared. We stop in front of the statue once more and a Negro, light skinned, like Absalom, with dark wavy hair steps forward. He seems to be the leader. Many here know him.

'That's William Wells-Brown,' says Absalom, 'and like Mr Henson, or William and Ellen Crafts standing next to him and many others, he travels all over England, Scotland and Ireland lecturing on the evils of slavery.'

Mr Wells-Brown spreads his arms wide. 'The American section here in Crystal Palace displays a variety of American products, cotton, tobacco, rice, but there is no reference to the three million slaves in the United States who help, who are in fact forced, to produce them.'

There's a wave of sound as people look around and they mutter and are a few boos. I'm not sure whether they're booing because of what he has said.

'We, escaped American slaves, have just walked arm in arm with white families from London, Bristol and Dublin. Surgeons, bankers and lawyers, joined by wives, children, and friends, something that we could never do back in America.'

'Isn't that the truth,' say one of the America exhibitors, moping his red face with his handkerchief, the other hand is on the gun by his side. 'You would not dare in the US of A. Your black butts would have been hauled into jail long before now. Now get away with you.'

I am not afraid. I know that he will not use his gun is such a public place.

'Prince Albert said in his speech, only two days ago at the opening ceremony, that the general idea of the Exhibition is the promotion of world peace but see how America's exhibit of Colt's repeating fire-arms features prominently here,' says Mr Henson shaking his head.

Mr Wells-Brown continues speaking. 'We say, United States of America should show side by side, the specimens of cotton, sugar and tobacco, and the human instruments of their production. The international image of the United States is one marked by slavery.'

'Slavery is over, young man,' shouts someone in the crowd.

'No, sir,' says Mr Wells-Brown. He points to the red-faced man who is still holding his gun. 'Ask him. Many of us here and in other parts of your country are fugitives. If we return to America, we can and will be captured and returned to our so-called masters and back into slavery.' He waves his hand around. 'The rice in sacks is South Carolina's gold. The balls of cotton produced by slave labor accounts for over half of America's exports. That fact is ignored in this exhibit of cotton and cotton fabrics, spun in your mills to make fine gowns for your women, fine shirts for your backs.'

By now the area is full of people. We're at the front, but I can feel the weight of the crowd on my shoulders. They are listening.

'Is that how Sir Henry gets his cotton?' asks Nellie.

'Yes, child,' says Josiah Henson. 'I picked many a bale of cotton in my time.'

'Look at this statue, *The Greek Slave*,' Mr Wells Brown says. 'The catalogue informs us that she is chained and a slave. Holding

the cross and the locket in her hand are symbolic. The cross of
Christianity, the locket, a reference to the slave's owner family and
their supposed love for her. This figure appeals to an American
public that values Christian religion and family sentiment. But we
challenge this works' status, an example of America's democratic
ideals.'

'We do,' say several people including Absalom and Mr Henson.

'We have a different reading of this statue,' says Mr Wells-
Brown 'What about our families? Do they love us any less as we
are torn from our mothers and fathers to be sold and resold? Our
hands too are bound.' He opens a bag and brings out a plate. In
the centre of the plate is a kneeling Negro, his hands in chains.
'This statue is companion to this,' he says waving the plate above
his head. 'This image is one some of you may recognize. It was on
many different things, broaches, hair pins, plates, sugar bowls and
so on. It was created for the Committee for the Abolition of the
Slave Trade, in 1787.' He stopped and showed the plate around. He
says, 'on it is written, "*Am I not a man and a brother?*" 1787. But sixty-
four years later we are still in chains. So now I ask you all again.'
Mr Brown kneels, lifts up his arms and says again, '*Am I not a man
and a brother?*'

There is a rustle around me. Absalom helps Mr Henson to
kneel too and though he cannot lift up his arms above his head, he
stretches them out. Absalom kneels, and I kneel with him. Nellie
too kneels by my side. One by one, men and women, black and
white, old and young, we all kneel, and raise our clasped hands.
Some, with tears running down their faces, we say again and again,
'*Am I not a man and a brother?*', and '*Am I not a woman and a sister?*'
The voices ring out, swell, and swirl around, the sound rising to the
gods, to the ancestors, far out across the oceans, to the very bones
in the bottom of the sea resting in the arms of *Mamiwata*. I hold
on to my *gri-gri* and pray, 'Maluuma speak to the ancestors for me.'

It is at that moment I look up into the gallery and see her; a small black girl, her dark blue cloak flung back, showing her lighter blue dress with a soft white lace collar. She's leaning over the railings almost as if she wants to jump over and join us. I tighten the hold on my *gri-gri*. It is the African Princess. She's here. She's almost within reach. A lady by her side pulls at her. 'Look over here, over here,' I whisper. She does not, so I stand up in the middle of the kneeling crowd. She looks past me, and my heart begins to beat so fast and so loud I feel that I will lose my senses.

Her face! I know that face. I know those marks on that face. I stretch out my hand. She turns to the right and waves, but not to me. I look behind me. A man is waving to her. And then she is leaving holding on to the woman's hand, laughing with two other little girls. I want to shout stop, but she is gone. I push through the people standing up and linking arms. Nellie grabs my arm. I try to shake her off, but she holds on.

'Let go,' I cry. 'I must get to her?'

'Get to who?'

'She's here, I've seen her. I must go to her before she disappears.'

'Who are you talking about?'

'My sister,' I say. 'I've seen my sister Salimatu.' I am crying and laughing. I do not know whether it from happiness or sadness.

# FAITH

# CHAPTER 51

*Dis na me saabant wa A done pick fa do me wok.*
*A lob um an A sho please wid um.*
Behold my servant, whom I have chosen; my beloved
in whom I am well pleased
Matthew 12:18

## May 1851

The whole household has gathered in the hallway and on the stairs to see the ladies and the gentlemen leave for the presentation of Missy and Isabella at St. James Palace. Their dresses covered with laces and silks, diamonds and feathers alone could pay the wages of all the servant for years.

While the servants' gape, I slip away. In the room I share with Nellie, I bring out the pen, ink and paper Nanny Dot has let me have.

'What do you want with pen and paper,' Nanny said when I begged her for them yesterday.

'I want to practice writing my name,' I lied.

Now I do not know what to write. How do I start it? Dear Salimatu? I bring the paper close, dip the pen in the ink and wipe the extra off on the pen wiper.

'Dear S,' I stop. Now they call her Sarah. But I find it hard to write that and think that I am writing to my sister. I look at what I have written and decide to leave it like that, just S. It can be for Salimatu, Sali, Sarah, Sister.

✦✦✦

*Dear S,*

*Four days ago, at the Great Exhibition, I see you again. The first time in five years. Did you see me? Did you know me?*

*I am your sister, Fatmata now called Faith. I have thought about you every day since you were taken away by Santigie.*

*Do you remember anything of life in our village, Talaremba where I helped our grandmother, Maluuma, birth you, Aina, the girl-child born with the cord around her neck, born with the caul covering her head? You are the second daughter, the third child of Isatu and Dauda, chief of the village. That is what those cuts on your face mean—that you are the daughter of a chief. I give thanks to Olorun, Oduadua and all the other gods that they have let me know, at last, that you are alive and treated well, as a princess. You were born high and your gods have lifted you higher.*

*My biggest wish now is to hold you, to be together once again.*

✦✦✦

Nellie rushes come in and I stop writing.

'Who you writing to? Absalom?' she says, staring at the words as if they will float off the paper and into her mind and understanding.

I know that she does not believe that the letter is for him but what else can she say.

I am silent but she waits. 'To my sister.' I say. My lips tremble. I

432

cannot believe that I have just sat and written to my sister, knowing that she is alive.

Nellie squats down at my feet, her skirt spreading out like a black hole for me to sink into. She takes hold of both my hands and pulls me round so that I face her.

'Faith, listen to me, that girl can't be your sister. She's the African Princess. All people know that.'

I pull my hands away. 'I saw her face, the marks and I know from the inside of me, that she is Salimatu.'

'You were not that close. How could see the marks on her face?'

'I know those mark because I saw our grandmother Maluuma put them there. I have them too. They are part of my ways, her ways. They say who we are.'

Nellie stares at me. 'You are a princess too? Then what you doing here? Why you not at the palace too?'

I shrug my shoulders. 'What does that matter, now. What good has it done me. Maluuma used to say that *"birds cannot fly with one wing."* All I want is to get her back.'

Nellie does not know what to say or do. She sits on her bed, pulls her shawl close. 'Even if she's your sister, you can't just walk up to the palace and say, I've come to see my sister, let me in. If we can't get into the workhouse, how can we get into a palace?'

She's right, no one will believe me. 'I don't know.' Scrunching my letter into a ball, I throw it into a corner and burst into tears.

✵✵✵✵

I must have fallen asleep because when I open my eyes, I am on top of the bed clothes, fully dressed and my boots on. Nellie is shaking me.

'Look what I have for you.' She gives me a note and even before I read it, I know that it is from Absalom.

'What does he say?'

Without thinking I sit up and read it out. 'Proverb 59:16. *He who finds a wife, finds what is good and receives favour from the Lord.*' My eyes widen and I clutch my *gir-gri*.

'Oh Lor' he asking you to marry him?'

'I think so.'

'He is, he is.' Nellie grabs me, pulls me of the bed and swings me around the room, half shouting, half singing, 'you're going to get married. You're going to get married.'

'Shh, you want the whole house to hear you?'

We both collapse onto the bed our arms around each other, laughing. Ah, but I'm going to miss Nellie when I go.

'Where did you find the note?'

'He give me it himself. He outside waiting for you.'

I grab my hat and shawl. 'Thanks Nellie.'

I am out of that room, down the back stairs and in the street before you could say Great Exhibition. I run into his arms and I don't care who sees me.

�֎֎֎֎

We walk to the little park in Berkeley Square. We sit on one of the benches and Absalom takes my hand. 'So, we going to do it? You going to marry me proper?'

I squeeze his hand and give him a look. 'I thought we already marry on the boat, Absalom Brown.'

He laughs and put his arm around my shoulder. 'Oh, yes we did!'

The way he says it and the look he gives me takes me right back. I could lay right there on the grass if he were to ask me, so hot and full of want, I am.

Though the dark is coming fast, I can see he ready too. I can feel his need as he pulls me to him and we both near going crazy. He kisses me long and hard and the kiss go deep, deep. When he lifts me on to his lap, I do not say him no. I forget everything I don't want to remember. The darkness push through the branches and leaves to cover us and together we reach where we must go.

After, he tells me that our wedding is all arranged for that Saturday and our passage to Africa booked.

'Sarah, I mean Salimatu,' I say. 'How can I go now and leave her.'

'We don't know that she's your sister. We're going to Freetown, where many of those captured by the slavers are taken, after being rescued by the British patrollers. We will look for your sister when we get there.'

My eyes fill up with tears. I feel great pain. 'Why won't you believe me? The African Princess is Salimatu. She is my sister. I know it. I feel it.' When he tries to put his arms around and I pull away from him. 'We'll not find Salimatu in Freetown because she's here in London, right now, sleeping in the palace.'

He gives me a long look and nods slowly. 'I believe you but there is nothing you can do about it. She is alive and well. Her life is different now. Will she even know you?'

He is right, she is a princess now. What life would she have with me, a runaway slave? I must let her go, for now. I feel for my gri-gri and hold it tight. Maybe one day. I stop. I cannot let myself think about one day. I have lost everything and everyone from my old life. Then for the first time in many moons, thoughts of my brothers pass through me. I grab hold of Absalom's hand, 'what if my brother Lansana, the one Santigie sold to the slavers, was rescued by the British?'

He smiles and squeezes my hand. 'It is possible. Many of those rescued have not gone home but settled in Freetown in their own villages, with new lives, new language, a new tribe. They call

435

themselves Krios. If your brother is in Freetown, we will find him. We will go to the commission and search for Lansana while we wait for your children to come join us.'

That is enough for now. I will think only of finding Lansana and having my three children back with me.

Absalom pulls me to him, and I hug him tight. I know then that I will never have to fight the world alone. He will always be by my side. Anyone seeing us would think we were one, joined together. Absalom kisses me and I kiss him right back, long and slow.

✿✿✿

I wake up early because again I feel sick. I get up but never make it to the chamber pot and there is sick all over me. On my hands and knees trying to clean it up I am sick again. Nellie is awake now.

'Leave it,' she says, 'I'll clean it.' She passes me a cup of water. I rinse out my mouth.

'It must be something I eat,' I say, but I don't look at her.

'Who you trying to fool. It's not the first time you been sick. I done hear you before. And look at you in your shimmy.' She says pointing to my belly. 'Think I can't tell? Me ma have five children after me. I know the signs. So, how far gone, six, seven weeks?'

I hang my head. 'Seven and a half.'

'Absalom?'

'You think I've been with anyone else?'

'No, but when?'

'We get together on the ship, coming.'

'They'll chuck you out without a character if the Madame know about it.'

'We were going to get married anyway.' I stretched out on the bed and decide that I had better tell Nellie everything. 'We want to, before we go to Africa.'

'Africa?' Nellie laughs. 'You funning me.'

'No. Child or no child. I'm not staying here.' I sit up and grab hold of her hand. 'You can't tell anyone though. Nobody. We going to get married and then go to Africa.'

Nellie's whole face seems to be awobble. 'When?'

'On Saturday. In three days, at Stoke Newington. Then we sail on *The Bathurst*, to a place called Freetown, in Africa. You hear what it's called? Free Town. Where people are free. And we going to buy my children's freedom. The Quakers going to help us.'

Nellie crying now, puts her arms around me and holds on tight. 'I don't want you to go.'

FAITH

# CHAPTER 52

*Den, de big tick curtain wa beena hang een God ouse split down de middle
fom top to bottom*
Behold, the veil of the temple was rent in twain from the
top to the bottom
Matthew 27:51

## May 1851

I say goodbye to no one, not even Nellie. I do not want her to
know exactly when I am going. It is enough that tonight she will
take my bag, packed with the little I own, and leave it under the
outside stairs. If she puts its way back no one will see it unless they
know to look for it. I almost cry when I see that while I had been
taking care of Henry-Francis for the last time, Nellie had come into
our room and sewn her new yellow ribbon to my grey dress with
little yellow flowers. I have but two handkerchiefs. I fold one and
put it under Nellie's thin pillow. I put the dress on and it is tight
across my breast. I look down at my stomach swelling and wonder
how it has not been noticed so far. I check my purse to see that I
have some money in it and the note I have written for Absalom
and check that the rest of my money is still sewn into the hem of
my coat. I smooth the bedclothes and leave.

I walk fast and jump on to the Green line bus at Regents Street.
I know how to get to Stoke Newington now. I wish Nellie was
with me, but Absalom and I, Mr and Mrs Brown, will come and
collect my bag later tonight. Tomorrow Absalom and I leave for
Gravesend, there to join *The Bathurst* and sail for Africa.

I am up and standing before the conductor calls out Stoke Newington. Off the omnibus I take a deep breath and walk down Church Street. It is much busier than it was last Sunday. There must be a market nearby for people are rushing by with baskets, bags, children, moving between horses and carriages, barrows and the many omnibuses coming and going. I make for St Mary's. I wonder if my note is still there. I will not go and look, I have a new one with me, a note that says all that I need to say to him.

Absalom had been surprised when I told him three nights ago that Nellie and I had been to Stoke Newington.

'I left a note for you on the notice board in case you went there.'

'Notice board, where?'

'At St Mary's Church. Didn't you see it.'

Absalom had thrown back his head and laughed. 'St Mary is not the Quaker Church. The Quakers do not have churches, or priest or ministers. They meet in the meeting house monthly. I have not been near the church.'

Today we will meet by the church, however, and together walk to the Quaker meeting house, to declare we now consider ourselves married in the sight of the friends. The quiet is making me feel as though this is happening to someone else. I watch people getting off every omnibus that stops. Then I see him across the street and my body tingles as I think of the night to come.

At the meeting house we sit and wait for God's spirit to lead people to speak. I try not to think about how different my marriage day would have been if I was back in Talaremba. There would've been food, music, and dancing the whole day. Madu would plait my hair and oil my body, Absalom would sit with Jaja drinking the best palm-wine waiting for me to appear. Even if I'd been on the plantation there would be some kind party as we jumped the broom, not this unjoyful quietness.

At last one of the elders stands and invites us to make our

commitment to each other in the presence of God and the friends. Then many speak, welcoming us, asking for God, their god's, blessing on our joining together freely and equally as lifelong partner.

When Absalom stands and says, 'in the presence of God and friends, I take this woman, Faith, to be my wife.' My heart swells with pride and happiness, for this is my man. My voice is strong and loud as I reply, 'I take this man, Absalom to be my husband.'

I hold on to my *gri-gri* and send a silent prayer to the ancestors, 'Maluuma, Madu and Jaja, hear me and watch over us.' Then it is over, we are married. Absalom and I are now man and wife. When we leave the meeting house, we hold hands as we walk to the omnibus stop.

Suddenly a little girl, no more than three years old, breaks from her mother and runs towards the middle of the street in front of a carriage. There are shouts of 'stop'. The horses' rear and the child slips. Absalom throws himself over her and tries to roll away from the horses. He does not see the omnibus coming from the other way. The horses come down one, two, three. The noise shoots through me. I cannot see Absalom for the crowd. He will get up, brush his beautiful coat down, straighten his cravat, laugh.

But that is not what is happening. I run into the street, push through the growing crowds. The child is howling in her mother's arms, but she is unhurt. I hear someone say, 'he looks bad.' There he is, I see him, on the ground, blood pouring out, the side of his head where one of the horses had kicked him. I fall to the ground, my knees in his blood and beg him to open his eyes. He tries but he cannot. They call for a doctor but what good will that do. I lean over him and kiss his lips.

'He just rolled under my horses' hooves,' says the driver of the omnibus, in a loud voice. 'Ask Fred, the conductor. It not easy controlling them horses when something like that happens.'

'Absalom, my love, I am here,' I say.

He gathers strength from I know not where and whispers, 'my wife.'

I am sobbing, and every tear feels like the blood is being squeezed from the heart of me, but I will not leave his side. I lift his head on to my lap and stroke his matted hair.

I am full of so many feelings I do not know which one to follow first. There is so much say before it is too late. I remember my note. The psalm I was going to give to him after our wedding. He must hear it. I grab hold of my *gri-gri* and call on Maluuma, all the ancestors that have gone before. I call on all the gods that are in the heavens, the old gods and the new, I call on Jesus, Jehovah and almighty God. They must all hear it and help save my man. *'But I will sing of your power; yes, I will sing aloud of your mercy in the morning; For you have been my defense and refuge in the day of my trouble.'*

The crowds are still there, mouths move, and I know that they are saying things but, I do not hear them. There is just the two of us, made into one. I fear he's fading fast. I sit in blood, and dirt from the street, crying and loving for both of us, as the pain fills every part of me.

There is one more thing I must tell him. I take his hand and press it on my stomach. His eyes flicker. He tries to speak. I bend over him and kiss him hard and breathe the words into him. 'Your child. Your child will be free.'

There is a smile. I swear there is a smile and then someone has picked him up and put him in a carriage.

'He ain't going to make it,' someone says. 'He's a goner.'

I open my mouth and the sound that comes out is so deep and wild, the very soul of me pours out and chases after his as it flies up to the gods. He is gone, but where? I am left to wander soulless.

'Absalom, my love, my husband.'

✧✧✧✧

Later, Nellie tells me what happened at the house. When I did not return on Saturday there was uproar. Some said I had run away, some said I had been killed, others were sure I had been captured and sold into slavery.

Only Nellie knows part of the story and she does not tell, at least not to anyone in the house. When she sees my things under the steps in the morning, she and Jack come looking for me. In Stoke Newington, they hear about the accident the day before, about the black woman crying and screaming at the almost white man who had been kicked by horses, saving a child.

They find me sitting in the graveyard behind St Mary's Church digging a hole.

'Fatmata,' cries Nellie. 'We've been looking for you. You been here all night? You be soaked through and through. Come. Let's get you out of here.'

Nellie's face is wet. I do not know if it is because she is crying or because it is raining.

'I am waiting for him,' I say. 'They will bring him here. I must have it ready.' I do not stop digging. No matter that I have no hoe, no shovel, this is the last thing I can do.

'What you talking about? He ain't never dead,' Nellie says kneeing down beside me and takes my hands, forcing me to stop. 'Stop, Faith. This is not the way. Look at your hands. Your fingers are bleeding.'

I stare at her. 'He's gone, gone to the ancestors. They took him away, but they'll bring him back. I must prepare where they can lay him down.'

'Oh, Lor',' says Nellie and I think she is crying. 'What they done with him?'

'I'll find out,' says Jack, 'but she can't stay here. Sunday service will start soon. People will be coming through this way.'

'Where can we take her?'

'Back to Charles Street. We cannot leave her, and you have to get back.'

'Oh, Jack. That Missy Clara'll kill her. If she know what I know.'

'Then don't tell them. Let them think she just got lost. Get her bag up to the room and that will be that.'

I hear what they are saying but I say nothing. What is life now without Absalom? I cannot go without leaving something near the place where Absalom joined the ancestors. I take out the psalm from my purse, I dig into my *gri-gri* and pull out the heart-stone that Maluuma gave me. I wrap the psalm around my heart and cover them with the earth. In a soft voice I sing the song he first heard me sing on the ship all those weeks ago.

'What that you saying? Faith, what's that?'

'The song to send the dead on their way. *Everyone come together, let us work hard; the grave not yet finished; let his heart be at peace.*'

'Stop,' says Nellie, 'we don't know he's dead.' I shake my head. I know. Nellie wasn't there. She didn't see him. She didn't hear them say 'he's a gonner.' I let Nellie put her arms around me, lift me up and walk me out of the churchyard. There is no fight in me. How are they to know that I have left the old me, with her hopes and her dreams, her heart in that hole.

✧✧✧

Next day Missy sends for me. She takes one look at me and she knows. I would have been gone by now if the Gods had not taken a hand and changed my life once more. She grabs hold of me and tries to shake me. 'Where have you been? Answer me.'

I no longer care what happens to me, so I tell her.

'I went to get married.'

'Married?' She shrieked so loudly I had to cover my ears. She hit the side of my face and my ears ring and made the inside of my head shake and scream no more.

'To whom? Where you did you meet him?' She shakes me, but I am silent. I will not speak. It is nothing to do with her.

My silence seems to enrage her. She hits me again and I fall over. I do not cry. It is when she goes to kick me in the stomach that I grab her ankle and pull her to the ground and there on the carpet we fight like two bitches, growling and snarling.

When they come in and pull us apart, I am screaming. 'you will not kill my baby. That is all I have left of him. You will not take this too.'

✿✿✿✿

I am locked in the cellar among the rats and the spiders. It smells of sewer. It is bad but what does it matter, the ship had been worse. They can do with me what they will. I have no way of knowing what has happened to Absalom.

I'm two days in that place before Nellie comes to see me, in the dark of the night. She is afraid of rats and would be in trouble if found out, still she creeps down here with news of Absalom. He is alive and in hospital with a broken leg and a broken head. I think that I will burst with happiness.

'O *Oduadua* I praise you, I thank you.' I cry. 'I must go to my husband.'

'They not going to let you out.'

'What's to happen to me?'

'You broke her nose. She's locked herself in her room. Her face is all swollen.'

'Are they calling the law?'

'I don't know but there's a lot of talk behind closed doors. So many people have sent cards saying that they cannot attend Miss Isabella's coming out ball that Lady Compton has had to cancel the ball for fear of it being half empty. You should hear her screaming around the house. She says, "how can they have overlooked a previous engagements. It's a lie. Mother make them come. It's Henry's fault, he should never have married her. I hate them." Lady Withenshaw is mad as hell because Sophia also will not get her ball now.'

✿✿✿✿

I don't know how I'm going to do it, but I will get out here and go to Absalom. I must. Three days later, in the dark of the night, I do get out, but only to be bundled into a carriage.

'*The Clarendon* sails in the morning,' I hear. 'Keep her down in the hull until you dock in America and take her straight back to the Plantation. Her Master will deal with her.'

'Yes, sir. I understand.'

'No, no. I must go to Absalom,' I scream again and again but there is no-one to help me and the carriage just rumbles and shakes out of London.

At the docks I am pulled out of the carriage. I stumble and fall to my knees. The sky is brightening into morning and a pale May sun breaks through the clouds. I look up at ships of all sizes moored at the dock, moving up and down to the swell of the sea. Then I see it and my heart seems to stop. I try to get away from the sailors, ignoring the pain from the cobble stones biting into my knees. A sailor grabs my arm and pulls me up. I fight and sob.

'No, no, no,' I cry, pointing to one of the ships. '*The Bathurst*, there it is. Take me to *The Bathurst*, please. That's the ship I should be sailing in.'

'Take her down, take her now,' says Mr Cartwright, Sir Henry's manager.

※※※

I feel movement and my stomach heaves. Although I cannot see or hear any voices. I know that the ship is pulling away. I am being transported once more. The tears flow. Sailing away from England, from Africa, from freedom and from my husband. I remember our dreams and wipe away my tears. I will find a way. I put one hand over my stomach, with the other I hold on to my *gri-gri*. I speak to my unborn child.

'You will soon be free. You'll not grow up a slave. This I swear. O *Oduadua* hear me. My children will be free.'

# SARAH

# CHAPTER 53

*When a plunge is to be made into the water, it is of no use lingering on the bank.*
*—David Copperfield, Charles Dickens*

## May 1851

*Friday, 9ᵗʰ May 1851, Winkfield Place.*
> *I thought that the whole family would be in the hall waiting to welcome me home from London but they were not. The train from Dundee broke down. They won't be back until tomorrow. Mrs Dixon and Tom are here. I'm glad.*

❊❊❊❊

'Shame, you could have stayed another day in London if we'd known in time. Edith's gone to see her folks, in Bermondsey,' says Cook. 'I have no one to go see and Tom won't leave his garden if you pays him, so here I am and right glad I am for your company, lovey.'

Sarah sighed. 'Can I stay in the kitchen with you? It's scary upstairs all by myself.'

'That you can. I'll make you something special to eat, shall I? What about a nice milky rice pudding mixed, with some finely-shredded beef-suet? I'm sure you'd like a bit of rice, wouldn't you? Harry used to tell me that's what blacks eat in Africa. At least

447

that's mostly what they had on the ships when they left Africa. Don't go off like potatoes and a bit of weevil don't do you no harm. He ate it till he could not stand the sight or taste of it.'

'Thank you, Mrs Dixon, I'd love some rice,' Sarah said, skipping to the back door.

'And where are you off to now?'

'Just into the garden.'

'Well don't stay out there too long and don't get yourself all filthy with your digging.'

'I won't start digging. I'm just going to look at something.'

'When you come back you can tell me all about what you done in London. Fancy, you gone to the Great Exhibition already. If it stays open for long, I might get myself down there to see the wonders of the world with me own eyes. They say they be taking folks down in coaches.'

Sarah slid out of the kitchen, ran to the far end of the garden, stopped, and looked around, frowning. Where was the hole, the patch of earth? Then she saw it. the A small tree had been planted there.

She felt someone come stand by her side. It was Tom.

'That there be an apple tree when it grown a bit more. Then it'll give this spot some shade,' he said before blowing a puff of smoke from the pipe he had clenched in his mouth. 'And when it start fruiting, it could help keep the Doctor away.' He laughed and wheezed and coughed.

Sarah glanced at him. He remembered. She had asked him whether the proverb about apples keeping the doctor away was true, and he had said, 'Well, Missy, I could not rightly say whether that be true or whether it be not.'

'Thank you, Tom.'

'By and by, if I were to put a bench under that tree, when it be grown a bit, mind, a person could sit them down, and think and remember to their hearts content.' He stuffed more tobacco into his pipe, nodded and walked away.

✿✿✿

This time it was Sarah who waited for her family to return. She stayed in the dark drawing room, pulling the curtain back to peek out every time she thought she heard the carriage. When at last they arrived, she couldn't wait for them to come inside but opened the front door and stood on the steps hopping from foot to foot.

'Sarah, my dear,' said Mama Forbes, hugging her, 'you're back. Good. Let's get in.'

In the hall, Sarah grabbed Emily's hand but although she smiled, Emily did not seem as excited to be home as Sarah had thought she would be. They looked different and now she felt apart from them, shy of all of them. Maybe it was because they were tired, wearing nothing but black and she wasn't. She hadn't thought about Mama Forbes, Mabel, Emily, even Anna, still wearing black. How could she have forgotten in just a week? She would get Edith to help her change into her black dress as soon as they went up to the nursery. Things would feel more like it should be, she was sure.

✿✿✿

Next morning during breakfast Sarah began to understand there were going to be changes now that Papa Forbes had died.

'Mama says that we're going to school,' said Emily suddenly.

Sarah dropped her spoon into her bowl of porridge so quickly liquid flew out and splattered her black dress. 'School? Why? What school? When?' She fired the question fast and sharp, not bothering to clean up the mess she'd made.

Emily laughed at the look on Sarah's face. 'I don't think we were supposed to know yet but Grandpa Forbes let it out the night before we left. Aunt Caroline and Aunt Laura are starting a school. I think that's where we'll go. Grandpa Forbes says we must give up Winkfield Place because Papa was no good with money and made bad investments on the railroad.'

Mabel hit the table with her fist, making Alice and Sarah jump and the plates rattle. 'He's wrong. Papa was good at everything.' She pushed her chair back and went to stare out of the window. Sarah saw Mabel's shoulders move. She was crying but Sarah didn't go to her.

'What does "bad investments" mean?' asked Emily.

'I don't know,' said Sarah still watching Mabel. Her mind full of the thought of moving from Winkfield Place.

'Freddie's leaving Eaton,' said Emily. 'He's going to join the naval cadets. Grandpa Forbes says it'll be good to have another Forbes in the Navy, besides Uncle George.'

Sarah bit at the side of her thumb. All these things planned, talked about, decided and she had been not there. When was Mama Forbes going to tell her that they were going to move, go to school? What about her German lessons? Would Mama still teach them the pianoforte? So many questions flying around in her mind.

✹✹✹✹

When she was sent for the next day, she knew what Mama Forbes was going to tell her.

She ran into the drawing room and though the curtains were still drawn, it was a little brighter now that the black coverings had been taken off the mirrors and pictures.

'Good morning Mama,' she said. Then she saw there was someone else with Mama, 'Oh, Good morning Lady Phipps.' She was surprised to see her. Edith had not said there was a visitor, and so early in the day. Mama Forbes looked as though she had been crying. Why? Had they been talking about Papa Forbes? Was that what had upset her? Sarah knew that they all still cried sometimes, when they talked about him. That must be it.

'Good Morning Sarah,' said Mama Forbes. 'Come and sit by me. Lady Phipps and I need to talk with you.'

Sarah sat and waited, looking from one to the other. Neither of them seemed to want to speak first. Then Mama Forbes said quickly, as though trying to get it all out on one breath, 'My dear, you'll be going away soon, very soon, in a week's time.'

Sarah smiled, 'I know, Mama, we're going to school in Scotland. Emily told me. She didn't say that it was next week, though.'

The two women glanced at each other and Mama Forbes sighed.

'You won't be going to school with the girls,' said Lady Phipps.

Sarah started to tremble. 'Why not? Why can't I go with Mabel and Emily?' she said, moving closer to Mama Forbes. 'I want to go to school with my sisters.'

'You'll go to school,' said Mama Forbes. She stopped speaking and looked at Lady Phipps. 'This is too much.'

'You'll be going to a different school, in a different place,' Lady Phipps said then. 'You'll be going to a school in Freetown, Sierra Leone, in Africa.'

'A country in Africa?' Sarah shouted, jumping up. 'I don't want to go to Africa, I want to stay here with you, Mama Forbes.' Sarah threw herself at Mama Forbes pinning her to the chair. 'Please, don't send me away, don't send me back to Africa. I'll be good. I promise. I'll do whatever you say Mama, please, please don't send me away. I don't want to be captured again.' Her sobs were loud, her face awash with tears, her whole body shaking as her sobs changed into such violent coughing she could hardly breathe.

Mama Forbes held her close, she too was crying now. 'Sarah, it is not I who is sending you away. I would have you stay with us forever, if I could, but I'm not your guardian, Her Majesty is, and she has sent Lady Phipps to inform me of her plans for you.'

'It's for your own good, Sarah,' said Lady Phipps, although she too had tears in her eyes. 'Her Majesty cares for you and believes that the inclement weather of England and Scotland, when Mrs Forbes and her family move there in June, would be injurious to you. Reverend and Mrs Schmid are missionaries going to Freetown, they will accompany you and see that you arrive safely. Queen Victoria will continue to be your guardian and will be in contact with the school. It is a missionary school and a safe place for you as you grow into a young woman.'

'No, no, no,' screamed Sarah. Mrs Forbes held her and rocked her.

✵✵✵

*Saturday, 10th May 1851, Winkfield Place.*

> *I know what is to become of me, now. Sent away again. To Africa. To be a slave again? They said I was free, but I am not. I wish I was dead. At least then I would be with Papa Forbes. Ancestors help me.*

✵✵✵

The next few days went too fast for Sarah, too fast for everyone. She cried herself out. They all did. Anna followed her around, saying, 'don't go Sarah, please don't go.'

Freddie banged the table and shouted at his mother, 'how could you let them do this, Mama? Tell them no, she stays with us.'

Mama Forbes cried, and he apologised for being rude then he went into the pantry, drank half a bottle of Papa Forbes special port and was sick. Mrs Dixon baked a special cake every day. Nanny Grace prayed and prayed, while Edith cried and sniffed.

Mabel cried too and said, 'you will always be my sister.'

Emily slept in Sarah's bed every night. Sarah's arms were covered in scratches.

# SARAH

# CHAPTER 54

*You were a part of the trade of your home, and were bought and sold like any other vendible thing your people dealt in.*
*—David Copperfield, Charles Dickens*

## May 1851

*5 Wimpole Street, Friday, 16th May*
  Tomorrow I leave England with Reverend and Mrs Schmid
  for school in Freetown. Another long journey across water,
  the second in a year.

  I went to Buckingham Palace this afternoon. Mama Queen
  gave me a heart-shaped locket with a picture of her inside.
  She said that she gives lockets to all her daughters on their
  birthday. I am her goddaughter. It is my birthday and
  goodbye present. I will wear it. Salimatu is coming with me
  she will wear the gri-gri.

  These are the people I am leaving.
  Mama Forbes, Emily, Anna, Freddie, Mabel, Nanny
  Grace, Edith, Mrs Dixon, Tommy, Miss Byles,
  Alice, Vicky, Bertie, Affie, Lenchen, Tilla,
  Daniel, Lady Melton, Jack, Nellie,
  Prince Albert and Mama Queen
  I have said goodbye to them all, but I do not want to go.

✿✿✿✿

Sarah gripped the railings, stood on the lowest deck-rope and leaned out to look down into another busy quay side. This time there was no call of the *Ochema* bird of parting. These calls were gulls crying for food, nothing to do with her going. There were no dugout canoes, no Kroo men, but most importantly, no Captain Forbes to take care of her.

'Get down. You cannot stay here.' She could hear the words Papa Forbes has shouted to her the first day on *HMS Bonetta* and her heart leapt. See, they were wrong, all of them. Papa Forbes had not gone to join his ancestors, he was here. He had come to get her, to stop them sending her away.

'Papa Forbes,' she cried turning around. But it wasn't him. It was a black man, his well-oiled hair, lay thick and wavy. She could tell he was not a sailor by his white neckerchief and well-fitted jacket. Her disappointment made her eyes sting and she staggered. The man reached out to steady her.

'Sorry if I startled you, but I've seen people fall overboard from leaning over like that.'

'Thank you, Sir.' Sarah muttered not looking at him.

They stood there, side-by-side not saying a word. For a long time, she'd searched for black people now here was one but she just wished he'd go away. She wanted to stay there and watch England fade away as they sailed.

'You're Sarah Forbes Bonetta, are you not?'

She gave him a quick look then. 'Yes sir. How do you know that?'

'Everyone knows who you are—the African Princess. They write about you in the newspapers all the time. I know, for example, that you've been staying with your guardian, Her Majesty and that you went, at least twice, to the Great Exhibition.'

Sarah looked up at him. 'Yes, that is all true.'

'I know that Captain Forbes, who rescued you and brought you to England, has passed away whilst at sea. I'm very sorry for your loss. It's always hard when someone you love joins the ancestors.' He touched her shoulder.

Sarah gripped the rope tighter and tears that were always sitting just behind her eyes spilled over. It was the first time anyone had used such words to her. He knew about the ancestors then. She put her hand to her chest and felt for her *gri-gri* with her caul in it. She was wearing it again as well as the locket from the Queen. If she was going on the ocean to Africa, she was taking no chances. She needed all the protection she could against *Mamiwata*. Look how she had been able to swallow up Papa Forbes.

'The newspapers don't know everything though,' he said, giving her a little smile. 'They don't know that you're on this ship, on your way to school in Freetown. I know because Reverend Schmid has told me. We're all travelling together to Freetown.'

'I don't want to go.' The words burst out of her.

'Why not, little sister?'

'I don't want King Gezo to get me again. Captain Forbes won't be there to save me this time.' She did not know why she was telling him this, but it felt good to say out loud what she was afraid might happen.

'You're safe.'

Safe, that word again. 'How do you know that?'

'I know these things. My name is James, Lieutenant James Davies.'

'Lieutenant in the Navy?' Sarah frowned. She had not known that there were black officers in the Navy.

'I joined the West African Squadron patrolling the coast against slave traders as soon as I could,' he said, his face became thoughtful. 'They rescued me when I was a child. They saved my life.'

A thought hit Sarah. 'Did you know my Papa Forbes,' she said urgently.

'Yes. I was a sailor on HMS *Bloodhound* with Captain Forbes. He was a great man.'

Sarah's eyes widened. He knew Papa Forbes. 'Can you take me to him, please?' The question burst out of her.

Lieutenant Davies shook his head. 'Little one, you know I can't. The Captain is with the ancestors now.'

'What will happen to me in Freetown?' cried Sarah.

'All will be well,' said James. 'Reverend Venn has arranged for you to go to Miss Sass. She runs a school for young African girls who will become good missionaries and who will go out to all parts of the world, teaching God's words.'

Was that the plan for her? She had known it was a missionary school, but no one had said anything about her becoming a missionary.

'I do not want to be a missionary,' she said loudly. 'I don't want to teach about God. I just want to stay here in England, with my family.'

'But your family are not here, they're in Africa, in Freetown. You are African, you'll never be English.'

That got her attention immediately. 'My family are in Freetown? You know them? When we get there, can you take me to them? To Fatmata?'

'Fatmata?'

'My sister. She looked after me in the forest then the Moors took me away. I went to many places before King Gezo's compound.'

'I don't know whether your birth family are there, but I do know that we're all family, all Africans together. British ships, captained by officers like your Captain Forbes patrolled the waters, fought the slave ships and re-captured us. Then they took us to Freetown. There are many of us in villages and towns in Sierra Leone now.

Who knows, Fatmata might have been one of those rescued.'

Sarah took a deep breath and for the first time in the week she relaxed. Maybe if Fatmata was in Freetown that was where she should go. Were the ancestors leading her to Fatmata?

She looked at the many ships in the harbour. Some of them were slowly moving out, starting their journeys. A large ship glided past them.

'Is that one going to Africa too?'

'No. That's *The Clarendon*, on its way to America. These ships go to all parts of the world, Australia, China, America, not just to Africa.'

Sarah was glad now that she was on *HMS Bathurst*, going to Freetown, and not going anywhere else. At least there she might find her true sister.

'When we get to Freetown, will you help me find Fatmata?'

'I will try. If she's there, we will find her.' He put out his hand. 'Come I must take you back to the good Reverend. *O ti wa ni ti lo ile*—you're going home.'

Sarah held her *gri-gri* and turned her back on the shore to the blue sea. She did not need to see England fade into the distance. She wanted to look forward. Sarah smiled. Salimatu took James's hand.

✿✿✿✿

*Saturday, 17th May, 1851. On The Bathurst*

> *Left Gravesend for Africa on The Bathurst this morning. Mama Queen says that I can come back when my cough gets*

*better but I do not know if I ever will or if I will see my friends and English family again. Who knows what will happen to me in Freetown. Maybe I will find Fatmata, my sister. Maybe not. But I am not alone. Salimatu comes with me. We are two in one, and we are going home. I am no longer afraid.*

# HISTORICAL NOTE

A note on the title, *Breaking the Maafa Chain*. 'Maafa' is the Swahili word for disaster but it has come to mean 'African Holocaust,' referring to the historical and ongoing violence toward and displacement of African people and their descendants.

✺✺✺

Although Sarah Forbes Bonetta did exist and there are some actual people, places, facts and events in this book, verified through extensive research, *Breaking the Maafa Chain* is a work of fiction and a product of my imagination.

I first heard about Sarah growing up in Sierra Leone. She seemed to have always been part of the folklore of family stories—the slave girl who grew up a princess, goddaughter to Queen Victoria and friends of the royal children. But I knew very little about who she was.

All I know of Sarah Forbes Bonetta's early life is that she was captured after a raid on her village and her parents were killed. From the markings on her face, Sarah was believed to be the daughter of a chief. No one knows what exactly happened to her siblings.

The novel is set in the mid-nineteenth century, towards the end of transatlantic slave trade. Slavery had long been abolished in England, but the other European and African countries did not have to abide by British laws. So, though illegal and risky, the transporting slaves via the 'Middle Passage' from Africa to America or the West Indies was still a lucrative business. Determined to stop the slave trade, however, Queen Victoria sent envoys to persuade the Africans to change and trade in agricultural products instead of people. The West Africa Squadron of the Royal Navy also patrolled the west coast attacking any slave-ships in the area. They rescued the newly captured slaves and took them to Freetown, Sierra Leone. There they soon established a colony of liberated slaves joining an already established colony made up of former slaves, the black poor from England, ex slaves from America and Nova Scotia and the Maroons from Jamaica.

Sarah, whose original name was Aina, has been captured during a raid in her village, Talaremba, near Okeadon and ends up in the court of King Gezo of Dahomey, (now Benin), a prolific slave trader. In 1850, Captain Forbes, the Captain of *HMS Bonetta*, is in the kingdom to persuade the King to give up the vast wealth he got from the illegal slave trade and go into palm-oil production. Although the Captain is unable to change the King's mind, he is able to rescue the eight-year-old child who is about to be sacrificed to Gezo's ancestors. The King, still wanting to remain on good terms with the British, decides to send the child as an embarrassing gift to Queen Victoria.

Captain Forbes names Aina, Sarah Forbes, after himself, and Bonetta after his ship. Queen Victoria asks to see Sarah and, impressed by her intelligence and sympathetic to the child's plight, the Queen decides to become her guardian and godmother. Sarah, known as the 'African Princess', friends with the royal children, frequents Windsor Castle and the other palaces.

But, after only a year, because of her poor health, Sarah is devastated to be sent back to Africa, to a missionary school in Freetown, Sierra Leone. She stays in Freetown for four years then

Queen Victoria unexpectedly sends for her to return to England where she continues to live the life of a princess. At nineteen she married John L. Davies and returned first to Freetown and later to Lagos, Nigeria. They had three children and the eldest was named after Queen Victoria, who agreed to be her godmother. Sarah died of tuberculosis in 1880.

Sarah's close relationship with Queen Victoria was known and understood at the time and she is mentioned in many of Queen Victoria's diary entries. There is, however, hardly anything about Sarah in the many Queen Victoria biographies. This omission intrigued me and with the growing interest in Queen Victoria, I became absorbed in exploring Sarah's significance within the aristocracy of Victorian England. I started my research by painstakingly going through books, letters, newspaper articles, online sources and Queen Victoria's diary.

*Breaking the Maafa Chain* tells the story of Sarah's early life and her year in Victoria England before being sent back to Africa. As I gathered more and more information Sarah's story began to emerge. I wondered what her life would have been like before she was transported to Victorian England, such a different world. What would she remember? What would have happened if she had been transported to America instead of England? How were black people viewed in Victorian England? What kind of racial tensions existed then?

The thought of the contrasting life Sarah could have had was fascinating. The idea of Aina (whom I call Salimatu) later named Sarah, and the completely fictional Fatmata, renamed Faith, was born. The story is narrated by both sisters and I use epigraphs to suggest the themes for each chapter. Fatmata's chapters have Yoruba sayings, rooting her in the language she has taken with her to the Gullah, South Carolina. Salimatu's epigraphs are English proverbs, connecting her to the new language she is learning. When

Fatmata becomes Faith, her epigraphs are taken from the Gullah Bible, the language she has been forced to learn. Sarah's epigraphs are quotations from Charles Dickens's *David Copperfield*.

In their narratives the sisters view their lives through different lenses as both try to find their way to freedom physically and emotionally in a rapidly changing world—one a Princess, the other a slave.

# ACKNOWLEDGEMENTS

I am truly grateful for all the people on whose shoulders I stand, whose words have touched me and whose ears I continually bend with my dreams and hopes.

Special thanks to my friends Guinevere Glasfurd and Siobhan Costello—wonderful writers who shared many memorable writing retreats with me—for their encouragement and honest feedback, always.

Thank you to my dear friend Irene Morris for her unflagging belief and support, forever ready to be my research travel companion, and to Nathan Morris for putting up with our constant chatter about this novel.

And to Caron Freeborn who first encouraged me to tell this story. So sorry that she is no longer here to see the finished version.

Thanks also to the judges of Lucy Cavendish First Novel competition who shortlisted the unfinished novel making believe for the first time that I could and should finish the novel.

To Myriad First Editions who selected me as winner of their competition. The prize, having an extract of *Breaking the Maafa Chain* in the *New Daughters of Africa* Anthology, gave me such confidence, knowing that my writing sits with some long admired, phenomenal writers.

To Bernardine Evaristo and Yvette Edwards for their inspiration and support.

Moya Ruskin and Baz Norton for opening their home to me and giving me space to write whenever I need it. To Tricia Abrahams for listening and always being there.

Thank you most of all to my children Jem, Joel and Zelda. This book is dedicated to them. They have been so patient, putting up with my disappearing to write but always being there to welcome me back, with love—and food.

# ABOUT THE AUTHOR

Anni Domingo is an Actress, Director and Writer, working in Radio, TV, Films and Theatre after training at Rose Bruford College of Speech and Drama. She appeared in Inua Ellam's *Three Sisters*, a play set in Nigeria during the Biafran War, at the National Theatre (UK) and toured Robert Icke's *The Doctor* to Australia early in 2020. She currently lectures Drama and Directing at St. Mary's University in Twickenham, Rose Bruford College and at RADA. Anni's poems and short stories are published in various anthologies and her plays are produced in the UK. An extract from her novel *Breaking the Maafa Chain* won the Myriad Editions First Novel competition in 2018 and is featured in the *New Daughters of Africa* (2019) anthology edited by Margaret Busby. Anni recently won a place at Hedgebrook Writers Retreat and Norwich National Writing Centre's Escalator programme enabling her to start working on *Ominira*, her second novel. *Breaking the Maafa Chain* is her first novel.